Praise for Sop[...]

"In short, jewel-like chapters, *Unforgivable Love* by Sophfronia Scott, a retelling of the classic *Dangerous Liaisons*, is the tale of a sexy summer's intrigue in the world of comfortable, glitteringly fashionable members of African-American high society in Jazz Age Harlem, New York. Scott's novel is a vivid, vibrant, and panoramic exploration of the hearts and minds of its mostly well-heeled characters and the universal themes of love, sex, and social intrigue. *Unforgivable Love* offers a delightful opportunity to spend time in the Harlem heyday, a period of post-war optimism and renaissance. Sophfronia Scott takes readers there and lets them wander and discover this exciting, historical time and place."

—Breena Clarke, author of the Oprah Book Club selection, *River, Cross My Heart*

"Scott's wonderful, original retelling of *Dangerous Liaisons* takes readers deep into the lives of her characters; Mae, Val, and Elizabeth are riveting and complex. You won't be able to stop reading this terrific, absorbing book."

—Karen E. Bender, author of *Refund*, finalist for the National Book Award

"*Unforgivable Love* is an unforgettable read. Scott's reimagining of *Dangerous Liaisons* into 1940s Harlem society is nothing short of inspired, with all the spice and spite and delight of the original, and more. Nuanced, haunting, elegant, this is a book I can't wait to read again—and then again."

—Robin Black, author of *Life Drawing*

"Picasso's 'Head of a Bull' was made simply by attaching a set of handle bars to bicycle seat; simple, yes. But a stunning leap of imagination. This is what *Unforgivable Love* brings to mind for me: Here is this eighteenth-century French tale remade into a panorama of mid-century Harlem, America—full of brilliant characters, a tale of love and lust and treachery, written with the rhythms of jazz, giving forth beautifully rendered rooms and streets and sounds. The remake is better than the original."

—Richard Bausch, award-winning author of *Before, During, After*

"*Unforgivable Love* is a fast-paced tale of intrigue, seduction, and betrayal. Sophfronia Scott leaves us breathless."

—Lee Martin, author of the Pulitzer Prize finalist *The Bright Forever*

"At once beautiful and ominous, visceral and ethereal, tragic and fulfilling, *Unforgivable Love* is a genuinely moving novel of love, loss, and the treacherous paths we make for ourselves when we let our passions run away with us. Sophfronia Scott has given us a book that will last—an elegant page turner that transcends time and place."

—Bret Lott, *New York Times* bestselling author of *Jewel*

"Complicated characters, unbearable tension, heartbreak, and betrayal make *Unforgivable Love* an absorbing read. Deeply poignant."

—Erika Robuck, national bestselling author of *Hemingway's Girl*

"*Unforgivable Love* is an exquisite, sexy, beautifully imagined novel in which Sophfronia Scott expertly recasts the intrigues and characters of *Dangerous Liaisons* in Harlem of the late 1940s. It's evident that Scott was deeply inspired by the spirit and events of Pierre de Laclos's classic novel, but she has claimed its subjects—romantic love and betrayal—as her own. Both a virtuosic homage and a thrilling retelling—*Unforgivable Love* is a stunning accomplishment."

—Christine Sneed, author of *The Virginity of Famous Men* and *Little Known Facts*

"*Unforgivable Love* is lyrical and lush, enchanting and energetic. With botttomless empathy and loving attention to detail, Sophfronia Scott embraces a classic and makes it her own."

—Tayari Jones, author of *Silver Sparrow* and *An American Marriage*

"*Unforgivable Love* is vibrant, thoughtful, and very sexy. It sneaks up on you and once you are under its spell, it won't let go."

—Martha Southgate, author of *The Fall of Rome*

"Why do the worst people always seem to win? In this remarkable retelling of the French classic *Les Liasions Dangereuses*, Sophfronia Scott brings scandal, manipulation, and perverse desire to (barely) postwar America. Never have I rooted against a protagonist so fervently, all the while taking secret pleasure in the subversion of virtue. But wait. Who really wins here? Beautifully written, sumptuously atmospheric, fearless in its cultural appropriation, *Unforgivable Love* is surely the breakout book for this thrilling new voice."

—Bill Roorbach, award-winning author of *Life Among Giants* and *The Girl of the Lake*

UNFORGIVABLE LOVE

Sophfronia Scott

WILLIAM MORROW
An Imprint of HarperCollins*Publishers*

HarperCollins books may be purchased for educational, business, or sales promotional use. For information, please e-mail the Special Markets Department at SPsales@harpercollins.com.

FIRST EDITION

Designed by Diahann Sturge

Library of Congress Cataloging-in-Publication Data has been applied for.

ISBN 978-0-06-265565-3

17 18 19 20 21   LSC   10 9 8 7 6 5 4 3 2

For Robert Vivian,
who asked about the light.
The light lives here . . .

Ships at a distance have every man's wish on board. For some they come in with the tide. For others they sail forever on the horizon, never out of sight, never landing until the Watcher turns his eyes away in resignation, his dreams mocked to death by Time. That is the life of men.

Now, women forget all those things they don't want to remember, and remember everything they don't want to forget. The dream is the truth. Then they act and do things accordingly.

—ZORA NEALE HURSTON
THEIR EYES WERE WATCHING GOD

And we are put on earth a little space,
That we may learn to bear the beams of love.

—WILLIAM BLAKE
"THE LITTLE BLACK BOY"

May we all feel the light of a brilliant love.

—DARRYL GREGORY
"PRAYER & HALLELUJAH"

PROLOGUE

Mae

Westchester, 1934

Why was Alice making her wait? Mae Malveaux lifted the hem of her thin cotton nightdress and walked barefoot across the lawn into the shade of a sheltering willow tree. The hammock shifted gently in the warm evening breeze, and the first stars decorated a purple-pink sky. It would be dark soon, and she didn't want to be outside by herself. She lay back in the hammock and hummed to herself, the colors above her head deepening. Soon she saw just the tree's slim green leaves.

Mae was glad she didn't have to be in Harlem sweating through her clothes on some fire escape. She would look up when she walked down the street and see under the skirts of women she knew from church. They sat there on the metal cages fanning themselves all day. She didn't want to be like that, exposed to the world like an animal at the zoo. And thank God, because of who she was, she didn't have to perspire in public.

Ever since her mother had looked at Mae's long dark plaits and perfect ten-year-old face and said, "Put Mae's picture on the pomade jars," there had been no need for her to be like anyone else. No reason to do what other people do.

She could live in a proper brownstone and not hear strangers' footsteps up above her head. She could come up to Westchester County and run half naked in the dark with the girl she loved more than her own pretty face. And for Mae Malveaux, that was saying something.

Now her silky dark hair flowed loose around her. She knew her mama would get mad if it frizzed up in the dewy air, but she didn't care.

Mae sat up. She heard the shushing of Alice's slippered feet rushing through the grass. Suddenly Alice collapsed over her leg, slapping herself on the ankle.

"Ouch! Damn mosquito! Mae! Why do we always have to be outside? You know you can come to my house. We can stay in my room."

Mae opened and closed her mouth. She decided not to try again to explain how indoors they belonged to other people. At least that's how life presented itself to Mae. Indoors she had to wear black stockings that clung to her legs like spiderwebs and endure dance instructors who poked at her when her step lagged a beat behind or her back remained unbending. But she had begun to suspect this wasn't the same for Alice, especially after Alice cut her hair into the shockingly mannish bob so many white women were wearing. Tall and vivacious with skin the color of cooked caramel, Alice strode through the world as if she were a white woman and entitled to every freedom of a black man.

Alice's face and hair were not printed on thousands of jars of hair product. Alice could skip coming out for a full year just because she didn't feel like getting dressed for the debutante ball. She had also experienced men, real men, not the bashful boy "gentleman callers" summoned by a mother and sitting chastely on a sofa. Mae knew for a fact Alice supped on the delights of Wayne Watts, one of the deacons at their Harlem church; Anthony Harris, owner of the Belle Fleur restaurant; and Nicholas King—the very sight of the well-muscled landlord made women draw breath in anticipation of his body threatening to burst through his clothing at any moment. Mae would listen to Alice's exploits in admiration and naked jealousy. At eighteen Alice was already her own woman while Mae, at twenty, doubted she ever would be.

So instead she just asked Alice, "Where have you been?"

"I wasn't feeling too well after dinner. Had to make my mama believe I was fine, that it was just something I ate."

Mae didn't ask why Alice wasn't feeling well. She didn't care. It only mattered that Alice had made her way to Mae there, now, and the feeling of loneliness that often opened up and threatened to swallow Mae whole had closed again.

"Come here," Mae whispered. "Lie down."

The willow fronds cascaded down around them and shielded them from prying eyes. They pulled their gowns down and lay topless. Their rounded breasts shimmered with sweat and shone like new suns in the rising moonlight.

"I heard my daddy playing jazz music in his room this afternoon," Alice said.

Mae snorted. "Mama calls it devil music."

"My mama too! Why do you think he was listening in his

room? She won't allow it in the rest of the house! It sure felt good, though. I heard it coming through my bedroom window. And to think they get to hear music like that in Paris all day long."

Mae nodded. Alice loved to talk about Paris, how they should pack steamer trunks, run off to New York City, and board a ship to cross the Atlantic. A few weeks ago Alice had jumped on top of Mae's bed and held a towel around her naked butt and waist like a sinfully short skirt.

"Can you imagine us in Paris, Mae?" She shook her rear in a shivering shimmy. "We would be queens! Josephine Baker would have nothing on us!"

Mae had pulled a chair over, put her feet up on the bed, and applauded and crowed at Alice's dance.

"Oh yeah! Show me some sugar!"

Alice had squatted low and let her plump bare breasts bounce against her chest. She stood again and kicked her legs up, one after the other, high into the air. Then she fell backwards and lay spread-eagle on the bed laughing.

"And you know," she'd added when she had caught her breath, "they're not afraid of blacks in France. People aren't penned up—none of this 'You live in that neighborhood and we'll live in this neighborhood.' You can be where you want to be. Keep the whole damn city in your pocket if you want. You'll see, Mae. One day we'll go to Paris together and you'll see."

Now Alice was quiet. Her eyes seemed lost staring into the branches above her. "I could've just laid there listening forever," she said of the jazz music. "That piano felt like it was talking to me. Talking in my heart."

"Alice, that's crazy." Mae laughed and snuggled closer. "You don't know what you're saying."

Alice stared at Mae for what seemed like a very long time. "Maybe I don't," she finally said. "Never mind that now. Let me see you walk. Walk for me."

Mae didn't want to leave her perfect place nestled against Alice's warm skin, but something about her friend's voice, her breathy, catlike purr, always made Mae's body obey. She dropped herself out of the hammock and skipped a few paces away.

"Remember, relax. Let your hips swing."

Mae closed her eyes and frowned. She couldn't remember how to relax. Everything Mae learned about her body made her straight and hard like an ironing board. Her mother never allowed any part of Mae, her hips in particular, to veer off center. She learned to walk with books on her head and her mother's hand on her spine. The icy touch held her taut and upright.

"Mae," she heard Alice whisper, "pretend you're me."

Mae took a deep breath that settled into the lower part of her body and made her right hip rise underneath her hand. She opened her eyes, gazed directly into Alice's, and swung one foot forward until it landed precisely in front of the other. The next foot swung out from behind and Mae placed it again in front and in line with the back foot. Her left arm swung through the air as she lowered her chin. Once she got her feet going and pounding out a rhythm, her body knew better what to do. After that it was like dancing. When she arrived back in front of Alice, Mae placed her hands on both hips, threw her head

back, and laughed with a joy that made her body tingle. Whenever she could unlock her body like this Mae felt like a god.

"That's my girl!" Alice crowed, and Mae threw herself
back down into the hammock. "When are you gonna use those
moves where it matters?"

Mae shook her head. Didn't Alice see it mattered now, more
than it ever would with anyone else? She couldn't see herself
walking for anyone but Alice. Alice had brought this body out
of Mae and as far as Mae was concerned, it belonged to Alice.
"Yeah, like Mama's ever gonna let me out of her sight long
enough to do that."

"You're here now, aren't you?" Alice sat up and looked
around. "And I don't see your mama anywhere out here."

"Yeah, well, this is different. There are no men around here
either."

Alice laughed. "Oh, Mae, you just don't see it, do you?"

"See what?"

"You've got more freedom, more choices, more chances
than you realize. If anything, that fishbowl your mama's got
you living in is gonna protect you so you can do even more."

"Alice, what are you talking about?"

"I'm talkin' about you being Mae Malveaux. Your mama's
got more money than all of Harlem and half of Westchester.
You've already got men lined up around your parlor and going
out the door of your brownstone."

"I don't want to marry any of them! All they want is our
money."

"But that's just it, you don't have to, Mae! You can have as
many of them as you want, keep them dangling for as long as
you want. Not one of them will say a damn word as long as they

think they can have that money. But you'll cut 'em loose before they realize they don't have a chance in hell."

Mae stared at Alice and asked a question for which, somewhere inside, she already knew the answer: "Why would I want to do that, Alice?"

A slow, icy smile sprouted in the corner of Alice's mouth and spread wide across her lips until it gleamed and struck Mae's heart cold.

"Just because it feels good, of course."

Mae lay back and let Alice's words run through her. When they came out the other side they bred possibilities that expanded like a wave of heat until they sat enormous and expectant on top of Mae's heart. She saw herself tearing open Nicholas King's shirt, running her hands along the hard ripples on his chest.

As if it wanted to practice a similar motion, Mae's finger floated across Alice's chest and traced the outline of the dark areola of one of her breasts that, magically, seemed fuller than Mae had ever seen them. Her thumb took the flesh of the nipple into a playful pinch, but Alice pushed Mae's arm away.

"Ow! Naw, Mae, that hurts!"

"It never used to hurt."

"Well, it do now."

"How come?"

"How come? Mae, don't you know anything? Because your breasts get tender—they hurt. That's just something that happens when you're gonna have a baby."

Mae stared, blinked, and then began to laugh hard, deep in the belly. It was this kind of humor that made her love Alice so—she made Mae feel good deep down like they were skipping through clouds and didn't care what anyone thought. But when she tried to move down to nuzzle into the space just under Alice's arm and above her breast, Mae found Alice's bright brown eyes staring back at her, hard and stony.

"What? What'd I do?"

"What are you laughing at? I just told you I'm gonna have a baby and that's supposed to be funny?"

"You're what? Alice, *no!*" Mae sat up so fast the hammock swung wildly. Alice got her feet on the ground and steadied herself and Mae.

"I told you I was sick tonight. Did that sound like a joke?"

"No." Mae stood up. She didn't know what else to do. "Alice, who's the daddy?"

"Nicholas King, I think, but it doesn't matter!" Alice shook her head. "Because I'm not having it!"

"Not having it? But how? Alice, what are you gonna do?"

"There are ways, Mae. I'm not givin' up my life, you can bet your sweet mama's fortune, I'm not!"

"How can you do something like that, Alice? Why would you?"

"Mae, one of these days you're gonna learn this world ain't made for colored women. You don't own nothing but what you can take for yourself. You got a mama who owns her world, so you don't have to worry about all that. But she knows what's what. How come she ain't married? Where's your daddy at, Mae?"

Mae couldn't respond. She only knew rumors, half-truths, and a baritone voice that still sang her to sleep in her dreams.

"At the end of the day, though, you'll still have people callin' you nigger behind your back, and most of them will be men. So why can't we take what we want, just like they do? Why can't we be in charge of our own lives, as long as we have our own money to do it? They think they can have it all for nothing, Mae. I will always make them pay."

Alice's face glowed like burning coal and Mae couldn't take her eyes off her. She was like Moses returned from the mountaintop and Mae wanted to know more and go where her friend had been. Then she heard the feet pounding and the earth seemed to shift as she saw Alice's mother charging toward them. When Alice finally turned it was too late. Della Evans's hand came down like lightning and whacked the side of her daughter's cheek.

"What the hell are you doing out here? Cover yourself up!" She stopped dead and looked closely at Alice's breasts as if she were seeing them for the first time. Mae could tell she wouldn't fail to see what Mae herself had missed. Alice shrunk back and pulled her gown up over her shoulders.

"Alice Evans, you tell me the truth right this minute! Do you have a baby in that belly?" She raised her hand again. "You tell me right now or I'll knock your ass into next year!"

Alice covered her head with her arms while Mae stood with her hand gripping the hammock, her nightgown still bunched up around her stomach.

"Y-yeah, Mama," she stammered. "Yes."

"Whore!" Mrs. Evans grabbed Alice's arm and pulled her close, then smacked her on the head and across the face. Alice's mother kept pulling her across the lawn and back to their house.

"Mrs. Evans, no! Stop!" Mae protested, not knowing what else to do to protect her friend. But the older woman's eyes flashed and Mae felt like a hole had been burned into her face.

"Mae Malveaux, you get your sass-ass back home before I get your mama and tell her you're out here walkin' around half naked!"

"But Alice!" She reached for her friend. Alice waved her off.

"Mae!" Alice spoke sharply. Tears flooded her eyes. "Go home! I'll be all right."

"Shut up! Just shut up!" Mrs. Evans pushed Alice ahead of her and they disappeared into the dark. The words rushing from her mouth dissolved so Mae couldn't tell what she was saying, but whatever they were, they still poured out hot and furious. And Mae was sure Alice was still crying.

There would be no getting rid of the baby now.

* * *

THE EVANSES DROVE back to Harlem the next day. Mae heard nothing from Alice for an entire month. Then came the day when Mama told her to pack—they were going back into the city a few days early.

"How come, Mama?"

"Oh, I thought you'd be happy to go. That Evans girl, your friend, is getting married to Ray Barton. About time that nice man found himself a wife. I hear they're moving to Detroit after the wedding."

"Ray Barton!" Mae's hand swept to her mouth and her fingers felt like ice. Alice would never marry a man like Ray Barton. Yes, he was well respected in their church community and he was imposing—he stood over six feet tall and had shoulders so broad that standing in front of him was like standing in front of a brick wall. He had survived the war,

but whether he had survived in one piece was another matter.
Both Mae and Alice knew he wasn't right in the head. The
dark lines under his eyes and the hollow look within them told
how a man could be snapped open like a new tin of hair pomade,
and his insides scooped out just as easily to be spread out glistening and melting under the burning gaze of the sun.

When the wedding ceremony began and Alice appeared at
the wide-open oak doors of the Fairfield Baptist Church, Mae
couldn't make out her friend. Alice was swathed in layers of
organdy to hide her shape and her face was covered with a long
white veil. It wasn't until after, at the reception, that Mae could
push toward Alice and have her worst fears confirmed. The
girl stood glassy-eyed as she stared past the faces of each happy
guest offering congratulations. But her look softened when
Mae reached her. Alice's spirit felt small, so small Mae could
hold it in the palm of her hand.

"Mae! My Mae!" They embraced, close enough for Mae to
hear Alice choke down a sob in her throat.

"How are you?" Mae whispered. "I'm sorry, I wanted to
help."

"Shush. I'm gonna be all right."

"But Detroit? It's so far. What am I going to do without you?"

"You will be all right."

Mae's knees shook. A cool grief began to sweep over her.

Alice, as if reading Mae, grabbed her by the shoulders and
lifted her up to stand taller. She turned Mae around and whispered in her ear. "See him?" she hissed urgently. *"See him?"*

Mae's eyes sped around the room. "Who, Alice, who?"

He stood leaning against a pillar, his lanky frame dressed
in a rich-looking suit and his pencil-thin mustache perfectly

groomed. His long fingers held his drink so lightly it seemed to float in the air beside him. Mae didn't know his name, but she knew it didn't matter.

"Mae, have him," Alice whispered. "Take him for me." She kissed Mae on the cheek and pushed her in his direction. Mae looked back into her friend's eyes and realized she would never see Alice again. She nodded.

Mae turned to him. She breathed down into her lower body and let her legs swing forward. Her hips swayed. As her hands moved up to them Mae raised her chest up and in that moment she felt a coal ignite in her heart. This man, whoever he was, would be the first to pay.

* * *

Val

Harlem, 1925

Val Jackson didn't want to walk any farther. Not when he already felt the hard leather rubbing on his toes so a blister could form at any moment. Not when the sun had already risen high enough to be in his eyes and burn his thirteen-year-old head. He wasn't running all over town to find the perfect empty street when this alley right here, bounded by Mr. Porter's pine board fence and the cellar walls of tall apartment buildings, was wide enough and close enough. They were stopping right now.

"Here!" he shouted to the boys just ahead of him. He

dropped his glove on the ground and bent over to retie his shoe. "We can play right here!"

"Naw, naw, ain't enough room. You crazy!" Short Red Johnson kept walking and pointed the way with his stick. "We gotta go out to the street like my mama said."

"Your mama'll be beatin' us over the head when you get your sorry butt run over! We're playing right here."

Besides, Val thought, *I don't have time for this.* That little shrimp didn't know what time was. He could run around in the streets till the sun went down and maybe even after that. Short Red's mama didn't sit at home reading all day, threatening to call him home the moment she came across words that made her think, *My son's got to know this!* Short Red wouldn't get dragged home to the kitchen table and a makeshift classroom, as though summer didn't matter and there wasn't enough time in the world to learn who thought what about colored people and what they needed to do with themselves.

Val rolled up the cuffs of his pants to keep them out of the dust. Some of the other boys stopped and made their own preparations.

"Shit," Short Red murmured. "All right."

They followed Val's lead because they didn't know any better. Val just had that way about him. They knew he wasn't the oldest—Tyrone, who was throwing down a potato sack for second base, would be fifteen next month. But Val was the best talker and the best player. If you wanted him on your side you just shut up so he knew you weren't gonna bother him too much.

He was the best looking too. Val had smooth deep-brown skin, high cheekbones, and a blinding smile. When he stared at you with shining eyes, you felt like you were the only person in the world, and you wanted to follow him around forever just so you could stay in that light.

"Short Red, you up first!" Tyrone stretched his muscled back like he was about to take a nap, not pitch a ball. The boy stepped up to the plate and Val bent over to wait for the ball. Sometimes it happened too fast—the swoosh of the bat as it whipped round through the air, the *crack* when it made contact with the ball, the drumming of running feet, the satisfying thump of the ball into the glove.

"Boy, that wasn't no strike! My grandma can pitch better than that and make corn bread while she's waitin' to bat!"

"Then you better get her out here 'cause I don't see no one else pitchin' and I need somethin' to eat!"

"My grandma got better things to do than teach you how to play your game!"

For Val the best part was when it was his turn to grip the stick in his hands and feel the sting in his palms when he thwacked the ball out into the street. It burned like hell but he could sing with the pain because it just felt right to be making use of his body. Didn't his mama understand that? Didn't she know all the times she was scolding him for not being able to sit still when he was supposed to be practicing scales on the piano that he was just trying to give in to his body's power? He had felt it coming on for months, like he was starting to get things he didn't have a use for yet. But he was understanding these new things wanted him to move, to be in his body and feel everything there was to feel: heat, cold, pain, sharpness, and that other thing—the sensation he had no name for. It made him shiver when he watched the older girls like April Jean strut

down the street with chests suddenly rising like they had baseballs stuffed underneath their shirts.

He didn't know what the feeling was, didn't know what to
do with it. One day he expected the shiver to come round full
force and explode out of his mouth with an exultant *Aaaahhhh!*
But until then he would swing the bat and sniff the leather of
his glove and whip balls out into the air. One day it would all be
clear to him—one day.

Not this day. On this day the sting in his hands would be
followed by the crashing sound of broken glass, his friends
swearing, and the hammering of their feet running away from
him. Val dropped the stick and looked up with resignation at
the broken window where Mrs. Walker's braided white head
soon appeared.

"Val Jackson! Val Jackson! You get your behind up here
right now, boy! Your daddy's gonna have your hide if I don't
tear it off first! You get up here now—don't you give me that
look, boy!"

You go ahead and get my daddy, Val thought. *And I can look
at you any way I please.* He didn't have to run like the other
boys, running scared like rabbits looking for a hole to jump
down. His mama was right—there were some things he didn't
know. And his body told him there were many things he
didn't understand. But this he knew for certain: this was Harlem.
His name was Valiant Jackson. And because of those two things
he didn't have to be afraid of nobody.

CHAPTER 1
Mae

Harlem, May 1947

Mae loved herself with a ferocity that came of feeding too hard and too long on her own exquisite beauty. She could smile in the rearview mirror of her car and see the alabaster beam reflected back from her picture in advertisements for Malveaux's Magic Hair Pomade plastered on every billboard and in the windows of every drugstore starting from West 53rd Street, going all the way up Manhattan and through Harlem for the next hundred blocks.

Even now she gazed happily into her vanity as her maid, Justice, applied the French pomade and arranged the dark folds of her hair into thick Victory curls perfectly framing her face. She never used the concoction her mother had created and made famous. Tired of having it smeared on her head since childhood, Mae had thrown away her own grease-filled powder-blue tin in the days after her mother's death.

She held out her wrists and Justice dabbed on fragrant dots

from the crystal bottle of Caron Fleurs de Rocaille perfume. Mae's cold-creamed skin glowed bright and her eyes danced with the sparkle of a girl, making her seem younger than her thirty-three years. She knew this feature made her irresistible. Mysteriously, each man thought he had discovered this light for himself and believed only he could see it in her. They never noticed her well-hidden contempt for their arrogance.

Mae was vigilant about her expressions. She learned long ago the faces she wore would always be more essential than any dress she put on, no matter if it were a Christian Dior or a Pierre Balmain. Her beauty was a formidable instrument because people liked to stare at her as they would a motion picture actress and, in the same vein, she could tell them any story she chose to project and they would believe it. So she practiced the lift of her cheeks, the turnings of her mouth, the shapes of her lips, and the conjured emotions that she flitted across her eyes. Her masterstroke came when she could wipe her face smooth and present a look of calm so numinous it bewitched her admirers into claiming her a goddess.

In rare instances, though, she suffered a rebellion to her visage of serenity. It was an errant twitch seated in the muscles of her lower-left eyelid. She always felt it right before it surfaced. It was as though the weight of all the folly the eye had beheld was suddenly too much for it. She saw how, though small and fast, it unmasked her disdain. Not everyone would notice, but someone less foolhardy—someone like Val Jackson—would never miss such a telling detail.

Regina, her white Polish maid, brought in Mae's long, satin Dior that had arrived from Paris the previous day. Mae stood, stepped into the gown, and enjoyed the feel of the gold fabric flowing down her body in a shimmering cascade. She placed one hand on Justice's shoulder and lifted her right foot with the grace of a ballerina. Regina took hold of Mae's ankle, guided her into leather slingback pumps, then pulled the strap through the buckle.

Too tight. Too tight.

"Ouch!" Mae lit out with her right hand, landing a blow upon the woman's ear and side of her face. Regina's arm rose in defense.

"I'm sorry, ma'am," she whispered. "I'm so sorry."

Mae looked away while she finished. The stacked heel added nearly two inches to her height so she had to sit again. This allowed Justice to fasten the necklace of marquise-cut diamonds while Regina clasped the diamond-and-platinum bracelet around Mae's thin wrist.

Mae occupied the largest brownstone on Sugar Hill. Designed by the noted architect Branford Waite, it featured a double-width façade and a broad stoop from the front door to the street. Perfect white shades on the windows muted the sun's glare during the day but let in plenty of light. The flower boxes on the ledges contained enough nicotiana, tuberose, and alyssum so their combined sweet fragrance would greet Mae each time she walked out the door.

That night she came gliding out of the building like a new moon rising. All down the block she knew quick hands snapped shutters closed then reopened them a crack so their owners could spy on her floating down the steps to where her man, Lawrence, held open the door to her forest-green Packard. She knew this because she knew exactly how her world was situated—how every single person thought, including and especially what they thought of her. She choreographed each step, each motion, and she moved through Harlem exactly as she pleased because of it. What good was money otherwise? She laughed at the predictability of society and how no one but her seemed to understand how to wield this delicious power. And since her mother died, and then her own husband, Mae reveled in the added sweet freedom of answering to no one.

She settled into the caramel cushions of the car's backseat. Lawrence steered in the direction of the Swan, her chosen nightclub. Mae knew in particular how it would be there. Lately the bandleader would make sure they didn't play Duke Ellington's gorgeous new piece, "Lady of the Lavender Mist," her favorite, unless she was in the room and ready to dance. Her usual party would be seated and waiting at her table. The air already hummed with the expectancy of an unseasonably warm Saturday night. The scene was set. It only needed her to make it come alive.

* * *

THE SWAN, OWNED by Ike Dunbar, the real estate business-man, held the distinction of being the only club in Harlem completely free of the lower classes. Mae appreciated how smart Dunbar had been in his thinking. As popular as the Savoy was with its crowds of whites slumming from downtown and big bands laying down the heat every night, the club allowed anyone in. Dunbar knew people like Mae wouldn't set foot in a place like that when it held even the smallest possibility she could end up dancing next to her maid. So he created the Swan to be different. She loved the place for it. The bouncers, many of them former prizefighters, wore tailored suits Dunbar ordered himself, and he introduced them to every single member of the Swan's clientele so they could greet them by name. It also made it easier to spot strangers who didn't belong so the bouncers could offer the right physical encouragement to leave the premises.

These same bouncers, without hesitation, grasped the door handles, beautiful ivory bars carved to look like curving swan necks, and pulled them open for Mae. She walked over mosaic tile depicting two swans facing each other, their necks entwined, and quickly crossed the foyer lit by a mammoth chandelier of sparkling crystal and brass. She climbed the narrow staircase to a balcony landing lined by a wall of thick black velvet curtains. Two men dressed in tuxedos, their dark curls trimmed close to their scalps, flanked the opening, and when Mae approached they held open the folds so she could step through. This revealed another piece of genius by Dunbar—a grand staircase made of ebony, the risers lit with tiny starlike lights. It went down to the main floor of the club so anyone arriving would make a stunning entrance.

When Mae descended the stairs she maintained an even, middle-distance gaze. She didn't want to look like she was assessing the room, which of course she was. And because all eyes were on her she knew to be careful. She certainly didn't want to acknowledge Ike Dunbar waiting for her, as usual, at the bottom of the stairs. People might think they were a couple and Mae wouldn't stand for that. But she allowed him to lead her to her table in reverential silence. He used to turn himself inside out trying to say something to make her laugh but she put a stop to that long ago. Instead he played the respectful escort while she enjoyed the sound of the trumpets and saxophones laying out notes so smooth she felt she could float upon them all the way to her table. A gentle haze of cigarette smoke mingled with the scent of whiskeys and gins. She smiled because she felt beautiful and whole in this careful pearl that was her world, but she pretended she smiled at nothing in particular. She shared her joy with no one.

She sensed the room holding its breath until she slid into her booth. The gentlemen stood. Her cousin Gladys Vaughn called out Mae's name before scooting her stout rear end over. The thick black and white cushioning rose up behind Mae and provided a dramatic backdrop. She took a cigarette from the box on the table and one of the men swiftly lit it for her before sitting carefully out of her line of sight. Mae liked being where she could see the whole room, and everyone could see her. Then the music, the dancing—the swirl—began again. At her table Mae surrounded herself with the safely boring, suitable for her position as a wealthy widow. They were all well-respected, churchgoing people yet connected enough to both provide her with important tidbits of information and broadcast certain bon mots when she needed to have the news out in the community.

Gladys, her lipstick too pink as always, wore a dark blue gown made of jersey, the only fabric forgiving enough to stretch with beauty, not tightness, over her thick body's ample curves. "Don't you look pretty?" she said. "I was saying you look like the sun coming through the room, didn't I?"

"She certainly did," Joe-Joe Johnson and Mantel Suggs replied in unison. They were Mae's safe admirers. She enjoyed having mature but good-looking men at her table. Mantel was a prominent physician; Joe-Joe was the photographer of record for their social circle. He was the only one she allowed to take her picture for the press. Both were sharp and handsome in their tuxedos and appropriately adoring of her, perhaps because she knew their secret: though both kept girlfriends, they preferred at the end of the night to go home—and to bed—with each other.

"Do you want the usual, Miss Malveaux?" Joe-Joe asked.

"Yes, thank you."

He signaled to a waiter but one was already pushing toward them a cart carrying a bottle of champagne in a silver bucket.

She'd call these people around her friends if she could, but in one way or another they piqued her too much. Across from her, Florence and Edward Mills sat close, raising their now refilled glasses in ridiculous toasts—"Here's to life!" They were much older than Mae, once friends of her mother's. Ed was both a lawyer and the son of a lawyer and had handled her mother's business. His happy, nervous energy tested Mae's patience. But the couple could sit on the other side of the table with their backs facing the room and didn't need to spin their heads in an obvious way like Gladys did. Sometimes Mae would look over and notice Ed and Flo holding hands under the table. The sight would always confuse her because she'd feel a pinch of contempt while at the same time wanting to cry. She survived these instances by observing how commonplace their sentimentality was and how quickly, she knew, it would disintegrate in the face of a searing, well-placed moment of cruelty.

So this was the mix Mae favored—a touch of high society from the Millses, respectable blood relative in Gladys, and handsome men to dress up the table. The rest of the room was stocked with the city's leading black politicians, doctors, lawyers, and real estate brokers. Every so often a journalist managed to slip in as someone's guest but no one liked an overt eavesdropper, so few were invited to return.

Gladys spoke nonstop, which ensured awkward pauses never dampened the table. She sipped her champagne and chattered away. Mae nodded, her head tilted toward her cousin with false intimacy, but already she was searching the room. Perhaps it was the feel of the gold dress against her thighs, or the perception of her own glowing, but Mae was in the mood to take in something special tonight. She didn't know what she wanted, though, and when she felt this way she was liable to take a man just because she could. Then later she'd regret it because he would turn out not to be worth the trouble and worse—not up to her standards.

Then the music changed and she heard him—the band had a new singer. She had never heard a voice so smooth, so rich. She forced herself to not look at him, but his voice seemed to pull her his way. She sent her white flare smile out to the room and even managed to converse a little with Gladys, but the singer poured honey in her ears all the while.

How many times had she heard "Nature Boy" in this room? What was so different about him? The song sounded bare, stripped down. When Mae finally gave in and allowed herself a glance she paused.

He was so young.

His smooth, fair skin shone and the stage lights made him angelic. He seemed to smile as he sang, drawing contentment from his music. His soft reddish curls framed his forehead. His body, strong and broad, anchored her eyes to the stage. The rest of the band listened as he sang accompanied only by the piano, bass, and simple rhythm guitar. Mae forced herself to turn away and picked up her champagne glass but still she listened.

The greatest thing you'll ever learn
Is just to love and be loved in return.

He sang the last lines like he believed the words. Did he really? She wanted to know and she wanted to know firsthand.

"What did you say about Cecily?" Mae leaned toward her cousin, determined to feign interest.

"I said she got up here on Thursday. From North Carolina."

"Why didn't you bring her tonight?"

"Here?" Gladys pulled her silk stole back up over her beefy brown shoulders. "Oh, honey, that girl's eyes would pop right out of her head before she even got her butt in that chair good. Then they'd be rolling around the room all night. She's been down South so long it'll take a while for her to get used to this kind of society. That's why I want you to talk to her a little. You can help her."

Mae doubted that. Her cousin's daughter was, at least when Mae last saw her, a gangly colt of a girl with big, dark, empty eyes. Mae found the thought of her dull. The fact that she had spent the past year on a farm in the South made her even more so.

"Cecily will be fine. She'll figure things out just like we all did growing up."

"Yes, but she doesn't have that kind of time. She's gonna be married not too long from now."

The fold of a tiny frown dented Mae's brow. "Married? Gladys, what are you talking about? She's so young."

"She's young, but not too young to get into trouble. And with all the money she's gonna have, the good-for-nothing men around here will get her before you know it."

Mae's fingers grasped her glass and she had to be careful she didn't crush the crystal in her hand. It was 1947. Why did their families think a black girl with money had to be tied to some older man like a store-bought daddy? Maybe, she thought, there were too many dirty old men too happy for the privilege. She had endured Brantwell Davis as a husband because he was quiet and suitably in love with her. The Howard-educated fool also happened to own many of the stores stocking the Malveaux products, which is why her mother thought him a good choice. But Mae didn't mourn when he toppled over in church, dead of a heart attack. She snatched back her maiden name within weeks of his funeral. "Well, then, who's going to marry her?"

"A respectable man with money of his own," Gladys said, raising her glass with a triumphant smirk. "Someone who will appreciate a good girl for what she is."

"And who exactly is that?"

"Frank Washington. Here he is right now."

Mae followed Gladys's gaze and saw Frank striding toward them, his arms out as though he were about to embrace them both. A chill ran down her bare shoulders and into her arms. Ice crystals blossomed on the surface of her skin. She couldn't believe the man had the audacity to come at her smiling like he was about to sell her Edgecombe Avenue. He knew better than to be familiar with her in public. But this fearless flaunting told her he didn't think she had a hold on him anymore.

They had been lovers once, good ones too. He appreciated her power, her money, and her instinct. He thought her shrewd to be so discreet in her relationships. He was happy to sleep with her but knew to be careful in public places. Still, she collected the usual insurance, as she did with all her lovers: little secrets, bits of information she knew were supposed to go no further than their bed. She always knew exactly where and how a man could be hurt so he wouldn't dare go boasting he'd had Mae Malveaux. Frank loved his position in society just as much as she did. He loved appearances even more. But he seemed to accept the terms of their relationship too cheerfully. She felt she always had to drop tiny hints to remind him of what she knew about his business—the illegitimate child he'd sent off to grow up daddy-less in Pittsburgh; the quiet payments he made to appraisers who valued properties the way he wanted them to.

Of the tiringly large number of marriage proposals she'd received since her husband's death, Frank's was the only one she would have considered with a serious mind. The base of his money was old and respectable. He had been born in New York and so had his parents. But then he had the ambition to make money of his own in this new Harlem, putting together real estate deals. He had helped half the churches in acquiring new property, often from him. And he had some flair, and enough of his own interests that he wouldn't always be around and stifling her.

Only Frank never proposed. She remembered that final night in his bed when she'd thought he'd been about to ask. They'd been talking about marriage and she had been half listening, already planning how to string out her indecision, how she would hold him on the threshold of anticipation every day, possibly for months, before finally saying yes.

"Everyone up here looks down on the South," he had said, lying back with his hands under his head. "I think it would be the best place in the world to get married."

"Well, yes, but why would you think that?" She didn't want a country wedding where they served corn pone and molasses.

"That's the only place you can find a girl, a really good girl. The women up here, even the young ones, know too much. They seen too much. A girl from a good family in the South would be pure as the driven snow. I'm gonna marry a girl like that someday."

Mae had had to work hard to absorb the shock of his words. Her fist had gripped the sheet into a ball and pulled it around her naked body, but she'd pretended to be getting up to get dressed as usual. She'd smiled, but cooled to him after that. She'd placed a kind of formality between them and finally, when she felt enough time had passed for him not to connect the event with her current action, she'd told him it was over. His complacency had made her burn. He hadn't asked why. He'd simply shaken her hand like he was walking away from a poker buddy. By the end of the week he was strutting arm in arm with that fat Delia Song, who used to run around with Val Jackson.

* * *

NOW HE WAS coming at her grinning because he'd found his Southern-fried virgin at last. Mae wanted to leap out of her skin and tear his throat open. Instead she smiled as she would to any admirer.

"Good evening, Mrs. Vaughn, Miss Malveaux."

Gladys beamed. "Hello, Frank, it's so good to see you! I want you to know Cecily is home safe and sound. She'll be in church tomorrow morning if you want to see her. She's gonna be so happy to see you again!"

Those last words felt like a big lie and the weight of them made Mae's eye twitch come on. She drew on her cigarette and turned away to blow the smoke into the air.

"That would be nice, thank you," said Frank. "It's good to know she's home where she belongs."

He turned to Mae. "Miss Malveaux, I have it on good authority the band is readying 'Lady of the Lavender Mist.' Would you like to dance it with me?"

Now she boiled because he had put her in an impossible situation. He was being much too familiar, wanting not only to dance, but to her favorite music no less! What was he out to prove tonight? She mashed her cigarette into a crystal ashtray and stared at him. He seemed to recognize the look because he immediately dipped his head into a slight bow and added, "If you don't mind putting up with a clumsy old fool like me."

She gave him a small, tight smile and nodded. Frank was a very good dancer and he knew it. She could say yes to his offer; he would pay too much attention to how good he looked on the floor. She once teased him that he should have been onstage, had missed his calling as a performer.

He waited as though he wanted an invitation to sit down but Mae looked past him and sipped from her glass. Finally he bowed again to Gladys's grinning and nodding and slunk off.

"When?" Mae asked Gladys.

"When what, honey?"

Mae moved her glass toward Joe-Joe for more champagne. "When will you have the wedding?"

Gladys's eyes widened as though she were a child and Mae had mentioned Christmas. "In about six months or so. Maybe even New Year's Day."

"New Year's Day?" Ed asked. He glanced at his wife—her mouth shrunk into a knot like she'd tasted something sour. "A lot of people still hold superstitions around New Year's." Then he laughed. "They might be afraid to leave home that day."

"Oh, they'll be there." Gladys waved a hand through the air. "Frank wants a big wedding even if we have to serve enough collards and black-eyed peas to feed half of Harlem."

"Of course he does," Mae said.

The information sealed her decision. She would crush Frank's plan. But how to do it? Yes, she had enough influence with her cousin to dissuade her from the marriage—it would take only a few well-placed hints or concerns. However, Mae wanted more. She wanted Frank's humiliation, to have him walk through Harlem with laughter trailing in his wake. She wanted his hypocrisy exposed, his name thoroughly ridiculed. That might be enough for her.

By the time she heard the first strains of the Duke Ellington tune and Frank Washington came over to claim her, Mae had made her plans. This allowed her to accept his hand graciously and take the dance floor in his arms. The grinning dummy couldn't fathom what was to come, and she was determined to make him pay for his ignorance.

The other couples made room for them and Mae was glad

because she was closer to the band and she knew the singer would be able to look at her. She danced for him. Frank spun her around and dipped her. She arched her back a tiny fraction more. Her chest plumed upward. When she came up again she felt full, full of strategies and opportunities. If Frank had lifted her at that moment she was certain she could have flown. Then he swung her out and she faced the singer dead-on. She sent the young crooner a look of asking and light and yearning. She knew he caught it because he was nearly a half beat late coming in with the next verse. She heard a tickle in his voice that proved him unnerved. He would want to know more. She had him. She would send her man Lawrence to retrieve him.

Suddenly Mae knew she would take this singer to Paris, even if he had been there before. She would make it all new for him. He would sing "Nature Boy" for her, just as he did it to-night, and he would teach her what those last two lines meant for him, why he could sing them the way he did, like he really believed the words were the secret he had been put on earth to discover. Was he really young enough to think like that? She would turn his spotlight on herself and absorb all these mysteries, if they did indeed exist in him. It was worth the exploration. At worst, he would turn out to be like any other man. She would enjoy him nonetheless.

Frank spun her around again and in the corner of her eye she noticed a tall dark-skinned man trotting down the grand staircase with the grace of an athlete.

Val Jackson had arrived.

It was just like him, she thought, to enter the Swan mid-song, when the dance floor was full and the focus away from the stairs. But then he seemed to enjoy blending into crowds unnoticed. He frequented baseball games, and—where had she first met him? On a busy concourse at the World's Fair in 1939. In other ways, more important ways, he was like her. Soon the room would fill with whispers and she'd feel them like a breeze changing direction. She needed only a quick glance over Frank's shoulder to see how good Val looked tonight. French cuffs gleamed from the sleeves of his tuxedo, matching the wattage of his smile, a smile that seemed like a miracle in the way it made his ebony-dark skin glow. Not many men could smile like that and not look like a fool.

Of course she wanted Val, how could she not? He was every-thing she was—wealthy, gorgeous, and, best of all, keenly aware the world had been made just for him. He walked through life the way Mae thought a black man should, not as someone who always had something to prove, but as someone who wanted everyone else to prove why they were worth his attention. Free-dom filled Val Jackson and he wasn't afraid to see the world from his high advantage and act on it. More important, he wasn't afraid of Mae, and this endeared him to her forever.

Val, like her, feared no one. Val didn't see her as someone to be conquered. He recognized her at once as a superior, and even appreciated how she had to be better, craftier, and smarter than he did because she was a woman. She loved him for being the only one who could endure the shining hard re-ality of her. She never slept with him—she had her reasons for this—but Mae and Val were each ravenous for an equal. They affirmed each other, proved the way they saw the world was true and that they were indeed gods, not false deities created in their own minds. Though they stayed carefully separated socially, she held Val close to her and never strayed far from him in her thoughts. She even cheered him on from afar. They were on a tremendous walk around the world, and she had no doubt he would meet her again when they were done with all the specious pursuits and ready to complete their journey together. She was certain, so certain, Val would be her last, sweetest, and final lover.

Mae did want love. She didn't care that it didn't last, didn't care how easily it could be broken. What she cared about was how every human being seemed to walk the earth clutching at love, but she couldn't do the same. She knew that shouldn't matter—she didn't want to be so ridiculous and so weak—yet she did desire love if only to have it in her hands, a rare bauble she could enjoy as she studied its strange hold on the world. But for Mae some entity always held love, ripe and shining, just out of her reach, letting her know with soul-slicing certainty that she wasn't good enough to have it.

The only person she had ever truly loved, Alice, had loved Mae enough to warn her about this. She had seen the work of Mae's mother—the cultivating and promoting of Mae's beauty, sending her daughter to sit in drawing rooms in the capitals of Europe, the search for a safe and respectable man for her to marry—all this would keep Mae from being mistreated and misplaced in the world, safe from the human frailties of hunger, want, greed, and need. But it also meant she was safe— painfully, genuinely, horrifically safe—from love.

When the dance with Frank was over she glowed with the delicious feeling she always had when assured she could have anything she wanted. She didn't even care if anyone thought the look came from dancing with Frank. She signaled for a waiter to summon Lawrence, who hung out near the kitchen anticipating her requests. In this moment of distraction she failed to notice Frank planting himself at her table. Already he was jawing at Gladys about Cecily and apologizing for how he would be away at least part of the summer on business. His hot air clouded the table. Mae took another cigarette and leaned over to Joe-Joe so he could light it.

She ignored Frank and focused instead on Val at the bar across the room. She watched him with her own interests at heart. She envied not the girl he paid attention to, but the way he could stalk his conquest so openly and be feared and admired for it. A woman couldn't do that and remain respectable. She had to be so much smarter. Lawrence came to the table and leaned in close so she could whisper directions to him.

Her tablemates were talking about the weather. Mae cringed.

"It's not as hot as it could be," Gladys was saying to Flo. "That's why I told Rose Jarreau I couldn't bring Cecily for a visit. So much to do with her before the season starts."

"Yes." Flo nodded. "She's so lucky to have a mama like you."

"Well, I told Rose if it gets hot again she'll see us before a drop of my sweat can hit the ground."

Polite laughter rolled around the table.

"Mae, why haven't you gone to the country?" asked Ed.

She smiled. "Now, why would I do that when all of you are here?"

"And that house of yours is air cooled," noted Gladys. "No need to run up out of the city."

"Besides, Gladys," Mae went on, "dear Cecily has already missed so much like you said. I want to do all I can to help her catch up." She looked Frank directly in the eye. "Yes, all I can."

Frank coughed nervously then sighed and stood. "I think I'll go have a word with Ike Dunbar. Excuse me, everyone. Enjoy your evening."

Mae nodded silently and watched him retreat. Something other than anger rose in her and she was enjoying it. She was on the precipice of something exquisite requiring all her formidable powers. One man, this young man, she would have. With the other, Frank, she would trod upon his desire like a worm under her heel. And she would use Val Jackson to do it. It wouldn't be enough to expose Frank's bastard or his shady business dealings. She had to destroy what he desired—or at least the feature he wanted most. The thought that she could orchestrate this while taking another lover made her feel like a man. She felt a glorious ache between her legs and she pressed her thighs together. Wasn't this what men did when they felt disrespected? And was she any less worthy of respect than a man? Frank had to learn this. It was important for anyone whom she allowed into her realm to understand this—you crossed her at a price.

Joe-Joe reached across the table to her. "Care to dance?"

"In a moment, Joe-Joe." She watched Val stand to lead a blue-gowned girl to the floor. "I don't like this song."

Lawrence returned then and leaned close to her ear. "It is done, ma'am," he whispered. "And his name is Sam Delany."

She nodded. Sam Delany had potential; he had a heart. The way he sang, it seemed he soaked up exactly what was in front of him and squeezed it out in the notes of his music. She guessed he wouldn't be incapable of love like Frank was. She was willing to bet he sang about love because he had beheld it, embraced it, absorbed every ounce of it until he shone like a beacon. Soon it would shine on her.

"Good," she whispered back. "Now, when the moment is right I want you to get a message to Val Jackson. Tell him when he's done wading through the mud to come see me after church tomorrow."

"Yes, ma'am."

CHAPTER 2
Val

Harlem, May 1947

Before Val Jackson had left for the Swan he'd sat in his office above his own club, the Diamond. The handsome walnut clock on the wall struck the half hour: nine thirty. He felt the bass throbbing in the floorboards under his feet. Half of Harlem danced beneath his good graces tonight but Val, pulling on his crisp white tuxedo shirt, thought only of Elizabeth Townsend, who was quietly situated at his aunt Rose's Westchester estate. She would be getting ready for bed about now.

His aunt always insisted on dinner at six—ridiculously early. Then she and Elizabeth would walk in the rose garden. Auntie turned in well before nine and that's when Elizabeth wandered the great house alone, sometimes reading in the library. Her husband called each night at nine, an annoying detail. Then she would dress in her nightclothes, a thin cotton gown—sleeveless, the maid Annie had said—and sit on the balcony outside her room and gaze up into the sky before going to bed. One night the housekeeper thought she heard Elizabeth praying out there.

Val fastened the silver cuff links at his wrists and recited Elizabeth's routine to himself twice more as he finished dressing. He knew all the details, thanks to his man Sebastian's unfailing ability to bribe just the right people in his aunt's household. Elizabeth would be in bed by ten p.m. sharp; that's what the latest report had said. He loved the potential of those two succulent hours between eight and ten. Just now, in May, they would be filled with air so thick with humidity no one's mind would want the trouble of thinking straight. The end of a hot summer day was when a woman's guard might be down just enough to entertain latent thoughts.

But that's what he enjoyed about this particular conquest. Elizabeth Townsend didn't have any latent, smoldering desires. He had watched her long enough to know this, seen her loving eyes trained on her straight-as-a-board husband and her arm looped through his. Val would change that. He knew he would be the one to light the match, and whatever thoughts burned in her from there would be entirely his own creation. For a few sweet moments he paused and allowed himself the pleasure of imagining Elizabeth in her bed, her bare skin sliding between the cotton of her nightgown and the famously soft sheets his aunt's home was known for. The prospect made him ache with satisfaction.

A long, slow smile ignited from one corner of his mouth and spread to the other as he sat down behind his desk and leaned back in the enormous burgundy leather chair. Was this what Satchel Paige felt like, coming to the mound to meet a fresh opponent after so many years? Was he rolling in the life of it, so excited that there was still someone worth pursuing even after he had bedded and tasted the best? Elizabeth Townsend was so damn perfect—not one of these pants down, legs up women easily charmed by his name alone. He would savor Elizabeth Townsend when the time came—and it would be so fine the streets of Harlem would want to open up and swallow him, engulfing him in praise and awe.

"Sebastian."

The butler answered so fast it was as though he'd come at Val's very thought. Without a word, he took his employer's left hand and, with a silver file, smoothed the nails and cleaned underneath them.

"Any news?" Val used his right hand to remove a Montecristo cigar from the mahogany humidor on his desk. Sebastian pulled a lighter from his pocket and lit it. The smoke encircled Val's head like a gentle fog and the spicy wood aroma filled the office as Val settled into his feel-good body for the night.

"Miss Malveaux, they say, will be at the Swan, sir."

Val drew on the cigar with a long, deep breath. Nice. He and his wayward love would play their game tonight. There was nothing better than when he and Mae got to perform before an audience.

Only one question remained—who would be their targets? Sebastian popped open a tin of Malveaux's pomade and touched his fingers to the gel. He dabbed the sweet-smelling hair dressing onto the edges of Val's dark curls. He brushed it through quickly, wiped his hands on a thick white towel, and then went to retrieve Val's tuxedo coat from where it hung behind the office door.

Val stood and held out an arm. The finely tailored piece

framed his physique, squaring off his broad shoulders and tapering down to his narrow waist. He approached the full-length mirror and stared. Sometimes Val pitied the world when he looked this good. He knew once he went out that door he could have anything he wanted and any difficulty could be solved with a ten-dollar bill. At thirty-five years old, he walked over Harlem like he walked on a fine Oriental rug.

He straightened the bow tie on his tuxedo.

"I'm ready," he told Sebastian. "You can pack up my things and take them to the apartment. I won't be coming back here."

"Yes, sir. Do you want your room ready? Will you have company tonight?"

"If you're talking about Miss Malveaux, I can't rightly say but there's always the chance. Keep the champagne on ice but if it's anyone else don't bother. Do the usual. You got that?"

"Yes, sir."

"And don't bother with the car. I'll walk to the Swan."

* * *

OUTSIDE ON 7TH Avenue the glorious boulevard opened up before Val. He loved it because the street sang to him, *home, home, home,* in complex, syncopated beats. The smells of every place he passed reached out, inviting him to remember everything he'd ever been. Fish frying at Sally Mo's put him back at his mama's table, his mouth watering for one more piece of her perfect cod. At Ewell's striped barbershop pole Val smelled soap and clove and walked again at his father's side, listening as Daddy repeated his instruction on how he himself would never be accepted in New York because that's just the way people felt about folks who moved up from down south. But because Val had been born in Harlem, life could be different for him. He would have money and birthright. "You will own these streets, son," Daddy had said. "And you can do whatever you want with them."

Val's favorite scent, though, he picked up only on certain women on certain blocks, late in the evening when it was time for them to be out looking for takers of what they had to offer. It put him in mind of Ella Jenkins, who took him by the hand one sweet spring night and, for the price of two nights' rent, made a man of him. After that his daddy could talk about money and birthright all he wanted. Val knew then he possessed a new power that crystallized every advantage he owned. And when he conquered Aletheia Collins he knew the power had turned him into a magnet so strong the world would always come to him.

When he was twenty-one no man could win the love of the black-haired siren who, rumor had it, left a well-to-do husband grieving for her in Pittsburgh because he didn't have enough where it mattered to satisfy her. When she walked down the street, the men could only stare, their catcalls stuck in their throats because her beauty went that deep. Her tiny waist flowed down to hips that bloomed out so full they made every male over the age of twelve want to worship the moon. She smelled of strawberries and the scent lured men to follow her around because it brought them memories of jam and summer and the life flowing through their veins. Her sleepy brown eyes never seemed to take in anything that pleased her, as though nothing would ever be new for her again. But Val wanted to be the man who would strike the match that would light up her face and make her berry-colored lips open for him.

So on the afternoon he saw her in a red cotton dress walking down 7th Avenue he knew how to take her. He stepped in front of her, looped an arm around her waist, and pulled her toward him. He felt her body tense, but instead of ducking like a man about to be slapped, he did nothing—no attempted kiss, no apology, no words at all. Instead he hummed, low, but loud enough for her to hear, "Stardust" and moved her around the sidewalk like it was no different from the polished wood floor of a dance hall. Val kept his gaze clamped on hers until he saw scale after scale fall from her eyes—first bewilderment, then rage, then challenge. But his stare showed that he knew full well who filled his arms and he understood and appreciated the gravity of her being. They bumped into shoppers bustling down the street with their packages until enough of them looked up and either stopped or shuffled toward the curb to give them space. The opening of this space, and the loose, unhurried motions of Val and Aletheia on the pavement drew people to windows and doors and the witnesses couldn't stop looking. It seemed like something from a movie set, but Val figured a woman like Aletheia required a strong dose of fairy tale. For all he knew, that's why she turned up her nose at the world. If a man wanted to take Aletheia Collins he had to be bigger than life. That's what Val aimed to be when he placed both hands on her face, his long fingers framing the curve of her heart-shaped beauty, and laid his own lips full on hers.

Val felt the electricity charging him up into the height of a god. Taking Aletheia to bed that night was almost, almost, anticlimactic by comparison because from that moment, on the street, he owned the real victory and his prize was not Aletheia, but the fierce, undying respect of the men around him.

Without raising a fist, a weapon, or even a five-dollar bill, Val proved himself a man to be reckoned with on the stage they grudgingly valued most. He did enjoy Aletheia. In fact she had been truly a delicacy, her body so primed and gorgeous that her love nearly sucked him out into her bottomless sea to drown. But every marveling glance around Val as he walked Harlem's streets sustained him. And the strength of those looks made Val bold enough to do the thing that caused the boys at the bar to holler and suck in their teeth: he dropped Aletheia just a few weeks later with no more thought than he would have given a dirty hankie. For a man to be able to take pussy like that was one thing, but to leave it at will was something every single one of them, if they were being swear-on-the-Bible honest, knew they couldn't do. They would be enslaved to the pleasures of a woman like Aletheia Collins until she moved on to someone else or died. But Val Jackson was the one who moved on, from one glorious conquest to the next with no fear of retribution. This new game made life for Val bright and urgent. He was a man—the man they wanted to be.

That night as the dusky musk smell lingered in the air Val felt like he was being born all over again.

In the Swan Val descended the stairs on the wave of a trombone crescendo and on the floor he saw Mae enveloped in the sound. Frank Washington twirled her and her feet touched on the two downbeats. Val loved this song too, loved how the trombone's swagger made a woman's hips sway, and the music seemed to hug her curves.

He paused and allowed his deep brown eyes to roam appreciatively over Mae's form. It could only be a moment—a casual observer would think he had barely glanced her way. But she would know. And if he didn't pay his split-second due now, Mae would settle accounts later.

The dance floor was polished to a high gloss. Across the room the bar took up an entire wall with four bartenders, each wearing a black shirt and white jacket, tending the length of it. Single young women, each one gowned and gorgeous, sat on cushioned seats at the bar and hoped one of the well-moneyed men in the room would invite her to sit at a table or, even better, to dance.

Val moved to the bar and an empty seat where he could comfortably scan the room. A line of pouty, lipstick-stained mouths turned in his direction. He ordered a gin and tonic, looked back across the room, and sighed.

The Swan was a playground to him most Saturday nights, but this night he could feel something prickly and impatient about himself. The sameness of the space and the people in it seemed to grate on his nerves, threatening to become unbearable. There was Hedley Wilson making a fool of himself, as usual, with his overcrowded table and seeking eyes, wanting to know who was watching him. Like anyone cared about his over-the-hill self. And the society molls, reveling in their red-boned glory, with their self-satisfied looks and understated diamonds, they turned their heads when Val looked in their direction, as though he wouldn't know how hot they were between their legs underneath their gowns.

Val recognized the feeling: it was again the strange discomfort crawling along the edges of his mind. He had felt it coming on ever since the Robinson game last month—the one in which Jackie Robinson had broken the color line in baseball. One month had passed since Robinson had stepped out of the Dodgers' dugout, dignified and silent. He'd taken up his spot at first base, hands on his knees, ready to play ball. But there had been no way to ignore the rush of noise sweeping the park—many cheers, yes, especially among Val and his friends—but Val could detect the jeers and the word "nigger" grating its nasty undercurrent through the sounds and he could see the tight white mouths of the Boston Braves and many even on Robinson's own team.

Val had wanted to act then, to run through the stands, up and down each section, tossing greenbacks into the white crowd to distract them, to give them the only thing they cared about, to hopefully protect Robinson from the white hot glare of their anger. But there wasn't enough money in the world to give these people what they *really* wanted—to have all these dark faces disappear so they wouldn't have to be confronted so often with their fear, bigotry, or fake tolerance ever again.

So Val had tried to cheer louder, to scream into this void and say this man wasn't going anywhere, that Robinson would show them. He'd clapped his hands over his head and stomped his feet.

Then Val had looked at Robinson again. He'd thought about all this extraordinary baseball player would soon do: the hits, the stolen bases glorifying his speed, showing them the game the way it was meant to be played. But then Robinson had stood up, lifted his cap, and, turning slowly, saluted all the people in the park. He'd gone back to his stance and Val had fallen silent. Somehow this gesture had been the right one. But even more than that, Val thought, it was important—not like money or social position. There was something about this man and the way he was that would matter more for his people— and it would matter long after he died. Val had wanted to shake off the feeling but he knew it seemed to be a piece that fit right into a puzzle that had troubled him more as he got older. This puzzle made him angry when he could change a look with a five-dollar bill or sit in places that once gave him satisfaction, such as the Swan, where he sat that night. These damn people were living out a stupid fantasy when the world was changing and there was so much more. . . .

Possibility.

That was the word, but Val didn't allow himself to think it just then. He refused to give birth to it tonight. If he did, the Swan would fall down on him like a load of dirt and he would be buried in this place so empty of possibility.

Instead he turned his attention to the lovely young thing wrapped tight in blue satin and sitting a few seats from him down the bar. Val picked up his drink and moved toward her and within a few steps the scent of the gardenia in her black pinned-up hair reached him and relaxed him. He lifted her hand and kissed it. When her lips split into a relieved and grateful smile, he knew he wouldn't have to introduce himself. He would learn her name, buy her a drink, and the night would proceed in the ordinary way with the end he knew so well. He relished the glances of envy he knew men were shooting his way because they knew they would have to buy many more drinks, work harder at being charming, and still have no certainty of the result Val Jackson would enjoy that evening. His reputation brightened the moment and he loved how, in this way, he could be so above other men. For now this feeling would help him accept the deadening predictability of this place until he could find whatever it was that would draw back the shadows and recall him to life.

CHAPTER 3
Mae

Harlem, May 1947—Sunday Morning

Mae Malveaux had washed every inch of her body except for a small area between her breasts. At that sweet spot she detected the combined scent of herself and this new lover. It would serve as a welcome distraction in church when the sermon went on too long. She stood in front of the full-length mirror and surveyed her figure. The globes of her chest were still firm and high; her waist tapered down into perfect narrowness while her hips and rear blossomed just enough, but not too much. Mae sighed with pleasure. Any other woman would be concerned about just when these voluptuous features would lose their bloom and drift earthwards in their added years. But Mae was still of the mind she wasn't like other women. In fact she knew no reason why some miracle couldn't occur just for her and make her the one person to elude the crush of time's wheel. Of course Mae was old enough to know better, to know such thinking was pure folly.

And she was still young enough to believe if miracles would apply to anyone, it would be to her.

Justice brought out the yellow dress and matching Dior jacket with the delightful peplum that flared out from the waist. Regina followed with Mae's undergarments, and the process of clothing their mistress began.

Sam Delany woke and seemed to be in shock to find such activity going on around him in the room. When he sat up Mae trained her eyes right on him in the mirror. He froze. His reaction pleased her so she spoke pleasantly, keeping her voice low and silky.

"Good morning." She didn't turn her head but continued to speak and no longer looked at him. "Sam, you're going to get dressed, go down the back stairs, into the cellar, and exit this building through the door taking you out into the alley. You will end up on the street completely on the other side of the block and far away from here. Do you understand?"

"Sure, Mae," he said but then stopped. Justice turned to him swiftly and a stiff shake of her head told him this was just the absolute wrong thing to say. "Uh, I mean, yes, ma'am. I do understand."

"Good." Mae turned to him then and smiled. "If you can manage that I might invite you back. But Sam, remember this: if you speak a word of this to anyone, you won't sing a note in public again. If you do it'll be with a harmonica behind a set of prison bars. It's your choice."

Mae carefully examined herself again in the full-length mirror. She nodded to Justice, who picked up a small white Bible from a table and handed it to Mae as she left the room, Justice and Regina close behind.

* * *

THE CHOIR, A small summer retinue swathed and sweating in dark purple robes, hummed the start of a tune, a cappella, to begin the service.

"When are they gonna get a new organist?" Gladys complained, adjusting herself on the hard pew where she sat between Mae and Cecily. "It's been months."

"You know Reverend Stiles," Mae said, and stared straight ahead. "He won't even think about something as trivial as an organist until the campaign is completed."

Gladys fanned herself with the wooden-handled piece of cardboard given to each of them when they entered the church. "He better get this service started soon before we all melt. Where is he anyway?"

Mae raised an eyebrow under the brim of her hat. "Probably primping."

CHAPTER 4
Val

Harlem, May 1947—Sunday Morning

The windows of Val's bedroom in his top-floor apartment faced fully east, as they did every place he ever lived. He didn't want it any other way. And he never let Sebastian or any other servant close the curtains. He always let the sun come through and, on some summer mornings, practically burn him out of bed. Val cherished that first blush of sunrise and how it grew into pure yellow light as it lifted itself up from behind the Harlem buildings. There was something about it that fed him, sustained him. He felt it coming through his eyes and flowing straight into his veins—better than the dope he once needled into his arms before he realized he could get the same feeling without crashing to the brink of death after each high.

On this Sunday morning in May, Val rose to meet the light. He stood naked in the glow for several minutes, his skin burnished and smooth all over, before he reached for his burgundy silk robe and wrapped it around the taut muscles of his body.

He stepped across the room to his dressing area and slid the heavy pocket doors closed behind him. Not once did he glance back at the young woman still sleeping in his bed, the sheets covering only her round bare bottom.

He slid the hangers along the rod in the closet so he could examine his suits and decide which one to wear. He heard the girl shift in the bed and sigh. She must be awake by now. She would be like all the others, lying there with a grin on her lips because of where she was, and thinking she'd finally been lucky. She'd probably begged to borrow her sister's dress and her aunt's earrings. Was probably dying to tell whoever she could all about him. He satisfied himself with how little he cared.

When he was dressed he returned to the room. She seemed to have gone through the trouble of arranging herself on the bed for full effect. She'd pulled the sheets around her like a sexy movie star, placing one long slender leg out and on display. When she saw him she gasped. He was polished head to toe and dressed in a dark blue pin-striped suit. She reached out her arms but he only looked down at his cuffs, tugging them out from his jacket. He opened the door.

Sebastian was at the threshold waiting and he stepped in quickly. The woman pulled her leg back under the sheets. He was holding a hanger of clothing—a simple brown dress with a small floral print, a hat, a slip, panties, and stockings that he presented to the woman by laying them carefully on the bed. Val stood out in the hall and waited.

"Those aren't my clothes!" he heard her protest.

"Your dress, miss, is in that box on the dresser," Sebastian said. "If you don't want the world to know what you were doing last night I suggest you not put it on and wear these instead."

He moved toward the door, grasped the knob, and looked at Val then back at the woman. "You may get something to eat from the cook in the kitchen, but afterward I trust you can find your own way out of the apartment."

"What about Val?"

Sebastian glanced through the door and down the hall. Val started walking.

"Mr. Jackson will by now be downstairs and once I join him we will be leaving. In fact I will go now so I don't keep him waiting."

"Leaving? Where the hell is he going?"

"To church. Goodbye, miss." He closed the door behind him.

* * *

FROM THE BALCONY Val spotted Elizabeth Townsend with the accuracy of a bird dog. He sat back in the pew, satisfied once more with the precision of his people's information, right down to the navy and yellow flower print of her pretty dress. He sighed. Unlike the other women so handsomely endowed, Elizabeth's gifts were not on display. Her neckline didn't venture below the simple scoop shape just under where her neck met her shoulders. But Val had no trouble seeing that she had much to offer—the fabric curved admirably over the generous mounds on her chest and moved in to hug her slim waist. Her fair skin still held the glow of youth and hope and Val wanted badly to add his own hue to this fresh palette.

Her hair, neither too short nor too long, rested in thick brown curls just above her shoulders. Her lipstick was an easy, unpresumptuous shade of pink. Her eyes he knew well from constant study—wide-set and large—the kind of eyes that demanded honesty. Val knew he would have to be at his best—smooth and pitch-perfect—to deliver a pure lie into those eyes. He could stare into a mirror and talk all day, but it wouldn't be the practice he needed. He would just have to be ready to endure those eyes when the moment arrived.

CHAPTER 5
Elizabeth

Harlem, May 1947—Sunday Morning

The car horn blared into Elizabeth Townsend's ears as the wood-paneled station wagon passed her on the left. She jumped a little on the seat but her hands remained glued to the wheel. She regretted not taking her friend Rose Jarreau up on her offer to use her driver and car, but Elizabeth didn't want to impose. Besides, Elizabeth thought, her own husband, Kyle, had left the black Ford coupe, a wedding gift from his parents, behind for her to use. But then he had also arranged for this long visit to Rose's home, not giving a thought to her monthly service in the Mount Nebo soup kitchen. She was determined to keep her commitment, so here she was, making the trip alone on a Sunday morning. Elizabeth continued driving too slowly down the highway.

She let go of the wheel for a moment to use the back of her white-gloved hand to dab at the sweat forming on her temples. Rose's Mercylands estate, with well-tended gardens, ramblin woodlands, and a shimmering lake, was beautiful, though, and Elizabeth was grateful to be there instead of cooped up in her lonely apartment with the heat of summer coming on. She blamed Kyle for the lonely part. Over the course of their eight-year marriage she grew used to his long absences south for his civil rights work, but last year Kyle decided they should switch churches and leave Fairfield Baptist, which she had attended since childhood, for the larger, more public Mount Nebo. He'd pointed out how the most prominent Harlem residents attended Mount Nebo, and he was getting to a point in his career where it was time for him and Elizabeth to take their place among them. Elizabeth preferred the warm familiarity of Fairfield's small congregation, but she was also of the mind that God would be with her wherever they went. She volunteered to help out in the soup kitchen, having decided she would meet as many people as she could, but she was hurt Kyle hadn't seemed to realize that he had now left her, at twenty-eight years old, without the comfort of her own church community.

Elizabeth murmured a prayer of forgiveness for Kyle and for her as she maneuvered the car. She had known this was what their life would be like—long periods of separation, for the greater good, Kyle had said. "We're like missionaries, Elizabeth. There's great work to be done in the South and here too. Our lives are going to mean something—we're going to be about something!"

Such words made her devoted to Kyle, as she'd been ever since she got paired with him at the Debutante's Cotillion as a teenager. She'd worn a dress of white organdy swathed around her like a flower blossom and a ribbon had held her hair piled high on her head. She was grateful for the white gloves, pushed above her elbows, because she worried about her palms sweating and making her lose her grip on her partner. She also worried she might slip in her white pumps on the polished floor, but Kyle, six inches taller than she, held her securely and never let her stumble. They had to dance a waltz to music by Tchaikovsky, but most of the other boys chafed at dancing to a piece with the word "fairy" in the title. Some of the mothers weren't happy about it either, but Hattie Sanders, the chief organizer, prevailed. Most of the boys took the floor with sour faces, but Kyle looked straight across at Elizabeth with a gentle smile that seemed to say, *It will be all right.* His fingers held her gloved hand and spun her like a water lily on a swirling pond. Elizabeth liked his confident touch—he made her feel light, as though she had wings. She thought he liked her too, but after the dance he only smiled and honored her with a curt bow. He blended back in with the boys on the other side of the ballroom and Elizabeth assumed she would never see him again.

The dance had been one of those perplexing times when Elizabeth longed for her mother. Her name was Uriah and whenever Elizabeth thought of her, she smelled warm cotton and remembered her mother ironing, which she'd done every Thursday. She'd let Elizabeth iron the handkerchiefs and pillowcases, showing her how to sprinkle water on them before pressing out the wrinkles and how to keep her fingers out of the way of the hot iron. Now and again Elizabeth burned herself anyway—she was always distracted by the drops of water as they tumbled off her mother's fingertips, catching tiny rainbows in the sunlight just before they touched down on the cloth.

Uriah was the reason Elizabeth was called Elizabeth and not Liz or Beth or Betsy. "I gave you a beautiful name so I could love it every time I heard it," she used to say. "And so you can love it every time you hear it."

Elizabeth did love to hear her name. The tiny buzz on the lips that came when people vocalized the "z" always thrilled her. It was like she was six years old and hearing her mother call her home for dinner. Elizabeth held her mother in this way, in the hearing of her own name, for years. And she still whispered "Uriah" to herself whenever she needed a blessing.

* * *

URIAH WOULD SIT and talk to Elizabeth before bedtime. Elizabeth loved looking up at her round brown cheeks and wanting to reach up to touch the metal curling pins in her hair. But when she was fourteen and Uriah began coughing up red sheets of blood, Elizabeth became the one sitting on the side of her mother's bed. Sometimes she crawled under the covers with her mother when she couldn't get warm, and Elizabeth would wrap her arms around her mother's thin, leathery skin, damp with the smell of sickness, and feel life in retreat like the tide pulling back from the sea.

One night Uriah patted Elizabeth's arms with spindly fingers. "It's all right, honey." Her voice sounded full of gravel and liquid, like a river was flooding up to drown her from within. "I figured I was just about done anyway."

"Done?" Elizabeth spoke the word into the back of her mother's damp nightgown. "What do you mean, Mama?"

"Done with the journey the Lord laid out for me. And it

sure has been nice. Look at all I got to do. I got to love a man like your father, love him in a way most people don't even get to know the word 'love.'"

Elizabeth could feel her mother's head turn back toward her and Elizabeth pressed her own forehead against her mother's spine.

"I got to have you. Even got to see you through to the point where you're practically grown so I know you're gonna be all right." She coughed hard and pushed her cheek into the pillow. Elizabeth squeezed her gently.

"Mama, how do you know when you're done?"

Her mother drew a breath and Elizabeth felt it shudder through her body. "Well, I guess because I can feel peaceful about things. I know I don't want for more. But I see what you're thinking, Elizabeth. What about watching you get married someday? Or having a baby? Honey, all that would have been icing on the cake. All that would have been nice but I don't need it. And I sure won't lie here making myself miserable because of it. Not when you're here with me, right now, and I know you're just fine."

Elizabeth squeezed her mother again, harder, and began to weep.

"Mama, I don't want you to be done. I don't want you to go."

Elizabeth felt her mother's lips, dry and chapped, against the skin of her forearm. "It's all right. I see where I'm going. I see it clearly, baby, like a bright light shining in front of me, calling me home. I'm not afraid. When your time comes you'll know it too. You'll see it's nothing to be scared of."

But Elizabeth could only think she would be angry if she saw such a light. She decided she would mistrust it with all her being. It was a flaming void for all she knew. And despite what her mother said, it seemed to be burning up what she loved and believed in most.

* * *

ELIZABETH'S FATHER, WALTER G. Moore, was in real estate, but after his wife died, he founded a weekly newspaper, the *New York Clarion,* because he wanted to encourage Harlem's blacks to own more businesses and control more of the money they spent every day for housing, food, and clothing. He had small ears and a receding hairline and wore round wire pince-nez. He enlisted his younger sister, Sadie, to help prepare Elizabeth for her social debut. Sadie took her shopping for the all-important white cotillion dress, but Elizabeth didn't feel comfortable enough to ask her what to do about Kyle Townsend.

Her father sent her to Vassar, where she studied English and art history. Elizabeth enjoyed the subjects but in her heart she hoped her education would lead her to helpful, meaningful work. She developed her writing skills and read widely to form her own opinions. When she felt she was ready, she asked her father if she could work for his newspaper.

He removed his glasses, pinched the bridge of his nose, and sighed.

"Elizabeth, it's not something girls usually do. It wouldn't be right for you."

"Why not?" She stood before his desk in the office. He closed the door, but she could still hear the buzz of the reporters talking and the clacking of their typewriter keys. Elizabeth had dressed carefully in a straight dark blue skirt and matching jacket. She squeezed the clasp of her pocketbook between her fingers to give her hands something to do.

He shifted uncomfortably in his chair. "Because a man asking questions is thoughtful and looking to learn something or say something. A woman asking questions is just plain nosy."

"What am I supposed to do, Daddy? If you won't give me a job, who will?"

"You have other talents, Elizabeth." He put his glasses back on and turned back to his typewriter.

Elizabeth knew he was talking about her faith. It was the only seed her father allowed her to nurture. She wore the apostles' attitude as naturally as she did her skin, and she dutifully sought the face of Jesus in the face of every person she met, no matter their station. Her faith upheld her—it was her life—but she didn't see how it could help her make a living.

One Sunday Elizabeth and her father arrived early for Fairfield Baptist's service, and found Reverend Mitchell arranging his sermon notes at the pulpit. When he saw the Moores he stepped down to greet them. The tall and elegant man seemed to Elizabeth to float down to them, his robes billowing lightly behind him.

"Good morning, Miss Elizabeth, Brother Moore!" He shook Elizabeth's hand and his slim, tan fingers were so long she thought they might wrap twice around her own.

"On your own today?" her father asked. He surveyed the small nave and the polished wood pews.

Elizabeth smiled and turned her head so Reverend Mitchell didn't see. She knew her father was looking for Deacon Phelps, whom he didn't like. Her father always groused about the deacon's heavy, pedantic Scripture reading. Though it was a small part at the beginning of each service, Walter Moore thought the deacon set the tone—and that Deacon Phelps set the tone so low they had to spend the rest of the service recovering from him each Sunday.

"The deacon is sick today," Reverend Mitchell said. He removed his glasses and polished them with an edge of his long sleeve in a self-important way. "I'll just read the Scripture as well. No problem there."

Walter Moore waved his hat in front of his daughter. "Why don't you let Elizabeth do it? I'm sure she wouldn't mind."

Her father looked at Elizabeth and winked. She frowned at him. Women in their church didn't often participate in such a visual manner unless they were singing—something Elizabeth had no talent for. But she would like to read. She had already glanced at the bulletin on the way into the sanctuary and noticed the Scripture reading was from the Book of Isaiah, one of her favorite parts of the Old Testament.

"Yes, Reverend," she said, nodding. "I can do it."

Reverend Mitchell looked back and forth between them twice before saying, slowly, "All right then. I would appreciate it. Why don't you go up to the lectern and have a look at it so you know what you're doing?"

When the time came for Elizabeth to read, she did her best to ignore the small flurry of whispering that followed her steps down the aisle. Her shoes sounded too loud, and the walk seemed too long, but once she stood in front of the Bible and placed her fingertips on the large "49" marking the chapter of Isaiah, she felt better. She began to read, her fingers following along the words.

"'Listen, O isles, unto me; and hearken, ye people, from far,'" Elizabeth said. She looked up from the page, found her father's face among the congregants, and smiled as she read the next lines. "'The Lord hath called me from the womb; from the bowels of my mother hath he made mention of my name.'"

She loved these parts of Isaiah. Since childhood Elizabeth always felt a nurturing presence all around her, and Isaiah seemed to affirm it for her as divine spirit. Isaiah enlivened her and made her feel she too was being called, like she could hear her own name in the wind. So she read the passage affectionately, like the words of a beloved summoning her.

"'And he hath made my mouth like a sharp sword; in the shadow of his hand hath he hid me, and made me a polished shaft; in his quiver hath he hid me.'"

Elizabeth glanced at the page, then looked out at the congregants again, careful to make eye contact with two or three people. She shook her head slightly and her right shoulder rose a bit as she read the next line with a sense of wonder, which was indeed how she saw it.

"'And said unto me, Thou art my servant, O Israel, in whom I will be glorified.'"

She found such amazement in that, to think God would think so much of her—and everyone. Would they hear that in her reading? She hoped so.

"'Then I said, I have laboured in vain, I have spent my strength for nought, and in vain: yet surely my judgment is with the Lord, and my work with my God.'"

To herself Elizabeth prayed that she would not labor in vain or waste her strength. But as long as she followed the spirit she trusted that would never happen.

"'And now, saith the Lord that formed me from the womb to be his servant, to bring Jacob again to him, Though Israel be not gathered, yet shall I be glorious in the eyes of the Lord, and my God shall be my strength.'"

Then, the next part, again—God speaking to His servant! Wonderful. Elizabeth thought she might not sound as reverent as Deacon Phelps, but figured she could only read as she would read the Bible to herself. She could only hope her love of the words filtered through.

"'And he said, It is a light thing that thou shouldest be my servant to raise up the tribes of Jacob, and to restore the preserved of Israel: I will also give thee for a light to the Gentiles, that thou mayest be my salvation unto the end of the earth.'"

She so wanted to be a light. When she read the Word she realized this, her standing there at the lectern, was a brief moment when she could be one. She looked up from the page again, tapped the Bible where she read, and smiled to the congregants.

"'Thus saith the Lord, the Redeemer of Israel, and his Holy One, to him whom man despiseth, to him whom the nation abhorreth, to a servant of rulers, Kings shall see and arise, princes also shall worship,'" she said. Elizabeth scanned the room carefully. She wanted to plant the final four words of the passage firmly into her listeners' minds like a sacred seed. She even dared to add her own slight emphasis. "'Because of the Lord that is faithful, and the Holy One of Israel, and *he shall choose thee.*'"

Elizabeth stepped down from the lectern into a pond of silence. No one looked directly at her. Heads hung down in prayer or stole sideways glances at her as she went by. She found her father beaming.

Reverend Mitchell stood to offer a prayer and welcome, but from the silence it seemed the congregants were already well into their own meditations. They listened to his sermon in the same quiet manner, resisting his attempts to rouse them. No one seemed to waken until the choir began to sing "Move On Up a Little Higher," and then everyone clapped to the music in a way that felt a little more joyous, as though they'd never thought to clap before.

Afterward, strangely enough, people addressed their compliments to her father, and not Elizabeth directly.

Mother Hines in her white dress and hat gripped Elizabeth's wrist with a marshmallow-soft hand and hunched over when she spoke to Walter Moore, like she was revealing a secret. "After hearing the Word like that, I didn't need no sermon!"

More people, in the same manner, made similar comments about being touched somehow by Elizabeth's reading in a way they couldn't put into words, but knew they'd be thinking about for a long time to come. It tickled Walter Moore to no end, especially when Reverend Mitchell made no comment of his own.

"He's not going to say anything, but it doesn't matter," he said to Elizabeth as they walked home that afternoon. "Everybody will know from now on what they're missing. Now they know what a good Scripture reading can really do."

Reverend Mitchell never asked Elizabeth to read again. But she grew in her community's esteem and the congregants admired the simple, shining example she set for everyone else.

Still, it discouraged Elizabeth to feel so close to divine light and hope and not see it reflected in the lives of so many of Harlem's struggling residents.

She returned to Vassar for her final semester with all this on her mind. She persistently wondered what her life would be, and prayed about whether she should teach, the only job that seemed suitable for an educated young Negro woman. Then that spring, when she was on the verge of graduating, Kyle Townsend returned to her life.

She heard the shout reverberate down the dormitory hall. "Elizabeth Moore! Elizabeth Moore! You have a gentleman caller."

She left her room puzzled. She touched a hand to her brown curls and smoothed the front of her green sweater. What man would come visit her other than her father? Elizabeth walked down the stairs and into the common room to find Kyle. He wore gray slacks and a red sweater over a crisp white shirt. She recalled hearing he had graduated from law school the previous year and he stood towering over her, even taller than when they first met.

"What are you doing here after all this time, Kyle Townsend?"

"I just wanted to talk to you. Can we sit outside?" His eyes slid toward the door like he already wanted to be on its other side.

A hint of daylight still remained when they sat on the bench under the crab apple tree in full bloom. The scent made Elizabeth strangely giddy, but she did her best to sit quietly while her surprise visitor spoke. For the first fifteen minutes or so Kyle looked at the ground as he explained to Elizabeth how he'd known right away at the cotillion she was a special girl, but he didn't want to try for her until he knew he could support them in a good life. Once he'd graduated from law school and had a job, he went to her home to look for her.

"Your father told me you were here, so here I am," he said. He shrugged his shoulders and his eyes finally met hers.

"How did you know I wouldn't have a boyfriend already?" Elizabeth gripped the edge of the bench, her ankles crossed beneath her.

"I didn't. I hoped you wouldn't. Prayed about it a lot."

She nodded. "So what do you want now?"

"I'm not asking for anything, Elizabeth." Kyle held his palms up like he wanted to show he wasn't hiding anything. "I just want to see you for a bit. And we'll see what happens. Okay?"

Elizabeth looked up at the stars beginning to come into view. They seemed starkly white, like ice crystals. She thought she didn't know what might happen. But she said, "Okay."

He sighed then and sat up like she had lifted the weight of the world off his chest. Then he began to talk as though she'd released his words.

"The world is so messed up, Elizabeth. I don't like how our people are being treated, here or in the South. But it is worse in the South. We have to acknowledge that. They string up black men with no more thought than hanging up their laundry. Like our lives aren't worth any more than the dirt on their clothes."

"I know! I see it in Harlem too." She wanted to talk about what her father highlighted in his newspaper, about the inequity of how the black population of Harlem paid rents to white landlords and frequented stores owned by white business owners. She wanted to ask Kyle what he thought of the fact that so much of their money did not return to their own community, but she paused. She saw a tightness in Kyle's face that made her realize he didn't like her interrupting him. She folded her hands in her lap and looked down at them in the dark. "I'm sorry. You go on."

"You're right, Elizabeth. The economics of our people is a serious issue as well. But I can't work on that and civil rights at the same time."

"No, of course not."

He sat back and crossed his legs and draped a long, ropy arm on the bench behind her.

"Anyway, I think with my work and all your efforts in the church, we could stand for something really special. We could bring attention to things just because of who we are and the way we stand up for what we believe. We won't be just another young couple bringing a bunch of babies into the world."

He looked at her quickly. "But we'll do that too when we're ready. We've got plenty of time for children."

Elizabeth nodded. "Yes."

She wasn't sure if Kyle's words were those usually reserved for courtship, but she liked what he said. He had a vision for them as a couple, as a family. That was good enough for her. It gave her a place to be in the world, as though he had marked a spot on the map and said, *This is where you belong.* And she accepted it, grateful to be protected and loved in a place where, as she saw each time she read her father's newspaper, there were so many, women especially, who went unprotected and unloved.

* * *

ELIZABETH TOWNSEND ARRIVED that Sunday morning, not late but not early enough to park close by. The side streets were so crowded she had to find a spot five blocks away. She was glad she had worn low-heeled shoes, but she moved slowly, trying not to sweat through her clothes before she got there.

The Mount Nebo Baptist Church rose up as a huge stone monument to its congregation's faith on the corner of St. Nicholas and Edgecombe Avenues. It featured two medieval-looking turrets and a footprint that took up half the block. The building once housed a white Episcopal church but as the growing Negro population seemed to assure a complete take-over of Harlem in the 1920s, that congregation relinquished it to the Mount Nebo advisory board for six hundred thousand dollars.

Having one of the wealthiest congregations in Harlem helped Mount Nebo grow further and now the church leaders sought to move their soup kitchen from the basement to a separate center across the street.

"Good morning, Mrs. Townsend." Howard Frisbee manned the open door, as he did every Sunday, with small bows and big gentle smiles. Elizabeth enjoyed seeing him because he was not only glad to be there, but also happy for every single person who made it in on Sunday.

"Nice crowd today, Howard." She offered her hand, and he took it into the softness of his own as she climbed the final step.

"Every soul a blessing, Mrs. Townsend, every soul a blessing."

CHAPTER 6
Cecily

Anselm, North Carolina, 1946

Cecily sat on a train headed south. The ride had lulled her into a deep and restful sleep. She didn't sense the movement of the cars slowing down so she felt grateful for the warm pressure of the porter's hand on her shoulder waking her as they pulled into Anselm. She sat dazed and humbled in her sleepy fog. Already her exile felt complete. She'd told her mother she didn't want to come down here and the swiftness with which she found herself on the train and out of Harlem still bewildered her. Cecily closed her eyes again.

Had it been two or three days since that funny spring breeze came drifting through the windows of their town house? She had never noticed air before in her seventeen years of being in the world. This breeze felt soft like a baby blanket and warm like the arm of a friend looped into her own. And it seemed to gently push and pull on her like a child wanting her to come out to play. Cecily had followed the breeze through the doors of empty rooms, down the hall, and past the parlor where her mother was giving directions to their servant, Gideon. She finally went out the front door and settled herself on the stoop. She stuck her legs straight out in front of her and lifted her skirt to her thighs so the breeze could reach her there and tickle the soft hair on the surface of her limbs. She leaned back, her elbows behind her and supporting her on the stone steps as she took in the trees just beginning to flower. That's when Royce Haywood walked by.

At least he was going to walk by, Cecily thought. He had his hands stuffed into the pockets of his jeans and his shirttail, untucked, fluttered about his waist. He wore a sour expression, his mouth twisted in a knot of unhappiness. He pushed one foot in front of the other in a way that seemed, to Cecily, very determined. But when Royce was just two or three houses down he saw Cecily. She noticed how his lips seemed to relax and his face, the color of browned butter, lifted toward her.

"Hey, Ceci."

"What's wrong with you, Royce?"

"Why does something have to be wrong with me?"

"Because you ain't calling me by my right name. You ain't called me nothing but Cecily since we were five years old."

Royce shrugged. Cecily didn't bother to sit up.

"Why do we always have to do everything the same?" he asked. "Don't you ever want to do different things?"

"I like my name just fine, thank you." Cecily had shocked herself. She'd never spoken to anyone like that before, let alone a boy. "Sassy" would be the word for it. She wasn't sure if that was a good thing but she did like the way Royce looked strange for a moment, his forehead all creased up, like he didn't know what to say. *Did I do that?* she wondered. Then he sat down on the stoop next to her and she liked that even better. He was close enough that she could smell him. His salty, musky scent mingled with the soft spring breeze.

"I didn't mean anything by it, Cecily. I just feel like I'm tired of being me sometimes."

"That's silly. How can you be anyone but you?"

"By changing! People change all the time. I can still be me but something different. I'm ready to be different."

Cecily wondered if it was possible to change parts of yourself—to put them on and take them off like you do with your clothes every day? Did it even happen to her just a moment ago? Then Royce went on as though he'd read her mind.

"We're changing, Cecily. Don't you feel it?"

She looked out into the street. The breeze pushed the petals from the pear tree blossoms down the pavement in a way that reminded her of drifting snow. "You mean like we're not children anymore." Cecily had meant that to be a question but as the words tumbled out of her mouth the truth of them stung her tongue and made it lie flat so she had no choice but to voice the words as fact.

"Yeah," Royce said. He leaned back and, like her, rested his elbows on the steps. "Something like that."

Part of her felt like she would obviously know this long before Royce did. Her period had started over two years ago. But she wasn't settled with it. Its appearance still surprised her unpleasantly even though her mama had told her it would happen each month and tried to remind her to get ready. However, Cecily still soiled her panties and had taken to hiding them, then throwing them away. This behavior didn't seem like something a grown woman would do but Cecily didn't know what else to do and was too ashamed to tell Mama. She could only feel her heart drop into her stomach each time she went to the bathroom, detected the metallic smell, and pulled down her underwear to find it stained ruby red. This part of her commiserated with Royce because it seemed they were supposed to be coming into something different but no one was telling them what it was.

And that's when he did it. Cecily still wasn't sure he had really done anything because all that happened was a movement of his hand. His fingers had ventured toward her thigh in a way that, Cecily thought, looked like he was about to brush an ant off her leg. It seemed to happen so slowly, like she was seeing it but really not sure of what she was seeing.

"Royce!"

The boy's hand snapped back like he'd burned it on a hot stove. He jumped to his feet. Cecily turned to see her mama come barreling down the stoop like the 7th Avenue Express bus. Cecily didn't know what to do because she didn't understand what Royce had done. He had his chin dipped low and his hands back in his pockets. But when Cecily looked at her mama again she was staring at her, not Royce. Cecily thought her face seemed to soften and Cecily was even more surprised when she turned and asked after Royce's parents like she would on any other day.

"They're fine, Mrs. Vaughn," Royce said, stammering.

"You better get along home. Cecily has to go in now."

She said it, Cecily thought, like she and Royce were still little kids playing in the street, and that made a warmth rush up into her cheeks.

"Yes, ma'am." Royce went down the last few steps and left but he didn't, Cecily noticed, walk in the direction of his house. He kept going on his way to wherever he was going before he saw her. She wondered, now genuinely curious, where that was.

* * *

TWO DAYS LATER, Cecily found herself on the train to Anselm to stay with her father's aunt Pearl and uncle Menard. Cecily blinked and looked around her. People gathered up satchels and the remainders of sack lunches as they moved into the aisles. She jumped in her seat when she heard a voice close by, just over her right ear.

"This is your stop, Miss. Don't dally. I'll get your bags but you got to get off. I promised your mama."

Cecily turned her head and managed to clear the fog in her brain just a little. The porter wore his hat tipped back so far on his head she could see the gray curls shining in his nest of black hair. His glasses made his light brown eyes twice the size and four times as disconcerting. But once he saw Cecily was awake he turned from her and disappeared around a corner and out the door. She rose and took hold of the black handbag she had kept carefully tucked between her body and the wall of the car. She fumbled with the wax paper left from her sandwich before finally folding it and putting it in the bag. She had eaten somewhere between Philadelphia and Washington. Cecily figured she must have dozed right afterward because there had been remnants of city outside the window—line upon line of squat wooden town houses with dirt patch backyards and rickety picket fences separating them—before she closed her eyes.

The train idled along wooden planks that marked where the tracks ended and the country road began. As she stepped off the car it seemed sunlight bounced off every surface. She shielded her eyes with her hands over her forehead. There didn't seem to be a bit of shade anywhere, not even under the trees. Cecily saw a cloud of dust swirling toward her and ahead there seemed to be a pickup truck and that truck's horn honked as it came to a stop near the platform.

"Over here!" called the woman behind the wheel. She waved through her open window at the porter, who was just about to drop Cecily's suitcases next to her. "Just throw 'em right in the back there!" The woman, Aunt Pearl, jumped down from the truck and covered the ground between her and her grand-niece in four loping strides. Her joints jutted forward and back, finger-snapping quick, and seemed to make light of the fact that the load they carried was anything but light. She wore denim coveralls and underneath a green short-sleeved collared shirt, unbuttoned just to the top of her ample bosom.

"Sessssily!" she cried, letting her tongue slide over the "S" sound for too long. She wrapped her thick bare arms around Cecily, engulfing her in a heady mix of smells: grass, fresh earth, flowers, and one other thing Cecily couldn't name but was certain was something like sugar mixed with cinnamon. "I haven't seen you since you were a little bit of a thing! And now look at ya. So tall! I bet you ain't even done growing yet." And just when Cecily couldn't tell whether she was being hugged or crushed, Aunt Pearl released her and opened the truck door.

"Well, come on, come on. I'm glad you're here, but we got to get going. Your uncle Menard will be wanting his supper before you know it."

"Thank you for having me," Cecily stammered as Aunt Pearl pressed some coins into the porter's hand. Cecily turned toward the open door.

The growl came first, rumbling dark and low from the front seat. Then the dog, which had been lying down, sat up on its haunches and barked sharply twice. Cecily jumped back and nearly fell over the porter behind her.

"Oh, hush up, Rex!"

Aunt Pearl reached into the truck and grasped the collar of the dog, a German shepherd, and pulled it out of the cab. "You've had it too good long enough. You got to ride in the back now where you belong. Get up there!"

The dog put up its huge paws and leapt into the back of the truck. Its fur was a mass of black and brown with patches of silver hair that caught the light when the dog flew up past Aunt Pearl and into the bed of the pickup.

"Don't be scared of Rex," Aunt Pearl said, taking Cecily's hand and pulling her toward the seat. "He's had us to himself forever, but he's just gonna have to get used to having company."

Cecily stepped up into the truck, her eyes still on the German shepherd. But it had lain down in the truck bed, away from her suitcases, and seemed to pay her no further mind. Suddenly Aunt Pearl was back behind the wheel, shifting gears, and kicking up more dust as she spun the truck back onto the road. Cecily coughed and rolled up her window.

"How's your mama?" Aunt Pearl asked and laughed. "Is she still as fat as me?"

Cecily smiled carefully but didn't know how to answer. True, her mother was big like Aunt Pearl. But where Mama was large, soft, and slow, Aunt Pearl seemed solid and spring-loaded, like a girl who could still jump rope. And Cecily was sure her great aunt had to be at least twenty years older than Mama, maybe more.

"She's all right," Cecily finally said. "I think she's mighty grateful for you taking me."

"Oh, we're happy for the company. My children are long grown. Then I met Menard and it's just me and him."

Cecily stared. "But I thought Uncle Menard was Daddy's uncle?"

"Yeah, your daddy knew Menard as his uncle, but Menard is my second husband. Left the first one when we got sick of looking at each other."

She laughed, but Cecily didn't understand why that should be so funny.

"The gals around here look at me cross-eyed like you're doing now, but I say get you a second husband if you can manage it. You mark my words! You don't know what I'm talking about now but you'll see when you've got that first one and you're done with him."

Aunt Pearl let loose with another gleeful laugh and leaned back in her seat in a way that caused her to smash down on the gas pedal. The engine roared and the truck leapt forward. Cecily found herself laughing a little too.

"I thought Menard and I might have our own babies. I hoped the Good Lord would bless us again—thought I'd be like Sarah in the Bible and have a baby in my old age. But that's all right."

She slowed the truck and began to turn into a long, dusty driveway next to a bright yellow farmhouse. Two oak trees on the lawn in front of the structure stood tall and strong like sentinels. A wooden porch, painted cherry red, stretched the length of the house and on it sat two rockers angled toward each other in an almost conspiratorial manner. Simple flowers filled the bed around the porch: black-eyed Susans, coneflower, daisies. Later Aunt Pearl would tell Cecily how she didn't have time for roses. "Can't have no fussy flowers around here," she would say. "Got so much else to do, my flowers have to be able to take care of themselves." Cecily would wonder if the same went for her.

A big red barn sat squat in the back and beyond it woods that seemed to go on and on. In front of the house, on the other side of the street, large patches of potatoes, squash, and cucumbers stretched out toward more woods that eventually rose up into a mountain ridge that ran down as far as Cecily could see and formed a kind of wall hugging the whole countryside. Aunt Pearl stopped the truck and Cecily heard the dog jump from the truck bed and land on the ground just behind her.

"Come on, let's get dinner started. Menard will bring your bags when he comes in from the fields."

Cecily felt like she had entered a different time frame where, no matter how hard she tried to catch up, she seemed to be always five seconds behind. She was still processing Aunt Pearl's words but Aunt Pearl was already on the porch steps. Cecily followed her. They entered a kitchen decorated with pink wallpaper with tiny pink rosebuds and green leaves running down in strips like ribbons. In the middle was a long wooden table and Aunt Pearl proceeded to set on top of it a large bowl, a sack of flour, and dishcloths.

"You can put your things down over there." She pointed to a bench just inside the door under a row of hooks on the wall. "You know how to make biscuits?"

Cecily shook her head.

"No? What about corn bread?"

Cecily shook her head again. She wasn't sure whether or not to tell Aunt Pearl that Mama always had Mrs. Jenkins make all their food.

"Well, that's all right, honey. Sit down here and watch me. I've got to hurry now, but tomorrow I can show you properly."

Aunt Pearl had kicked off her shoes and moved around on the shiny floor with broad bare feet. She seemed to be even faster than she was before. The flour went into the bowl, then chunks of butter, then a little milk. The next thing Cecily knew Aunt Pearl had a perfect white mound of dough under her hands, like she'd seized a piece of cloud from the sky. She pressed into it with the heel of her hands, pulled it back over with her fingers, then rolled it up until it was rounded again. She took a wooden rolling pin and worked it back and forth over the white mound until it was flat but not thin. She took a small jar, dipped the top of it in the sack of flour, then shook it off and handed it to Cecily.

"Here, you can cut out the biscuits. Like this." She held Cecily by the wrist with one hand and took Cecily's hand with her other and pressed the mouth of the jar into the dough. Cecily could feel just how much to push down and then turn back and forth until it released a perfect circle.

"Keep doing that." Aunt Pearl turned away and pulled a long flat pan from behind a curtain covering the area under the sink. She dipped the corner of a dishrag into a tub of lard on the counter near the sink and rubbed it all over the surface of the pan. "Put them on there when you're done. Line them up nice, that's it."

Aunt Pearl turned away again and busied herself with the stove and washing vegetables in the sink. Cecily focused on her task. After she had cut the third biscuit the dough began to stick to the rim of the jar. She looked at Aunt Pearl but decided on her own to dip the jar into the sack of flour. When she shook the jar off, though, she realized too late she had gotten flour in the jar. She dumped a small pile on the table. But since Aunt Pearl had strewn flour across the surface of the table before rolling out the dough she figured that was all right. She kept cutting out the biscuits. Just as she was about to tell Aunt Pearl she was done, her aunt was there, next to her, gathering up the leftover pieces of dough and magically putting them back together again into a new ball. Once again she rolled it out and Cecily had a new flat piece to cut from. When Cecily had filled the pan Aunt Pearl whisked it into the oven.

The kitchen filled with warm, comforting smells: pork simmered in a pot of pinto beans, the biscuits rose in the oven, coffee percolated on the stove. Cecily's stomach rumbled.

When Uncle Menard came in he had both of Cecily's suitcases under his arms, just like Aunt Pearl said he would. He dropped them, and Aunt Pearl jogged across the kitchen to him and caught him up in the same kind of bear hug she had given Cecily. He laughed and smacked her on her backside in a way that made Cecily want to look away. But he was laughing as he came over and offered his hand.

"How do you do? I am *so happy* you have the opportunity to meet me!"

Cecily shook his hand and smiled, uncertain. "Yes. Thank you."

Uncle Menard laughed again and went to the sink to wash his hands. He was bald except for a fringe of short white curls running behind his ears and circling the lower back of his head. He had small dark eyes he made even smaller when he spread a wide gentle smile across his face. The air around him smelled of tobacco.

That evening they ate and talked loudly and laughed more than Cecily had ever seen people laugh her whole life. It felt like a party. She asked about the farm and Uncle Menard explained how they grew tobacco and cotton, the most profitable cash crops in the South. On smaller plots they planted greens—both turnip and collard—winter squash, spinach, and sweet potatoes. The size of the property had grown over the years, starting with an ancestor of Pearl's who bought land and made the right white friends who allowed him to hold on to it and even acquire more in tough times. During the Depression Aunt Pearl and her brothers had scoffed at the New Deal programs that had been terrible for other black families. But even owning so much land, they knew nothing was safe and they took nothing for granted. Men with rifles patrolled the fields day and night at harvest time and even then they still had to put out fires set by white people who didn't think it right that blacks should have what Pearl's family had. Cecily wondered aloud why they stayed.

Aunt Pearl shook her head and looked at her as though Cecily should already know the answer. "If we left, Cecily, then the better place would always be somewhere else."

The rest of the evening they listened to Uncle Menard tell stories about the men he worked with and how they nagged and teased one another. Cecily put her plate, sopped clean of gravy, aside and put her elbows on the table—something Mama would never allow.

"And that Odom was always asking me about my comb," Uncle Menard said. "'Menard, can I borrow your comb?' Always asking me like that." Menard rubbed his shiny pate. "One day I got tired of it and I went down to the dime store and bought me a comb. When Odom asked for it I pulled it out of my pocket, just as nice as you please, and handed it to him."

Cecily smiled and nodded. A good end to the story, she thought. Uncle Menard had shown him.

"He took that comb and started running it through that nappy head of his." Menard mimed the actions of a man turning his head this way and that, grooming a full head of hair.

Cecily laughed and looked at Aunt Pearl. She was perched on the edge of her seat. She had her elbows on the table, her hands under her chin, and her eyes twinkled as she watched Uncle Menard.

"Then he handed the comb back to me and said, 'Thank you, Menard!' and I said, 'Thank goodness, I need that back bad!' and I took off my shoes and started scratching that comb into my toes! I said, 'This is the only way I can reach down there when my feet start itching!'"

Cecily stared in wonder as Aunt Pearl laughed and Uncle Menard's shoulders shook from holding back his own glee.

"You should've seen that Odom's face! He went running over there and dunked his whole head into the water barrel! He was rubbing at his head like a dog with fleas!"

Uncle Menard gave in to the waves of laughter overtaking

him and pounded his fist on the table. Cecily laughed so hard her stomach muscles felt weak. But Aunt Pearl outdid them all. Her whole body laughed—she swung her bare feet up into the air in front of her like a V and clapped her hands and bent over sideways as the laughter rolled out of her. Cecily had never seen anyone laugh like that before. She didn't know if her own body even knew how to do that. But she didn't care because the moment seemed to shine. Cecily didn't think about Mama or missing Harlem or the fact she really didn't know the people sitting there laughing with her. She just felt good.

"That was so funny," Cecily said later as she dried the wet plates Aunt Pearl handed her from the sink.

"Oh, that story? Menard has told that one about a hundred times!"

"To you?"

"Yeah, to me. Who else is he going to tell it to? Sometimes we have guests like you, but he tells it to me all the time."

"And you still laugh like that?"

"It's still a funny story! And he likes telling it to me. There's nothing wrong with that. It's just a way we have of enjoying each other's company. Isn't that a good thing?"

Cecily nodded. She began to realize how little she knew of how men and women could be with each other. When her own father passed she had been old enough to feel the loss, but not old enough to remember noticing whether or not her parents had been affectionate, or how they had looked at or spoken to each other. If you were going to be with the same person, day in and day out, for years and years Cecily supposed you couldn't help but hear the same stories from each other. Aunt Pearl was showing her how a person could choose how they took it all in. Cecily didn't know why, but it seemed another thing for her to feel good about.

* * *

THE ROOM WHERE Cecily would sleep looked out over the backyard. By the time she had changed into her nightgown and stood by the window it was too dark for her to see anything out there. She twisted her fingers in the fabric of the light green curtains. Cecily didn't like the dark and this dark outside her window was beyond what she thought possible. It was black like the darkness of a hole that wasn't satisfied with just being a hole so it had to suck you in and make you part of the darkness. She was glad of the glass between her and that blackness but still she put her other hand on the window just to see. Would she feel it pulling her out?

Then she heard the scratching at the door.

It sounded like a heavy scraping, like something wanted to take the paint off the wood. Cecily opened the door and gasped when Rex loped into the room, like it had been his room first. The dog looked up at Cecily, like he was expecting her to do something, but she couldn't move. She wanted to call Aunt Pearl, but that seemed a babyish thing to do. But Cecily did want to cry. She wanted to cry for her mama and to be in her own room and to take a hot bath. She realized she was even afraid to move her pinky toe to shift her weight as she stood.

Finally, when she felt so weary she thought she would fall over, Cecily reached out and put her hand on the bed. She found the softness of the coverlet. The dog looked at the bed and then at Cecily and panted. Slowly she raised the covers, lifted her knee, and began to inch herself underneath them.

Rex jumped.

Cecily yelped and dove under the blankets, hoping they would protect her by keeping the dog from biting all the way through to her skin. But instead she felt a heaviness at her feet, near the bottom of the bed. She looked out. Rex had settled himself there, his body curled into a neat roundness and his head on the covers. Cecily fell back on the pillows and pulled the covers up all around her. And that's how she went to sleep, staring into the eyes of a German shepherd who only gazed back until they both lost consciousness.

In the morning Cecily woke up to the sound of singing. She realized it was Aunt Pearl. She went to the window and saw the darkness had gone and light was dancing all over the backyard. Aunt Pearl was hanging laundry out on a clothesline.

Cecily unpacked but she could have left most of her things in the bags. The night before, Aunt Pearl deemed the clothing too fancy for the farm and handed Cecily a folded stack of cotton dresses, a stiff shirt like the one Aunt Pearl had worn the day before, and a large pair of denim coveralls.

"Those were Danny's," she said of the coveralls. "You're taller than any of my girls were so his will fit you better than theirs."

Cecily put on one of the cotton dresses, pale blue with a little pocket just over her left breast. After breakfast when she was filled with coffee and eggs and biscuits smothered in sausage gravy, the lessons began.

* * *

AUNT PEARL'S DAYS were full of cooking and driving and cleaning and, on some days, working in the fields alongside the hired hands. But Cecily soon learned there was an easy rhythm about everything she did. It just made plain sense how they would bake bread for the week's sandwiches on Monday, drive out the lunches on Tuesday, Wednesday, and Friday, and wash clothing on Thursday. And even though Aunt Pearl had to show her how to do everything, she took Cecily into her work routine as though the girl already knew it—as if she only needed reminding. This settled Cecily and made her not so afraid of making mistakes. In time she even grew confident—she liked feeling she could be useful, that she could be a part of a known result like a dinner on the table or a truckload of sack lunches.

Cecily learned how to spin food in her hands. Apples went round under her knife and the peel came off bit by bit until it fell to the kitchen table in a heavy spiral. Collards, bunched up in her fist, spun through her knife producing perfect strips of greens that filled up the sink, where she rinsed them in water and stuffed them into a pot for the stove. She learned food tasted different when you had worked it with your own hands. It tasted good, deep-down good. Sometimes Cecily felt a hunger so keen it seemed like a void had scraped her stomach raw like she had never properly filled it—didn't even know what it was to be filled.

Soon, like Aunt Pearl, Cecily stopped wearing shoes around the house and in the yard. At first she didn't like the way the morning dew made the grass slick and slimy under her feet, but she came to appreciate how cool it felt as summer came on and the days grew hotter. There seemed to be a kind of freedom to her and Aunt Pearl standing in the sun, wearing what they wanted, laughing like they were both young girls as they picked tomatoes in the garden or hung the laundry in the yard. Aunt Pearl taught Cecily how to use the washing machine, how to crank the clothing through the rollers to squeeze the water out of it so it could better dry on the clothesline. She talked about her children, about Uncle Menard's appetite, whether he'd remember to get that shoulder of pork ready for her to get on the stove Saturday so it could cook down all day and be done for Sunday dinner.

On certain days Aunt Pearl took the lunches without Cecily. On those days she stayed and helped in the fields, but this was work she would not be teaching the girl.

"Your mama would have my hide," she told Cecily. "She don't want your hands hard or your skin blackened in the sun from doing this kind of work. You're better off staying here and taking care of yourself."

And Cecily didn't mind because when she did go out to the fields with Aunt Pearl she felt a strangeness she didn't like. The first time she was stunned to see so many men. They were already anticipating the truck's arrival and were putting down tools or shedding sacks, and claiming shady spots under nearby trees. The truck pulled up, and Cecily watched them moving about—men tall and short, slim and stout, men as old as Uncle Menard and boys surely no older than herself.

When she would step out of the truck it seemed her skin burned from a flash of light—light that came, she was certain, from the eyes of every single one of those men as they focused on her for one hot moment, then quickly turned away. Cecily saw them talking to each other, continuing their motions as though they had done nothing more than notice a robin perched on a fence rail. But she could sense she had their acute attention, and she moved with feet of clay as though they had caught her in the heaviness of their collective gaze. Her breasts tingled against the rough fabric of her shirt, and this feeling told her she had entered a different place—had arrived here just as surely as when she stepped off the train in Anselm. But she was even more of a stranger in this place—and the thought bewildered her because her body seemed to be telling her she was supposed to be here, that there was something familiar about it even though the landmarks were foreign and the language unknown.

Cecily put a hand on the side of the truck and steadied herself, then shuffled toward Aunt Pearl, who was grabbing the first crate of lunch sacks.

"Don't you pay these men no mind," Aunt Pearl said. "Some of them act like they'd never seen a girl your age before." She yelled out to a man who wore a red bandana peeping out from under his straw hat and who seemed frozen in his spot. "Cole! Get over here and help me with this food if you all expect to get anything to eat before the sun goes down."

He came forward and took the crate from Aunt Pearl and she took another and moved toward the men under the tree. Cecily went to the rear of the truck and tried to pull a crate to her but it was heavy. The man Aunt Pearl called Cole came back, reached his long ropy arms past her, and slid the crate to himself. He lifted it liked it weighed no more than a dozen eggs. As he turned and whisked the crate away from her, Cecily smelled his sweat in the air where he had stood.

Her instinct seemed to awaken. She heard *Jump!* in her mind and she turned, placed her hands on the open door of the truck bed, and hoisted herself up into it. She began sliding crates to the end of the bed so Aunt Pearl and Cole could grab them. She felt better—she was higher up and out of reach. The eyes, she knew, were still on her and somehow that seemed okay. As long as they didn't get close enough for her to sense their power, she would be fine.

* * *

CECILY HAD AN ache for thinking space, somewhere to go where she could sort through all the changes happening to her. The change she noticed most of all, the one she appreciated most but understood the least, was how here in Anselm she had come to recognize when her blood flow was about to come. She didn't have to mark her calendar like her mama had shown her. She realized she felt her body moving through stages, month after month, like it had been talking to her all this time, and she was finally in a place quiet enough where she could hear it. One week her body would feel like it was gathering up in preparation for something. She wanted to eat more biscuits or an extra helping of pancakes. She felt the softness near the bottom of her belly like everything wanted to focus on this one essential spot of her being. In a few days the gentle ache, right at the bottom of her abdomen, would come and Cecily knew to get ready then, to put protection in her underwear, because her body was about to let it all go—the blood, the food, everything it had been holding on to. When it was over she felt light again.

Cecily had no answer for what was happening, and in the months to come she found she didn't have words for a lot of things. But she discovered she did have more words than before—words for how the sky made her feel, words for the changing quality of the light from season to season. But she had no one to give these words to.

She would sit on the porch in one of the rocking chairs and consider her changes and her longing to know more. One day in late August as she looked across the road and toward the woods it occurred to her there might be some quiet over there, somewhere far off between the trees—in fact she was sure a quiet might even be calling to her. It was like an emptiness beckoning her, pulling her toward it so she might be the one to fill it. Cecily stepped off the porch and started walking. Rex got up from where he lay near her feet and accompanied her. They crossed the road and went in the direction of the woods. Her shoes sank into the soft ground and her nose filled with the smell of ripening vegetation. Birdsong, calm and cheerful, seemed to affirm the way.

She walked until she made her way into the woods. The leaves, grown thick in the summer heat, seemed to close behind her like a curtain. As she walked the ground dropped down toward the banks of a river that flowed across the back part of the county and formed the border between Anselm and Portage, the next town over. She came to a stand of evergreens with long red trunks that stood like toy soldiers just up from the river's edge. The foliage was higher there and the light bright. Cecily sat herself down on the roots of a tree. It was quiet there aside from the sound of the water flowing past her. Aunt Pearl had said no one was ever down there because the good fishing spots were all miles farther downstream. Cecily felt the silence and soon she thought about all the new things settling into her. She kept coming back to a simple word: "good." Everything around her just felt good: her aunt's singing, the food they ate, the trees all around her, the smell of the earth as they tilled the fields.

She thought about all of this as the days wore on and her walks to the water became frequent. When she sat by the river Cecily didn't think about where she had been before—about Harlem or her mama or their life there. She didn't think about where she would be the next day. She liked knowing she was fine just where she was. And she did feel fine, especially once she found a good place to sit and Rex would walk himself around in a circle three or four times then settle down next to Cecily. She stroked the short wiry hairs of the dog's shiny coat and felt the rapid heartbeat that seemed to work in rhythm with his panting.

There was a part of Cecily completely aware of not being afraid in this place—that it was inevitable, and she had come all these miles to be in this sweet spot, her toes curving into the moss as present and necessary as any of the trees around her.

She learned that if she sat long enough and still enough the birds and animals around her would go about their business like she wasn't there. The squirrels chattered in the branches above her head. Once in the early evening a deer walked along the riverbank across from her and stared. Birds landed just out of arm's reach.

And then, one day she saw a man—a white man.

She had been sitting as usual when she heard the unmistakable rustling of bush and leaves that told of an animal of some sort making its way to the riverside. She knew to hold still and wait, that whatever came, if it did see her, would pay her no mind and keep doing what it needed to do.

But when she saw the thing had two legs she pulled her knees into her chest and tried to make herself small. To Cecily he was as wild and rare as an animal might be because he was so pale, pale like the belly of a fish from the river. He was short legged, and he moved quickly along the mossy banks. His hair, light brown, was too long and uncombed. At first he seemed hurried, the way he had come bashing through the branches. But he sat down on the bank, almost in the water. He was quiet, much like Cecily was when she was doing her own thinking, except it seemed he was talking to someone. In fact she was quite sure he was talking to someone even though his lips didn't move and all his limbs were still. He was too far down from Cecily to get a good look at his face.

She thought about going closer but then, quite suddenly, he stood, tore off his shirt, and threw himself into the water with such force Cecily feared he'd hit his head and drown and his body would come floating down to rest at her feet. He thrashed around in the water, loud and hard and mad, like he'd dropped something in there and had to find it right away. Whether he ever found it or not Cecily didn't know, but he kept on going for what seemed like forever. When he stopped all Cecily heard was the sound of him breathing hard. He pulled himself out of the water, scrambled back up the bank, and disappeared. At first she thought she should run, but he was on the other bank, going in the opposite direction. He wasn't coming after her. So she kept sitting and thinking until it was her usual time to go back to the house.

The next time the white man appeared, Cecily did pull herself to the other side of a tree trunk to conceal herself better. She saw him execute the same odd ritual, as he would again and again in the days to come. He didn't come every day. Cecily thought he seemed far from where he should be, as though he didn't live nearby. But he must belong somewhere, she figured, because other than his long hair nothing about him seemed overgrown or filthy. He didn't have a beard.

Cecily got used to his presence much as she did with any other presence in the woods. On a sunny day the thrashing made it look like he was tossing rainbows as the water all around him caught the light. Sometimes he'd float on his back and stare into the sky. Cecily knew she should be afraid of him—and she kept herself far enough away behind bushes or trees so he couldn't see her. But there were times she heard his splash much farther down from where she was, and instead of staying safely in her place she followed the sound to find him—to watch him. She knew she should be frightened of the man, not only because of his whiteness, but also because his behavior proved him to be beyond the boundaries everyone else stayed within to make sense of the world. Yet it seemed to Cecily whatever the man thrashed against and mumbled to had nothing to do with her. It was something inside him, something that couldn't be de-scribed with words but still felt strangely familiar to her. So she watched him, thinking maybe it would be possible to see inside a person—thinking maybe she could learn something from him about what was going on inside herself.

One unseasonably hot day in early October Cecily went into the woods. Thunderstorms the night before had drenched the ground but water still hung thick and heavy in the air as though it were draped over clotheslines. In the woods the branches bent down with their overgrown foliage and the earth underneath her felt old and alive. She went all the way down to the river, took off her shoes, and stepped in to soak her feet in the cool water. When she heard the manic rustling sound, at first she thought nothing of it. It wasn't the usual sound of the white man or that of anyone else coming. Maybe squirrels were quarreling as they often did in the leaves just before they chased each other back up into the trees. But the sound didn't stop and it seemed larger, more rhythmic—intentional.

Her feet still in the water, Cecily peered through the canopy of wet leaves on the opposite bank, and when she found the place where the motion was she also found the brightness of skin. It was the white man but he was naked and lying face-down in the dirt. He was writhing as though he were having a fit and trying to burrow himself into the ground. Cecily took a step closer then stopped. She didn't move, didn't dare make a sound, but she couldn't take her eyes from his skin.

She saw the places where it was brown, the places where, moving up his limbs, the skin was blinding white. She wondered if he would die there if she didn't call for help. She wondered what they would say to her if she did. Cecily opened her mouth to speak but the voice she heard wasn't her own. It was his, releasing a soft, wordless cry. Then he turned over and seemed exhausted. He had dirt all over him but Cecily saw something on him, white and glistening, spread all across his belly. She couldn't leave. His head fell back and his eyes seemed to roll up into the trees and toward the sky.

Rex barked.

Rex never barked in these woods, not even when chasing squirrels, but the sound came out sharp and clear like he wanted to call to the man and scold him. The man sat up fast and for the first time Cecily saw his eyes, though glazed, were a shocking shade of blue mixed of sky and water and cornflower. She'd never seen eyes like that before and they held her rooted in the muddy water. She wasn't sure if he could see her. He seemed still in the thrall of his dream, his vision turned inward. But the light in his eyes, in the red glowing of his face, made Cecily believe he saw through the curtain of leaves just as well as she could. Suddenly she became painfully aware of her bare feet and bare legs under her dress. She ran.

Cecily ran all the way back to the house and it wasn't until she reached the porch that she realized she had left her shoes on the riverbank. She went back the next day to look for them, but they were gone.

In the nights afterward when she was safely in bed, in the blackness, Cecily thought about what she had witnessed. If she had been able to tell her mama about it, she would have heard the words—"nasty," "dirty"—that surely this man was crazy. Cecily would have taken these words into herself and believed them. But with no one to give her these words she was left to her own thoughts. And though she didn't fully understand what she had seen, her body told her more when her right hand would drift downward under the covers and settle in the soft moistness between her thighs.

* * *

CECILY DIDN'T SEE the man again. She still walked to the river with Rex, only she tried to do so more quietly. And when she sat she did so longer and with expectation, but he didn't return. It could have been because he knew she'd seen him but more likely, she thought, the coming cold had driven him away. The late season heat had finally released its hold on the countryside and one morning, about a month later, Cecily awoke to the sight of the lawn glazed white with frost.

"It's time to get you some boots," Aunt Pearl said after breakfast. "We'll have to go to Portage, but that's all right. I wouldn't buy boots from any store but Ames's anyhow."

They drove into the town on a Saturday afternoon. Aunt Pearl liked the Ames shoe store because the owner sold to blacks in a comfortable back storage room that was fixed up nice, just like the front. Cecily liked it because it was warm and there was a cushioned bench for them to sit and wait on. She heard customers talking in the other part of the store. A salesman finally came through the door and stepped from behind a rack of shoes. He wore dark brown pants with a leather belt and a white shirt with pens in the chest pocket and the sleeves rolled up to his elbows. Cecily lowered her gaze shyly as he approached, but when Aunt Pearl began to introduce Cecily she looked up enough to see his face. The light of his shocking blue eyes welded Cecily to her seat.

It was the man from the banks of the river.

Cecily dug her fingers into the fabric of the cushion beneath her. She saw no sign of recognition. His right hand moved up slowly to tug at his ear and scratch the skin just behind it. She listened to Aunt Pearl call him Mr. Travis and introduce Cecily as her grandniece from the city and explain how she would need boots, nothing fancy, for the winter. He nodded and sighed as though he'd just heard this request for the fifth time that day.

"I'll see what we have."

His voice was higher than Cecily had expected it to be, like some part of the sigh never left his body but was left singing there in the upper register of his throat. He sounded calm, gentle—none of the power she had felt whenever his body had thrashed about in the river.

The boots he brought to her weren't much to look at—just black with a plain zipper up the front. They came up to just over her ankles and were topped with a fur cuff that felt warm. He took Cecily's stocking-clad foot and guided it into a boot. She held her breath when he lifted her leg, placed the foot against his left shoulder.

"Just push your heel down in there."

She hesitated at first, but as she put pressure against him she realized he felt solid, like a wall. She pushed her foot more and it slid into the bottom of the boot.

"That looks just about perfect, Mr. Travis! And you didn't even have to measure her foot. How's that feel, Cecily?"

She could only nod. The boot was a perfect fit. Its mate went on just as easily and Mr. Travis stood and took Cecily's hand so she stood and walked around in them. His fingers felt strong as they pulled her up from the bench.

"Well, I've been doing this a long time," he said in the breathy, sighing voice.

Cecily sat down again and removed the boots. Mr. Travis placed them in a large paper bag. He rolled the top and handed it to Cecily. She felt like she could finally look him in the eyes, those eyes that looked like they had absorbed every inch of the sky. He seemed to return the look pointedly, with a firm nod of his head, as though Cecily and he had just agreed on something. She nodded too, surprised she didn't feel embarrassed or scared.

"Thank you," she said softly.

"You have a good day now," he said to Aunt Pearl.

Cecily wore the boots when the cold began to cling to the land and the leaves no longer shielded her in the woods. But still she made her way down to the river. If she met him again she hoped to speak to Mr. Travis, to say something kind and comforting. But she didn't see him again and perhaps it was just as well. She didn't know what those kind and comforting words should be. She also got the sense he knew them better than she did.

CHAPTER 7
Cecíly

Harlem, May 1947—Sunday Morning

In the heat, Cecily found it hard to focus on the minister's voice. Her eyelids kept drooping. She had the full breasts, lips, and hips of a woman but, sitting stoop-shouldered next to her mother, felt she looked more like a girl. The pink dress she wore hung awkwardly on her body and she crossed and uncrossed her long arms in front of her like she didn't know what to do with them. A part of her was still stuck in Anselm, the day she returned from her walk and found Mama sitting back in a kitchen chair, spreading open like a magnolia flower. Aunt Pearl had been closed up and tight and not smiling. At that point Cecily had been in Anselm for over a year and was feeling settled.

"It's time for Cecily to come on back home," her mother had said, sighing and tired from the heat.

"The peaches were going to be good this year," Aunt Pearl had said quietly. Cecily knew she had been thinking about the

cobbler they had planned to make together and how she had yet
to show her niece how to make whipped cream.

Now that she was back in the city, Cecily felt hot and tired
all the time. Her feet hurt from the new pumps Mama had
bought for her but that Cecily still didn't know how to walk
in right. She wondered if she could slip the shoes off under the
pew without her noticing. Mama had bought the shoes right
before they met that man, Frank Washington, who had been
so nice to Cecily, but she kept wondering why they were talking
to this old man. He had come over to them again this morning
and now sat just across the aisle from her, smiling like he knew
something she didn't. Cecily refused to look at him. She dozed
off and on throughout the service thinking, in her brief moments of sleep, she was in the South again. In Anselm the grass
had been soft beneath her feet and she knew how to look for
crickets as nighttime fell.

Cecily missed spending her mornings in the kitchen with
Aunt Pearl, learning how much water to add to the flour when
making biscuit dough, how to soak beans before putting them
on to cook, how to can tomatoes for the winter. And she still
thought of her afternoons out with Rex, and the river in the
woods, and, though she had told no one about him, Mr. Travis.

She thought about him because in Harlem Cecily felt like
she had been cut off from some important part of herself that
he seemed to know on his own, for himself. She was just beginning to figure it out before Mama came and got her. Now
she felt out of place, even though Harlem had been the place
where she grew up. What troubled her most was there seemed
to be fewer ways to mark time here, aside from a clock and a

calendar. The buildings stood between her and the sun's daily walk across the sky. The flowers couldn't tell her the season because the ones she saw were often forced to bloom out of time. It was only May yet summer seemed to be bearing down already in a rage of endless heat. The people here were always insisting on their own time—time for drinks, time for church, time for dinner, time to dance, time to play bridge.

On the farm they woke and slept with the sun. They planted when the earth knew it was time, and they reaped when the ground was ready to give it up. Her seventeen-year-old body seemed to welcome these natural rhythms.

Now, at home, she seemed to get the signs all wrong. Her arm still stung from the memory of Mama's smack from the day before. Cecily thought she had been so clever—she missed the smell of the fresh air in her clothes and had taken it upon herself to dry her own laundry outside. But she had hung the garments where people could see. Mama had yelled about how Cecily should know better, how they weren't living in a tenement on 116th Street. The fact that Cecily didn't understand—they had always hung their clothes out in Anselm and it didn't seem to bother anybody—only upset her mother more.

That's when Mama said they had to go see her cousin Mae.

Her mother nudged her and Cecily realized she had been asleep. The minister was saying, "And we give thanks this day oh Lord for our generous flock who maintain your house."

The collection plates were going around. Gladys nudged Cecily again. The girl, still yawning, pulled the bill her mother had given her out of the little blue purse and placed it on the plate. She tried to hand it to Mae, but one of the ushers swooped over her and took the plate before Mae could touch it. He held it as she placed a crisp hundred-dollar bill onto it with her manicured hand.

Cecily looked up and noticed the good-looking man in the balcony. There was something familiar about him, but she didn't know why. It seemed to her he might be looking down her dress and the thought gave her a funny feeling. It made her scared, but not really scared. It was something else and she didn't have a name for it.

She realized she felt that way all the time now, like suddenly there were no names for a lot of the things she saw and felt. It was like she was on the brink of something about to happen, like she was sitting in the dark of a movie house and waiting for the show to start. When? When would it begin?

"Now I have some good news to share with all of you," the minister went on. "As you all know, the drive to raise funds to build an addition to our church to accommodate our growing congregation had stalled in recent weeks. Well, I'm happy to report that we recently received a *very* generous donation in the amount of *twen-ty-five thou-sand dol-lars!*" He made sure to punch every syllable and paused to wipe his brow dramatically with a handkerchief. "That has, I am grateful to say, totally made up for the shortfall and we'll be breaking ground on the project in the coming weeks."

Murmurs of approval moved through the room and many heads turned Mae's way. Cecily shifted in her seat. It felt like they were all looking at her.

"The donor is listed as 'Anonymous,' but I think we've all known this donor to be modest and protective of her privacy and we will respect that." He smiled at Mae. Cecily thought

Mae looked annoyed but she acknowledged him with the slightest nod of her head. Cecily bowed her head to disguise the tiny smile forming on her own lips.

* * *

"EXCELLENT SERMON, REVEREND," Mae said afterward as they crossed the threshold. "So inspirational."

"Thank you, Miss Malveaux. As always, we are blessed with your inspirational presence." He kissed Mae's hand and held on to it just a little too long. She gently pulled it away before he released it, and she walked down the steps to where Lawrence and the car waited for her at the curb. Gladys followed but she wanted to give Reverend Stiles her own assessment of the service.

"And it was so right, Reverend! I was just telling Cecily the other day you can't be too careful about choosing the people to have around you." Gladys paused. Just then she saw the movement of Mae's wrist, first toward her and then away, motioning her to the car. Then the arm disappeared through the window.

"Well, it was a lovely sermon. Come, Cecily, we don't want to keep Mae waiting." Gladys took Cecily's arm and they hurried down the steps.

CHAPTER 8
Val

Harlem, May 1947—Sunday Morning

Val and Sebastian sauntered out of the church just in time to see the green Packard pull away.

"Sebastian," Val said quietly. "Get the car, please."

"Right away, sir."

Sebastian walked down the steps and Val moved to the side of the doorway, opposite from where Reverend Stiles stood. Val put on his hat and clasped his hands behind his back. He enjoyed watching the flow of parishioners coming out of the church. It was like a rainbow tipped on its side because the women wore every color under the sun. Their hats, some small and jeweled, others large swirls of lace and feathers, bobbed and danced on nodding, smiling heads. The men in their suits were like thick, dark blocks inserted at various intervals to corral the riot of color. Val felt the warmth of the late spring day on his face and relaxed.

He looked over to where the minister still collected compliments for his weekly outpouring of fire and brimstone. Reverend Stiles took time in between his greetings to glare at Val over his wire-rimmed glasses. Val smiled and winked at him.

"How ya doing, Reverend! I see you're keeping the flock fine, as always!"

He nodded at Val but didn't answer. Instead he took the hand of Elizabeth Townsend, who had come through the doorway. They smiled at each other. Val wanted to hear what they were saying, but the voices and footsteps of the people between them made it impossible. After a few minutes she joined the flow of parishioners and walked down the street. Val watched the backs of her legs and the swooshing of her skirt against them.

When the crowd finally thinned Reverend Stiles stared at him a few moments longer before delivering a terse, "Good day, Mr. Jackson." Val winked at the retreating minister, then strolled down the steps in the direction Elizabeth had gone. He knew she was headed for the back lower-level entrance of the church.

The hallway off the entrance was narrow and darkened by the wood paneling. Dim yellow bulbs lit the passage. Soon it would be filled with a line of men, women, and children waiting to be fed in the church's soup kitchen. Val made his way down the hall, turned right, then stepped through the open double-door threshold of the large gathering room. It was set up with rows of long tables and at one end an open kitchen buzzed with the work of the churchwomen preparing the meal. A line of windows along the top of the room let in natural light and made the basement space more inviting.

Val lingered near the doorway, just out of sight, and finally spotted Elizabeth. She had just finished greeting her sister volunteers and was getting ready to help. She moved with quick and careful hands. She put her hat on a shelf and took a long white apron from one of many hooks along the back kitchen wall. She touched her hair briefly then began some occupation that called for her to turn her back to Val. All he could see were her shoulders sloped downward and her arms moving with assurance and skill. There was a lightness about her that he liked. It made him think holding her would be like possessing a butterfly in the palm of his hand—hard to grasp, easy to crush.

He heard a car horn bleating in short bursts through the windows above his head. He knew it was Sebastian. He stared at Elizabeth a moment longer, then went back down the hall and up the steps. Sebastian pulled the Cadillac toward him in a slow crawl. When the car stopped, Val got in.

"To Miss Malveaux's?" Sebastian asked. He put the car in gear and paused with his foot on the brake.

"Yes, but no rush," Val said. He leaned back into the seat. "Mae can afford to wait a little. It'll be good for her."

CHAPTER 9
Cecily

Harlem, May 1947—Sunday Morning

Cecily wanted desperately to sit down. The high heels pinched her feet and seemed to hurt more than they did at church. Her cousin's white maid—Mae called her Regina—laid out a tea set bordered with pretty blue flowers. She wanted to study the cups and take off her shoes but Mama insisted on walking her through all of Mae's parlor-floor rooms.

"All of this furniture, honey?" she was saying, pointing to the golden side chairs placed against the wall in the living room. "It's made to look like the same furniture in a king's palace in France. These candlesticks"—she pointed to the heavy round pillars on either side of the mantel—"are from England. I remember when Mae's mama came back with these. Saw her unpack them myself."

During the tour Mae didn't speak or move from her seat at the table. Cecily had the feeling Mae was watching her, maybe even sizing her up. She could barely look Mae in the eye. There was something about her that made Cecily feel like looking at Mae would be like gazing into the sun. She was glad to focus instead on all the beautiful things her mother showed her. She lingered over the paintings on the walls and ran her fingers over the piano keys of the Steinway. But the pain in her feet forced her to hold on to tables and chairs as she moved around. She felt like a baby still learning to walk.

Finally Mae spoke. She waved a graceful hand toward her. "Please sit down, Cecily. Gladys, come have some tea. You make me tired just watching this poor girl on her feet."

The tea tasted bitter to Cecily's lips but she was afraid to ask for sugar. However, sitting across from Mae and Mama, she managed to summon the courage to get a good look at her famous cousin. Her only memories of Mae were from her childhood—faint images of someone very pretty, like a fairy, and how she could make a room seem full of light. But Cecily had never been allowed to stay in those rooms. She was always being taken to bed or sent to the kitchen to eat. Sitting with Mae now Cecily found herself trying to understand the difference between Mae and Mama. Cecily knew her family had money. She didn't know how much, but her family did possess wealth. Her mother frequented the same bridge parties and church meetings as Mae. Cecily knew they sat together at the Swan, the most exclusive club in Harlem.

But money seemed to do different things for Mae. Cecily noticed she moved coolly, slowly, and deliberately through a room. She had so many elegant ways about her. Mama seemed to be always on the verge of nearly crashing into a person or a piece of furniture wherever she walked. In Mae's presence Cecily became uncomfortably aware of how Mama seemed to talk too loud and too fast. Even having a delicate cup of tea in her hands didn't slow her down. Mae's yellow dress seemed simple yet sophisticated. Mama's polka-dot dress felt too busy.

"I knew the moment Cecily arrived that we had to come see you, Mae," Mama said after draining her cup. "I don't regret the time she spent in North Carolina. It's a safer place for a young girl to grow up. But now I have so many plans for her and she is not at all ready. She's missed the debutante balls and had no instruction in dancing or music. I knew you could help us."

"Indeed." Mae raised an eyebrow.

"Mae is so wonderful about these things," Mama said to Cecily. "She has all the right connections! Langston, Cab, Ella—all the right people! The best of Harlem! And Mae knows exactly what we need to do to make you presentable. Lord knows she has more time than anyone else since her poor Brantwell died. How long has it been, Mae?"

Cecily noticed Mae winced at the mention of "poor Brantwell."

"Six years" was all she replied.

"And who's been running the business since then?"

Mae sipped her tea. "I have, along with a board of advisors of course. That's how my mother would have wanted it."

Mama took her fork and speared a tiny sandwich on the platter in front of her. She added two more. "Well, we all know your mama was as smart as a whip! Making her own hair product, then coming up with the idea to put your face on every single can when you were just a baby! Everyone always said your mama made the business, but your face made the money!"

Mae smiled but said nothing.

Cecily looked around, unsure of what to focus on. She thought about eating something herself. Then Mae placed a reassuring hand on Cecily's knee. She wondered if Mae could tell she had taken off her shoes.

"Don't worry, my dear, it won't be so bad," Mae said. "We'll start with finding you a music teacher. Is that all right, Gladys?"

Mama chewed loudly. "Perfect!"

"And maybe we'll do a little shopping. You'll see how that makes it fun to be a woman, among other things." She smiled and leaned on her elbow, hand under her chin.

Regina came in bearing a full kettle of hot water. She filled the teapot, then spoke quietly to Mae.

"Mr. Val Jackson is here, ma'am."

"He is? Hmm." Mae raised her eyebrows. She looked at Mama and smiled. "What could he possibly want? Send Mr. Jackson in."

"Oh, that man!" said Mama. "I can't stand the sight of him. Mae, why in God's name would you have him up here in your house? Did you see him in church this morning, leering down on all of us like the dog he is? I don't know why Reverend Stiles puts up with it."

Mae set her teacup on the table. "And yet he attends your Winter Ball every year at your invitation."

Cecily looked at her mother. "Why do you invite him, Mama, if you don't like him?"

Mama suddenly looked like she needed to do something with her hands. She picked up the teapot and refilled all their cups.

She said, "Honey, you're gonna learn soon enough money opens every door in Harlem. A lot of people don't like Mr. Jackson, but they certainly love his money."

Mae chuckled. "But it only gets him so far."

"That's because it's dirty money," Mama said. She put down the teapot and pointed a finger at no one in particular. "His daddy and his granddaddy—both bootleggers."

"They run the numbers right out of that club of his," said Mae. "That's why he'll never have what he really wants."

Cecily opened her mouth to ask what Mr. Jackson wanted but Mama, hearing the man's footsteps near the door, quickly hushed her.

"He wants to own a baseball team," she hissed. "But nobody with gambling in their background gets to buy into a team no matter how much money they got."

CHAPTER 10
Val

Harlem, May 1947—Sunday Morning

When Val Jackson walked in, his hat held over his chest and his smile filling the room, Gladys greeted him with such cheer one would have thought it was her parlor, not her cousin's. "Oh, Mr. Jackson! What a nice surprise!"

"Yes," said Mae. "Quite the surprise."

Val bowed and smiled. "Oh, there's no way I'd ever run up out of this city without paying my respects to you, Miss Malveaux."

Mae's chin tilted up. "Leaving the city?"

He was pleased he had gotten her attention. He took her hand, ran his thumb over its soft skin, and kissed it. "Not forever, ma'am, not forever. I'm going to visit my aunt Rose at her Westchester estate. She's invited me up to escape this heat."

"Oh, Mrs. Jarreau has invited us too!" declared Gladys warmly. "Cecily, Mrs. Jarreau owns half of Harlem. She and her husband were buying real estate before most colored people knew the meaning of the words. Your daddy handled a lot of her business. Unfortunately we haven't been able to take her up on her generous offer; there's been so much to do with Cecily. You remember my daughter, don't you? She's been visiting with our people down in North Carolina."

Val feigned surprise. "This is little Cecily? No! I don't believe it!" He positioned himself behind the girl, his hands on the back of her chair. "The last time I saw you was at one of your mama's parties, sitting up there on the steps listening to everybody when you were probably supposed to be in bed!"

Gladys chafed and moved her mouth as if to say something. He looked at her like her next words might be the best thing he'd hear all day. "Yes, well . . ." She sipped her tea instead.

Mae, to his delight, artfully filled in for her. "Well, I wish someone would invite me out for some good clean air. Lord knows how stuffy it can get in Harlem when it warms up. It was positively sweltering in that church this morning!"

"I'd be happy to put in a good word for you with Aunt Rose." He leaned over Cecily's shoulder toward Mae.

"Don't be ridiculous. I was joking."

"Yes, honey, you can go up to your own country house any time you want," said Gladys, looking hard at Val. "Mae, it's time for us to go. I told old Mrs. Walker we'd stop by and holler at her before Sunday dinner. Come on, Cecily."

The girl pouted, he noticed, with a deliciously plump lip.

"Oh, Mama, do we have to? I'm so tired."

"You should get your rest," Val said. "It'd be a mighty shame to see those pretty eyes tired."

Gladys stared at him as she stood. He stepped out of the

way so she could reach her daughter and pull Cecily to her feet. "Mae, we'll be in touch?"

"Of course."

Cecily stumbled. He saw she had taken off one of her shoes under the table. Her cheeks colored and she dove down to find it and came up wobbling. Val reached for her other arm and steadied her.

"You take care now," he said.

Cecily barely got out a tiny "thank you" before Gladys whisked her away and out the door.

Val started to laugh, but Mae put a finger to her lips. She went to the window and watched as Lawrence escorted Gladys and Cecily into the car. When they were safely on their way, Mae gave in and they both let loose with satisfying mirth. He enjoyed being with her like this, above anything and everyone who couldn't be what they were.

"All right, Val, what's this bull about going to Westchester? You never leave during baseball season and everyone knows Rose Jarreau is already leaving everything to you."

"Oh, baby, will you miss me?"

Mae's spine stiffened. She touched the side of his face then gave it a playful, but significant, slap. "*Don't* call me that. But of course I will. Especially now—I need you. That's why I called you over here. You know I don't like you hanging around. I have my reputation to think of."

The slap didn't hurt but it woke him up. It reminded him to be careful. He turned away from her and sat on the sofa. "I'm at your service." Mae went to a box on the mantel, took out a cigarette, and lit it. When she had drawn the smoke into her lungs and released it she said, "Remember when Frank Washington and I ended things last year?"

"That old prick? So what?" Val put his hands behind his head and crossed his ankles.

"And where did he go? Off with that jelly-bellied lover of yours."

He nodded. When he had been distracted with other pursuits Frank did manage to pluck Delia Song, a dancer from the World's Fair who had attained a certain level of fame and notoriety after that event.

"I was glad her fat ass was gone."

"Or so you wanted everyone to think." Mae sat down next to him and offered the smoking cigarette. He took it and tapped it over a crystal ashtray on the table next to him. He drew on it.

"Like I said, so what?"

"Well, the old prick is getting married." She leaned back on her side of the sofa and touched a toe to his thigh. He blew out smoke in a thin white stream.

"To her? Who the hell cares?"

"No, no, no. She's not his type. Not really. Frank always had a weakness for the virginal type—young and fresh. The rest he only toys with."

"Like he did with you."

"And . . ." She looked at Val, her gaze hard as ice.

He knew that look. He likened it to what a bull must look like right before it charges. He steeled himself by laughing again. Then he sat up and stubbed out the cigarette.

"And Lord have mercy on the man who toys with Mae Malveaux!"

"Exactly."

"Ah, yes, I love it!" He rubbed his hands together. "Ladies and gentlemen, sweet revenge is our game and our beautiful ace Mae Malveaux is on the mound. Let's sit back and enjoy the heat!"

"Oh, you'll get to play too," said Mae, pushing at Val's shoulder. "I know who Frank has chosen as his intended."

Val frowned for a moment, then his eyes lit up. "You're kidding!"

Mae laughed and leaned back into the sofa again. "Yes. Our little hothouse flower from the South: Cecily Vaughn. I want you to seduce her. Get her pregnant if you like, I don't care. I just want it to be clear to Mr. Washington on his wedding night that he's the biggest fool in Harlem if not all of New York City."

"Very nice." He nodded slowly, thinking.

"Frank is leaving tomorrow for Martha's Vineyard for the entire month. That should give you plenty of time. And you would enjoy yourself. She's so ready."

Val sighed. He got up and helped himself to bourbon at Mae's cocktail cart. "And so easy. Too easy."

"What?" She got up and followed him.

"Come on, Mae, this is beneath me, you know it is." He dropped ice into his drink from a silver bucket. "I'm not some hard-up boy off the street. I'm a man who needs a challenge. That girl will have her skirt up and her legs open for the first man who looks at her cockeyed."

"Ha!" She turned her back on him and threw herself onto the sofa.

"You know I'm right! You wanna talk reputation, well, I

have a reputation to think of. I'm not an ordinary man. I *don't* bed ordinary women. And Lord knows there's nothing out of the ordinary about Cecily Vaughn." He sipped his drink then put it down. He pulled a cushioned ottoman over to Mae and sat down in front of her. He lifted her leg, the fullness of her calf fitting perfectly into his hand. His fingers brushed Mae's thigh and he began to slowly move them a half inch up her skirt. "My conquest has to have something extra special about her."

Mae sat up and pulled her leg back. "Aren't you being a little presumptuous? Unless—" She paused and looked up as though she had to pull an answer hanging right in front of her. "Yes! You have a totally different conquest in mind?"

Val picked up his glass and went to the window. He sipped his whiskey.

"Tell me."

He stayed silent.

"You know I'll find out soon enough." Mae got up and stood behind him. She ran her well-manicured fingers down his spine.

He said nothing.

"Val." She pinched the back of his arm.

"All right, all right. Look, it's nothing, Mae. Come on, it's nothing!"

Her eyes thinned to needles. Before they could pierce him he spoke fast.

"If it's that important to you, I'll do it."

She crossed her arms and seemed to reappraise him. "You will?"

"Sure. I'm not gonna be gone that long, a couple of days, that's it."

He lifted his hand to smooth a small lock of hair near her temple. She smiled and seemed to accept this tiny pleasure before retreating a safe distance to pour her own drink.

"Thank you," she said.

He returned to the sofa and leaned back with his hands behind his head. The lie had been an improvisation, but necessary. His Elizabeth Townsend project was still too new and too fragile to have Mae anywhere near it.

CHAPTER II
Val

Mercylands, Late May 1947

The hot sun reached through the windows of the north-bound Cadillac, and Val Jackson closed his eyes. With Sebastian at the wheel he was content to give in to the sleepiness without a struggle. There was nothing outside he needed to see, no part of the landscape he didn't already know as well as his own face. When he was a boy he would make the journey to his aunt's estate sitting sideways on the car seat, his forehead pressed against the cool glass of the window. He had always tried to pinpoint the exact spot where all traces of the city fell away and the trees asserted their domination. He thought there might be a kind of magic in that change, that he could even possess it at the moment of its happening. If he put his hand out the window at just the right time he might even catch it, he believed, like a swift line drive into his baseball glove.

If the landscape was changing and shedding itself of city elements, then he must be doing the same. But he didn't know what he had to leave behind or what it meant. Why would his mother always insist it was good for him to spend time at Aunt Rose's every summer if something didn't actually happen to him with each going? And why, when she and his father returned weeks later to retrieve him, did she examine him so carefully? Her soft brown eyes would sweep over him from his head to his toes while she smiled and asked him a stream of questions. "Who did you play with? How many fish did you catch? Did you like the books I sent? You didn't have time to write me more than two letters? Where are your shoes?"

He would answer, often with many more words than necessary, because he had loved talking to her and because he could feel the warmth of her undivided attention. Her face would glow when she laughed at his stories and when his father placed his straw fedora on Val's head and it would slip over his eyes. Val would push the hat back on his forehead and keep on talking. What was he revealing to her in his chatter? Had he changed and could she tell? What would he say to her after this summer? This kind of thinking always kept his mind occupied on the long drive, but years later he could see it had been childish. His mother had probably meant the trip was good for him because he would enjoy playing outdoors more in the country, and childless Aunt Rose, who was really Val's mother's aunt, had liked having him around. And it had been better for him to be there than running in the streets of Harlem where anything could happen.

As a teenager he had gone in protest. When he turned sixteen his father had begun to teach him his business. This infused Val with a sense of movement—the motion of people from place to place, of dollars being spent, of product being made and delivered. This movement all sprang from his father's direction. At times he would figuratively give Val the wheel and allow his son to oversee a project or a delivery. Val liked having people look up to him and do his bidding. After such attention he couldn't bear the quiet of Mercylands even if he was allowed to have his own friends visit. His mother had cajoled him that last summer, just before he turned eighteen, by saying it would be the last time he had to go.

And it had been, but not for the reason he'd expected. His parents had said goodbye, left him for his stay at Aunt Rose's, and never returned. The accident, caused by a speeding fifty-year-old banker crossing the centerline on a curving piece of road, had consumed more than one car and three other lives besides those of his mother and father. He hadn't known the meaning of the word "grief" but suddenly the patch of Oriental carpet in his aunt's library where he fell to his knees became his classroom in the ways of loss. He'd tried desperately to reassemble in his mind a picture of his mother's smile because he couldn't believe he would never see it again. The faces of both his parents had slipped through his fingers like fog and he'd feared the effect would be permanent.

But Aunt Rose's face—her high forehead and translucent eyes the color of strong tea, the same eyes as his mother's—had steadied him. She'd steered him through the planning of the wakes and then the funeral, but had made it clear he had to be the one to give the directions. He'd been the one to walk behind his parents' caskets and stand next to Reverend Cooper on a grassy knoll in Woodlawn Cemetery while the minister uttered words that Val guessed were supposed to help.

"'I am the resurrection, and the life: he that believeth in me, though he were dead, yet shall he live: And whosoever liveth and believeth in me shall never die.'"

Val had thanked all the mourners and left feeling small and alone in the back of the long dark car. It was only later, when it was all over and he and Aunt Rose walked along the tree-lined lanes of Mercylands, that he understood why she had guided him so. At that point she could have stepped in and taken over everything—his money, his father's businesses. That day she made it clear to him she wasn't going to do it.

"Your daddy was no dummy," she'd said. She had nudged him in the side and winked at him. "You probably know more about what he was doing than any lawyer or anybody else he had working with him. Am I right or wrong?"

Val had nodded and forced a small laugh. "You're right." His father had, in fact, insisted Val come to his office every day after school. He'd talked about numbers, showed Val ledgers, and introduced Val to his employees. But more than anything, he'd stressed to Val the importance of generating income. They lived a certain way only because this money was being made. There was no such thing as infinite supply. If he wanted to maintain his lifestyle, and the fawning preference people gave him, the money had to come in, and from more avenues. It also helped to have many legal entities going to mask their illegal interests, which were often more profitable.

Once he understood business was no more than a colossal numbers game, just like baseball, Val took to it with the acumen of a born entrepreneur. If he could hold a season's worth of batting statistics for the Dodgers' starting lineup in his brain, an accounting ledger would be a small thing to conquer.

"I know you have more sense in your head than most boys

your age," Aunt Rose said, and she sighed. She held out her
right hand with the fingers splayed like a tiny wing so she could
caress the leaves of the shrubs as she walked. "What's three or
four years? The work you have to do will be no different then
than it is now. You may as well start doing it."

"Yes, Aunt Rose," he said quietly and stared down the
lane in front of him. The world suddenly felt open to him, and
empty in a way that invited him to fill it however he pleased.
In that moment he understood his childhood interest in the
changing landscape and realized such transitions were mean-
ingless. He could move from one world to another with no
more effort than it took to walk from room to room. Already
he had gone from being his parents' child to their surviving
heir. If any magic did come of such a drastic change, and the
many more sure to come, he knew he had to conjure it from
his own choice of how he would appear once he stepped into
the situation. He was in complete control. Who did he want
to be? There must have been something he was on the verge
of becoming—that person his mother saw taking shape under her watchful eyes. But he didn't know who that person
was—he couldn't see himself through her eyes and he couldn't
ask what she'd seen and what had made her smile. It was all
lost to him.

He did know the feeling of walking down the street with
his father. It was like they had together formed a great magnet.
He could sense heads turning, bodies bending toward them
as though he and his father had reconfigured the very air that
people breathed and they were compelled to adjust themselves
accordingly. He liked how that felt. And if he were forced to
admit it, he would say he wanted most to know how it felt to

wield that power alone without his father propping him up like he had when he'd taught him how to ride a bike. The thought made him stand straighter as he imagined how he might walk down Lenox Avenue in the coming days.

As though sensing his thoughts, Aunt Rose had stopped walking and touched his elbow to make him look at her. When he did he saw her face was hard but beaming with so much love he felt he needed to hide. It was too bright for him to stand still in the glare.

"I'll help you if you ask for help. But I want you to act like you got some sense," she said. The words felt solid and stern—a hand placed on his chest to keep him from running wild.

"Yes, ma'am," he whispered and bowed his head. She reached up and touched his chin. The skin of her honey brown fingers was soft and warm.

"It's time for you to be a man," she said, nodding as though she wanted to be certain he understood her. "It's come sooner than your mama would have wanted, but I won't stand in the way."

At the mention of his mother he had hugged Aunt Rose. He'd wanted to cry, but he hadn't.

* * *

THE CRUNCH OF gravel beneath the Cadillac's tires woke him and signaled his arrival at Mercylands. He sat up and looked out the window. The rhododendron and azalea bushes crowded the sides of the way, greeting him with a riot of pink, red, and white. The well-tended plantings seemed thicker, more lush, and he realized this was because so much time had passed since his last summer visit. Had it been two years or three? He made brief appearances throughout the year, but Aunt Rose would still scold him. He wasn't concerned. She would be happy just to see him and voicing her displeasure would add to her enjoyment. He looked down the drive. The canopy of tall sugar maples hid the mansion until the last possible moment. His aunt loved beauty, but not ostentatious display. When she and Uncle Lou built Mercylands forty years earlier, the spoils of his fortune earned in shrewd real estate deals, she hadn't wanted a stone behemoth like the homes built by the Roosevelts and Vanderbilts farther north.

"Crazy white people," she'd once told him when she saw a photo of Hyde Park in a local paper. "Why would you want to live in a place that looks like a mausoleum?"

So Mercylands, while large, had all the charm of an English cottage. She had ordered the stucco painted white, and insisted green shutters be placed on all the windows. The front door, tall oak panels flanked by thick stone columns of similar height, was plain. There was no grand stairway, no broad sweeping entrance. On the other side of the door was a floor of red stone tile and a simple hall decorated with wallpaper covered in cherry blossoms. A small statue of Pan stood perched on a waist-high stone pedestal. The effect was inviting, not intimidating. When Val used to bring girlfriends the house always had the desired effect, inspiring awe but not to the point where a woman couldn't picture herself at home. Of course the place could also bring out any hidden greediness in a girl's personality, but to Val it was all useful information to act on.

He didn't go through the door. Instead he climbed out of the car and, without thinking, began to retrace his boyhood steps.

In the past whenever he first arrived on his aunt's one hundred and twenty-one acres he would run around to the back of the mansion where a vast lawn swept away from the broad terrace like an emerald ocean. He would make a tour of the grounds, then eventually go into the house through the French doors of the terrace and greet Aunt Rose as though he'd only gone out to play an hour ago. Now as he reached the lawn and realized what he was doing he decided it wasn't a bad thing. If he didn't immediately present himself to Aunt Rose and Elizabeth Townsend, his aunt would of course know the reason and tell her guest about her nephew's charming old rituals. She would relate stories of Val hitting balls into her tomato plants or how badly he scraped his knees trying to learn how to ride a bike on the gravel drive. This would cast him in a fair light and let his conquest see him as a man capable of nostalgia and sentiment—a good beginning. With any luck Mrs. Townsend might already be curious and looking for him from one of the large drawing room windows that opened onto the terrace.

He walked up and down the lawn that had long been the site of countless baseball games—imagined ones when he was young, then real ones when he was old enough to invite other boys over to play. He knelt, pulled up a few blades of grass with his fingers, and crushed them beneath his nose. Each year he had looked for signs of previous base markings but Aunt Rose's gardeners had always been diligent about repairing whatever damage he'd done the previous summer. He used to reason the muddy or flat yellow spots weren't his fault. The lawn was too perfect and too inviting once the fragrance of fresh-cut grass penetrated his senses. He also knew his aunt could have incorporated any or all of the lawn into the elaborate gardens that

decorated other parts of the property, but he was certain she reserved the grass for him. It was her joy to watch him play from
the comfort of the terrace, where she often sat drinking tea or a
gin and tonic underneath the green-and-white-striped awning.

He turned his back to the house and walked across the lawn
until it sloped gently downward to a gravel walkway about five
feet wide that led into the woods of Mercylands. When the path
ended he walked on mossy ground until he came to the large
shining lake Aunt Rose called Gethsemane. Milkweed and
ferns were just beginning to rise along the surrounding banks
and Val heard crickets and peepers telling him, as they always
did, that the lake was alive and healthy. When he was older he
had brought girlfriends there, then picked them up and threatened to throw them into the water. He had laughed at how they
would kick and scream, not because they feared drowning—
which he found doubly funny because most of them couldn't
swim—but because they feared the ruin of their straightened
hair.

If he had taken the path in the other direction he would have
come to the formal walkways leading to Aunt Rose's gardens
and greenhouse at the other end of the property. Over there
she kept nature perfectly tamed into geometrically trimmed
shrubbery and beds of flowers whose names he didn't know.
His mother and Aunt Rose had constantly warned him to stay
away from the blooms with his baseballs and bats. In the same
direction, if one stood in the massive windowed cupola topping
Aunt Rose's house and if the workers kept the trees properly
pruned, a view could be seen of the Hudson River flowing plac-
idly on its way to New York City as though this was always
the way it should be—whatever existed here in this idyllic place

went against the current and inevitably had to return to the city and reality again.

Of course he preferred the woods. He understood the wild, uncultivated life there—turtles and fish and crickets and grasshoppers and praying mantises. He used to love the sound of the breeze tickling the leaves over his head, but today he wasn't listening. He looked at his watch and thought about how much time needed to pass before he went into the house. He appreciated the quiet. He'd forgotten how easy it was to think when the sounds of the city fell away.

Now he could better see in his mind the path to Elizabeth Townsend's heart, and he could consider it more clearly than he ever had before. It was so perfect they should both be at Mercylands when the property was at its best. He savored the challenge of her, as though he were about to begin a double-header featuring undefeated teams. And he held home-field advantage.

Every aspect of the place would serve his purpose. Mercylands moved to Aunt Rose's rhythm. It wasn't slow, exactly, but it was a tempo that said, "There's no reason to hurry here." In the past he would have done something to rev up the energy—invite friends, play loud music—all of which he knew Aunt Rose enjoyed as a good change. For this visit, though, such actions would be counter to his plans. He wanted all to be as usual—Aunt Rose and her lovely guest spending time in her garden, especially now as the roses came into their own. They would play cards, take walks, and, when the weather allowed, enjoy meals on the terrace. The size of the mansion would aid his cause too, with its excellent assortment of public and private spaces. The drawing room itself was large enough that you might separate yourself and enjoy a solitary activity such as reading, but still be within earshot to participate in a conversation when the right opportunity presented itself.

He especially needed this feature so he could observe Elizabeth Townsend and listen to her from a safe distance. From the information he'd been receiving he'd been able to glean a few things about her habits, but to learn the woman, the whole woman inside and out, he had to study her. He was looking forward to it, to uncovering that one quaking sphere of emptiness within her so he could step in and, to her, magically fill a space she didn't even know was there.

He had a few guesses about what might be missing in her life. He relished having the chance to guess. It was like a delicious probing through layers of silken folds and rough tracts of wool or steel. Discovering the need was like finding a woman's pearl—delicate and translucent and worried smooth by her hold on it, by her fear of showing it to the light of day. He thought too many women walked around with their need fully on display, sewn into their too-tight dresses or painted into the bright red of their lipstick, need that often melted down into burning, ravenous hunger threatening to devour any man senseless enough to step into such a yawning void.

Every woman performed, without realizing, her own dance of the seven veils. He always watched from a distance, a distance that felt safe to her. Layer by layer she would reveal herself. He would provide careful prodding when necessary, but he knew the best thing to do would be to hold back. Once he sensed her emptiness, then came the miracle—when he could mold himself into the fulfillment of this need. It was the true challenge because it took some doing. If he were too obvious, making foolish declarations and promises too soon, she wouldn't trust it. The work had to be subtle so only she would notice it. It would be her own discovery, and this was a kind of gift to her because there was always joy in such a discovery, in thinking you know something, have detected a patch of light where everyone else saw only darkness.

Once she had made the discovery, the pearl cracked and he could step into it and slide on down as though into a tub of warm water. He could have a woman then. If he was lucky the struggle went on a little longer. But he would win. He would always win. There was some satisfaction in that, but now he cherished stepping on the edge of not knowing if he might win, and Elizabeth offered that prospect. He was aware of the edge because—and this was the thought he kept stuffed down in the pit of his stomach—he didn't want to know what losing looked like. There was something unbearable and bitter about the idea. He refused to consider the possibility.

* * *

WHEN HE FINALLY approached the house he did so at an angle that made him able to see anyone standing at a window before they saw him. He had used this method before when sneaking into the house, usually not alone. As he drew closer he made out the shape of a slim figure. She seemed to have her hands behind her back. Her posture had a feeling of expectancy. She looked like someone waiting—waiting for him. He intentionally took his time as he climbed the steps to the terrace. On his face he composed a look of calm distraction—he wanted to seem thoughtful, as though he'd been brooding while out on the grounds.

He stepped through the French doors, careful to ignore Elizabeth Townsend standing at the windows to his left. He looked straight ahead and moved to Aunt Rose, who stood near a sofa and was pulling a sweater on over her shoulders. She grinned like a girl and kissed his cheek and tugged at his ear like she owned him. "Val, where have you been?" Her forehead, still unlined, met her hairline of smoky dark curls like a beach of brown sand. Her lips, stained a deep blackberry, set off the dark honey shade of her skin. Val admired that she still wore makeup, still moved through her world with the ease and confidence that came of wisdom, real wisdom. She was so unlike the silly old women who strutted around church pretending they knew something about the world just because they possessed the dumb luck that so far had allowed them to sidestep death by accident, illness, or assault.

After being out in the sun his eyes had to adjust to being indoors, but not much. The large drawing room was painted the palest shade of blue and it had a white ceiling of plaster carved into elaborate patterns of garlands that looked like cake frosting. It was naturally bright and light just as he remembered it. He could clearly see Elizabeth Townsend's slightly tousled brown curls and the simple cut of her yellow short-sleeved blouse.

"You've missed lunch!" Aunt Rose was saying. She drew him into a tight hug and laughed. "Belle made the chicken salad you like because I told her you would be here. She about broke her arm whipping up eggs for the mayonnaise. You better go in the kitchen and get some or she'll have your hide—and mine!"

"Then that's exactly what I'll do." He kissed his aunt's powdered cheek and winked at her. "Can't have Belle mad at me. She'll have me eating liver for days!"

She looped her left arm through his and waved her right arm toward her friend. "Elizabeth and I were just about to go out for a walk. This is Mrs. Elizabeth Townsend."

When he moved toward the guest, Aunt Rose tugged on his elbow before she released his arm. "You know her husband, Kyle, don't you?" Her left eye narrowed to a slit and the right eyebrow lifted into a shrewd arch. Ordinarily he would ignore such a look, but now it suited his plan to prove her warning unnecessary.

"Yes, from church, but this is the first time I've had the pleasure. Nice to meet you, Mrs. Townsend." He smiled, but with no more warmth or attention than he would give a male stranger of no interest. He presented his hand to Elizabeth for the briefest of handshakes. When she touched him he was careful to notice the shape and size of her hands—not too small, medium, soft but surprisingly strong. He could feel her long middle finger wrap around his hand as she shook it. Her face opened to him like a refreshing window. Her eyes, smile, and expression all looked so honest and free. He saw no hint of flirtation or calculation, only a friendly sort of kindness.

"Thank you! I've heard a lot about you." She paused as though regretting her choice of words and a rush of color flooded her cheeks. "From Rose, I mean." She glanced quickly at his aunt. "Such nice things about your growing up here."

His stomach muscles tightened and his heart thumped hard. He wanted to put her at ease, to say something to show she didn't have to feel embarrassed. But the reaction he felt in his heart shocked him and he forced himself to rein it in. If he showed her too much attention it would mess up all his careful thinking for this first meeting. He stuffed his hands into his pants pockets and stepped back to put some distance between them.

"I can only imagine." He nodded and turned to his aunt. The safest move would be to focus on her again. "So, where are you going for your walk?"

Aunt Rose pointed out an area through the French doors to the left, where her gardens began. "Oh, just down the lane a bit. I want to show her the dwarf lilacs in the courtyard with the limestone walk. They bloomed late this year. It was so cold up here a few weeks ago. Now they're all out and it smells like heaven. I told Elizabeth they were probably just waiting to bloom for her." She looked at her friend and smiled.

He resisted the urge to agree. Then Elizabeth spoke again.

"But I don't want to intrude if you want to spend time with Rose. You just got here and I know you haven't seen each other in a while." She clasped her arms behind her back like she didn't know what to do with her hands. Her voice had a careless, lovely lilt about it that made it feel familiar to him somehow. Her chin dipped when she looked down at the carpet and a curl flopped over her right eye. She pulled it back without a thought and let it sit messily on the top of her head.

He thought about how many times he had witnessed a similar motion. It was almost always followed by the woman seeking a place in which to view her reflection—a mirror, a window, a piece of silverware—so she would know her hair had not gone awry. He looked at Elizabeth and waited for another blush, another note of unease, but she only showed the wide-eyed, pleasant face that expected his response.

He was incredulous. *My God,* he thought. *This woman has no idea how pretty she is.* He realized he could himself uncover things for Elizabeth she had yet to know about herself. The potential for the game rose in his sights and it pleased him—all the more reason to stick with his plan. He felt impelled to join them, and with any other woman he would have done so. He would have spoken more, asked questions, engaged her in further conversation. But for Elizabeth Townsend he only smiled indifferently.

"No, you two go on," he said. He opened one of the doors to the terrace for them and stepped aside. "Don't worry about me. Aunt Rose and I will catch up in a bit. And I've got that chicken salad waiting for me. Enjoy your walk." He kissed his aunt again before she walked through the door and he was careful to smile, not stare, when Elizabeth passed him.

CHAPTER 12
Elízabeth

Mercylands, Late May 1947

She tried to be attentive to Rose as her host showed her the romantic stone walls enclosing parts of her garden and the thick green leaves and tiny white flowers, climbing hydrangea, clinging to its cracks. Rose spoke of the shrubbery shaped in voluptuous cylinders and pyramids to match the ones she had seen on a trip to Florence, and of the bunches of purple irises grown from rhizomes given to her by an Ohio relative.

But Elizabeth's thoughts remained in the house with the nephew who would now reside with her and Rose. If she were anywhere else she might have been more concerned about living under the same roof as a nightclub owner who, rumor had it, ran numbers rackets and an illegal liquor market, and seduced women with the fearsome skill of a merciless Casanova. But Rose reacted with such joy at the news of his visit—she ordered a new radio for his room so he could listen to baseball games, and had the piano in the library tuned—Elizabeth couldn't help but be curious.

Then to see the man at last—with a smile so bright it seared her brain. Why else would the first words to come tumbling out of her mouth be so stupid? She was sure she'd given him the impression they'd been gossiping about him. But he hadn't seemed to notice. In fact she was surprised he was so friendly and gentlemanlike. She had seen the way he sat apart from everyone else in church and she'd always thought he had a rakish attitude. There were times when he even had his feet propped up on the back of the pew in front of him during Reverend Stiles's sermons. She expected such a man to speak with arrogance, to have a tone of disrespect in his every word. He was, after all, in complete control of his world and could behave however he liked.

But to see him with his aunt, who could tug his ear and treat him as though he were still a nine-year-old—Elizabeth realized she had to begin parsing out the rumors of Val Jackson and separate them from her actual experience of him. It wasn't fair to prejudge him. Perhaps he was no more than a boyish cad who needed a good scolding. She couldn't imagine Rose would put up with the kind of behavior that seemed to be the basis of his reputation. At any rate, she made up her mind to consider herself safe from him.

The call she'd received from her friend Gladys the day before, though, made it clear she should take nothing about Val Jackson for granted. "I heard he was on his way up there," Gladys had said. "You just watch yourself, girl. He'll mess with you because he can. That's all there is to it." What would Kyle say if he knew Val Jackson was at Mercylands? Well, he would know—she would tell him during their next telephone call. She would listen carefully for his reaction, but she was sure it would be no different from her own—no cause to worry. She sat too far outside Val Jackson's sphere of interest.

How could she ever fall prey to him? She was happily married, a fact well known, and she certainly wasn't one of those women who went in search of affairs. He must know that because he barely looked at her when he arrived. She ran a hand through her hair. And, she realized, she didn't give him much to see. She brushed away a piece of lint from her pants and noticed their boxy, unflattering cut. It was a good thing she and Rose were outside—if she saw her own reflection she'd probably cringe to see the image she had presented to Val Jackson, who was used to collecting the most beautiful women in Harlem. She didn't need him to think her pretty, but for her own self-respect, she thought, she should pay more attention to how she appeared. She was a grown woman—she could take better care of herself. She rubbed her nose and tugged at the collar of her shirt. Well, there was nothing she could do about the way her eyes seemed too far apart on her face or how her hair seemed to have a mind of its own, but she could try to be a little neater about her clothing.

"Oh look!" Rose clapped her hands together and drew them to her mouth as if she were about to pray. "Ho ho! Lord, what a sight!"

Elizabeth saw they had come upon a row of lilac bushes—she could smell their perfume, sweet and delicate, as it hung in the air. But what was she seeing? The lavender color of the flowers was overwhelmed with a fluttering orange mist. When she and Rose drew closer, she saw the movement on the branches was not a mist but butterflies. The bushes were covered in butterflies. They rested on the lilacs as though on purple clouds.

"How beautiful!" Elizabeth said.

She had never seen so many butterflies all at once, and guessed they were freshly transformed. There must be a littering of cocoon skins somewhere in Rose's garden, left behind in the butterflies' search for their first sustenance. She leaned over the winged insects and peered at them closely. She saw their tiny tongues, like thin black wires, unfurl and pierce the tender heart of each lilac flower. They drank deep. The branches shivered with their consumption, and she wondered what it would feel like to be so gloriously and willingly drained. To realize all that you are can be the single perfect fulfillment of another being—and then to have that being drawn to you, completely aware of the presence of that perfection and knowing with a blessed certainty it would not be turned away empty-handed. Could the precision of nature be any more humbling?

Rose put an arm around her shoulders and with surprising strength pulled Elizabeth toward her. Elizabeth realized for the first time in several days she didn't feel anxious—in that moment Kyle was exactly where he was supposed to be, and so was she. She was not alone. She could relax at Mercylands and be surrounded by an unexpected wealth of little miracles, like this one that reminded her of the hope and beauty of God's creation. She wouldn't have experienced this in their Harlem apartment, where her eyes would have been continually turned down into the pages of a book, hungrily seeking the same feelings but never finding them. Books told her what the world could be and should be. But standing there with Rose and witnessing the bounteous feast explained in utter clarity what the world truly was. The butterflies felt like life to her, abundant life, and indeed seemed to reflect the excited, expectant fluttering of her own heart. But what did she expect? She didn't know. She only had a vague sense of something on the way, something very near or on the horizon. The butterflies had come, it seemed, to affirm this notion and mirror her hope of being fulfilled.

* * *

WHEN THEY WENT back to the house, Elizabeth excused herself so Rose could have time with her nephew. She also wanted to change her clothes for dinner, and stood for several minutes examining the contents of her closet before deciding to wear a simple short-sleeved shirtdress of light blue crepe with a sash at the waist and four brown wooden buttons down the front. She tied her hair back with a ribbon and slid her feet into a pair of beige slingback sandals with a low wedge heel. When she studied herself in the oval full-length mirror, she decided the effect was just what she wanted—nice, neat, and modest.

In the dining room Rose, already seated and wearing an orange-and-blue-patterned shawl around her shoulders, smiled at Elizabeth. "Oh, don't you look nice?" she said. Val, in khaki pants and a crisp white shirt, stood and pulled a chair out for Elizabeth but said nothing and only nodded to her as she sat down. They passed around plates of fried fish, roasted tomatoes, and green beans. Rose went on to tell Val about the butterflies and he listened while he ate. He smiled and exclaimed when his aunt's talk called for it, but Elizabeth thought he said very little. Then, after announcing he needed to make a telephone call, he excused himself and left the table before they were done. Elizabeth smoothed the front of her skirt and asked for milk and sugar when Rose's servants brought in the coffee service.

When they had finished their dinner, Elizabeth and Rose went to the drawing room. Val was lying on a cream-colored sofa set against the far wall. When Elizabeth saw him she hesitated to move farther into the room.

"Oh, are we disturbing him?" she asked.

Rose sailed past her and picked up a beige-and-blue cushion from one of the chairs.

"That boy's not asleep, he's puttin' on." She chucked the pillow at Val so it landed on his upper chest. He sat up at once and even managed to catch it up in his right arm.

"Hey!" he said and laughed. "I was resting my eyes."

Rose pulled the shawl, which had slipped down, back up around her shoulders and pointed at him playfully. "You're too young to be resting. I'm the one who should be resting. You haven't done enough in this world to be needing rest."

Val rubbed his stomach. "I ate that whole plate of fish, didn't I? I always need a nap after Belle's dinners. Don't you?"

Elizabeth, helping Rose to lower herself onto a blue-gray upholstered sofa near Val's, started when she realized he was speaking to her.

"Me? Oh no, I'm afraid I eat like a bird." She smiled at Rose and sat next to her. "I mean the food here is absolutely delicious, but I try not to stuff myself."

Val nodded as though encouraging her to go on. "That's harder to do here, isn't it?"

"Yes." Her hand patted her own stomach and she puffed her cheeks full of air. "I practically have to turn my plate over to keep myself from going for seconds."

"See there!" he said, as though that proved something to his aunt. He stood and went over to the small bar cart a servant had placed there just before dinner. He put ice into a short glass tumbler and poured himself a drink from a thick crystal bottle. "Aunt Rose? Mrs. Townsend?"

"I'll have a nip of that brandy, Val," Rose said.

Elizabeth shook her head. "Nothing for me, thank you."

"Elizabeth doesn't drink," Rose said. She patted her guest on the knee.

"Are you a teetotaler?" Val asked. He poured brandy into a wide, round-bottomed glass.

"No, at least not in that sense." She shook her head and twisted her mouth as though she'd drunk something bitter. "I don't like the taste of it, that's all."

"I can understand that." Val handed the brandy to Rose and sat again on the adjacent sofa. "Why take up a vice if you can't enjoy it?"

Elizabeth never thought of a vice as something to be enjoyed. She smiled uncomfortably and looked at her hands, fingers laced together, in her lap. She thought about what else she could say and finally blurted out the first question that came to mind.

"What brings you to Mercylands, Mr. Jackson?" She tried to ask it as lightly and easily as possible.

He and Rose laughed and she felt a warmth rise to her cheeks. "You mean my aunt's company isn't enough?"

She tried to laugh too, but thought her effort sounded silly and insincere. She shook her head. "No," she said. "I didn't mean that."

"It's all right, I'm just teasing you." He took a sip from his glass and pressed his lips together as he swallowed. "She's told you I used to spend my summers here—over half my life. Right?"

"Yes."

"I've missed being here." He got up and kissed Rose's forehead. "I've missed you. Harlem can be a whole lot of mess in the summer—the heat, people sitting on stoops, nowhere to go, nothing to do but fall in love or pick fights with the people who are in love. Thought I should get my butt up out of there before I got in trouble."

Elizabeth wondered at his choice of words—was Val Jackson in love with someone? Was he capable of falling in love? But she didn't know him well enough to ask such questions out loud.

Rose was chuckling at him. "Good thinking—your mama's thinking."

"Yes, well, I've always been something of a mama's boy. I'll confess it." He smiled and clinked glasses with Rose before sitting down again. The intimacy of the gesture made Elizabeth get up and turn away to look through the open French doors. Outside the lawn was fading into the low light of dusk.

"Hey, that reminds me," Val was saying. "I brought you something."

Elizabeth turned to see him put his glass down and stride to the other side of the room, where he lifted the cover of a polished walnut cabinet. She realized it was a record player. He picked up a white paper sleeve on the table near the cabinet and removed the disc inside it and placed it on the turntable.

"It's a new Ella Fitzgerald song," he said once he placed the needle on the record.

He took his seat again and a wave of brass sound, slow and lazy, washed through the room like a lulling brook. Then the singer's voice, impossibly low and velvety, came wading through it.

I want a Sunday kind of love . . .

Rose leaned back and rested her head on the sofa. "Oh, Val," she said. She smiled and closed her eyes. "This is nice."

Elizabeth looked outside again and leaned against the doorframe while she listened. Rose was right—the music was nice. Its rhythm felt familiar, even soothing to her. She breathed in the evening air, moist with dew, and her left hand floated up to rest on the frame as though on the shoulder of an unseen partner. Soon she became aware of herself rocking slightly, imperceptibly, back and forth, as though the music had slipped inside her. She wanted to sit down before Rose and Val noticed, and when she moved toward the sofa she felt her feet step and drift gently on the tones of trombones.

She sat in the overstuffed chair opposite Val's sofa. A saxophone punctuated the air with a fist of soft notes. She slowly surveyed the room around her, carefully taking in the colorful tapestry, porcelain vases, and Oriental carpet before daring to look directly at Val Jackson.

His elbows rested on his knees, his hands holding his whiskey in front of him, and he was smiling at the sight of his aunt. He seemed to be enjoying her enjoyment of the song.

At home Elizabeth and Kyle rarely took time to listen to music. It wasn't that her husband disliked it—rather, he claimed he liked it too much. Whenever she turned on the radio, however quietly, he would say it distracted him from his reading. And there never seemed to be a free half hour when he wasn't work-

ing, when they could sit, as she did now, and let the music work
its magic. She stretched her arms on the chair's round armrests
and sighed quietly.

> *I asked the Lord above please send me someone to love*
> *A special Sunday kind of love.*

The last lines surprised her. They sounded like a kind of
prayer, but she wondered if it was a proper one. Was it right
to pray for love? She could see praying for a husband or a
family—these were blessings made numerous times throughout the Bible. The Lord brought forth the right mates and even
women past childbearing age, like Sarah, conceived children.
But this didn't seem to be the kind of love the singer wanted—
she desired a lover, a lover to "show her the way," whatever that
meant. What would the Lord have to say about that?

Rose seemed to have similar thoughts. As the final notes
faded she sat up and giggled. "That's a good one—*ask the Lord
above*—someone needs to tell that to these women today. The
Lord can probably do a better job of finding them a good man
than any tight dress they squeeze over their rear ends."

Val drained his glass. "May as well get the Lord involved—
he's all up in everything else!" He put the glass down and eyed
the bar cart again.

"I don't know." Elizabeth raised her arms above her head
and stretched. "It's hard enough to ask for the everyday things.
Sometimes I'm just grateful I wake up in the morning and
that's enough."

"Oh, but then you're not really living by the Good Book,
are you?" Val said. He got up and returned to the bar cart.

He picked up a bottle and pointed it at her. "'Ask and ye shall receive.' Sounds to me like the Lord wants you to put in your requests. Right, Aunt Rose?" He poured himself another drink.

"You're right about that, honey." She took a sip of her brandy then shook her head. "But I sure love me some Ella."

"I knew you'd like it as soon as I heard it," he said warmly.

A comfortable silence fell over them. Elizabeth was about to stifle a yawn when the sound of a telephone ringing rippled through the room. A servant soon followed.

"Mrs. Townsend, Mr. Townsend is on the telephone calling long distance."

"Yes, of course. My goodness, I didn't realize it was that late already. Excuse me."

She stood and turned to go but then, remembering her manners, said, "I'll probably go right to bed after I talk to Kyle. So I'll say good night now. Is that all right, Rose?"

"Of course it is, dear." Rose motioned with her nonbrandy hand as if she would whisk Elizabeth away. "Tell Kyle I hope he's taking good care of himself down there."

Elizabeth looked at Val and nodded shyly. "Good night. Thank you for bringing that lovely music."

He held up his glass as though to toast her, and smiled. "I'm glad you enjoyed it."

She took the call in her bedroom. When she told Kyle of Val Jackson being at Mercylands, her husband snorted. "Visiting his aunt! He's probably ducking some gang or the law."

"Well." She felt behind her for a chair and pulled it to her so she could sit at her desk. "He did mention something about avoiding trouble."

"See there? I told you. How many men his age do you see living with their aunts of their own free will?" He laughed edgily, igniting something in her that felt like resentment.

"They say he's more trouble around women," she said quietly, cupping the receiver in both hands.

"Well, it's just you and Rose there, right?"

"Yes."

"Then you've got nothing to worry about," he said briskly.

He delivered a string of details about his case and the people he'd interviewed and the uncooperative authorities that made everything harder and take longer than it should.

After she hung up the telephone she pulled the ribbon from her hair and unbuttoned her dress. When she removed it she found herself standing in front of the full-length mirror in her slip. One of the straps slipped down on her shoulder and she tugged at the other so the slip slid to the floor. She stepped out of it and meant to kick off her shoes, but instead she stared at her image in the mirror and studied her figure.

She thought of the butterflies feeding on the lilacs. Fulfillment—that would be something to pray for. And she could believe God would want it for her. Because for all the fire-breathing sermons she heard in church, she had the sense, a comforting, loving sense, that God didn't go around seeking to damn people. She was sure He wanted His creations to live and enjoy the gifts He gave them, and she was certain He would provide whatever she asked. But in that moment she realized she almost never prayed for herself. She prayed for her mother's soul, her father's continued health, Kyle's safe return, the well-being of her friends. She prayed for the poor, the sick, and the lost. Maybe, she thought, she never knew what to request before.

She stared at her reflection—the pale hips beneath her white underpants, her breasts encased in her brassiere—and thought of what it would mean to be fulfilled.

CHAPTER 13
Val

Mercylands, June 1947

Val Jackson waited in his room. It was the kind of day he'd been waiting for: hot, even unseasonably so for the first week of June. The humidity made the air so thick you could hold it in your hand. All motion at Mercylands—gardening, cleaning, cooking—slowed and the house sat silent, soaking up the heat like a sponge. On days like this his aunt would order a light lunch, a salad full of tomatoes and cucumbers. She would drink only lemonade. Then afterward she would go upstairs and lie still across her bed, every window in the room open. A fan would move the air around, giving the illusion of a breeze. Today he had accompanied her upstairs and said he would listen to a game in his room. Indeed he was listening— the Dodgers were playing the Pittsburgh Pirates—but he had toyed with the volume knob until the sound level was just right. He wanted it loud enough to hear the score when he wanted to hear it, but not so loud that he couldn't hear footsteps or a voice in the hallway. The Dodgers were winning so the broadcast attracted less of his attention. Now he sat in his undershirt and khaki pants with his feet up on his desk. He wore a baseball glove on his left hand and was tossing a ball into it so the ball thwacked the deep leather pocket and zinged the top of his palm with a satisfying sting.

He had been at Mercylands nearly a week and he figured now would be the right time to encounter Elizabeth Townsend alone. He waited because at lunch she didn't say what she would do while he and his aunt were upstairs. Whatever she chose to do, he wanted to give her the chance to settle into the activity, let enough time pass so he could join her in a manner that seemed as innocent as possible.

But if she remained in her room—which was likely given the hot weather—then he would have to figure out how to cross paths with her.

Sebastian knocked softly and entered.

"Sir, Mrs. Townsend has been on the terrace for the past half hour. She's reading."

Val removed his glove, tucked the ball inside it, and handed it to Sebastian. He put his feet down but sat a moment longer looking out the window. "What's she reading?"

"Not sure." Sebastian examined the glove, turning it over and over. "Annie, her maid, said she brought the book down from her room. Do you need this oiled, sir?"

"No, it's fine." He grinned. Sebastian noticed everything. "And thanks."

He liked that he and Elizabeth would be outside in broad daylight. The book, whatever it was, would provide a safe, convenient opening for conversation. He stood, went over to the valet stand, and removed the short-sleeved red shirt he'd hung there earlier. He put it on and straightened the collar around his neck. He started to button it but, after another glance in the mirror, decided to leave the shirt open. He put his hands in his pockets, considered his reflection, and decided he looked casual enough. Sebastian opened the door and Val walked out.

* * *

THROUGH THE DRAWING room windows he could see Elizabeth Townsend on the terrace with a tray of glasses and a large pitcher of lemonade on the table in front of her. She sat so far back into her chair's cushions she was nearly reclining. She wore a light dress with a blue-and-white gingham-checked print. Her slim legs, crossed at the ankles, stretched out from underneath her skirt, and her feet, Val was delighted to see, were bare. Her sandals sat a few inches in front of her, where they must have landed when she kicked them off.

"Hello," she said when he stepped through the French doors. She smiled and put her hand up to her forehead as though to shield her eyes from the sun. "How was the game?"

He shrugged. "Good, it's over," he lied. "Dodgers won," he guessed. He smiled and pointed to the empty seat across the table from her. "May I join you?"

She sat up, her forefinger still marking the place in her book. She used a foot to pull her sandals toward her but, he noticed, she didn't put them on. "Yes, of course." She waved over the chair with her book-free hand.

"Whew! Hot out here." He grinned and flapped the sides of his unbuttoned shirt before he sat down.

"Oh, I don't mind. I hate being cold. To me this is heavenly."

He nodded, but said nothing.

"What about you?" she asked. Her eyes crinkled at the edges and she wriggled her nose. "Does the heat bother you?"

"Me? Remember, I like baseball. Baseball is nothing if it's not standing around under the hot sun. It's the best part."

She laughed. *Good,* he thought. *Good.*

He pulled the pitcher of lemonade toward him and poured a glass. He offered it to her, but she shook her head. "I don't think my aunt expected it to get this hot so soon."

"Is she all right?" She bit her lip slightly and he liked the way the soft flesh reddened under her teeth.

"Oh yeah, she's used to days like this. She's resting, probably with every window open and a fan blowing on her."

"And I guess if it's going to be hot, better to be here than in Harlem. It's so beautiful here." She looked out across the lawn and his eyes followed her. The bottle-green blades shimmered in the afternoon light.

"I'll drink to that." He raised the glass of lemonade and winked at her. She shifted in her seat and looked down at the book in her hand.

"Whatcha got there?" He took a long drink and swallowed. "From my aunt's library?"

"No, I brought it with me. It's a novel. *The Street* by Ann Petry."

He nodded and leaned closer as though he wanted to see the book's cover. "What's it about?"

She handed him the book. "A woman living on 116th Street. She's alone and trying to raise her little boy all by herself."

"You mean like right now?" He examined the cover. On the

top-left corner a drawing of a woman's head with thick red lips and blue-black hair stretched across the book's spine and cover so only half her face appeared on the front.

Elizabeth nodded. "Well, yes, it is contemporary."

"In Harlem?"

She nodded again.

"Then why read it?" He slid the book across the table back to her, then took another long pull of his lemonade.

She looked confused, which caused a deep V line at the top of her nose, just between her eyebrows. "I'm not sure what you mean."

"Why read a book when you can see that story yourself every day, from the moment you set foot out your door?"

"It's not just about the story." She shifted again in her seat and one of her hands floated up to scratch her forehead. "It's a statement about the way we live."

"You live like that, do you? On 116th Street?" He smiled and savored the chance to tease her.

"Well, no. But people we know do. People who come to our church do."

"You don't know what you think about the way we live?" He leaned toward her and nearly winked again, but thought better of it and didn't.

"I do know, but it's good to see how someone else sees things. Don't you agree?" She tilted her head to the right. This made her unruly curls drop over her left eye and she pulled them back.

He shrugged. Why should he care about what some writer had to say about streets he knew as well as or even better than she did? A person only had to open their eyes, see what's going on, and then decide what they were going to do or not do. He wrote checks when he felt like it. He stepped aside, too, when it was none of his business. Why would you have to wait for someone else's words?

But the way she looked at him made him feel like he was once again at a table, across from his mother, on one of the many times she had summoned him from playing outside. She would make him sit down then push the book she'd been reading across the table until it was square under his nose. One day it would be Marcus Garvey. On another day it might be Zora Neale Hurston, or some lines from a poem by Langston Hughes.

"Look at that, Val," she'd say. "What do you think of what Mr. Hughes wrote here?"

He had thought he would make sure he was never in a situation where anyone could tell him where to sit. But instead he read quietly and told his mother his thoughts on the book until he had assured her he knew that he, too, was America.

Elizabeth was still talking, now about someone named Lutie. "But it's all connected. It's all connected to the world at large." He realized she was talking about the character in the book. "Her loneliness echoes the abandonment of every single woman in the world. Her son is the face of every hungry child."

He put his elbow up on the table, held his glass in front of him, and gestured toward her with it. "Maybe so, but I can't be concerned with the world beyond my influence. That kind of thinking can drive you crazy. Puts you in a place of always trying to do more than you can—you try to do the impossible, solve everyone's problems." He drained the glass, put it down, then leaned back in his chair as though he'd made his point and done it well.

She folded her hands on top of the book on the table and leaned toward him. "Forgive me for saying so, Mr. Jackson, but you don't seem concerned with any aspect of the world, whether you have influence in it or not."

Something inside him froze, like a bag of ice lodged in his abdomen. He knew he should look away from her and defuse the moment, but he couldn't move. He stared straight into her eyes. "That's because the rest of the world doesn't give a damn about what happens to Negroes, let alone Negroes in Harlem. If they want to know anything it's where we are, so they can run the other way."

This wasn't the kind of talk he thought he would have with her. He wanted to go back to the weather, or discuss the pattern on her pretty dress, or tell her a story about falling off the terrace when he was twelve. He would rather talk about anything else. But with each statement he couldn't help himself. The words wanted to stand on her proving ground and they spilled out of him like prisoners from a jailbreak. He was going too far, revealing too much.

If this were a conversation with Mae she would have sensed her dominance by now and would be looking for the first opportunity to crush him. But then he would better know how to handle such talk with Mae. It would be easier. She would operate from ego, which meant he would have some chance of defending himself by poking at the slight openings in her ego where he might find her vulnerable. He would know when he had found the spot by the look in her eyes, blank and cold like a closed window. Then he could reach inside, grasp the heart of her false belief, and shred it with his fingers.

But Elizabeth spoke from passion and true belief, not ego. He could only stare, knowing that if he didn't move away soon he would be cut to ribbons by the gleaming sharp edges of her words.

"What if we are the ones who need to give a damn?" she asked. Her right hand moved to her chest, her fingertips touching the small bones at the base of her throat. "Everything that's happened these past twenty years—the stock market crash, the Depression, the war. Some people might say Harlem reflects all of it. I say it's the other way around. Harlem was a part of making it all happen."

"I don't get what you're saying." And he really didn't. But that didn't stop him from pushing on. He kept his eyes level and forced his tone to stay as even as he could make it. "Last I checked no Negro was given any say about whether or not we went to war. Most don't own stocks so we had nothing to do with the market collapse, and a colored child going hungry didn't start a breadline."

Her hands opened like birds taking wing, like she would grasp the whole sky in her palms. She looked at him with widened eyes. "What we do matters. How we think matters. How do we know it didn't all happen because of the way we went about our own lives? That countries aren't more willing to go to war because drunk men in one of your clubs are willing to pull guns on each other? That children aren't starving because of the way we starve ourselves?"

Her look unnerved him and he made a swift decision. It

might be better to let her keep talking. "So you tell me, Mrs. Townsend." He lifted his chin like he was inviting a right hook to the jaw. "Where do I come in?"

It was the wrong thing. His tone was a shade too careless, and a little too cool. His words yanked her by the heartstrings and she reared up from the table as though she had wings on her back. Her face glowed like she would spit fire.

"You breathe!" she insisted, her hands on her hips. "Don't you?" Her head tilted toward him like her right ear wanted to yank the answer out of him. "You have a brain that can put two and two together. You have eyes to see. I say if Miss Petry can make us care about this one lonely woman who isn't even real maybe someone will be more willing to help an actual person. And that could improve a family, then an apartment building, then maybe a neighborhood."

He shook his head. She wasn't yelling but the way she spoke she seemed to think what she was saying was the most obvious thing in the world and she was downright bewildered that he didn't know it already. He wanted to duck underneath the table, but not because he was afraid of her. What he was feeling was worse, much worse, because it twisted his stomach inside him like a wrung-out washcloth—he was ashamed.

"Yes, Mr. Jackson, you see what I'm getting at now." She touched an index finger to the table and tapped it as she slowly enunciated her words. "Eventually we can change the world. I do believe that. I have every faith in it. For you to think like that is shortsighted. The world won't always be the way it is now. My husband works like a crazy man to bring on that day of change. And until it comes it is up to every individual to be a citizen of this world, not just the Negro community, because that is exactly what we are."

She was done with him. Even before she bent down to pick up her shoes, hooking her fingers around the heel straps, he could tell she was done with him. Her voice rang with the finality of a church bell at the end of a service. He should have gotten up too, he knew that, and he even moved his hands to push himself up out of the chair. But in her bare feet she moved lightly, quickly, and before he knew it she had stepped through the French doors and was gone.

He leaned back and let his head drop down over the top of his chair so he could consider the clouds drifting above him. It was a safe place to direct his gaze. If he focused on the table he knew he would grab a glass and smash it on the terrace floor. The book too still lay on the table. The half-faced woman's eye on the spine stared back at him. He wanted to throw it through the French doors, into the house. But instead he needed to think about why he wanted to act like this in the first place. What had she done to him?

They'd slipped too quickly out of polite conversation—he hadn't been ready for the turn of the tide. And he was caught off guard by the chance to voice thoughts that, he assumed, had no place to go before. His crowd didn't sit around discussing books or social issues. She had surprised him and whenever he found himself unprepared he always thought the best thing to do was tell the truth. It would be the easiest thing to remember if the words got thrown back at him later. But he wasn't sure himself about this truth and didn't know if he wanted her handling it.

He sat up and shook his head hard to clear it. He was thinking too much about what happened, about the argument itself.
He leaned forward, his elbows on his knees, and concentrated
on his fingers as he interlaced them in front of him. What had
he seen? She was confident, and strong—much stronger than
he'd thought she would be. That wasn't a problem; he'd had
strong women before. But he sensed something extra in Elizabeth, like a complex set of tumblers that might not allow him
to unlock her.

Then he felt it—doubt formed like a small dark cloud
on the table before him. It seemed to spread across the top
and was so thick and persistent that it made him get up and
jog down the terrace steps to get away from it. He continued
walking across the lawn and thinking. He refused to doubt
he could have Elizabeth Townsend, refused to believe some
aspect of her would be impregnable to him. He was sure he
just had to adjust his tactics.

The sun bore down on his bare head and he pulled his shirt
off. He went back to his main observation—she was strong.
And yet how had he been approaching her? *Cautiously,* he
thought. Figuratively, he was stepping toward her as though
she were a bird on a limb, hoping to coax her from her branch
and onto his finger. He saw now how wrong this was—and
how unlike him. Wasn't it always a losing proposition when a
team entered a championship game and tried to play in a way
other than what got them there in the first place? He had been
doing the same—playing to lose. He would have to engage her
on his terms, his way. And strike repeatedly.

He came to a bed of flowers that looked like daisies with dark
pink petals. He pulled one toward him, wrapping the thin stem

around his right index finger until the tip turned white. But was he right about this? How would she respond? He decided he would have to test her somehow, even before he planned anything else. He needed to see if he could ignite some physical sensation in her, and in turn unsettle the mind she obviously controlled well. Her response would tell him how to make the next move and the one after that. He tugged the flower and snapped it off from its stem. He let it drop to the ground and he crushed it underfoot as he turned to walk back to the house.

CHAPTER 14
Elizabeth

Mercylands, June 1947

Elizabeth knew from the sweat beading on her forehead underneath her straw hat it must be well over 80 degrees. It wasn't even ten o'clock, but she and Rose had decided this would be the coolest part of the day to cut some flowers. Her friend sat on a low canvas seat just within reach of the largest dahlias. Elizabeth, wearing long leather gloves to protect her from the thorns, stood near her cutting roses. They placed their choices in large buckets of water. She dabbed her cheek with the back of her gloved hand and checked to see how Rose was faring in the heat. She wore a short-sleeved shift made of pale blue cotton, her arms bare because, she told Elizabeth, she still had faith the sun would do what it was supposed to do and tan her up nice. Indeed, the browning of her sun-kissed arms lent a look of health to her parchment-thin skin. Anyone who didn't know her might easily think this vibrant woman was a good ten to fifteen years younger than she was. Rose laughed that way. Her eyes sparkled that way. Her cheeks bloomed that way. Elizabeth hoped she would look so well in her seventies.

She liked this woman. She enjoyed the slow, well-considered nature of their activities—sitting with Rose doing needlework, cutting flowers as they did now, talking about books. Rose looked up at Elizabeth and smiled. Elizabeth hadn't told her about being on the terrace with Val two days before. Maybe because she didn't have words for what had happened. It hadn't exactly been a fight—more like a disagreement, she figured. She knew she was impatient with certain topics.

Certain aspects of the world bewildered her. The war had felt like ongoing heartbreak, especially when she saw men returning broken in body and spirit, like trees after a storm. But the smaller interactions hurt even more, hurt to the point of anger, because she saw how unnecessary they were, how people chose to treat each other poorly, and knew how to inflict pain so well.

Perhaps that's what ignited her about *The Street*. So many people could have reached out and helped Lutie and, at least in the part she'd read thus far, no one did. The woman had no one. The other characters extended their hands only when it would serve them. Then to hear Val Jackson—a man who could easily offer help to so many—speak so callously, it was just unacceptable. If he really thought that way, then he was far worse than people said.

He may have sensed her feelings because he seemed to recede from her and Rose in the past day or so. He didn't eat with them the night of their conversation or the next morning. Today at breakfast he spoke only to Rose and said he would be out on the grounds after the meal. He seemed chastened and a part of Elizabeth felt she had wrongly slapped his wrist with her foibles. She wasn't sure how to alleviate this—or even if she wanted to—but she decided she would try to be kinder when they spoke again.

When the baseball crashed into the bushes near where she and her friend worked, Elizabeth jumped. The torn leaves and crushed blooms released their scent into the hot air. Rose, still perfectly balanced on her canvas seat, looked up and she and Elizabeth both turned. Val was jogging over to them with an apologetic smile on his face and a baseball bat over his shoulder. Behind him, on the lawn, Elizabeth could see his man, Sebastian, wearing a baseball glove. She was intrigued to see Val running and the difference the motion brought to his demeanor. He glowed and seemed somehow more vital.

"Val, please!" Rose said. "Can't you boys be more careful?"

Val bent over and kissed her on the cheek. Elizabeth got the sense they had played out this scene countless times over the years. "I'm so sorry, Aunt Rose! I'm sorry! I didn't know Sebastian would be such a lousy catcher." He got down on his knees in his khaki pants and white T-shirt and started looking in the bushes near Elizabeth. "Did you see where it went?" he asked her.

"Over there, I think." She pointed to the right. He crawled around her ankles to the area she indicated and peered into the roses.

As Val looked for the ball Elizabeth pulled off her gloves. She sat on the ground near Val and watched him, pushing her straw hat back on her head.

"I'm sorry we had that—that misunderstanding the other day," she said.

"You are?" He glanced at her then reached into the bush. "Ouch!" He pulled his arm back and she could see white, chalklike lines where the thorns had scratched him.

"Yes." She folded her hands on her lap. "Look, we don't know each other. I was judging you—"

"And harshly, I'd say," he said, interrupting her. He examined the marks on his arm and looked into the bush again.

"Well, I've heard—" she began then stopped. She didn't want to sound defensive. She twisted the gloves in her hands, frowned, then tried again. "You know, Rose introduced us when you got here, but I'd seen you before at church."

Val looked up from under the bush and smiled. "You've seen me?"

"Yes. You sit upstairs as far away as possible." Elizabeth wiped her hands on the green-and-white-striped apron she wore over her simple linen dress. "You never participate in the service. I've always wondered why."

Val smiled broader. "You've wondered about me? Well, I don't know if you want to be telling people that. I'm a man with a certain kind of reputation."

"Yes, I know! When I said I was coming here a friend told me to watch out for you."

Val frowned and stood up on his knees. "Oh? Who told you that?"

"None of your business." Elizabeth heard the sharpness in her voice and looked down at her hands. "I'm—I'm sorry."

"Well, if you have people warning you about me, then you can understand how a man like me wouldn't be welcome in church." Val went back to his search for the ball. "I try to lie low, take in the Good Word, don't bother anybody. You can appreciate that, right?" He tilted his head closer to the ground. "Look, there it is. You've got gloves, can you get it? These thorns will tear my arm up if I try to reach in there."

She got on her knees and looked into the rosebush where he was pointing. The ball sat like a big white egg lodged between the rose's thick canes. "But I'm not like that," she said. She pulled on her gloves and gently pushed her hand through the leaves. "I don't believe in keeping someone out of a congregation because of their past. I'm of the mind Christ came for the sinners, not just the righteous. The door must stay open for those who need God the most." She extracted the ball and handed it to him.

"Yeah, you've pegged me right. I am most in need." He stood and brushed the dirt from the knees of his pants. "Thank you."

"You're welcome, but I didn't really do anything."

"Oh." Val touched her on the shoulder lightly with just one finger. "You've already done more than you know. More than you know!" He laughed and started to walk away but stopped as though he'd forgotten something. "Hey, you want to hit a few?"

Elizabeth shook her head. "Oh, I wouldn't know how. I don't know anything about baseball."

"That's okay, I'll show you. Come on."

She hesitated then helped herself up from the ground. "Excuse me, Rose, I'll be right back."

Rose didn't look up. She plunged a cut stem into the bucket by her side. Her hands took hold of another flower and she placed the shears around its stem at an angle. She snipped it. "Of course, dear."

Elizabeth followed Val back to where Sebastian was waiting. He tossed the ball to Sebastian then turned to her. "Here,"
Val said, pressing the bat into her hands. The heavy wood
dropped to the ground, bending her wrist. She felt the tiny
muscles strain.

"Ouch! That hurt!"

"No! You gotta hold it up! Hold it up!" Val took Elizabeth's
other hand and made her wrap both around the end of the bat.
"Okay, now look at Sebastian. Over there, look at Sebastian!
He's going to pitch the ball to you."

Elizabeth held the bat up in front of her like a club. It felt so
heavy she thought she would drop it. Sebastian shrugged and
shook his head.

"You gotta get in your stance. Here, separate your feet like
this." Val stood in front of Elizabeth. "Put one foot here and
one foot here." He waited until she had matched the placement
of his feet. "Now bend your knees like this." He modeled the
movement for her. She imitated him but once she did she forgot
to hold up the bat. It flailed uselessly in her hands. "Here, let's
try this," he said.

Val positioned himself behind her and brought his arms
around her shoulders. He put his hands where hers gripped the
wood. "Okay, now pull it back like this."

He was too close.

His thick biceps felt like steel bands around her arms. She
couldn't move. Elizabeth tried to turn her head toward him to
protest. He had her encased with his body. Her heart thumped
fast.

"Bend those knees and put your body into it! Swing it
around this way." He made the bat sweep through the air in

front of her. His body twisted and she twisted with him. She felt the muscles of his groin, hard and insistent, pressing into her backside. *No!*

Elizabeth released the bat and pushed his arms down and off her. "Stop it! Stop it!" She didn't say anything else. She couldn't say anything else. She only wanted distance, as much distance as possible between them, so she started walking. She felt a rush of blood flood her face. She didn't notice how easily he had let her go.

He was calling her.

"What'd I do? What'd I do? Hey!"

She didn't look back.

CHAPTER 15
Val

Mercylands, June 1947

Val had enjoyed watching her walk away that fast. The motion of her legs had given her butt a rhythmic movement he found endearing. This next expanse of time would be important and he wanted her to spend it alone. He knew she would make some quick excuse to his aunt and retreat to her room. That was exactly where he wanted her to be, thinking of him.

For now he contented himself with a cigarette on the terrace. He watched the shadows grow longer over the great green lawn while he smoked and savored the day's gains. For the first time, he had held her. Sure, she was holding a bat and he was making a big show of guiding her swing, but it was physical contact. He placed his hands on the cool stone slab shelf, supported by curvy columns and running the length of the terrace. The warmth from her skin ran down out of his fingertips and into the stone. She had smelled of cocoa butter, rose hips, and something he'd forgotten. He closed his eyes to summon the scent from his memory—the smell of skin warmed by the sun.

She smelled like summer and life. He recognized it from his own skin, his elbow so close to his face as he prepared to bat when he played ball in the streets as a child; his kneecaps as he leaned over them, sitting on a stoop waiting for his mother to bring him a cold cup of fresh lemonade. But at this Val shook his head. This was an unnecessary detail. He wouldn't access something so familiar to him.

What was more important—his test had worked. He'd felt her heart beating like a caged bird in her chest. Her skin tensed beneath him once he had his arms around her. All this meant she could be affected by him, stirred by him. If she had been indifferent and stood like a pillar, cold and unmoving, he would have had little hope of succeeding. But now hope shone bright and it lit his way clearly.

Sebastian poked his head through the open French doors. "Sir, I was able to reach Reverend Stiles. He's on the telephone now. You can use the line in the library."

"Thank you, Sebastian."

Val stubbed out his cigarette in the thick glass ashtray on the table and went inside. The library, floor to ceiling, was covered in oak paneling except where it was all shelving filled with row upon row of volumes—his aunt's beloved collection. He crossed the red-and-gold Oriental carpet and picked up the heavy black receiver from the desk.

"Reverend Stiles! Val Jackson."

"Hello, Brother Jackson!"

His voice boomed through the line too heartily for Val's taste. He pulled the receiver away from his ear.

"Reverend, I'd like you to come up to Mercylands after the service on Sunday to visit for a day or two. That is, if you're available?"

"Of course! I'd be delighted to see you and Mrs. Jarreau. She's all right, I hope?"

Val leaned against the desk, his back to the door. "Oh, my aunt is fine, Reverend, just fine. She'll be happy to see you. I just wanted to talk to you about a couple of things."

"Then I'll be there."

"Good. I'm not coming down for the service, but I'll send my driver to pick you up. Is three o'clock okay?"

"Yes it is, thank you. It'll be nice to have a break from the city. It's boiling hot here."

"Great, then I'll see you day after tomorrow."

"Yes. You have a blessed evening."

"Goodbye."

He went up to his room and stood at the open window overlooking Gethsemane Lake. Sebastian, as Val knew he would, soon followed.

"Sir."

Val turned, his arms crossed. "Okay, Sebastian, here's what we're going to do. I'll take dinner in my room tonight and tomorrow. But I'll be downstairs for breakfast. You got that?"

"Yes, sir."

"And when I get down there I want at least three newspapers waiting for me at my place at the table. I want the *Times*. The others can be whatever you can get."

"Yes, sir." Sebastian took a small notebook and pen from his pants pocket and began to write.

"On Sunday I want you to drive down and pick up Reverend Stiles. He's going to join us for a couple of days. Let my aunt know so she can have a room ready."

"Yes, sir."

"I'm going to lie low for a bit until he gets here. If my aunt or Mrs. Townsend ask about me, tell them I'm taking a walk or I'm in my room reading. Got that?"

"Yes, sir." Sebastian looked up from his notebook, an eyebrow raised. "Do you want me to get any particular books for you?"

Val paused and thought. He shoved his hands into his pockets and looked out the window again, considering his options. Then he nodded and turned back to Sebastian.

"Get me a Bible. And whatever my aunt has by Langston Hughes, bring that too. That's good thinking, thank you."

"I'm glad to help, sir. Is that all?" Sebastian finished his notes but still held the pen to the paper.

"No, that's it. Thanks."

Sebastian nodded, spun on his well-polished heel, then paused. He put a hand in his jacket pocket, pulled out a small envelope, and turned back to Val.

"I forgot to tell you, sir. This arrived in today's mail." He handed the envelope to Val and left the room, closing the door quietly behind him.

The tips of Val's fingers went cold. He stared at the familiar handwriting for a moment before tearing the note open. A shiny red "M" decorated the top of the card. She'd written nothing on it other than a large swirling question mark. He put it back in its envelope and took his lighter out of his pocket. When the flame licked high enough to consume half the card, he dropped it onto a large ashtray on the desk.

Val looked out the window again and a strong breeze, the

first in a few days, blew into the room. It made the leaves on the trees whisper excitedly as though they too relished a pause from the heat. He was glad for it—he wanted his aunt and her friend to be comfortable. Elizabeth would retreat after today and he needed to do the same. But he knew he could beat her at this because she wouldn't want to leave Aunt Rose alone, especially once she realized Val wouldn't be with Rose. It was the perfect situation now. He would be able to orchestrate his moves from his room, but Elizabeth would think she was acting all on her own.

He thought of how light she'd felt in his arms. Her wrists— little, thin, birdlike wrists—delighted him. He took a cigarette from the pack on his desk and lit it. He exhaled out the window and watched the blue stream of smoke float toward the lawn. A short burst of laughter rose up from his throat. He really hadn't meant to press so hard against her but he couldn't stop himself. How easy it could have been with any other woman to push her against something, the terrace rail for instance, just the right height, and then slide her skirt up above the dimpled knees, over the soft round thighs, up over the firm tomato shape of her ass and remove the annoying undergarments until she was fully exposed and open to him.

He had taken women like that before—yes, too many times. And wasn't that what he enjoyed about the prospect of Elizabeth? That it would be different with her? But different how? He honestly didn't know, but the fact that it was a mystery lying somewhere on a near horizon drew him in. This riddle tasted delicious, like the sweetness of a piece of butter brittle in his mouth in the moment before crushing it with his teeth. He would wait. He could wait. This waiting he loved.

CHAPTER 16
Elizabeth

Mercylands, June 1947

Elizabeth felt like a child who had been warned many times away from a hot stove, but whose confidence had made her careless. Now she was singed and humbled. She kicked at the rug in her bedroom and paced in frustration. She had been so ridiculous. How could she let him stand so close to her—*like that?*

She kept pacing. The movement comforted her. Even berating herself was easier than allowing herself to quiet down. She knew she would do that, eventually, and she wasn't looking forward to the contemplation that would follow. Because in quiet moments she had to consider the strange feeling that this man—this Val Jackson—had been skirting around the edges of her consciousness much longer than she realized, perhaps even before she noticed him sitting in the upper pews at church. There was something about him that seemed familiar, even inevitable, but how could that be? She knew nothing about him apart from the gossip she heard from friends.

A thought came to her and Elizabeth began rummaging in her things for Gladys's most recent letter, but had she brought it to Westchester with her? It would help to read it now, to read her friend's reassuring words one more time.

When she couldn't find it she went to her desk and pulled out paper and a pen from the drawer in front of her. She scrawled the letter quickly but the words mentioned only the pleasant grounds and Rose Jarreau's abilities as a warm and gracious hostess. At the end she wrote, "Write soon and tell me how you are." If she could have put more urgency behind the sentence without alarming her friend she would have. But Elizabeth knew she wouldn't have to mention Val Jackson; Gladys already knew he was there and would send the reinforcing words Elizabeth required.

She rang for the maid even before finishing the letter, and sealed it as Annie stood waiting.

"Annie, has the afternoon mail gone out yet?"

"No, ma'am."

"Take this, please, and make sure it goes today."

"I sure will, Mrs. Townsend."

With the letter posted, Elizabeth sensed calm returning to her. She placed her palms flat on the desk and stretched her arms out in front of her. She faced the windows but the balcony and her seated position prevented her from seeing anyone walking the grounds. Was he still out there?

She played the scene in her mind again, his arms around her, his voice just inches behind her right earlobe. She noticed there was a juvenile quality to what happened. What if he was just being playful and silly—no different from a high school boy seeing how far he could go? Elizabeth pulled herself forward and laid her forehead on the desk. Maybe she had made too much of it, being indignant, running away like that. It would only give him reason to tease her in the days to come. She had to pull things back. She would have to go down to dinner and show him he had not upset her in any lasting way. If he brought it up, she would laugh and correct him lightly. She was sure Rose would support her in this, and Elizabeth would follow her lead. Nothing her nephew did ever seemed to ruffle Rose. Elizabeth wanted to learn how to cultivate the same even temper.

She folded her forearms on the desk and put her head down on top of them. Her breathing quieted and she felt the earlier thoughts return. Why did he seem familiar? She closed her eyes and his arms again encircled her. Maybe the feeling was merely an echo of what she knew of Kyle's embrace. But the moment she considered this answer she sensed it was wrong. There was always a hesitance about Kyle's touch that seemed to emphasize their individual natures. Whenever they entwined it felt like both of them needed to make accommodation for the other, being careful not to delve too far or too close.

But with Val she sensed a clicking together like magnets, like his arms being around her was a perfectly natural occurrence. He had smelled of sweat, but she recognized more in his scent—a combination of earth and ocean, flowers and wood, something very alive, indeed akin to life itself. The thought of it brightened her eyes, as though someone had snapped their fingers in front of her face, awakening her. Even now a warmth flowed through her and the skin stretched along the top of her back tingled. *This can't be,* she thought. *This cannot be right.*

Her hands rolled into fists and she pressed her head against her forearms. She would bury this notion, whatever it was, and she was determined to do it at once. This man was nothing to her. Val Jackson was vile, intolerable, and in a few days she would have written words from Gladys affirming her in this thinking. Really she didn't even have to speak to him if she didn't want to for the remainder of her visit.

Elizabeth repeated these thoughts to herself until they began to whirl in her mind like a vortex. And she used this spinning steel of words to drill into the ground deep. She could feel her notion of oneness with Val tumble into the resulting hole. And now the thoughts reminding her of what he was fell into that hole, again and again, until any thought of being close to him had sunk deep, deep down into her being, never to rise again. She raised her head and turned so her right cheek lay on her arms. Her eyes drooped with the heaviness of her work and the warmth of the room. Soon she fell asleep.

* * *

SHE SAT UP slowly when she heard the quiet knock at the door. She rubbed her eyes and looked out the window. It wasn't dark out, but the light had shifted enough to tell her it was early evening. A gurgling sound rolled through her stomach and she realized she had missed lunch.

Annie opened the door enough to poke her head through.

"Mrs. Townsend, are you ready to get dressed for dinner?"

"Yes, Annie, come in." When Elizabeth had first arrived, she'd declined these offers. She could very well dress herself. But when she noticed Annie's look of disappointment each time she sent the maid away, Elizabeth realized she was keeping her from doing her job. Having company in the house probably meant extra work and extra wages for everyone. So she allowed Annie in and discovered a warm, comforting experience she never expected. Annie who, Elizabeth guessed, was just a few years older than her made her feel as though she were dressing for a party every night. She complimented Elizabeth on her clothes, quickly ironed or mended any item requiring attention, and had the added skill of hairdressing. Elizabeth trusted Annie, the hot comb in the maid's pudgy brown fingers, to press out the fuzzy tufts close to her temples and the nape of her neck. Considering how much time Elizabeth and Rose spent sweating in the garden under the summer sun, Annie had to perform this task a couple of times a week.

Annie also chatted freely, and this soothed Elizabeth's nerves and eased her into the quiet she wanted to have at dinner. Still, she jerked her head when Annie mentioned Mr. Jackson.

"I'm sorry, ma'am, did I burn you?"

"No, Annie." Elizabeth pulled the thick white towel closer around her neck and held the ends bunched in a fist under her chin. "What were you saying about Mr. Jackson?"

"It's nice he's here. It's always so lively when Mr. Jackson visits."

Elizabeth closed her eyes. "Yes, I'm sure."

"Mrs. Jarreau will miss him at dinner tonight."

Elizabeth opened her eyes and tilted her head up toward Annie. She could feel the heat of the retreating hot comb just above her left ear. "Mr. Jackson won't be at dinner?"

"No, ma'am. He sent word he'll be eating in his room. The kitchen staff are preparing a tray for him now."

"Oh." Elizabeth lowered her chin and closed her eyes tight. Annie brought the comb close to her temple and tugged gently at the tight curls there. While she did so Elizabeth chewed over this new piece of information with some relief. She wouldn't have to deal with him at all, at least not for tonight. Even as she winced under the comb she could feel the muscles down her back relaxing.

* * *

SUNDAY DAWNED COOLER than the previous days. A fine breeze blew through Mercylands, pushing away the thick, water-laden air that had hampered Elizabeth and all of the mansion's inhabitants. In the afternoon Elizabeth and Rose were able to sit comfortably out on the terrace for the first time in nearly a week.

"Thank you, Jesus," Rose said. She lowered herself into her chair and leaned back as though giving permission for the wind to flow over her. "That cool air sure feels nice."

"Amen to that," Elizabeth replied. She sat and looked down the length of the terrace and then over the lawn. They hadn't seen Val much over the past two days and Elizabeth saw no sign of him now. When he did come to meals, such as breakfast that morning, he stayed hidden behind the newspapers he read. He still spoke to Rose with affection, but only acknowledged Elizabeth when she entered or left the room.

Was he upset with her? But then she remembered in thinking this way she would be assigning herself an imaginary power—that she could move his emotions with her actions. Val Jackson, she was sure, thought no more of her than he did any other woman. It was more likely that in keeping to himself and staying in his room he was finally settling in, and this was what his visits to Mercylands were really like. She assumed this because Rose didn't seem to think there was anything strange about his behavior. Elizabeth should be glad she didn't have to encounter him more than necessary.

The servant Avery stepped through the French doors, his hands wrapped around the handles of a large wooden tray. On it he carried glasses and a large pitcher of lemonade stuffed with mint leaves. He put the tray on the table and picked up a small blue-handled strainer next to the pitcher. He placed it over a glass and poured the lemonade through. He repeated this with a second glass and when both glasses were full, he handed them to Rose and Elizabeth.

"Ma'am, Reverend Stiles's room is ready." He made a small bow and lowered his eyes.

Rose reached for her lemonade. "Thank you, Avery. He should be here soon."

Elizabeth waited for Avery to go back inside before she asked her question. "Reverend Stiles is on his way?"

"Yes. Val invited him. Even sent his car to get him." Rose laughed and shook her head. "The old coot! He has a car of his own, but after riding up here in Val's Cadillac, I bet he's already plotting how to get himself one just like it. But the only way he will is if Val gives him that one when he's done with it."

"Would he really do that?"

"There's no telling what that boy will do. He can be as generous as an angel, but most of the time he goes around bedeviling people like he doesn't have anything better to do. If he were still nine years old, I'd probably take a switch to him!" Rose laughed again and nearly spilled her drink.

Elizabeth smiled and sipped her lemonade. The mint stung her tongue with a cool brightness. She caught a stray leaf in the side of her mouth and chewed on it. She wanted to ask why Rose would take a switch to Val and why he'd invited Reverend Stiles to Mercylands, but she had the sense she was beginning to skirt an unseen boundary.

The French doors opened and Sebastian walked through, holding them open.

"Mrs. Jarreau, here's Reverend Stiles."

The minister wore a short-sleeved white shirt and brown slacks and he held a straw fedora in his hands. He smiled widely and warmly.

"Here," said Sebastian, plucking the hat from him, "let me take that for you. I'll go find Mr. Jackson and tell him you're here."

"Thank you, Sebastian!" Reverend Stiles's smile grew broader as though it would split his face in two. "Rose! It is such an honor to be here." He looked at her over the top of his wire-rimmed glasses. "It's been a long time! But you look lovely. In fact you've never been prettier."

"Oh, you hush now with all that! Sit yourself down. Say hello to Elizabeth." She waved her hands in Elizabeth's direction.

"I was just about to do that. Hello, Elizabeth," he said. He sat in a chair between them. "So happy to see you here. Rose, this is one of my favorite parishioners. Always ready to lend a hand, always putting out the good word about the church and our work."

"That's kind of you to say so," said Elizabeth. "Here, let me." She poured a glass of lemonade just as she had seen Avery do it, then handed the glass to Reverend Stiles.

"Thank you."

"How was your ride up?" Rose asked. She winked at Elizabeth.

"You know, I don't think I've ever been in a car that rode so smooth! I enjoyed it, I'll say that."

Elizabeth smiled into her glass.

"So what do you and Val have cooking?" Rose peered at the minister over her glasses.

Reverend Stiles held up his empty hands. "I honestly don't know, Rose. The boy just said he needed to talk to me."

Rose swirled the lemonade in her glass then took a drink. "Well, as long as you don't talk him into trouble that's fine with me."

"Trouble? What are you talking about, trouble? You know the Good Lord moves me to do no harm and only His will. I'll go anywhere to stretch out my hand and lift up one of His sheep. I would—"

"All right." Rose flapped a hand at him to shush him. "You've already done your sermon for today. Remember the Lord also rested on the seventh day."

"Amen to that!" He smiled, sat back, and drank his lemonade.

"How was church today?" Elizabeth asked.

"It was fine, just fine." Then Reverend Stiles frowned. "But Mother Harris burned one of the coffeepots when she was getting ready for the fellowship hour. Boiled it bone dry then burned it after that."

"Oh no!"

"Nobody got hurt, but the smell came out of the kitchen and the whole fellowship room stank so bad no one wanted to stay down there. J.D. was still airing it out when I left."

They all laughed and were still laughing when Val walked out onto the terrace. He kissed his aunt's cheek, nodded to Elizabeth, then shook Reverend Stiles's hand and thanked him for coming. Elizabeth thought there was something muted about him. The tone of his voice didn't ring as brightly and his smile seemed perfunctory. It was like he was standing behind a screen that filtered out all the glow of him. He didn't accept a drink and he didn't sit down with them. Instead he perched himself on the wide stone terrace railing near his aunt. He participated in their small talk but his gaze stayed trained on Reverend Stiles. Elizabeth thought there was something unsettled about his look, something that sat just behind his eyes. She couldn't help wondering about this while at the same time chastising herself for doing so.

Finally Val stood up. "Reverend Stiles, come on and take a walk with me. It'll be good to stretch your legs after that long ride."

"All right then." The minister got up and rubbed his hands together like he knew he was about to go to work. "Excuse us, ladies." He nodded at Rose and Elizabeth then followed Val down the stone steps.

Rose watched them go and she chuckled.

"What is it?" Elizabeth asked. She smiled too. "Why are you laughing?"

"It's just funny how sometimes Mohammed will just bring the mountain to him. Any other person would wait and go to church, but Val must have something he wants to get out of his head now."

"Well, he can do that, right? Val's in that position. He can ask for anything he wants."

A small cloud dropped down and darkened Rose's forehead. She leaned toward Elizabeth and pressed her right index finger on the table in front of her.

"What Val does is no special thing. Anyone in this world can ask for what they want. They just don't do it."

Elizabeth shook her head.

"I'm sorry, Rose, I don't understand."

Rose sat back and crossed her arms. Her eyes narrowed until she squinted. "Val *asks* for what he wants. People envy him because they're too scared or too lazy to ask for what they want. If you ask me, it's pure laziness. People sit around thinking the world is going to hand them something, like the world owes them something."

Elizabeth stared at her glass and ran her finger around the rim. "I never thought of it that way."

Rose leaned toward her.

"You think Reverend Stiles wouldn't come to you if you called him? He just sat right there and said you were one of his favorite parishioners. You think he values you less than he does Val?"

She stared at her host a moment before she shook her head and lowered her chin. "No, I guess not."

Rose sat up straight again. "No, he doesn't. He'd be right on your doorstep or anyone else's. But Val is the one who asked. People don't think to ask for anything. They don't want to be told no. Then they sit there and stew because somebody like Val has the nerve to do what they won't do. I get tired of the way people act sometimes."

Elizabeth sipped her lemonade. How much of what she heard about Val Jackson grew from the roots of jealousy? Rose was speaking of a pastor's visit, but Elizabeth wondered how much of Val's lore might stem from those same emotions. They could easily generate from a man who felt spurned because Val won the woman he didn't approach; a woman scorned because she wasn't the one he sought; anyone who coveted his wealth and position, though it was dubious because of his clubs and other dealings. She had no way to assess the truth of all this. Her conjectures circled aimlessly in her mind.

What was a man? Was he his thoughts and deeds? Was he the way he treated others? Was he the way he treated her, Elizabeth? Was he his reputation or perhaps some combination of all these aspects? Was he the things he said to her or was he the boy who kissed his aunt's cheek with such affection? For her own part Elizabeth thought he behaved poorly just once or maybe twice. She supposed she would need to observe him, even talk to him more, if she was to arrive at her own right conclusions. What harm could come of it? Both Rose and Reverend Stiles regarded him well. If she had something to fear wouldn't they be the ones warning her against him?

Besides, she thought, why should she allow faceless rumors or even Gladys's caution to tell her what to think? She, like Rose, often tired of the way people behaved. It was too much like what she read in *The Street*—people acting out of their own interests with no thought to kindness or grace. But what did it mean to extend graciousness to Val Jackson? What would it look like?

* * *

OVER THE NEXT two days she watched and waited. Val and Reverend Stiles continued their private talks. At first she was grateful to have Val's attention focused elsewhere. She relaxed and didn't worry about what to say to him or how to say it. They exchanged easy pleasantries at meals. His meetings with the pastor intrigued her. Whenever she came upon them on the grounds Val was not smiling or laughing. He walked with his hands behind his back and wore a thoughtful look on his face. She would nod in their direction but she didn't want to interrupt their talk.

Was Reverend Stiles counseling Val? Was he on his way to making some sort of change in his life? That would explain his posture, his contemplative attitude. If this were true, what did it mean? And why was it happening? She wanted so much to talk to Reverend Stiles herself, she could chew through her fingernails as she thought about it. But she also knew such a conversation was impossible. It would be interference, even a betrayal of confidence. She would never do that.

Her eagerness, she knew, grew from her recognition of a clear path. She was on familiar ground. She knew how a person might seek a place at God's table and she had counseled many a friend looking for spiritual guidance. She could help Val. In fact she considered it her Christian duty to encourage him. If a man of his means could change his life, it would affect so many people for the good. A changed Val Jackson might make different decisions about what to do with his money. He could help fund the pastoral missions of the church. He would inspire others—he could be a real light to behold. Thinking of the possibilities made her more self-assured. *If you save one soul it's as if you've saved a whole universe.* There would be nothing wrong about befriending him if she could steer him a little toward good. She decided she would pay closer attention and look for small ways she might gain more insight on his intentions.

* * *

REVEREND STILES RETURNED to Harlem on Wednesday. Elizabeth thought this would mean she and Rose would see more of Val, but he still kept to himself. This confused her more than ever because he wasn't isolated in his room. He seemed to be out and about more, leaving the house at different times. What was he doing? She couldn't ask Rose.

Rose's maid, Annie, finally presented her with the chance to talk about Val. She felt something spin in her stomach when the woman laid out Elizabeth's dress for the evening and mentioned Val while she did so. Again, she said how wonderful it was to have him at Mercylands.

"He's always so busy," Annie said. She put the dress, a dark blue silk decorated with silver embroidery, on the bed and ran her hands over the skirt to smooth it. "He makes it so lively here."

"Busy?" Elizabeth pulled a slip down over her head and adjusted it around her hips. "What do you mean?"

"Oh yes." Annie unbuttoned the dress on the bed and held it up for Elizabeth to step into it. "He's usually up at the crack of dawn, out doing who knows what." She helped pull the garment up and began buttoning it again.

Elizabeth looked in the mirror at Annie's reflection and smiled. "Annie, if he's out so early, what makes you think he hasn't been out all night?" It probably wasn't right for her to discuss Val with a maid, but she liked being able to talk about him with someone.

Annie reached up and pulled back on Elizabeth's unruly locks so she could subdue them under bobby pins. "Well, you know, that is something. I don't rightly know. But where would he be all night around here? This isn't Harlem."

"Exactly. So where would he go so early in the morning?"

This time it was Annie's turn to smile. "When you're Valiant Jackson I'm sure you find good places to be."

Elizabeth laughed. She liked what she saw in the mirror— her hair tamed but still youthful and the dress accenting her figure's slimness. "Yes. It does make me curious, though."

Annie gathered Elizabeth's laundry from the hamper. "Well, it might be too bold of me to say this, ma'am, but if you really want to know, why don't you find out?"

Elizabeth turned to her. "How would I do that, Annie?"

"You brought your own car up here, didn't you?" She placed the soiled clothing in a basket, picked it up, and waited for an answer.

"Yes." Elizabeth thought for a moment then held up a hand to signal Annie she didn't need to say more. She loved the idea. Not because she wanted to know where he was going—she did—but more because if she succeeded she would, at the very least, have something of her own in her pocket to throw back at Val when he teased her. He did have a certain reputation, after all, and she could always call on that—and her newfound proof of whatever it was—to keep him at arm's length if needed. She sighed and relaxed. When she left her room to go downstairs for dinner she wondered how early she should rise the next day.

CHAPTER 17
Mae

Harlem, June 1947

It took careful consideration on Mae's part to give up her current lover for this endeavor. She stood in the church watching Sam Delany at the organ rehearsing the choir, and thought of his eagerness to please her, his pure, appreciative, puppylike devotion. She hadn't enjoyed such youthful attention in a long time. But the word "youthful" made her think of Frank Washington, and the thought of Frank Washington brought a wash of green over her eyesight and made the tops of her ears burn. The revenge, she finally decided, was more than worth it.

Still, she wouldn't have to make this sacrifice if Val had returned when he said he would. This was his fault. He'd run off to Westchester to hide something from her. How could he even think she wouldn't find out what it was? She knew him like she knew her own mind. This made his lie—and she was certain it was a lie—a dual sin. He lied to her and inconvenienced her. It was only fair he should pay double the price. But he would have to wait. Her new plan had holes. It could fail with a minor misstep. It required all of her attention.

Gladys was late, as usual. The choir was singing a spirited hymn when she barreled in at last, fanning herself and mopping her brow with a handkerchief. By then Mae was too exasperated with her to listen to her excuses.

"Gladys, are you serious about Cecily taking music lessons?" Mae asked.

"You know I am."

She nodded at the young man at the organ. "Then there's no better choice for her teacher than Samuel Delany," said Mae. "He comes highly recommended from Reverend Stiles."

Gladys seated herself in a pew and leaned forward to get a better look. Then she put on her glasses and peered at him carefully. "Isn't that the new singer from the Swan?"

"Gladys, you have such a good eye. I think he is. So now you know for yourself how talented he is."

"But a nightclub singer, Mae?"

"Would he be here if Reverend Stiles didn't think him trustworthy? We trust Reverend Stiles so I'm sure we can trust Sam, aren't you?"

Gladys sat back and nodded. "Well, you're right about that."

Mae smiled. "Where's Cecily?"

"She's in the car."

"I think they're almost done. We can take Sam out to meet her then, all right?"

* * *

OUTSIDE, MAE WAS glad to see that Cecily, coming out of the car at her mother's prompting, looked less awkward than usual. She wore a simple dark blue dress and she was managing to stand in her heels without rolling onto the sides of her ankles. When Sam came bounding down the steps to join them, Mae thought this would be as easy as putting a piece of cheese in front of a mouse.

"Samuel Delany," she said. She placed a hand lightly on his arm. "I'd like to introduce my cousin, Gladys Vaughn, and her daughter, Cecily."

"How do you do, Mrs. Vaughn?" he said. He shook Gladys's hand and smiled broadly.

When he turned to Cecily, Mae noted how he paused and stared a moment at the girl before offering his hand. She was also satisfied with how deeply Cecily blushed. "Very nice to meet you," he said, bowing.

"Will you come see us tomorrow?" Gladys wanted to know. "We can talk about the details then and you can see our fine piano. We live on West 136th Street. All right?"

"Yes, I will, thank you."

Mae smiled. "Good," she said. "Very good."

CHAPTER 18
Val

Mercylands, June 1947

Annie had said "crack of dawn" but the sun had been up for two hours when Sebastian started and then finished loading the trunk of Val's car. He nodded at Val when Val, dressed in a white T-shirt and khaki pants, walked out onto the driveway. Sebastian opened the rear car door and Val slid over the seat.

"You sure she's gonna be out there?" Val asked. Sebastian got behind the wheel and Val turned to look back through the rear window.

"Yes, sir. They took her car out already. And she told Annie again last night she wondered what you were doing with your mornings. I think the implication was you're meeting a lady friend."

Sebastian started the car and slowly navigated down the curving driveway, careful to stay away from the rhododendron branches hanging low nearby. He drove out of the gate, turned, and proceeded down the road. Val stayed low and peered out the back window until he detected the black coupe. It pulled out from a side road behind them and followed the Cadillac. It seemed to be keeping a careful distance from them.

"And here she comes!" Val smiled and turned around. He settled himself into his seat for the ride. Inviting Reverend Stiles had been the right move. In fact it had worked out even better than he'd expected.

During his walks and meetings with the minister Val found he didn't need to say much. He would ask a question such as "What presages change in a man's life?" and Reverend Stiles was happy to go on and answer at length without much prompting.

"A man like that starts off by withdrawing from the world," he had responded. He held his arms open wide as though he would embrace a globe. Then he pulled his palms together as though in prayer.

Val walked with his hands behind his back. He raised his eyebrows at this answer. "Why would he do that, Reverend?"

The minister raised the index finger of his right hand to the sky. "Because he's starting to hear the Lord's call." Reverend Stiles pointed the same finger to his ear. "He needs silence so he can hear it better. So he can figure out what the Lord is saying to him, what He wants him to do."

Reverend Stiles went on to talk of Christ heading off into the wilderness after receiving baptism from John. He spoke about fasting and contemplation—and temptation. Val did listen closely to all of it. He saw it as a way of researching his role. He knew there would come a time when he'd have to cut back on his meals and cultivate a starved, earnest look. Of course it would be for Elizabeth's benefit. She would have no reason to doubt the evidence of her eyes if he gave her the appearance of a man wasting away for want of spiritual food. He would be less threatening and she would feel more confident about engaging him. And when she did he planned to give her words, words with just enough truth for her to believe them.

Only a little truth was necessary. He wondered why more people didn't see that telling a big lie was like dropping a stick house down in front of a person and telling them it was a mansion. They'd have no faith in it because they'd played no role in putting the house there. Soon they'd see the cracks between the sticks and then the house would be blown down and the lie obliterated.

But if you tell a little bit of truth, you don't have to do much because the person you've given the truth to will build the house for you. They add to it their own observations, their own knowledge, because they know the veracity of your little bit of truth and it gives them confidence in the rest.

He looked in the rearview mirror again, but this time he examined his face. He could stand to lose a few pounds. While his face didn't look fat, it did have a softness around the jawline indicating the fullness of a healthy body. If he erased just a bit of it he was sure the difference would be enough for Elizabeth to notice.

"What happens after?" he had asked Reverend Stiles.

"Like Christ, the man comes back and begins to fulfill his mission, whatever he has gleaned it to be." Reverend Stiles waved a hand through the air again as though a long scroll of paper had unfurled in front of him and on it was a list of possible missions. Val took it to be his proposal for what he'd like to see Val do at Mount Nebo. He talked about stewardship, the vestry, the youth ministry, the soup kitchen. At the mention of the soup kitchen Val stopped listening. What would he look like in line behind trays of steaming dishes serving food with Elizabeth? He couldn't allow things to come to that—he would never live it down. But Val did like what Reverend Stiles was saying about mission. That day he had put Sebastian to work to find the right opportunity. He succeeded admirably, as always, and the payoff would arrive this morning with Elizabeth on the scene to witness everything.

For here was proof his strategy was working. She was curious, and curiosity meant she was thinking about him—a lot. Perhaps more than she realized. He was grateful for it, for her attention. If she were any other woman he would have chalked it up to nosiness and self-interest. But Elizabeth Townsend wasn't like that. He'd bet it a hundred times a day and twice that on Sunday. She was curious because she took an interest in his welfare. He knew this had to be true and the thought touched him. Here she was, following him! Already she had stepped outside of herself. Did she see that? Did she even recognize she had begun a journey that would take her far beyond the road they traveled on now? He wanted to know what she was thinking as she drove.

He liked the lightness in the way Elizabeth Townsend did things—it made him want to laugh—the demure way she nodded her head whenever she crossed paths with him and Reverend Stiles, the question mark that seemed to dance across her face when he said "good morning" or "good evening" to her and nothing more when she sat down at the dining room table. She was never testy or annoyed. She seemed even, perhaps, a tiny bit hurt.

Hurt would be good. It would give him the chance to salve the hurt with a little of his own attention, and that would open the door to so much more. Because the heart was never satisfied with a little bit of caring. It was a greedy lump of muscle, quick to feast on the tiniest morsel of sincere admiration. But once the heart consumed that admiration, it always wanted more— demanded more. Val counted on this. Soon he would make her aware of his devotion—the table was set for it. He had to ready himself to weather her protests that were sure to follow. But he was sure that would be all he had to do. Her curiosity—and greedy heart—would handle the rest.

He laughed and stole a glance in Sebastian's rearview mirror. He felt the satisfaction of a child, with string in hand, walking and pulling along a favorite fire truck or a toy puppy on wheels. "Be careful," Val said. "We don't want to lose her."

He lowered the window to his right and looked out. Already the sun had burned away the morning mist but he still smelled the water sticking thick in the air. The roadside vegetation hung low and swept the sides of the Cadillac as it passed. It would be hot again, but not until later. He was glad they were doing this before the heat of the day set in.

CHAPTER 19
Elizabeth

Westchester, June 1947

Elizabeth had been grateful for the early morning mist that draped over the road but now it was disappearing. She didn't know how to stay close enough to the car ahead without being seen. She gripped the wheel, leaned toward the windshield, and bit her lower lip. What was she doing? What would he say to her if he caught her? She was beginning to think following Val was a foolish idea, but she had gone too far to turn back. And she was curious because she truly thought she would see him coming home after staying out all night.

Another surprise: they went farther than Elizabeth expected. Wherever they were going she did not consider it local. The roads were becoming more urban, less country. Were they going back to the city? If they left Westchester County, Elizabeth decided, she would have to turn back. How would she explain being in Harlem, especially if someone she knew saw her?

She was relieved when Val's car finally stopped in the town of Mount Vernon, turning into the parking lot of a squat stone building with another side area paved and surrounded by a chain-link fence. The grounds seemed to be full of people. Elizabeth let her car roll slowly past the building. She saw large white letters painted over the main door: "Mount Vernon Boys' Club." Looking ahead she realized she could make a turn and come around to the other side of the building. When she did that Elizabeth saw she could park on the street across from the lot—close enough to see without being seen. She turned off the engine and leaned across the front seat.

Elizabeth smiled, then found herself laughing. The lot was full of boys—beautiful, smiling, eager black children who all seemed to be excited to see Val. They held bats, gloves, and balls—baseballs! Val seemed to be giving directions and suddenly the boys were running in a whirl around him until half were positioned in various spots in the lot and the other half stood behind the safety of the chain-link fence.

One boy stood near the fence with a bat, waiting. Sebastian kneeled near the boy, a glove on his hand and a metal mask over his face. Val stood a few feet away with another boy, who held a baseball. The boy watched and mimicked Val's movements. His spindly leg, like a colt's, rose into the air and then came down as he kicked out his other leg. He swung his arm as if to throw the ball, but he still held it in his fingers. He nodded at Val and Val stood back. This time the boy pulled up fully and followed through, pitching the ball at the batter, who swung and missed. Sebastian caught the ball and the boys behind the pitcher cheered.

Val smiled, patted the boy on the back, and said something

to him that made the boy grin with obvious joy. This was how the morning went on, the game continuing and pausing when the boys needed coaching. Elizabeth didn't know enough about what they were doing to follow it all, but she couldn't stop watching either. At one point it seemed Val's eyes had roamed over to her and she gasped. But she realized she was reacting to her own insecurity. There were too many children and she was too far away to attract Val's attention. However, there was no reason to stay longer. She had her answer, even if it wasn't what she'd expected. The best thing for her to do was get back to Rose's house before Val did. She started the car, her eyes still on the makeshift baseball game as she steered down the street.

* * *

THE REST OF the day Elizabeth wore her newfound knowledge like a comforting quilt around her shoulders. Val seemed safer, perhaps, not the villain everyone believed he was. She enjoyed listening to the familiar banter Rose maintained with her nephew throughout dinner, and paid careful attention as she ate her tomato salad and roast chicken. She was becoming more certain she could hold her own in conversation with Val without further troubles.

At the end of the meal Avery brought out coffee and, as usual, the evening newspaper for Val. He leaned back in his seat and opened the broad pages in front of him.

"How are your Dodgers doing these days?" Rose asked.

"Doing fine, doing fine. My man Mr. Robinson will keep them in the hunt for the pennant; I know that sure as I know my own name."

"Do you follow baseball, Elizabeth?" Rose raised her cup to her lips.

Elizabeth carefully doctored her own coffee with milk and a bit of sugar. "No, Rose. Kyle's never been interested so I've never had reason to go to a game."

"Val can't get enough. And he thinks Jackie Robinson walks on water, don't you, honey?"

"Oh, him I know!" Elizabeth said before Val could answer. "Everyone knows Jackie Robinson."

"And why shouldn't they?" Val said, putting his paper down. "The man's a giant. I can't believe you've never been to a game."

"Not everyone has to have the same tastes as you," Rose said. She stood slowly and kissed him on the forehead. "I'm tired. I think I'll drag these old bones upstairs and call it a day."

"Let me help you, Aunt Rose."

"No, no, I'm fine, honey. Sit and enjoy your coffee. I'll see you in the morning. You'll be up early again?"

"As always. You know how much I love the morning. It's just filled with possibilities."

"Possibilities?" Rose smiled. "Is that her name? Good night."

Val put a hand against his cheek and rolled his eyes. "Aunt Rose! What a dirty mind!" He laughed before half rising to kiss his aunt again. "Good night, babe!"

"Good night, Rose," said Elizabeth.

Val sat down and sipped his coffee. Elizabeth gave hers another stir, but when she raised the cup and her eyes, she saw Val's smile gone. He was staring at her with such focus she turned her head as though he had shone a light into her face. She covered by coughing, then turning back to him. She forced herself to maintain a Rose-like composure.

"I know Jackie Robinson is a great man. But why do you admire him so much? Especially a man with your . . ." Elizabeth ran a hand through her hair and looked away.

"My reputation?"

She coughed again. "Yes."

Val didn't move. His stare remained. "Look, I used to think character was a commodity," he said. "I thought as long as I had money, I could be as evil as I wanted to be. It didn't seem to matter and nobody seemed to care. Now Jackie Robinson, he showed me I was wrong. It doesn't matter how much money he makes, but *who* he is is everything! He's got to be good and he's got to be a good man. Why? Because it's gonna mean something for our people long after we're dead and gone. Ain't no amount of money can buy meaning. No amount."

He picked up his paper again. Elizabeth realized she could let him disappear behind it and he would leave her alone. But knowing this only made her feel bolder and she advanced. She sat back and crossed her legs, hoping to assume his same casual attitude.

"I saw you with those boys this morning."

"Yeah?" He put the paper down. "And you didn't even defend me in front of Aunt Rose just now. But how did you know?"

Elizabeth reached for the coffeepot and refilled her cup. It gave her an excuse not to look at him. "I followed you."

"Followed me?" Val laughed. "Oh, Mrs. Townsend, you better be careful! People are gonna talk!"

"I was just curious."

"About what?"

Elizabeth stayed silent and stirred her coffee, unsure of how to answer.

"Looks like Aunt Rose isn't the only one with a dirty mind!"

"I wanted to know if you were really as terrible as people say. I had to know for myself, only now I don't know what to think. The man I saw out there with those boys didn't look heartless or mean."

"Heartless and mean? Okay, let me solve the mystery for you." Val sat up and leaned toward her. "I won't lie—I've been living out of bounds. I run with a rough crowd and we only see people as prospects and victims. But now I'm trying to get up from all of that. I'm trying to follow somebody's good example and it's getting all messed up by people telling you lies and nosing in on my business. Who's been doing that anyway?"

"I'm not telling you."

"So you've said." Val got up, shoved his hands into his pockets, and walked over to the windows.

Again, Elizabeth couldn't resist the question in her mind. "Whose example?"

"What?"

"You said you were following somebody's good example. Who is it?"

"Oh, you're gonna keep nosing around in my business too?"

Elizabeth smiled. "Well, yes."

Val turned around to face her. He took his hands from his pockets, pulled his chin up, and looked directly into her eyes. "All right then. It's you."

Elizabeth thought she had stopped breathing. She had nothing—no words, no motion. She was anchored to the chair and her eyes locked to his.

"You asked. I've told you." He spoke in quick, calm words. "I won't lie. I've lied my whole life. But I see truth in you all the time. I see you sweating in that church basement, feeding those people, giving them love, inspiring love, being an angel. I want to be like that. I want to master that kind of emotion. I want to be like you. I love you."

Suddenly he moved and the table was no longer between them. He was on her side, reaching toward her, grabbing her hands, and holding her tightly.

"And I can't do a damn thing about it. Tell me what to do. I'll do anything you say. Please, baby, just tell me what to do. I need you."

She pulled back. Would she have to fight him? Would she have the strength?

The phone rang.

Its echo and subsequent rings filled the air above them, dissolving a spell.

"That's my husband."

Val backed up, his eyes never leaving her face. He would let her go, but she would have to move. Elizabeth got to her feet and wobbled for a moment, her right foot turned inward. She knew if she could turn her head, if she could stop looking at him, she would be able to walk, to leave. Her eyes found the wallpaper behind him, and she allowed her view to be swung by the pattern of printed flowers and trailing vines. She followed the green vines to help her head turn and then used them to lead her to the door and out of the room.

* * *

WHEN SHE HAD gone Val walked around the table again, back to his chair. He looked out the windows and took another sip from his coffee cup. Darkness began to fill the room, and Sebastian came in and turned on a lamp.

"Is there anything else I can get for you tonight, sir?"

"Yeah." Val nodded slowly. "Find out who's been bad-mouthing me to Mrs. Townsend."

"Yes, sir."

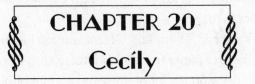

CHAPTER 20
Cecíly

Harlem, June 1947

When she and Sam sat together at the piano, Cecily felt as though the different parts of her that didn't make sense came together all at once. She was whole and, for once, absolutely herself. She knew she would be able to give him the words she hadn't been able to share with anyone else, and she knew without question he would understand. Cecily didn't know how this could be, but she was happy, happy in a way she had not felt for a very long time. He even helped her shape time differently so they mastered the minutes of their company. Cecily found with Sam time didn't move too slowly or too fast—in a certain way time didn't matter because she didn't care what would happen in the next day or even the next hour.

He had seemed so hesitant during their first lesson. He barely looked at Cecily when he spoke and he stood over her pointing at the music instead of sitting with her. She thought it was because he didn't really want to teach her, that he was acting as a favor for Mae. He asked her about her musical knowledge and she felt silly admitting she sang in church, but only when she could mimic the good voice of someone behind her or near her in a neighboring pew. She didn't know how to find the notes on her own.

"That's not bad," Sam said. "It means you have a good ear." He took a piece of paper from his briefcase and, using the piano as his desk, drew on it a set of lines and a series of black dots on sticks. Then he marked each dot with a capital letter.

"Here are the note names for a treble clef staff," he told her. "Let's start with that."

Cecily looked at the paper then put it up on the stand in front of her on the piano. She folded her hands in her lap and waited.

Sam cleared his throat. "Miss Cecily, you have to put your hands on the keys. This way."

"Oh!"

He placed her fingers over the keys and pointed out middle C. Then he pointed to the dots on the paper. "That's this note here. Your fingers cover the keys like this. Here's how you do the first part of the scale."

Sam's fingers, curved and strong, met Cecily's and tapped over the keys in a tiny dance.

"Let's just do the right hand for now. You try it."

She touched the keys softly, and the sound from the piano emerged just as quietly. Suddenly she needed more thought to make her fingers move independently of each other, but soon they did in an awkward clawlike motion where one finger seemed determined to high-step over the others. She managed to strike one key after another and she could hear the partial scale expressed beneath her fingers. She looked up at Sam and smiled.

He stepped back as though stunned. Then he nodded.

"Yes, that's it. Here." He came around the piano and perched on the edge of the bench. Cecily slid over to make room for him.

He took hold of Cecily's right hand and she felt a shift like a tiny spinning wheel in the bottom of her stomach. His hands felt impossibly soft and she wanted her fingers to stay there, warm and enveloped like under the blankets in bed. She smelled the starch in his shirt mingled with a dash of a spicy cologne. The scent seemed to awaken her, just as the porter on the train to Anselm had done all those months ago, to tell her she had arrived—and not arrived at any old place, but at home.

Sam shaped her fingers and moved them in his own so she could get a feel for how she should touch the keys.

She worried about Mama and how she could easily crush this feeling and break Cecily up into little unknown pieces again like when she had taken her back from Anselm. But she tried not to think too much about that possibility nor did she trouble herself with what she and Sam could become. She only cared about the golden hour they shared each week sitting next to each other. She carried the little slip of paper he had secretly given her tucked into an inner fold of her pocketbook. In moments when Mama was occupied, Cecily would take out the paper and read it over and over.

Cecily,

From now on whenever I sing, I sing for you. I love you.

Sam

This paper should have sparked so many questions in her: What did it mean? What could they do? Would they ever be together? And those times when the week wore on and she did not have the opportunity to read the words as much as she wanted, these questions did needle her. But then Thursday would come and they would sit at the piano and all of the questions fell away. Sometimes she could even enjoy the lesson and pay attention to what he was telling her. But usually she was working to hear what he couldn't tell her, looking for messages he might try to pass to her. Her playing suffered for it, she knew, but that was all right. She practiced more during the week.

Dear Sam,

I just want to keep saying thank you—I want to write it over and over again all over this paper. I love you, Sam! I will work hard, I will become a good piano player because I don't want to give Mama cause to send you away. Please let me know what else I can do for you. You make me feel like I can do anything.

Yours truly,
Cecily

After each practice Sam would write out a list for her of what she had to study that week. One day when she opened her book to practice, she found two sheets of paper instead of one. The one was her list. The other taught her what it meant to feel delight.

O Cecily!

Did you know your name feels like a song on my lips? I sing it every day and I thought I was a happy man. I thought it was enough. But now I know you love me and my cup runneth over. What can we do? The way I see it, we can only take what God gives us for now. You keep being you, I'll keep being me. We'll find our way, I just know it. Write to me again.

Your Sam

Their lessons changed after that letter. He brought her beautiful music, even if it was beyond her capabilities, so he could play it for her. They would begin with Cecily's scales and exercises to keep Mama from being suspicious. Then quietly Sam would begin a song and whisper the words to Cecily as though he were wrapping each lyric in a cloud and presenting it to her as a delicate gift. On the day he sang "Nature Boy," Cecily's heart broke and re-formed, broke and re-formed, over and over until he was done. The song seemed like a secret, one that explained the world to her with a single line:

The greatest thing you'll ever learn
Is just to love and be loved in return.

How far had the boy gone to learn this? "Very far," the song said. Cecily counted herself lucky because Sam came to her each week to deliver this message and prove its truth to her.

Their letters continued. She slipped her letters into his coat pocket—Sam was careful to hand his coat to her before Gideon got his hands on it. He would leave his letters for her between the pages of her music books in her piano bench. Mama praised her eagerness to practice when really Cecily tore through her materials in search of his handwritten sheets.

Dear Cecily,

Did you wonder why I acted so strangely at our first lesson? I was afraid! You have this light in your eyes, did you know that? It's like you're seeing every-thing in the world for the very first time! I didn't know what I would look like with that light shining on me—I was scared of how you would see me. You might think I'm just some shiftless club singer moonlighting at your church. Or worse—someone trying to take advantage of you, someone not to be trusted. But when I finally got the nerve to look in your face—damn! So much trust and honesty in your sweet face! I realized all I had to do was be the man you deserve and you would see it—you would see me with all your beautiful mercy and grace. And I knew I could do that. You fill me with such hope. Do you know that?

Until next week,
Sam

Dear Sam,

All this time I thought I was doing something wrong! I was embarrassed because I didn't know what I was doing and I thought you'd tell Mama she was wasting her money. I don't know what to say about all you write. I see things with my eyes, just like anyone else. But you do feel familiar to me, like I've been waiting for you. Does that sound crazy? I just know Mama wouldn't understand. How can we make her understand? Maybe we should wait until she knows you better to tell her about us? But what do we tell her? We have to be careful, she's always watching us, even when she's acting like she's not.

You make me feel like I did when I lived in Anselm with my aunt and uncle. I felt like I knew my own mind there, and my aunt Pearl treated me like I did too. Maybe life just moved slower there and I had time to think about things and take it all in. Here nothing makes sense and everyone moves too fast for me. I feel stupid—I can never catch up. But you slow time down for me. You make me feel like life is fine—it's going to be all right. And it will, won't it?

I love you,
Cecily

For all their writing, though, it was that first small note Cecily reread the most. It was easy to conceal so she carried it with her. The longer letters she returned to the piano bench, but the first note was her touchstone, the proof that told her the reality of Sam's love. Knowing he loved her, she could tolerate going all over the city with Mama for dance lessons and shopping and boring tea parties during which she couldn't keep herself from yawning. If at the end of the day she could pull out that slip of paper and read it again, she knew she could do anything. Sam sustained her, helped her hold her head up and walk the way she thought a woman might walk.

Yet her heart ached, because she couldn't say her love out loud. She thought her chest would burst with the joy and sorrow welling up within her. She yearned for a friend with whom she could sit and whisper or laugh. This someone could read Sam's letters with her and say whether they both decoded the same meaning from his words. She could then tell Cecily what to write in her own letters so she could reassure Sam with every word she committed to ink. Cecily missed her aunt Pearl. She missed their talks at the kitchen table as they worked their hands through mounds of dough, or in the backyard folding sheets freshly dried off the clothesline. She wanted to ask Aunt Pearl if one day Sam would tell her the same story over and over again, like Uncle Menard did with Aunt Pearl. Would Cecily be able to laugh with such joy each time he did? She didn't know the answer, but she did know she was more than willing to learn it.

When she read his letters, Cecily pictured Sam, his fingers folded around the pen, and how he must sit hunched over the paper, same as her, and line by line, how he wrote her and their love into being. She wondered if it was the same for a painter watching a scene come to life out of the colors underneath his brush. It must be the same kind of magic, exactly the same. How else could she feel so divine, so created herself?

Was this what Mama always feared, that someone like Sam would come along and re-create Cecily into a person Mama didn't know? But how much was creation and how much was this Cecily already changing? Was this what becoming a woman really meant? Because it seemed to her Mama kept looking for the little girl in Cecily, and Cecily was having a harder and harder time locating that child herself. When had she put down her Ruthie doll and forgotten to pick her up again? When had she stopped thinking about penny candy, and how long she could hold a lemon mint in her mouth before it melted on her tongue? And when had the fairy-tale prince stepped out of her childhood books and taken the shape of Sam Delany? Sometimes it seemed it happened over the course of years. Sometimes it seemed it all happened with a single breath. But it didn't matter because there was no turning back. She had stepped through a door and heard the echo of it closing firmly behind her.

CHAPTER 21
Mae

Harlem, June 1947

Mae paused on the steps outside the Vaughn brownstone and listened. Cecily would be in the middle of her piano lesson with Sam and Mae knew the next set of notes floating through the parlor window would tell her how far the teacher and his pupil had progressed. If she heard some insipid childish music she would know Cecily was still immaturely banging away and Sam was carelessly letting her do it. If she heard anything resembling a real tune she would know Sam was being respectful and dutiful—but not what Mae needed him to be.

If, however, she heard "Nature Boy," even if it was just one line, Sam was better than she had given him credit for, because it meant he was actively, furtively pursuing Cecily. Whether the silly girl knew it or not would be another matter, but Mae wouldn't worry about that just yet. She knew to ignore the hard spot on her heart, the part of her that didn't want Sam to play the song, couldn't bear the thought of his light directed so wastefully. It thumped in a way she found distasteful, even shameful, because she had no use for it. She dispensed the unwanted energy by tapping the stone stoop rail impatiently with the palm of her hand. Mae didn't like having to depend on the actions of others. One person, at most two, could be moved as she pleased. Any more than that and she had to spread out her chances and gamble on what they might do on their own.

Val should have accommodated her; it was as simple as that. The disappointment he had caused struck deep, shockingly so. But she wasn't ready to cut it off with Val—not yet. She needed him to come back to her.

She would have cursed Val's name but then the notes came. They listed out slowly, with hesitation, and held a kind of quiet sweetness. The tune was not "Nature Boy," but still Mae felt a gladness that made her confident as she continued up the steps. When she entered the parlor she took in the scene with satisfaction. Gladys sat on the other side of the room, her eyes focused only on the yellow yarn in her hands as she crocheted. Sam and Cecily sat side by side on the piano bench, their thighs just touching. Mae saw Sam place his right hand on top of Cecily's and noticed how slowly one of his fingers slid down the skin of one of the girl's.

"No, Cecily," he said gently. "Start here. This note."

Cecily said nothing, her gaze locked on Sam as she began playing again, this time hitting every other note wrong. Mae grimaced at the sounds but inside her heart leapt. It was time for her next move. She observed one moment more before blaring out her own bright "Hello!" and enjoyed the way Sam and Cecily jumped in their seat. The warm rose color spread fast over the girl's face.

* * *

"ARE YOU READY?" Mae had proposed the shopping trip a few days ago. The timing had turned out better than she had expected, especially when, after waving goodbye to Sam, Cecily dissolved into a melodramatic mess in the car. Mae said nothing. She crossed her legs and looked out the window. Cecily performed some crazed combination of giggling and sobbing. Mae sighed as though such displays were a common occurrence in her car, no different from a passing storm. She only had to wait for it to end—and they always did.

Mae leaned forward.

"Stop in the park," she told Lawrence. "Miss Cecily and I are going for a little walk."

"Yes, ma'am."

Mae smiled, as this change in course was enough to bring Cecily out of herself. The girl sat up and looked around as though she'd forgotten where she was. Mae squeezed Cecily's knee.

"Feel better?"

Cecily shrugged and nodded and accepted the handkerchief Mae offered. "Why are we stopping?" The car slowed on a tree-lined drive in the northern end of Central Park.

"Because you look like you could use the air," Mae said as Lawrence came around to open the door. "And a friend."

Cecily stepped onto the paved park path and began a fast trot as though she were on some expedition to the other side of the world. Mae stood by the car and watched as the girl, her head down, marched on for several steps before realizing Mae wasn't beside her. She looked back, embarrassed.

"Cecily, where are you rushing off to?"

She looked around, helpless, not knowing what to say or even how to stand. Her hands flew about in front of her, clasping and unclasping, in search of a place to settle. "I'm sorry."

Mae strolled to Cecily at a luxurious pace, her heels hitting the pavement with the steadiness of a metronome. Mae wondered if the girl could hear the rhythm. Would she ever be able to, or even desire to, imitate it? When she reached Cecily she took the girl's arm and Cecily, as though learning how to dance, tried carefully to match Mae's gait.

"Now," Mae continued. "What was all that fussing about?" She took Cecily by the elbow and guided her over to a shadier side of the walk.

"Sam loves me!" The words poured out of the girl like a glowing stream and her arms splayed out wide so she could splash in the depths.

Mae wanted to laugh at this but only raised an eyebrow. "Does your mother know?"

"No! I'm scared to tell her. I know she has plans for me."

They paused for two boys chasing a ball kicked across Mae and Cecily's path. Mae watched them thump over the grass. Then she nodded to Cecily.

"Including marriage."

"Marriage!" Cecily wiped her damp forehead with the back of her hand.

"She didn't tell you? Frank Washington. You must know him . . ."

"Sure, he comes around the house a lot. Mama always wants me to spend time with him. He seems nice but . . ."

"But what?"

Cecily flailed at the air with her hands, searching for words. "He's so old!"

Mae shrugged and crossed her arms. "Be that as it may, he has a bank account full of very young money. And poor Sam doesn't have a cent to his name."

"What am I gonna do? You have to help me, Cousin Mae. I don't wanna marry some ugly old man!"

Again, Mae suppressed a smile. Walking with the girl brought on a sting of memory, one full of intimacy and knowing. She muffled the thought and shoved it to the back of her brain. She needed to focus. The emotions of the young were so volatile—Mae knew she had to lay the bricks for these next steps carefully. The trust was already there. The affection for Sam? Clearly present. Mae need only work the wires just enough to get Cecily to act. But she mustn't make her overact. She mustn't run to her mother or make some ridiculously desperate declaration to Sam. Cecily had to be given enough support, enough hope, to see that moderate action was all that was necessary to get what she wanted—and what Mae wanted.

She stopped and put both hands on Cecily's shoulders. The warm breeze blew their hair in their faces. "You really think you love Sam?"

"I do! And I know he loves me. We write to each other all the time."

Mae frowned. "You do? How do you do that without your mother knowing?"

"I put mine in his coat pocket when I'm hanging it up. He leaves his letters for me in my music book in the piano bench."

Mae couldn't help but smile then. There was pride in the way Cecily revealed this bit of information—that was good. Mae decided to feed and boost this little failing.

"Very clever! Did you write to him today?"

"Yes!" Cecily kicked at a rock on the walk. She skipped a little into the air. "I didn't have time to say much. I told him I loved him and couldn't wait to see him again."

Mae wanted to shake her head but held still. This girl's blend of ingenuity and stupidity seemed to have no end. "Well, perhaps there's something we can do . . ." Mae trailed off and waited for Cecily to pick up the thought.

"But what?" Her arm shook in Mae's with her trembling.

"I could work on changing your mother's mind. It would take some time. She really has her heart set on you and Frank."

"You can do it, Cousin Mae! Mama always listens to you."

"Oh, but this is very different, Cecily. There's nothing obvious to turn her against Frank, and there's even less reason for her to think Sam would be an appropriate match."

"You'll try, though, right? Please tell me you'll try! I don't know what me and Sam would do if you don't!"

Mae paused and carefully placed her eyes elsewhere: on the shiny black paint of a lamppost, on the face of the white police officer who did not tip his hat to them, on the polished body of the Packard coming slowly around a curve as Lawrence drove up to meet them. She released a heavy, purposeful sigh.

"All right, Cecily, I will try. But you and Sam must help me. You can't give your mother anything to be suspicious about. And you have to promise me to be on your best behavior with each other—no sneaking around or being alone with him."

"Oh, you can trust us."

"How can I really know that, Cecily? It's so hard to control yourselves, young love and all."

Cecily began to pout.

"All right, let's do this. From now on you must tell me everything and show me everything he writes to you. Only then can I be certain your mother won't have anything to hold against you."

She stopped and placed a hand on Cecily's shoulder. This time Mae's smile flared cold and sweet.

"And I mean everything. Do you understand? You must trust me completely so I can trust you."

"Oh, of course! Thank you, Cousin Mae! Thank you! Thank you!"

They were in league now. The shared secret sealed it and Mae's triumph seemed reflected in Cecily's grateful glow.

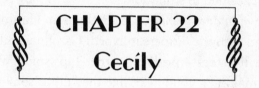

CHAPTER 22
Cecíly

Harlem, June 1947

Now that she knew she was expected to marry Frank Washington, Cecily's tendency to be nice to the man waned as her impatience thickened. He had the annoying habit of visiting right before her music lessons. This gave her precious little time to write to Sam and place the note where he could find it. On this particular day Frank was asking her about her cooking and how much she had learned during her time in the South.

"We used to have a cook who was from Alabama," Frank said. "She'd go home to visit her family and come back with a haul of fresh peaches. She'd make us peach cobbler with some of them and can the rest so she could bake with them all winter. Do you know how to do that?"

"What?"

"Can food, in jars. Like preserves and tomatoes and collard greens."

"Oh." Cecily thought about the pots of boiling water and

how she and her aunt had waited for the jar lids to seal. It
seemed far away and had little to do with sitting in her mother's
parlor in Harlem. What she did notice was how Frank Washington just seemed to smile at her.

All this man does is smile, Cecily thought. He smiled at her
like she had seen the farmers in North Carolina smile at newly
purchased livestock—pride in ownership, smug with themselves for making a good deal, like they'd put something over
on someone. Frank Washington's look made her feel penned
up like livestock. How different from the way Sam looked at
her. She barely heard Frank talk for thinking about it.

Sam made her feel like a locked-up part of her—a part she'd
never known was there—had been let loose. It made her feel
like her muscles didn't know how to work anymore, like she
could fall down just at the sight of him. And when playing the
piano her fingers never found the right notes when he was so
near.

When her mother finally walked Frank to the door, Cecily
rushed to the table. She could barely think what to write so she
scribbled the words she was already saying to him in her head:

Dear Sam,

> *Did you see that moon last night? A moon like that
> in the South would make the grass look blue! I hope
> we can walk in the night like that sometime. I have to
> write this fast. I wish we could talk in the open. Write
> to me soon.*

C.

She folded the paper quickly and stuffed it in her pocket and leaned against the wall to still her hurried breathing. He would be here any minute now. She remembered how excited she had been to find his first note in the music book, and how amazed she'd been to see her name in his handwriting.

These sheets began to fill the bench and she would feign practicing but really she would be studying the loops of his handwriting. It had the unusual feature of slanting backwards, from left to right, like the letters were falling back into each other's arms. Then, how precious to see her name written out in those very loops, her name laid out under his hands, as though her name and, in turn, she herself, were clay about to be remade into something more, perhaps something beautiful.

CHAPTER 23
Val

Mercylands, June 1947

The pile of baseballs had dwindled down to six or seven, all nestled in the grass at Val's feet. He picked one up, tossed it into the air, and swung through. He watched the ball sail across the green before turning his head toward the house. He hadn't seen Elizabeth all day. At first he was annoyed when Annie appeared in the dining room at breakfast to deliver Elizabeth's thin excuse of having a headache. Being disappointed was childish, but he had been looking forward to the pleasure of sparring with her in silence—watching her try to avoid his eyes, listening to her talk quiet nonsense to Aunt Rose so she could pretend she was all right.

Last night he had gone to the trouble of writing a note to her. It took a few tries because he thought he sounded too angry in the earlier attempts. Maybe he was a little ticked off—he had every right to be, she had run from him like he was a dog chasing her—but he didn't want to expose himself to her like that. He had slipped the folded piece of paper under her door himself. He knew he couldn't send Sebastian. What if she opened the door to give it back? He wanted to be there for the chance to argue with her if she resisted. The finished note read:

Dear Mrs. Townsend,

I can't believe I'm doing this—sneaking down the halls of my own aunt's house! Slipping notes under a bedroom door, which is what I'll have to do with this because after tonight I know you won't accept it from my hands. I won't sleep tonight, that's for sure. How could I after seeing that look on your face? You looked afraid and I don't get it. What do you have to fear from me? I only admitted—in a moment of weakness you don't even seem to pity me for—I love you. That's all I did and I see you're gonna make me pay for it. I should have kept my mouth shut and kept doing what I was doing: enjoying the love and letting it work its power on me. Did I even bother you before? No. I was happy to watch you, a perfect woman in body and spirit, and to behave for once like a man who might deserve you. I can't even do that now.

Look, I'm writing this to say I'm sorry, but who's really the wounded party here? You tell me, Mrs. Townsend. You tell me.

V.

When he put the note under her door nothing happened. It was after midnight, but he knew she was awake. He heard her pacing the floor. He'd thought he would see her at breakfast. She disappointed him, though, and didn't come down. She took lunch in her room too.

Then he realized his note might be *keeping* her away. She might be trying to figure out how to answer him. He laughed to think of what she might say in a letter. He imagined her bending over backwards with every word to make sure she appeared proper, to not give him any ideas. He almost felt bad for her. She would work so hard on something that had no chance of succeeding with him, at least not in the way she wanted.

But, really, he had no hope for a letter, not yet anyway. That's why, he reasoned, she had to come downstairs sometime soon. She probably wanted to confront him, to make a stand for herself.

He bent down and picked up another ball. When he straightened up he caught the motion of yellow—her yellow shirt—just out of the corner of his eye. She was walking on the paths near one of the garden beds. He dropped the bat and walked toward her. Val removed his batting gloves as he approached and after a few moments he realized her movement had stopped. She saw him—in fact she was staring at him, hard. He noticed how she didn't look to run away, but held her arms straight down and resolute beside her. Yes—he was going to love this.

"Mrs. Townsend!" He happily drew out every syllable of her married name. "Where have you been hiding all day?"

"What? Is that supposed to be a joke?" She seemed to dance

a little, shifting from one foot to the next. "How can you ask me that after what you pulled last night? You're as bad as people say you are! Worse!"

"Now, wait a minute! You saw my note." He stuffed his gloves into his back pocket and held out his arms as though to prove he had nothing to hide. "What did I do? What did I do that was so bad? I didn't even try to kiss you! I told the truth. I stated a fact, that's all I did."

Her hands balled into fists she pumped down at her sides. Her chin jutted up toward him. "So you say, but that's what's so bad. How can a man like you even understand real love? I'm married and the only reason I can see for you to say something like that would be to mess with my peace of mind."

"Oh, I understand love." He crossed his arms and lowered his chin so he was almost looking down on her. "Just not the way you do. I see it as a bigger thing. Bigger than the world. Limitless. It's a waste when you share that kind of love with only one person."

"I believe it's a waste when you don't. What's life about if you can't be devoted to one person? It's like each of us is filled with this special water." Elizabeth stopped and looked around her. She seemed to see what she needed just past Val and ducked behind him to grab a steel watering can. She dipped her hand into it and shook her wet fingers over the dirt. The water rolled into dusty beads on the surface of the ground. "You could sprinkle the water all over the place and see your drops dry up and disappear. Or you could pour it all into one place where it can make something live."

She grabbed the handle of the can and dumped it out fast.

The water splashed over Val's feet and made him leap away from her.

"Hey!"

Elizabeth threw the can aside and pointed at the ground between them. "At the end of the day, Val, did you make something live? Or is your water dried up and gone? That's how you measure a life."

Her face burned like the sun and Val almost lost control. He felt the strength drain from his legs and he wanted to collapse to his knees in front of her. He stared into her eyes, only her eyes, and spoke slowly to steady himself.

"But Mrs. Townsend, what if you've poured all the water in the wrong place?"

She frowned and blinked like she was hearing him speak in tongues. "What?"

"Come on! I've been running around this garden ever since I learned to walk. I know what a lot of these flowers look like in the spring. At first everything is just a bunch of green leaves. You can't tell what's a flower and what's a weed until they bloom."

"So?"

"So what if you watered what turns out to be a weed?" He waved his arms over the tall pink-petaled flowers nearest to him. "What if you watered a weed and it starts growing and spreading its seed and before you know it, there's even more weeds and they're choking the life out of every pretty thing in here?"

Val saw from her deepening frown he had aimed well. Whatever argument she'd been working on was gummed up in her head. Her mouth opened and closed. Then she dared try to dismiss him with a feeble wave of her hand.

"This is ridiculous," she said. "It doesn't matter. I have my place."

She walked away but Val, sensing ground to be gained, stayed with her step for step.

"Then what are we supposed to do, you and me?" he asked. "I think we have a situation here, don't you?"

She stopped and looked past him as though the answer were somewhere behind him just over his left shoulder. He loved this struggle, loved watching her try so hard to put a yes or no to something that too many women before her had decided to make easy and inevitable. The tension vibrated between them and Val's blood rushed like an ancient river through to his extremities. If he could have suspended her and himself in that space, in that moment, he would have done so gladly. He awaited her next words, and it was like watching a spark about to kiss the edge of a match.

He didn't expect to be burned.

She tilted her head so she could face him directly. She opened and closed her fists at her sides but the rest of her stood still. "I think you should leave. And if you won't, I will."

"Damn."

Val said the word softly, mostly to himself. She had taken advantage of him! He thought the question he asked was generous—he'd left plenty of room for them to talk in a comfortable way. But she used it against him. She had bunted when he was waiting for a full swing and now he was scrambling in the dirt to recover the ball. He decided right then and there that when this was all over and he bragged about her to his friends, he wouldn't stand for anyone feeling sorry for the little hellcat. He would tell them about this moment and how she gave even better than what she got. This, of course, had always been a danger, that she or even his aunt might make him go home. Last night had been a risk, yes, but he hadn't expected it to turn bad on him so fast. He stuffed his hands in his pockets and took a step or two back from her. He began to rethink his plans. He even surprised himself when he started to feel better quite quickly. Retreat wasn't always bad—in fact he might have an interesting choice of tactics that would work better at a distance.

"Fine." He measured out his words and gave each the proper weight. He nodded at her slowly. "I'll go. But I'm not taking back anything I said. You're not going to make me sorry for loving you. My love is a fact. It's gonna stay that way. Goodbye, Mrs. Townsend."

He turned and walked away from her—not too fast because he didn't want to seem agitated, and slow enough to give her time to take in what he'd said, then follow with her protest. It took her only a few seconds.

"But you can't love me! You have to stop!"

When she said the word "stop" he took it as a command. He halted his steps, faced her squarely, and shook his head. He even laughed a little.

"You are so mean."

Her eyes widened. "What? I'm mean?"

Val shook his head again and shaped his features into what he hoped would read as a mix of helplessness and frustration. Then he took what he thought was an inspired risk: his index finger shot out, full of accusation, and touched Elizabeth on the hard flat bone right above her chest.

"Loving you is the one good thing that has ever happened

to me, and you want me to give it up. That ain't right. And I'm not gonna do it. It's my love, it's my business, it's none of yours. Leave me alone."

She pushed away his hand. "Please! I'm trying to be a friend."

"Friend? You're saying we're gonna be friends? I wonder what that would look like." He scanned the grounds around them as though a picture might pop up and give him the answer. "I'll go back to the city, maybe write to you so we can stay friends."

"You can't write to me!"

"Oh, now you're gonna dictate terms!" Val laughed fully now and planted his fists on his hips. "I'm sorry, lady, but the mail is the mail! I can put a letter in an envelope with your name and address and a stamp on it and it gets delivered. Now, once it gets to you, you can do what you like. Read it or throw it away. You can't stop me from having that when you won't give a guy anything else."

Her chin dipped down to her chest and for a moment she looked like a scolded child. "Now you're making fun of me."

Val decided to dare again to touch her, this time on the shoulder, with his index finger. He liked how the motion seemed to lend a serious but not threatening tone to what he would say next.

"Look, I will go. I will write. And we'll see just how friendly this can be."

He disconnected himself from her and strode into the house. He thought he heard a muffled, exasperated sound squeak from Elizabeth's throat, but he didn't look back. He was done. She'd made her request, and he'd told her what to expect because of it. That was that.

He felt a tinge of anger that his leaving was so necessary, but what he sensed beneath his anger disturbed him more—it was a sourness in the core of his stomach and it made his insides churn when he realized he would not see Elizabeth the next day or for some time after. He knew it wasn't right to be feeling like that; it would be giving her too much control. But the fact that he had no control over it made him want to spit. He decided to focus on leaving and deal with how he felt later.

When Val returned to his room he found Sebastian bent over what looked like a large teapot on an electric hot plate. He wore white gloves and held, by its edges, a blue envelope. He suspended the back of the envelope over the wisps of white steam rising from the pot.

"What are you doing?"

"Sir, I think this letter contains the information about Mrs. Townsend you've been waiting for."

Val watched the operation. "How did you get it?"

"I got Annie to look the other way while I borrowed the mail. It has to be back on the hall table in thirty minutes."

"How much did she set you back?"

"Ten dollars, sir."

"Worth it," Val said, taking the envelope and throwing himself onto the sofa to read its contents.

He scanned past the sentences about church and volunteers and how hot the weather was until he came across his name and read the lines attached to it:

> *Honey, I hope for your sake Val Jackson is, as you*
> *say, minding his own business because you don't want*

*him in yours! That man poisons everything he touches
and he's usually touching other women.*

Val winced at the signature.

"Gladys Vaughn. Son of a bitch!"

Sebastian's gloved hands swiped the letter from Val's fingers
just before they clenched. A moment later and the paper would
have been crushed.

"I'll return this now, sir."

"When you're done with that, Sebastian, order the car." Val
rose and unbuttoned his shirt. He walked into the bathroom
for a shower. "Pack everything. We're going back to the apartment." He paused. "And call Louise. Have her drop by later
this week. Maybe Friday."

* * *

THE WHISKEY MADE the tip of Val's tongue feel like it glowed.
He lay back on the pillow and enjoyed the view of Louise's naked loveliness draped across the bed. He reached for his glass
and sipped again. The Louis Jordan song on the record player
drifted through the room.

*Early in the morning
And I ain't got nothing but the blues.*

He was glad he had sent for Louise. Being able to release his
pent-up energy into her willing arms made it easier for him to
focus.

"Why haven't you called me, Val?" Louise's thick black curls crushed against the mattress as she turned over and propped herself up on her arm.

He put his glass back on the bedside table. "I told you, I've been out of town."

She laughed, her head lolling back against the pillow. "But you didn't write."

He kissed her. "That's because you can't read."

"Oh you!" She pinched the lobe of his ear between her fingertips. "I can read!"

He stared at her. "You know, I need to write a letter right now. Here, you can help."

"What are you talking about? I'm right here."

"The letter isn't for you." The idea felt sweet as it came to Val's lips. "Just a minute." He slipped out from under the sheets and walked naked across the room to his desk. When he came back with the paper and pen he made Louise lie on her stomach. He placed the sheet of stationery on her back and sat next to her, his knees drawn up beneath him. He leaned into her ear. "Hold still," he whispered.

The paper was thick enough and Val found that if he angled the pen carefully it wouldn't poke through. As he wrote he thought how he liked the feel of the words, like he was talking to himself. Louise giggled.

"I said hold still."

"But it tickles!"

He filled out the page and found himself expressing what on the surface looked like a bit of hope. How would Elizabeth read it?

Dear Mrs. Townsend,

I hope you're sleeping well. I know I'm not. Ever since I left you I've been riding on love and it has taken me on a journey so satisfying that I can see and feel it all around me. Everything seems alive and soaked in love; even the desk I'm writing on now moves like waves beneath my hands. I wish you could see the world like this. You're probably mad at me just for thinking you could. I still don't understand why you made me leave my aunt's house, but see how well I can obey? This is what love does to people—it makes them better than what they are. I know you don't see that right now and I'm sorry, really sorry, you have me sitting on the bad side of your mind. I haven't done anything other than admit the truth, that I love you. And now I'm being punished for it. Just when I was feeling whole, like I'd been given a part of myself back, you cruelly took it away again. Of course this part is you. If I didn't know it before, I know it now because I'm writing this and feeling like I'm talking to you just as I would talk to myself. Are you my other self? I'll spend all night not sleeping and thinking about the answer. I will say this: it makes me feel good knowing morning will come soon. The light will open my windows and when I go to them I'll look into that rising sun and do you know what I'll see, Elizabeth? I'll see the possibility of redeeming myself in your eyes.

Yours,
Valiant Jackson

Louise laughed and nearly spilled bourbon in the bed when she read the part about being soaked in love. "My Lord, Val, is she going to get any of this?"

"Yes and no," Val replied. He carefully took the letter from Louise and folded it. This was in fact his exact hope.

CHAPTER 24
Elizabeth

Mercylands, Late June 1947

Elizabeth Townsend felt peaceful in the house after Val was gone. She watched from the library when his car rolled down the drive and out through the gates. As he drew farther away, a calm settled over everything. She sighed and allowed a bit of satisfaction to permeate her being. She was, after all, the victor left in possession of the field.

As that day passed, though, and then the next, she was uneasy to find the peace of the house was not reflected within her. She slept badly. One night she dreamed she sat in a museum exhibition staring at a massive baroque painting teeming with huge naked men and women. The people seemed overblown with flesh and their corpulent bodies crawled, caressed, and toppled over each other. But the canvas, enormous as it was, could not contain all the voluptuousness and Elizabeth was horrified to watch the figures spill from the frame. Heaps of skin, a sea of humanity, rolled and bubbled at her feet. Suddenly a swarm of thick fat fingers grasped her ankle and Elizabeth could only suck in breath—she couldn't even scream—before the hands pulled her into the void. She awoke feeling sick and filthy.

Elizabeth was walking up and down the length of Rose's library considering this dream when the mail arrived and Annie placed an envelope in her hands. Elizabeth recognized his handwriting at once. She said, "Thank you," and immediately took the letter to the terrace to read. Somehow she knew she needed to be outdoors with space to breathe just in case something did come out of the envelope that would consume all the air in a room.

She thought the words had a perplexing strangeness to them and suspected Val was making fun of her. She noticed he addressed her in the beginning as "Mrs. Townsend," but by the end she was "Elizabeth." Had he ever spoken her name before? She began to walk through all their past encounters in her mind before she stopped herself. She didn't need to do that. Why should it matter whether or not he'd ever called her by name?

But in thinking this she found herself wondering what her name would sound like coming from his mouth. She imagined he would smile, always smile, when he said it, and that brought her to thinking about his smile. He didn't smile the way other men smiled at women—either out of politeness or from a rude absence of mind from being caught up in indecent thoughts. When Val smiled there seemed to be something of pleasure about him, that he was truly enjoying what he was doing or what he beheld. If this were true, what was she saying about herself? Was she blatantly assuming Val enjoyed looking at her, enjoyed her presence? If so, then she had to acknowledge, by her own thinking and observation, his actions toward her were authentic.

Elizabeth sat down on the terrace. It was quiet. There were no men trimming shrubs, no servants dusting and cleaning. Birds chirped in the trees across the lawn. She sat in the silence and told herself in asking him to leave she'd done what was appropriate for a married woman to do. She even smiled and wondered what Kyle would say about her thinking—was it clear? Was it logical? Did she deserve to put herself on trial, which is what she seemed to be doing, sitting there arguing with herself?

Herself.

Other self.

What did he mean by that?

Elizabeth read Val's letter again. He wasn't sleeping well either, but for entirely different reasons. At least that's what she wanted to believe. Why did he say she was his other self and what would it mean to be inexplicably bound to someone that way? She and Val were not the same, of course, but what if by some odd sort of miracle they were two parts of the same piece? What if she held his virtuous, faithful side while he possessed her darker aspects—parts of her she didn't even know?

Once more she tried to stop her train of thought. It was inappropriate, but it intrigued her. There was something about the letter that made her unable to dismiss it right away. He'd also used the word "redeem." She believed in redemption, but could any be found for a soul that had already fallen so far and so hard? And could she, Elizabeth, truly be a vehicle for such rescue? Could she redeem him with an honest show of friendship? Would he accept only her friendship or know how to befriend a woman when he'd spent his life using women?

But could this be her role, to teach him how to be a friend?

It seemed to her Val's view of the world was limited—black or white, win or lose, nothing in between. Such a view spoke to her of emptiness and lack, which she found sad because she knew the world overflowed with an abundance of spirit and love. If she offered Val just a little in the form of her friendship, would it be enough for him to sense abundance?

Elizabeth laughed and fanned herself with the letter. How silly of her to think she could teach Val Jackson about abundance by offering him only a little affection. But it did make her see the true nature of her quandary—to get involved with Val Jackson did have an all-or-nothing quality. His needs and her way of faith would not have it any other way. She reminded herself, though, that Val was a man, not a soup kitchen project. And she was not a minister or a saint. So in an all-or-nothing proposition she could give him nothing. He was not her responsibility—her heart and allegiance belonged elsewhere.

What she needed to pray over and confess was the bit of satisfaction feeding her ego. Val Jackson was known for his taste and reputation. Wasn't it something that he noticed her, was impressed by her, just because of who she was? It reminded her of that day reading Scripture in church, and being surprised by how many people she could touch just by reading about God in the way she read to herself. Val Jackson, if he was being sincere, felt moved to change his life just from Elizabeth's example. She felt some pride there, yes. She also recognized the need to tamp down that particular deadly sin.

. . . *see how well I can obey?*

Yes. He didn't argue with her, didn't try to stall a day or even a few hours with a manufactured excuse. He dismissed himself quickly, dutifully. She had witnessed him saying goodbye to Rose. She even thought his face seemed shadowed in sadness, as though he were truly unhappy to be leaving his aunt. She felt bad for him but, she thought, he should admit some responsibility in making her feel uncomfortable in the first place. How could he say he didn't understand? She refused to fall prey to this sleight of hand that would make his poor behavior disappear.

I love you.

Of course these words were part of his ruse. Even if he was trying to tell the truth she could only believe he was deceiving himself. She wondered if he ever thought about how long his love outlasted any of his conquests. Perhaps he honestly felt it at the time—she was willing to give him the benefit of the doubt—but she was sure he just as honestly let the love go when he was done with it. Elizabeth would not conjure anger with him for this, though, only pity. If this was what he did, repeatedly throughout his life, he must be exhausted by the cycle now, and starving from the spiritual famine brought on by such behavior. But this line of thinking only brought her back to where she was before—that this all meant it was inevitable he should show up hungry on her doorstep. What right did she have to turn him away? And did she really have the sustenance he required?

He'd signed the letter "Valiant"—a beautiful name. She wanted to believe somewhere within his heart there was the essence of something princely and noble. Maybe it was just a wish or a hope his parents had made for him in calling him that, just as her mother had made for her.

"Uriah."

Elizabeth breathed her mother's name and prayed for guidance. Then she wondered if it was necessary. Val was gone. Kyle would return and there would be no reason to be alone with Val Jackson again—she would never be in the same room with him other than at church. So everything would be just as it was before. To know this should have comforted her, but Elizabeth only saw a grayness descending like a fog on the horizon. Her tongue suddenly felt like sandpaper rolled up in her mouth. Her stomach contracted.

"I should burn this," she said out loud. But Elizabeth folded the thick paper once again, replaced it in its envelope, and tucked it into the pocket of her dress. Then she turned her back on the sunshine and entered the house.

The library desk, hewn from ancient oak, anchored the room with its size and gravity. Elizabeth circled it slowly, repeatedly, as though considering an adversary. The tips of her fingers strayed over the tray of stationery placed neatly at the top center of the writing surface, opposite the chair. She wondered if it would be all right to answer his letter. If she were to aid him, she thought, this might be the best way to do it—from a safe distance, with plenty of time to consider her words.

Yes.

And rules—there would have to be rules. If she kept matters clear, if she provided boundaries to help them both stand where they needed to stand, it could help. If she insisted he banish the subject of love from his talk and she was only a supportive friend for him and nothing more, then perhaps she could remain close enough to help him—and to learn what potential had taken root within her.

She sat down at the desk and removed a sheet of paper from the tray. She took a pen from the center drawer and held it suspended over the page. Then she found the words she wanted.

Dear Mr. Jackson,

I wouldn't be writing this, but so much of what you wrote to me was unfair. I have to defend myself. You made me sound small, unfeeling, and un-Christian. I am not mad at you. In fact I'm the one acting out of your best interest. I suspect you already know this. If you are to continue the path you began with Reverend Stiles you must see how I would only be a distraction and not the inspiration you seem to think. Please accept my decision—which you have honored well. Thank you.

I must also ask, if you insist on continuing to write to me, that you honor this request too: please stop bringing up the subject of love. If you want to be friends, truly, then the word "love" can't be involved. I'm sure you would want to say it is platonic love or Christian love or a chaste love, but I believe you would be trying to fool both of us. You wouldn't accept that— even if this is what you intend you'd try to turn it into something else eventually. Why go down that road at all? Anyway, once you get some rest I'm sure you will see all this more clearly.

God bless you,
E. Townsend

She was tempted to write more, to ask him directly what he meant by "other self" and so much else. But this was enough for now. She folded the paper, addressed an envelope. When she slid the letter into the envelope she found herself imagining him taking the letter out. She blinked to shake the vision from her mind but then a thought came in fast to replace it. She put the envelope in her pocket where his letter still rested and went out into the hall. Avery was carrying a tray of glasses toward the dining room.

"Avery, I'd like to get my car if that's all right."

"Yes, ma'am," he said. He tilted his head to the right as though he wanted to ask her a question, but instead he nodded. "I'll have it brought to the door."

She drove to the nearest town and parked next to the first postbox she saw. She got out and took the letter from her pocket. Once she dropped it into the box she felt a thump in her chest. She had released something and realized what would come next was already out there and out of her control. It also unleashed a time of waiting she was painfully aware of. Now she calculated the time it would take for the letter to be picked up and how long it would take to arrive in Harlem and then to his mailbox. How long would it take him to answer? How would he respond?

These thoughts played like a jazz record in the background while her existence at Mercylands continued. She gardened with Rose, took their usual walks, and enjoyed meals. But all the time she thought about how far her letter had traveled and when it would arrive beneath his gaze.

* * *

THREE DAYS LATER, on the first of July, she returned to her
room after a walk with Rose and found a small stack of mail
on the bedside table. There was a card from Gladys, a thin envelope from Kyle, and a few notes and invitations from friends
from church. There was also a thick beige envelope covered in
handwriting unmistakably Val's, the lines sharp and jagged
like lightning bolts. She dropped the rest of the mail on her bed
and opened his letter. She sucked in breath and covered her
mouth with her hand. What she read made her fingers and the
tops of her ears burn.

Mrs. Townsend,

*You know what I'm sick of? I'm sick to death of
people insisting on distinctions when it comes to love.
What kind of love is it? How stupid. What does it
matter? Does anyone ask what part of God they honor
most? Do you have to choose between Father, Son,
and the Holy Ghost? No! It's impossible because it's
one and the same.*

*Any love, if it is real, will tear apart bonds and
sever connections because such love sees how wrong
it is to demand singularity in the first place. Christ
even said so—He knew His brand of love would rend
hearts and families. But what would be left? An open-
ness so complete and so clear that it would mend even
as it rends.*

*I know you know this too. That's why you're tor-
turing me with this junk about not using the word. You
know how powerful it is—you know there's only one*

*love. So why are you messing with me about it? I can
act like my love doesn't exist. You want me to lie to you
like that? Because I can do it, I can lie to you all day.
My old self did it well. But I want to believe you want
something better for me—something better for my soul.*

*And since we're talking about truth-telling let's
get one thing straight. You talk about my reputation
and you have your friends warning you about me. But
you seduced me. I'm the one to be pitied. I didn't have
anybody to protect me from your radiance and your
kindness. Nobody reminded me to be careful because
I'd never known such a woman before. I'm completely
under your thumb. All I can say is I'll do my best to
please you. That's just how I love you.*

V. Jackson

She had done too much. It had been a mistake to write him,
she saw it immediately. She felt a kind of wildness wanting to
spring from her chest and argue with him on every point of the
letter. And once again he would respond in kind. It would never
stop. They would bounce their words back and forth like red
rubber balls until one of them gave up and she didn't see that
happening. She had to end this. She sat down and wrote:

Mr. Jackson,

*You've already made me regret writing to you. Your
irrational answer tells me I can't talk to you. I'm sorry
I even tried. You don't want to see how impossible this*

*is for me, how my whole life could be rent in two, to
use your words. But I suppose it doesn't matter. For all
your talk about redemption, you still act like a selfish
man and you don't even see it.*

*As I said before, I write in defense of myself. I won't
respond anymore.*

E. Townsend

But as the ink flowed from her pen she sensed a futility
about the words it formed. She knew she was the one tightening
the string. With every thought of him, with every pen stroke,
he drew closer to her, and she pulled the ties in such a way she
could see them becoming hopelessly knotted. This was already
the point where she needed to drop the strings altogether—
the point where it would be easy to do so. She could go back to
seeing Val Jackson as an interesting stranger and give him no
more or less notice than civility required. This was the safest,
most sensible plan. If he wanted to repent and live a Christian
life she could be satisfied to watch it happen from a distance. If
her mere example had been enough to put him on the path, she
surely wasn't needed as an active agent to help him complete
the journey, if that was indeed what was going on with him.

And yet the strings remained in her hands and Val Jackson
in her thoughts and she had to think seriously about why she
chose to allow him to remain. Something must be missing for
her, something he could provide in abundance. She wanted to
know what it was, but feared it at the same time. She finished
scrawling the note and folded it. She decided it must be worth
it—why else would she stand so close to the flame?

CHAPTER 25
Mae

Harlem, July 1947

Val got up again, the third time since the maid poured the coffee. He didn't seem to be capable of keeping his seat while relating to Mae the contents of Gladys's letters. She considered his story an interesting development, unexpected and delicious. She savored the energy that forced her wayward friend to pace up and down her living room. *So much potential.* Mae picked up her cup and blew gently into it. She knew she only had to move carefully, minutely, to channel Val's disappointment to where she wanted it to go.

"Your cousin messed me up good with Elizabeth Townsend and now she's gonna pay the price. That bitch will be one sorry mama when I'm done with her."

Mae said nothing and sipped her black coffee. She wouldn't make it easy for him. He had thrown away the opportunity that would have compelled her to do so. And he'd done it for another woman no less. He had to know he would have to make his offer up front and at the same time admit to his failure and his need to partner with her.

"Who is she to you, Val? Isn't she married to that lawyer, the one who's a deacon at the church?"

"That's her."

"I see." Mae put her cup down, folded her hands in her lap, and nodded her approval.

"Yes!" Val turned and smiled. "I knew you would. Elizabeth Townsend, pure as the driven snow, known for her rock-solid marriage, and so Christian they'd probably make her a saint if she died tomorrow."

Mae nodded again. "And how is it going? Not well I'm assuming." She picked up her cup and looked out the window. "She made you stay long enough to lie to me."

He went very still. She could sense it without seeing him. Then he took two slow, deliberate steps and stood behind her. He placed a hand on her left shoulder.

"It's not like that," he said.

She tipped her head to the side, enough to allow her cheek to brush against the back of his hand. "Where is Kyle Townsend anyway?"

"Handling a civil rights case in Alabama."

She turned and looked him up and down slowly as though she were a surgeon, knife in hand, considering where to cut first. She laughed. "She's stupid. She's married. You only have to step over some idiot husband to get to her. There's nothing special about that even if you did succeed."

He sat down and leaned toward her, his elbows braced on top of his thighs. "Okay. Yeah. I'd say the same if this were any other woman. But like I said, Mrs. Townsend is practically a saint. And I want her to stay that way. I want her to hold on to her goody-two-shoes beliefs and still hand her heart over to me. You can appreciate that, can't you, Mae? Betrayal—you're down for that, right?"

She put her cup on the table and leaned toward him. She put a hand on his knee and smiled. "Actually I find being cruel much more becoming. And so much more satisfying."

He took up her hand and held her fingers to his lips. "But for the time being I'm here and available."

"You'll help me?" His mouth felt warm and she suppressed the urge to devour him.

"I'm at your service, Mae." A slow smile spread across his face. "Always."

She pulled her hand away and sat up. He took the cue and made his tone more businesslike. "How is it going?"

She crossed her arms and frowned. "Slowly."

"That's what happens when you send in a rookie. Time for you to switch pitchers."

She looked at him with widened eyes. "Indeed? Well, that's convenient because I told Sam you would help him keep in touch with Cecily. Deliver his letters, that sort of thing."

"Are you kidding me? I'm not gonna be his messenger boy!" He got up and went over to the cocktail cart. He pulled the top off the bourbon, poured a splash into the glass, and drank it all at once. "Besides, why does he need someone to do that for him? It seems to me he's been keeping his hand in the pot all on his own."

A twitch of Mae's lower eyelid betrayed her annoyance but she recovered well, she thought, by dabbing her mouth with her linen napkin. "Well, yes, but that's all he's been doing. He's ridiculously inept. It's about to get a lot more difficult for him, though, and I'm hoping that will move things along."

Val shrugged. "Then what do you need me for?"

Mae sighed and stood. She joined him at the cart and took the glass from his hand. "I see I'm going to have to make this more interesting for you." She poured her own splash of liquor into the glass and drank it down.

"What are you talking about?"

She ran her fingers over the front of his shirt. "What if I made it possible for you to take care of my business and finish your own little project at the same time?"

"How are you gonna do that?"

She let her hand drop down to his belt buckle. She tapped on the metal with her fingernail. "Never mind what I'll do. Can you perform?"

He put a hand over hers. "You know I can."

She looked up at him. "All right then."

"All right, what?"

"Take care of this business. Then come back and get your prize."

Val's mouth split into a big grin. "You don't mean?"

"I do mean it. For us. Yes." She slid a hand behind his head and pulled him toward her so she could plant a tiny kiss just below his right ear. She felt his breath, a deep exhale fragrant with bourbon, against her skin.

"Now you're talking." He moved closer but she pressed a hand, firm and resolute, into his chest.

"I'll want proof, Val."

"Of course."

She smiled, pulled away from him, and moved back to the table.

"You still haven't told me how this is going to work," he said.

"Just wait."

The doorbell rang and she picked up Val's cup and saucer. When Justice came in to announce the visitor, Mae handed the items to her.

"Mrs. Vaughn is here," Justice said.

Mae pointed toward the set of French doors at the other end of the room and flicked her hands toward Val to shoo him away. "You'll see," Mae said to him. Then, turning to her maid, she said, "Send her in, Justice, but get rid of these dishes first."

CHAPTER 26
Val

Harlem, July 1947

Val slipped through the doors separating the parlor from Mae's library. He stood back just enough to see without being seen. Mae turned to him and smiled. Her glowing face sent a kind of fire to Val's knees and they nearly buckled. He gripped the edge of a large mahogany table behind him.

It had been two or three years after their first encounter at the World's Fair. Mae's husband, Brantwell Davis, had dropped dead of a heart attack right there next to Mae in their front pew at church. From his perch in the balcony Val had noticed Davis's head tip gently to the right. He'd thought the guy had been about to fall asleep and he'd prepared himself for a good laugh. But Davis had slumped over, his head landing heavy like a stone in Mae's lap. The shock had been sufficient enough to earn Mae the never-ending sympathy of every soul in the parish. And she repaid it a few weeks later by hosting a party open to the community to celebrate Davis's life. All of

Harlem, it seemed, had shown up to pay their respects. Val had attended the party and watched and listened. He thought soon he and Mae might get together, maybe even be a public couple. When he first saw her glide into the room, looking less than mournful with the generous curves of her body swathed in a forest green gown that draped around her shoulders and showcased the round tops of her breasts, his thought started to feel more like a hope. He even toyed with the idea of asking Mae to marry him.

He skirted the perimeter of the room, his ears tuned to the sound of her voice. When he finally decided to make his move and cross over to where she stood, he saw it—her face, staring straight at him with a luminescence like a beam that could have knocked him off his feet.

She smiled and he nearly dropped his drink. He had wanted to run to her then and fall to his knees and stay there, happy to follow her like a dog for the rest of his life. But before he could take a step, her look changed. It didn't last long—a few seconds at most—then a mask formed over her features, hardening her face into a warning sign Val clearly read as: *Don't you dare come near me.*

Val paused, his feet adhered to the rug. He was so stunned he didn't notice the man behind him, the one who stole up to him and whispered, "Sir?"

Val turned but before he got a look at the speaker, the man pressed a small card into Val's hand and disappeared, edging out and down the stairs toward the kitchen entrance. He looked at the card: a magnificent black swirl of ink formed the initials "M.M." An even bolder swoosh of handwritten ink added the word "Later."

But he didn't see Mae later that night despite waiting for hours in his car down the street for further instructions. A few days later she sent a note:

Don't worry, my love. Nothing will change.

They'd continued as they had before, enjoying separate pursuits and sharing the details in midnight sessions over drinks at her house. He hadn't cared, though, because it had been enough. It was who they were.

But as he stood in Mae's parlor Val saw that luminescence in her again, for just a moment, and he wondered if "later" would finally arrive. Would he have her in the only way he'd never had her before? The idea excited and scared him all at the same time. The scared feeling deepened when he saw how quickly Mae's smile disappeared. In an instant a deep furrow formed on her brow and she looked sad, even concerned. She turned this face to greet her loving cousin and right away took Gladys's hands into her own.

"Mae! What's happened? What's wrong? And why couldn't you tell me over the phone?"

"I didn't know what else to do. I thought that Cecily . . ."

"What about Cecily?"

"I was worried she'd overhear. And I knew you'd be so upset . . . I was afraid of what you might do when you heard."

"Heard what?"

"Gladys, calm down. It's just that . . . Well, I think something is going on between Cecily and Sam Delany."

Val nearly snorted but caught himself in time.

"Oh, you must be joking!" Gladys laughed. "How could

there be? They've never even been alone together. Lordy, Mae, why in the world would you think that?"

"Well, maybe your mailman's been drinking."

Mae calmly walked away from Gladys and sat at the table again.

"What makes you say that?" She moved toward Mae, her hands on her ample hips.

"Because someone has been delivering letters into the piano bench in your parlor. I happened to notice them the other day when Cecily offered to play something for me and she opened it to get her music. I didn't know what to think, but who else could they be from but Sam?"

Val watched, impressed. Mae suppressed a smile and the blood drained from her cousin's face. Gladys Vaughn exploded.

"I will whip the living daylights out of that gal!"

She bolted for the door, but Mae rose in time to restrain her. Val covered his mouth to stifle his laughter.

"Stop it, Gladys, you'll do no such thing." Mae gripped her cousin's fleshy arm. "I knew you'd blow up like this. Look, hear me out. You can't tell her I told you. One of us has to stay in her good graces so we can know the truth of what's going on, no matter what. Wouldn't you agree?"

Gladys looked a little unsure but said, "Yes."

"I'm glad you think so too. Now, I have an idea." She pulled Gladys back to the sofa and got her to sit. Mae did the same. "It might help to cool things off a little. Why don't you just take her out of temptation's way? Didn't you say Rose Jarreau invited you up to her house in Westchester?"

What the . . . ? Val, behind Gladys's back, began waving a frantic hand at Mae. He mouthed the words, "No! No!" She ignored him.

"Yes, she did."

Mae touched Gladys's knee.

"Then accept her invitation. Take Cecily out of the city for a couple of weeks. When she comes back we'll be deep into the fall season, there will be so many parties, so much to do that she'll forget all about Sam Delany."

Gladys took a heavy breath and nodded. "All right. I'll do it, Mae. You're right, honey, as usual. I'll do it. Lord help me if I didn't have you." She took Mae's hands and squeezed them. Then she hugged her. Mae winced over her shoulder. "I better go now so we can get ready."

"Remember, don't be too hard on her. And don't let her know you found out from me."

Val watched Gladys's chin bob against Mae's shoulder when she nodded.

"Yes, yes. I'll let you know as soon as we get back," said Gladys.

"Thank you, dear."

When she had gone Val threw himself onto the sofa. Mae came in smiling at him again.

"Why the hell did you do that?"

"Look, you were totally out of the game. I just put you back in! And what better way to counteract Gladys's meddling than you contradicting her in person?"

He crossed his arms and frowned up at the ceiling. He hated that she was right, but he couldn't be mad. After all, she'd just made it possible for him to win—and have her.

"You're something else, you know that?"

"I do know." Mae sat down, arranging herself next to him and allowing him to put an arm around her. He felt some pleasure in doing it. He took the chance to examine her profile. Her lips rested together in the line of a satisfied smile.

He asked, "How'd you get to be so . . ."

"So what?" She raised her dark eyes to his face and for the moment they looked soft and harmless.

"So . . . you."

"Oh, Val, you don't even know." She plucked a bit of lint from his pant leg. "Men get away with so much. They mess around with us and just burn our little lives to the ground. It was only a matter of time before a phoenix rose from the ashes."

She looked at him and smiled. "Let's just say I'm here to get back our own."

He nodded. That part of the story he already knew. He'd watched it play out for eight years. "Yeah, I get that. But I want to know how."

She leaned her head back against his arm and sighed. "This world wasn't made for women. Certainly not black women. My best friend got pregnant when she was eighteen. Her parents forced her to marry some idiot with money so they could keep up appearances. After that I could tell she was a prisoner. I saw the shackles holding her. She was frozen—smiled at me like she was a piece of glass. I promised myself I would never live like that, like I had to be grateful for whatever scraps of respectability got thrown my way."

"So what did you do?"

Mae shrugged. "I watched. I learned. That's the best thing about being undervalued—plenty of time to see and learn. I listened. I learned exactly what buttons to push to get a man. I learned what I had to say to protect myself. I studied the white women in New York and Paris to learn how to look respectable. I went down South for a while to taste the blues, music that taught me how to seduce." She laughed. "Then I went to church to learn how to lie about it all." She patted him on the thigh. "I'm good, Val. You know that. And I never lose. Some idiots, like that Paul Kingsley, had to learn the hard way."

Val raised his eyebrows. "Paul Kingsley? Isn't he that army sergeant who tried to break into your house?"

"Break in? We'd already been to bed! And it had been wonderful. I was looking forward to having him as a distraction for a few months."

"What happened?"

Mae waved her hand in the air like she was swatting away a fly. "He was getting dressed and he started talking like the simpleton he was. Saying he was going to tell his friends how he'd had the great Mae Malveaux and all that bullshit. Stupid, just stupid. He obviously didn't know whom he was dealing with." Mae laughed. "I just smiled at him then stuck my head out the window and started screaming. Of course he wasted time trying to reason with me. He probably could have been gone before the police arrived but then, as I said, he was stupid."

"And everyone thought he was breaking in to assault you?"

"Yes, of course."

Mae studied the ruby red polish on her fingernails. Val stared at her in wonder.

"But Paul Kingsley didn't just get arrested. He was court-martialed too."

Mae shrugged.

"He deserved whatever happened to him. My point, Val, is it's all about appearances. They believe me because I appear right. Like at church. They think I donate all that money because it looks like I do. How simple can it be? People prefer pretty pictures."

Val nodded. "You're the designated hitter."

"I score every time." Mae sighed. "No one talks; no one escapes."

Val raised a hand and touched her face. His fingers followed the curve of her jawline.

"Did I? Was that what happened with us?"

Mae raised herself up on an elbow and looked straight into his eyes.

"You . . . oh you . . ." She smiled and caressed his hand. "I knew you the minute I saw you that night at the World's Fair. I recognized my true equal. I said to myself, 'Mae, there is a man not fooled or held captive by the conventions of our time.' I saw us standing together on the mountaintop. I saw how we would bring down the world."

She fell silent but her brilliant brown eyes stayed locked on Val. He realized he had recognized the same when he first saw Mae—his equal. He always knew that to conquer her he would have to conquer himself. The scent of gardenia from her hair cast a veil over Val's mind. He dipped his head toward her. His mouth grazed the plump pink softness of her lips. Then Mae's hand, hard and cold like an armored door, slammed onto his chest.

"Now, you have to go," she said.

"Back to Westchester?"

"Back to Westchester." She pushed his arm away from her.

"Remember, we both want our revenge and that is where you have to go to get it. And finish that other little project—for us."

"Well, yes, but your star player could use a little warm-up session." He smiled and tugged at the sleeve of her dress.

She smacked his hand. "Then go home and take a hot shower. Whatever it takes. Goodbye, Val."

She lifted herself lightly from the sofa, swept out of the room, and was gone. The skin where she'd struck him stung.

CHAPTER 27
Cecily

Westchester, July 1947

The Buick sped north just as fast and smooth as the train that had carried Cecily south to Anselm all those months ago. This time, though, she didn't have the comfort of being alone to think clearly about what was happening. Mama sat next to her, resolute as a boulder.

Cecily tucked herself as far as she could into the corner of the backseat. She wanted to put as much space as she could between herself and her mama, but since Mama didn't notice what she was doing it was a feeble form of protest. Cecily's cheeks still burned with embarrassment. Why was she always going away, and in the direction opposite from where her life seemed to be headed? Mama had yanked Cecily out of the house like a carrot from the ground.

She pondered again what she might have done to expose herself and Sam to her mama's anger. Cecily had been getting ready for her lesson, but she hadn't been writing Sam a letter or drawing tiny hearts on the music sheets or any other silly notion she indulged in while waiting for Sam. She had, in fact, been practicing, her head bent over her hands, her fingers curved and trying to mimic the loose and easy way Sam's hands floated above the keys.

That day she had heard the front door slam and turned to see Mama rushing at her, same as she had rushed at Cecily and Royce before putting her on the train to Anselm. Only nothing slowed or stopped Mama this time. She ducked her head, leaned a heavy shoulder into Cecily, and shoved the girl off the piano bench. Cecily hit the floor on her left hip and elbow, the pain sparking tears in her eyes. She felt bad enough, like a baby sitting there rubbing her sore arm and mewling. But then her mother opened the bench and seized Sam's letters. She started reading them! The look Mama gave her— Cecily didn't know why she didn't turn to ashes right then and there, her mother glared so hard.

"Ooooh! No, Mama, no! Please, God, no!" Cecily cried. She managed to get to her feet and reach out to her mother like she wanted to explain but didn't know how. Really she wanted to run out of the room, but Cecily surprised herself by holding her ground, messy tears and all. She thought it was because she knew Sam would be there soon and whatever happened next, it would be best for them to stand together.

But she wasn't prepared for how badly her mother would treat Sam. She unleashed a torrent of un-Christian language and made Sam out to be some sort of lowlife who had crept into their house instead of having been invited.

"You must be out of your mind," she said, "if you think I'm gonna let my daughter get involved with some no-account club singer."

Sam, his face ashen, had stammered, "Mrs. Vaughn, I didn't plan on all this happening."

"All *what* happening?" She advanced on him, her hands on her hips. "Just what have you done?"

"Nothing! We haven't done anything!"

"Uh-huh, and that's how it's gonna stay." She shook a finger at Sam. Her whole body seemed to shake with it. "You get out of this house now. You don't speak to my daughter—you don't even look at her ever again."

As Sam left, Cecily thought the room seemed to darken, like a cloud had passed over the sun. In her mind she pleaded with him, *Don't go Sam, don't go. Stand up for me; don't leave me here.*

For about an hour Cecily was able to console herself by thinking at least she would be able to see Sam at church. Her mother couldn't ruin that chance; she couldn't make them fire the organ player. Only Mae could do something like that.

The thought of her cousin made Cecily suck in her breath. Mama was sure to tell Mae about Sam. What if Mae thought Cecily hadn't obeyed her instructions? She'd think Cecily had let her down and the thought was unbearable. She knew she had to write to her as soon as possible. Maybe, and this was a small hope that made Cecily feel just a tiny bit better, Mae could still help them. But then her mother barged into her room and told her to pack her suitcase. They were leaving to go to Rose Jarreau's.

In the backseat, Cecily sank deeper into a heap of devastation. She curled up against the car door and flipped the ashtray cover open and closed.

"Sit up, girl! Stop acting like you don't have any sense." Mama slapped Cecily's leg. Cecily did, but turned away to stare at the Hudson River flowing next to them on the road north. The water reminded her of Mr. Travis, but she couldn't think of him too clearly, not with Mama sitting so close to her. Cecily still didn't understand how Mama had found out about the letters. Who was to say Cecily hadn't given them away herself with a look on her face or a thought so vivid Mama could read it in Cecily's head as easily as if she were reading it in her eyes? Now she was being taken away again. Was this why Mr. Travis went out to the woods and into the water, because in his regular life he couldn't be in his body the way he wanted to be? Cecily had no way of knowing if this were true, but if it was, it seemed to her another way that the mysterious white man made sense to her—spoke sense, even, without uttering a single word.

When the car pulled through the gates of the Jarreau estate, both Cecily and her mother were shocked by the unusual sight on the vast lawn of a woman swinging a bat. She threw a baseball into the air, too high, and swung the bat at it like she was about to beat a carpet. Her body didn't seem to know how to move with the long piece of wood in her hands and she looked, well, silly. "Mama," said Cecily, rolling down her window, "isn't that Mrs. Townsend?"

CHAPTER 28
Elizabeth

Mercylands, July 1947

She had found the ball and bat while wandering the too-quiet house that day. Rose was in the library returning telephone calls so Elizabeth sat for a while in her room and read. But after only a page or two she wanted to move about. She paced around a little then opened the door and strolled the length of the hallway. She paused at the stairs and considered going back to her room but decided to continue down to the first floor and go outside. She discovered a foyer where the servants allowed certain equipment to accumulate: boots, raincoats, umbrellas. She was just about to step through the door when she noticed a baseball and a bat. Elizabeth quickly looked around, but knew she was being silly—Val wasn't there.

Often, though, it felt like he was there—quite present in fact. His letters didn't stop. Sometimes there were just a few lines on the same thick paper. "Thinking of you. Val." Other times they took on a playful tone. One of the letters, postmarked from Chicago, had gone on for pages describing nearly every single play of the All-Star baseball game he had attended at Wrigley Field. He complained about Jackie Robinson not being on the roster. On the bottom of the last page, in large block lettering, he had drawn "42" with arrows pointing to it. "Jackie Robinson's number!" he'd written. That did make her laugh. It looked like something out of a schoolboy's notebook. She liked how he was engaging in an activity he obviously enjoyed. But why was he so in love with the game? As far as she could see it was about knocking around some big pincushion of a ball with a hunk of wood. She supposed boys with sticks always wanted to be hitting something. That must be the natural attraction. When she thought of the boyish aspects of Val she almost regretted the harsh tone of her last letter. She must have sounded like a teacher scolding him.

She had hoped once he went back to the city Val would lose interest in her and start chasing some other woman. Wasn't that what he usually did anyway? She only had to wait him out.

She picked up the ball and bat and took them out to the lawn. She threw the ball up and tried to grasp the bat in the way Val had shown her, but she missed. She tried again, and again the ball fell to her feet as she swiped at the air. The third time she managed to make contact and, shocked by how the handle vibrated and stung her hands, she nearly dropped the bat. The ball scooted across the grass and she laughed softly. She realized she would have to retrieve it. She walked over, picked up the ball, and continued her way down the lawn. She kept trying to hit the ball, sometimes swinging badly, but she began to enjoy having something to do. She hummed to herself in the sunshine. *I want a Sunday kind of love.*

"Elizabeth!"

Sweat rushed into her fingertips. She knew she wasn't doing anything wrong, but in that moment she didn't feel right either. She put her hands behind her back and stuffed down the song humming in her throat. She turned and there was Gladys rolling toward her on thick and swollen ankles. A gentle warmth settled over Elizabeth like a cloak. She was glad to see her friend.

When Elizabeth and Kyle had started attending Mount Nebo, Gladys's had been the first kind face Elizabeth encountered in the sea of strangers. She had invited the Townsends to sit with her during the coffee hour and she chatted incessantly about the church. She had been delighted to learn they were also connected to Rose Jarreau and downright giddy when Elizabeth said she wanted to help out with the mission and outreach committee Gladys chaired.

"Lord, girl, you'd be such a blessing!" Gladys had crowed and thrown her hands in the air.

Gladys turned out to be a helpful guide to their new community. She knew everyone of importance and loved to talk so her information flowed freely. She was a widow with an empty home and time on her hands. Elizabeth soon learned having female company was the blessing Gladys really desired. She had sent her daughter, Cecily, to live with relatives in the South but, she confided, hadn't anticipated how much she would miss the girl.

"The house just seems so darn dark without her," Gladys had said.

Now here was the daughter, tall and long-legged, striding across the grass in her mother's wake but following slow and stoop-shouldered as though bowed by a heaviness.

Elizabeth dropped the bat and embraced Gladys's large and comforting torso. "What are you doing here?" She held Gladys's hand and noticed the shadow of sweat staining the brown floral-print dress just under her friend's armpit.

"It was just getting too hot in the city. I thought it might be a nice change for a bit to come up and visit Rose, isn't that right, Cecily?" Gladys smiled and waved her free hand in her daughter's direction.

Cecily, her chin down and her lower lip puffed out in defiance, said nothing.

"Let's go find Rose," Elizabeth said. She tugged Gladys's hand and they walked toward the terrace. "She should be done with her telephone calls right about now. I know she'll be happy to see you both."

"What about all this?" Cecily's voice, unfamiliar and high-pitched, startled Elizabeth. She and Gladys turned to see Cecily nudging the baseball in the grass with the toe of her black-strapped shoe.

Elizabeth stared at the ball and bat for a moment and ignored the tiny glint of shame creeping up into her cheeks. "Don't worry," she told Cecily. "Deacon or Avery will come out and put them away."

* * *

THAT EVENING IN Gladys's room Elizabeth sat perched on the side of the bed and watched her friend unpack her clothes. Gladys drifted slowly between the suitcase and dresser drawers, then from the suitcase to the closet, unfurling the fashionable swaths of fabric that were her dresses. She sighed as though she wanted to exhale the weight of the world's sorrow from her chest.

"What's wrong, Gladys?" Elizabeth reached forward and touched her friend's arm.

Gladys glanced up before she turned to deposit a neatly folded stack of white cotton underpants in her top dresser drawer. "Oh, it's Cecily," she said with her back to Elizabeth. Then, after turning around, she added, "I found out that singer I hired to give her music lessons has been writing to her. Teaching her about more than any damn piano!"

"What do you mean?" Elizabeth gripped the pale blue bedcover with her fingers.

"He didn't get her into bed, if that's what you're thinking. But she's acting like she's in love, the little fool. Like she has any idea what love is."

It was what Elizabeth had been thinking but she said nothing.

"My cousin Mae, it was her idea to bring Cecily here for a spell. Help her get over it."

Elizabeth's left hand floated up to her chest. *Love rends.* Is this what Val had been talking about? Cecily loved someone. The thought of it, to Elizabeth, felt young and optimistic, but from what she saw the results were far from favorable. This love had caused Cecily to be separated from the man. And there was a rift between Gladys and Cecily too. Elizabeth thought about the distance she had witnessed between mother and daughter as they walked across the grass that afternoon.

But Val had also said love mends. Where would the mending be for Cecily, divided as she was from those closest to her? Elizabeth felt sad for the poor girl. She wanted to hold her up to Val as an example—he was only half right. Love destroys. His

own imagined affection could only do the same. She was thinking about crafting a letter in which she sent him these thoughts
when Gladys startled her with the mention of his name. When
she heard it Elizabeth slipped her right hand, balled into a tense
fist, behind her back.

"Here I was worrying you about Val Jackson," she said.
Gladys shook out a dress and dropped it back into the suitcase
again. Her mouth was twisted into a tiny cyclone of dejection.
"And I didn't even know what was going on in my own house."

Elizabeth opened her fingers again and offered her hands to
Gladys. "Don't worry," she said. "We're all here together now.
You and Cecily will feel better soon."

Gladys came over and took her hands. The way she held
on to her made Elizabeth feel as though she were pulling her
friend from quicksand.

* * *

WITH GLADYS AND Cecily's paired presence, the house buzzed
with new life. The women took walks together, played cards
in the garden under a pink-and-white-striped canvas tent, and
sat sewing or crocheting well into the evening. At times Cecily
sulked, standing with her arms crossed, her eyes fixed somewhere beyond the gates of Mercylands. Elizabeth noticed that
whenever Cecily was like this Gladys, who always had something to say, increased her talkativeness as if she wanted to
make up for her daughter's silence.

Because of all this activity—or perhaps in spite of it—
Elizabeth found she craved silence once again. She took on the
habit of rising early and retrieving the ball and bat from their

storage room off the kitchen. Belle, kneading bread dough or washing strawberries, would nod at her when Elizabeth crossed the kitchen floor. Once outside she would toss the ball up, hit it (for she was getting good at knowing when to swing the bat), pick up the ball, and hit it again in the direction she was going. She would walk the grounds in this manner until it was time for breakfast. It was only during this time that she allowed herself to think about Val. His letters, oddly enough, had stopped the day Gladys arrived. She knew she should be glad of it, but she couldn't help but wonder why. Had he decided her lack of response made her not worth the trouble? Perhaps he really had found someone else to pursue. Elizabeth figured the latter was probably closest to the truth.

One day Elizabeth woke to the put-putting sound of motors. She heard the deep voice of Deacon, Rose's head gardener, barking instructions. She figured his crew was mowing the lawn and probably trimming the bushes too. She stayed in bed and enjoyed the rumbling of voices and the smell of cut grass when it reached her open window. Her room felt so pleasant Elizabeth decided to remain there. She rang for toast and tea. She also sent a message that she was fine; she just wanted to spend the morning reading and would be downstairs in time for lunch.

By eleven thirty Elizabeth had consumed her breakfast, showered, dressed, and read six chapters of Ann Petry's *The Street*. Then she prayed over the novel's pages once again because they reminded her of how bewildering the world was to her. All of Harlem gossiped about how well the author captured the neighborhood, but Elizabeth saw it as a sad truth. When she came to the part where Lutie had to leave her eight-year-old son home by himself so she could pursue a job, Elizabeth put the book down, heartbroken. When she finally left her room and walked downstairs the house still seemed as active as when she first woke. Elizabeth was even more curious when she found Gladys and Cecily going outside. The sound of more men's voices, and their laughter, rolled up from the lawn. Rose stood by the terrace doors and wrapped herself with a light scarf around her shoulders.

"I'm so glad Val has returned!" Rose said and smiled like a girl going to her first party.

Elizabeth frowned, glanced out to the terrace, and saw nothing. "He's come back?"

Rose laughed. "Yes. He probably just got bored being alone and sitting around with only the two of us. We're not good company for him, old as I am and you being married and all. But now he's brought some friends up from the city to play." She made a waving motion that seemed to indicate she wanted Elizabeth to follow her outdoors, but Elizabeth stood glued to the drawing room floor.

"Has he?"

Rose waved to her again and nodded and smiled. "But we won't be left out. He's invited us to watch."

Elizabeth felt like someone had thrown a cement block into the gearing of her brain and she couldn't quite process Rose's words. "He has? And you're going?"

"Of course, my dear. Come on, we don't want to miss the beginning."

Rose took Elizabeth's arm and together they walked out into a glorious sunny day. They went down the terrace steps, onto the grass, and out beyond the tiny slope where the yard opened up and leveled. Elizabeth saw, with wonder, the lawn had been transformed. The green had been cut short and brilliant white lines like confectionary sugar on the grass marked the unmistakable shape of a baseball diamond. Thick beige bases lay in their own chalk boxes and a man with a chunk of black strapped to his chest and what looked like a wire cage on top of his head swept home plate with a tiny hand broom. Men dressed in T-shirts tossed balls back and forth and caught them in gloves. Elizabeth saw Gladys and Cecily already seated at a safe distance from the field in Adirondack chairs. Two empty ones awaited Rose and Elizabeth.

"Ah, ladies! Welcome!" Val was jogging toward them from the diamond. Elizabeth saw drops of sweat along his hairline and his face glowed in the sun. He looked well, healthy, and she was glad, strangely glad, to see him so.

He took his aunt's arm from Elizabeth's and helped Rose into her chair.

"Thank you, dear," she said. Rose settled back into her seat, rubbed her hands together, and grinned.

Val presented a seat to Elizabeth and she, leaning toward him as she sat, whispered, "You said you would leave."

"And I did." He took her hand and gave it a quick squeeze before he dropped it. "But I kept thinking how sad it was you've never seen a baseball game. It's about time you did!"

Before she could say anything else Val delivered one of his brilliant, blinding smiles and jogged off to pick up the bat at home plate. He took a few practice swings, exaggerating the batting stance he had taught Elizabeth, looking back at her as he did. She held her features steady, determined to show his teasing would have no effect on her.

The first baseman, however, seemed to be the one annoyed by Val's antics.

"Man, quit messing around and hit the damn ball!"

"All right," Val said, waving him off, "all right!"

The pitcher threw the ball and Elizabeth jumped at the loud crack punctuating the air as bat hit ball. The women clapped their hands and Rose even cheered as Val ran the bases. "That's the way to do it, Val!"

And so the game went on. In the field Val executed a dramatic dive to field a ground ball. On another play, a man from the opposing team slid into home, was called safe, and Val and his teammates argued over the call for a good five minutes. The women laughed and seemed to relax even as the players proved how seriously they took the game. A phonograph set up in a nearby window piped music including "Let the Good Times Roll" and lent a festive note to the scene. Belle and Avery brought out cold chicken sandwiches and lemonade spiced with mint leaves. Everyone was having a grand time, and Elizabeth was relieved she could enjoy the afternoon as well. As the game went on she felt less and less the focus of Val's attention. He seemed to melt into the company of his male friends and little existed for him outside the white lines. After a while she stopped worrying about whether her face looked too happy or too pleased. It didn't matter how she looked because she had disappeared. Then she found herself wondering whether this was a good thing or not.

CHAPTER 29
Val

Mercylands, July 1947

Val Jackson, who measured every moment according to its usefulness in his plans, quickly noted Cecily lagging behind as she and the other women headed back to the house. He tossed his glove to one of the men clearing the lawn and moved to catch up with her.

He knew very well he was at the full-blown height of his power. His body felt energetic and strong, radiating his every note of charisma and beauty. Some of this, he knew, was due to his return, which he happily considered triumphant. Staging the baseball game had been a brilliant and necessary piece of inspiration. It allowed him to stake his presence in a fun and joyous atmosphere. If he had merely shown up and walked in on the women, at tea for instance, the resulting tension would have flowed enough to poison the whole room. Val pictured Gladys giving him the evil eye, nonstop, over the scones.

The game had provided the added advantage of Elizabeth

getting to see him again in a nonthreatening light. He was sure this would be enough to soften any pique she probably felt about him coming back. Yes, it had all worked so well. And now the baseball game had primed him for the bigger game to come. There was wonderful work to do, and he was ready.

He caught up to Cecily, touched her on the arm, and whispered, "Sam is gonna call tonight."

"When?" The girl was so easily drawn in.

"Midnight. Come to my room, I have a private line. It won't ring in the rest of the house. Don't be late."

He walked past her and joined Elizabeth, Rose, and Gladys, opening the doors for them as they went inside.

* * *

WHEN VAL DRESSED for dinner he put on his white jacket and wanted to laugh because he knew that by slipping on this coat he too easily stacked the deck in his favor. His deep brown skin, set off by the jacket, made him glow like polished mahogany. He knew Elizabeth would notice, Cecily would stare, his aunt would approve, and Gladys might even try to be nice to him. Val grinned to himself, grabbed his cigarettes, and went out to the terrace for a smoke before dinner.

Elizabeth was already there. In fact she seemed to have been there awhile, looking out across the grounds, lost in thought. Val was pleased to have the chance to give her the first look at him in his evening splendor. He stood in front of her and leaned against the stone casually as he lit a cigarette.

"It's almost dinnertime," he told her. "Everyone else has changed already. You better get a move on."

She turned to him and crossed her arms. Her mouth was a perfect thin line of reserve.

"Why are you still here?"

"Why are you so mad?"

"Because I can only be your friend and you don't want that."

"No, no, no, my dear Mrs. Townsend." Val shook his head and laughed. "That's not it at all. Don't you get it?" He drew on his cigarette. "The way I used to be? Yeah, I would've been your friend. Then in two hot minutes, maybe less, I would've been trying to make you into something else. But because of you, I'm different now." He waved the cigarette and the blue smoke encircled him. "I don't lie about love. Being your friend would be a lie. I'd be pretending my love doesn't exist. I'm sorry, but I can't do that."

She crossed her arms and shook her head. "Ha! Of course you can't. You just do what you want. You don't care what happens to me or my peace of mind."

"Your peace of mind?" He took a step toward her. "Elizabeth, I said I love you. That means I care about nothing but your peace of mind. If anything, I'm the one getting stomped on here because you sit there and act like you want to be my friend."

"Act like?"

"Yeah! Listen to how you're talking to me. What is that? Don't sound like a friend to me."

Elizabeth put a hand out in front of her. "Let's just stop right here because this conversation isn't getting us anywhere." She turned to go in.

"You're absolutely right."

She paused. For a moment it seemed she had forgotten what she was about to do. Without looking at him she said, "Mr. Jackson?"

"Mrs. Townsend? Yes?" Val leaned forward and waited.

"Nothing." She turned back to him, her face pale. "I'm sorry."

Val smiled.

"Look, Elizabeth, don't worry. We're two adults. We can be nice to each other, at least for a few days. I think we can handle that. We'll get by. Okay?"

"Okay."

She nodded and he thought her expression, with her long lashes downcast, seemed to soften.

"All right then. I'll see you at dinner."

* * *

THAT NIGHT, JUST before midnight, Val sat in his room silently, listening for Cecily's approaching steps. She would have to leave her room, make it down the hall past Gladys's room without being heard, then cross the landing that would bring her to the wing of the house where Val's suite was located. The conversation with Elizabeth lingered in his thoughts and the sweetness of it made him feel the slightest hesitation for what he was about to do. He tamped it down by recalling Gladys's busybody words and thinking about how he would have been much further along with Elizabeth if it hadn't been for Gladys. If she had minded her own business he wouldn't have to be in hers now.

Within a few minutes he heard the soft tapping of feet in

slippers approaching his room. He opened the door in answer to her quiet knock and noted her moment of shock when she saw he was shirtless under his robe.

"Has Sam called yet?"

Val put a finger to his lips. He pulled her in, closed the door, and pointed to the phone on his desk. As if on cue it rang and Cecily, delighted, ran over and answered it. Val, from behind, continued to watch her intently.

"Oh, Sam! I miss you so much! Do you miss me too?"

Val moved to the door and locked it.

The call lasted about twenty minutes—interminably long to Val but he knew how to be patient. He leaned against a wall near the desk and occupied himself with observing the thinness of Cecily's cotton nightgown and the light robe she wore that had fallen open as she spoke.

"When will you call me again?"

She listened.

"Okay, I'll be patient. But call me as soon as you can, all right, Sam?"

Cecily hung up the phone, and Val moved toward her so he could place himself perfectly in the wake of her glee. She clapped her hands and threw her arms around him.

"Oh, thank you, Mr. Jackson! Thank you so much! Sam thanks you too!"

"Now, hold on here! Sam doesn't have to thank me. But you can show me as much gratitude as you want."

"He sounded so great! I thought for sure he would be mad at me for letting Mama bring me all the way up here. But he said you told him it was only temporary and the best thing to do and he understands! How can I ever repay you?"

She crossed her arms and rubbed her left ankle with her right foot in a way Val found strangely endearing.

"Now, that's an interesting question. How can you repay me, Cecily? What do you have to offer?"

He took her elbow and leaned down to kiss her but she pulled back.

"What, not even a kiss?"

She stared at him a moment then tried to make a dash for the door. Val grabbed her wrist and clamped a hand over her mouth just as she was about to scream. He pulled her close and held her tightly so he could speak low into her ear.

"Why do you want to do that? Huh? What's gonna happen when they come? What are you going to say? It's after midnight. You're in my room! You came here on your own. I think they'll believe me when I say you knew what you came here for."

Her eyes widened and filled with tears, but she nodded to show she understood. "What do you want?"

"Well, to take you up on your offer. To be thanked. I think you can start by giving me a kiss."

She sucked in her breath. "All right."

She offered up her lips and he kissed them. "All right?"

"Very nice." He smiled. "Now, how about a hug?"

"But we just hugged!"

"Yes, but I know a better one. Let me show you."

Val turned Cecily around and wrapped his arms around her from behind. He held her stiff and bony frame against him. His left arm reached across her chest and cupped her breasts; his right hand grasped her around the hips. She endured this but then Val allowed his right hand to travel down and up under her nightgown. She tried to squirm away, but his left arm tightened like a vise. His index and middle finger found between her legs the warm soft cotton of her panties. For a full minute his fingers remained there, sliding back and forth over the material. Cecily gasped but said nothing. When he felt the stony tension in her body lessen a little Val slowly moved his hand into the panties but kept the same stroking motion. He kissed the back of her neck. She began to whisper in a breathless staccato.

"Mister . . . Jackson . . . Mister . . . Jackson . . ." The last note in her voice went up to a kind of half-silent, high-pitched whine.

He plunged his middle finger, now sticky and moist, deep inside her. He pumped it a few times before her muscles finally melted and she collapsed against him into a soft and lovely mound.

They fell onto the sofa and he, his finger still moving inside her, placed his mouth there too. Her hips bucked up. He held on and then he didn't need to because her hands were on his head pulling him closer. Suddenly both of her arms flew back against the cushions and a sound, low and hoarse, a kind of "ahhhhh" escaped her throat. Val rose up and slid Cecily underneath him. The rest, as he had always known, would be easy now.

CHAPTER 30
Cecily

Mercylands, July 1947

Cecily's eyes stayed fixed upon the plate of grits and scrambled eggs in front of her. The sounds of a morning swirled around her—clinking forks struck china, coffee filled cups, a knife sliced through fresh bread. But Cecily knew if she abandoned her anchor, the perfect circle covered in yellow and white, she would get swept away into the noise and be lost. She couldn't respond to any of it, not even to say "good morning" or "yes, ma'am" to Mama, who stood at the sideboard filling her plate with bacon, eggs, and sweet rolls. Part of Cecily didn't understand how life was proceeding like everything was just as it was yesterday while the other part of her was relieved that it was. She had worried Mama would notice her slow descent on the staircase, how painful it was for Cecily to part her legs the few necessary increments to allow her to move down one step after another. Or see how still she sat now, perfectly still, lest she rekindle the burning sensation in the soft folds of her middle.

Gladys put a plate of sausages down next to Cecily's eggs and grits.

"Here, honey, eat that. You haven't touched a thing yet. It's a shame with all this good food here."

"Maybe she prefers something sweet?" Val Jackson said. He strolled in and dropped a folded newspaper at his place next to Mrs. Jarreau and kissed his aunt on the cheek. He seated himself and reached for the cup of coffee just poured for him. Both Mrs. Jarreau and Mrs. Townsend, who sat across from him, acknowledged him with "good morning" and continued to speak, but Cecily refused to listen. She didn't want to take the chance of hearing anything that would draw her away from her plate.

She gripped her fork, determined to not look at him, to make a start on the food and appear normal. But suddenly she was certain she smelled him—*smelled him*—as a sweet dark scent, like licorice, drifted toward her. She put her fork down and grasped her hands under the table. Mama was back at the sideboard again.

"There are some nice sweet rolls right here and they're still warm." She licked icing from her fingers and put another loaded plate in front of Cecily. The smacking sound Mama made turned a key in Cecily's stomach and she wanted to retch. Tears welled in the back of her throat. She was drifting away from them. Holding on to the plate, even with both hands, would be no good.

"Cecily!" His voice seemed to smack into her ears.

Her head snapped up.

"If you're not gonna eat those rolls, may I have one?" He smiled at her.

She stared. He'd spoken her name, and she was horrified. Not because she was forced to look at him, to peel her attention from the only focus holding her steady. No. Cecily Vaughn crumbled because when Val Jackson said her name the small soft knob of skin deep inside her middle responded. She thought she felt it resonating in tiny waves reaching out for him.

She pulled away from the table and ran.

CHAPTER 31
Mae

Harlem, Mid-July 1947

Mae shifted in her chair and as she crossed her legs the silk of her peignoir slid higher on her thigh. She leaned forward and breathed in the scent of the gardenias Justice had placed on the vanity an hour before. Mae was waiting for the succession of calls she knew would come. Val worked quickly, especially when pissed and vindictive, as he was when he slipped out of her parlor two days ago. Gladys would be frantic and Cecily desperate. Since Cecily's desperation couldn't further Mae's purpose and would be tedious too, she would wait to hear from Gladys, who was in a better position to furnish Mae with the key she required.

She rang the bell for Justice. "Very soon," she told the maid, "I will receive a phone call, most likely two. If one is from Cecily Vaughn, I don't want to speak with her. Tell her whatever you want and hang up. When her mother calls, I will talk to her. Do you understand?"

"Yes, ma'am."

Mae knew that when these calls arrived, her revenge would be accomplished, Frank Washington's bride deflowered. But she didn't want to sit at home and consider the work done because in the past two days she'd discovered so many more moves that remained unplayed, and these could bring her so much more than revenge. The game was different now. After all these years it was at last significant, perhaps even, she was willing to admit, vital. Because finally, finally, Mae sensed the machinations would shift and fall like dominoes irreparably in her favor and she would have the light and love—real love—she craved.

When Cecily and Gladys had left for the country Mae had summoned Sam to her, but not for the purpose of lovemaking. She had allowed him to come to her and she'd endured his misery knowing, when she chose, how she would make it evaporate into hot Harlem air. But she waited, wanting him to put aside Cecily on his own, and to understand how his heart and mind lay elsewhere, with Mae. He'd drunk champagne from crystal in her parlor, danced to jazz to soothe his soul. Even in feeling the ache of Cecily's loss, he had nurtured the hurt and blessed it, so much so that when Mae observed this she found a question slipping out of her before she could stop it.

"How can you stand it, Sam? If it hurts so damn much, why do you stand it?"

He looked at her with a clear, guileless expression of wonder on his face and his response just about broke her in two. "It's how I know I'm alive, Mae."

As much as this moved Mae, she would not sleep with

Sam again until she was assured of his devotion. She refused to be his consolation like that. But there was a sweetness to his vulnerability she enjoyed. It melted away his earlier fear of her and in its place she saw respect and, yes, real affection growing. Their situation was quite new for her—almost like a friendship. What's more she saw clearly a time coming when this affection would ripen into true love. His love would mean something because Sam knew what it meant to love. He would not allow such love to wither into indifference or the need to control her. Mae saw he possessed a vast spotlight and soon she would have it trained on her. She admitted as much to herself only at night with cool satin sheets pulled around her to chill the hunger of her skin calling out to him. But during the day she planned for him, strategized for him as she awaited her foray into the country.

When the call she wanted finally came, Mae, before taking the telephone, instructed Justice to begin packing her suitcase. She picked up the receiver and smiled into the air so her voice might mimic the gesture into the line.

"Gladys! Did you make it up there all right?"

"Yes, but it just seems like Cecily is getting worse." Mae could almost hear the sweat beads forming on her cousin's upper lip and the muffled sound of her wiping them away with a handkerchief.

"What are you talking about?"

"She's been sulky for a few days and I've just been waiting for it to pass. Pouting like a baby."

"Yes, well, you're right. It will pass."

"But today she stopped eating! She sat there today looking

at her food like it made her the saddest thing in the world. Ran right upstairs after breakfast and now she won't come out of her room."

Mae allowed herself to laugh but just a little. Mothers were so terrible at bending their children to their will, she thought. She figured it was because they took too much for granted. They thought they knew something because they had dropped a bundle from between their legs. If they truly knew their offspring, if they only paid attention to them and understood their desires, mothers could use that knowledge very well to get children to do what they wanted them to do, go where mothers wanted them to go.

"Well, you had to expect something like this, Gladys. Sam was her first love after all. It's not like you just took away a teddy bear."

"I know, but will you come talk to her?" Mae sensed movement—Gladys seemed to be pacing or throwing up her hands. Whatever she was doing, Mae thought, it told of exasperation, a good sign. "If somebody doesn't get through to that girl soon I won't know what to do with her."

"Me come to Westchester? But I haven't been invited." Mae curled the phone cord between her fingers and pressed her lips together.

"I already spoke to Rose and she told me it would be fine for you to come. 'The more the merrier,' that's exactly what she said."

Mae smiled. "All right, Gladys. I'll be there soon."

* * *

HER OPERATION BY necessity would be a delicate one. She had to soothe, heal, and cut all at the same time, making sure what remained of Cecily was only what Mae wanted to remain. And that Cecily would act on her new direction right away. But Mae sensed the work would be easier when she entered Cecily's darkened room, because the girl wasn't in bed hiding under the sheets and crying.

She was barefoot, but dressed in jeans and a blue button-down shirt as she paced back and forth. Mae guessed Cecily wasn't in the room to hide. No, she was in the room to think because she didn't know what to do with herself, didn't know how to act or what she wanted. Mae could handle confusion. Pure resistance—if she had not been able even to gain entrance to Cecily's room—would have been another matter.

"Go wash your face," Mae told her after she accepted Cecily's awkward, desperate hug. "Then we'll have our talk."

While Cecily obeyed, Mae pulled back the curtains of the room and was pleased to discover Cecily's windows overlooked the lawn where Val and his friends were playing baseball. She opened a window and the smell of fresh-cut grass rolled in. Mae settled herself on the window seat and motioned for Cecily to sit with her. As she did Mae was careful to note if Cecily looked out the window, whether she particularly noticed the men playing ball, and if she reacted with any hint of loathing toward Val. Mae thought the girl seemed wary but was not afraid to keep him in view. Then Cecily started talking and spilled a load of drama at Mae's feet. Mae leaned back and sighed as though Cecily had told her the oldest story in the world.

Still, at the right moment, she put a hand on Cecily's knee and conjured a look of pure concern.

"So he forced himself on you?"

Cecily paused and scratched her head. "No, not exactly," she said slowly.

"But you resisted him?"

Her hands flew up. "Yes! No. I tried. I was trying!"

She looked the girl directly in the eye and drew out her words deliberately. "Did you tell him 'no'?"

Cecily looked down at her hands and shrugged. "I didn't know what to say, and there were times when I couldn't talk—I thought I couldn't breathe!" She threw a pleading look at Mae. "I feel so nasty. And it hurt! Why did it hurt so much?"

Mae nodded slowly. "Did it hurt the whole time?"

Cecily's face froze.

Mae moved her head closer to Cecily's and whispered in her ear.

"You said you couldn't breathe. Was he strangling you, smothering you?"

The girl touched her silent lips with her fingertips and shook her head slightly. Mae leaned back again and allowed her eyes to drift toward the window. She crossed her arms.

"Then I must believe something else was going on, and that something else is the real reason I'm here."

Cecily's hand went to move over her eyes, but Mae snatched it and held it fast. She spoke again in the calm, deliberate voice. "You listen to me. You did nothing wrong. Do you understand?"

The girl nodded, but Mae saw she was unconvinced.

"What happened to you is as natural as eating, as necessary as breathing, yet there are women who would give their eye-teeth to feel in their bodies what you felt. They almost never get to feel that, if they ever did in the first place."

Cecily shrugged and shook her head. "How come they don't?"

"Because they're made to feel ashamed of their bodies, like men are the only ones who are supposed to feel something."

Cecily's hand relaxed as Mae held tighter with both of her own. "If Val made you feel good, then he's a better man than what they say about him. You're very lucky, Cecily." Mae watched the girl's eyes now turn outward, seeking to place Val out on the field. She chose her next words carefully. She rubbed Cecily's hands.

"I think what you want to know now is what to do next. Do you want to make love to him again?"

Cecily said nothing, but Mae took this as a good sign. She released the girl's hand and looked out the windows too, but trained her gaze on the lazy white clouds casting shadows into the room as they passed over the sun.

"This isn't about Sam anymore. It's about who you want to be as a grown woman—and you are a woman now. You've got to know your desire and what's going to make you happy. That happiness can be tied up in one man or you can find it in several. But it will always be your choice—not your mama's, not Frank Washington's, not mine. Once you understand who you are, you won't have to care about what they or anyone else thinks because you'll be able to sit right with yourself."

The girl shook her head. "I don't know what I want. You have to tell me what to do, Cousin Mae. You have to help me."

"Look at me. Cecily, is that what you really want?"

The girl nodded. "Yes, of course."

"All right then. Keep sleeping with Val Jackson."

"What?!"

Mae sat up straighter and hardened her face. Cecily's hand

covered her own mouth like she wanted to take back the excla-
mation.

"Don't be stupid. Look at what you have here. You've got
a chance to make your mother think you've forgotten about
Sam." She pointed out Val in the field. "You have a pleasant
distraction that will make what you say to her ring true. And
you'll get some very nice practice for after."

"After?" Cecily frowned.

"After you marry Frank Washington."

"But what about Sam?"

Mae nodded and looked away from her. "And you'll still get
to see Sam after you are married."

"How am I going to do that? Sam wouldn't do that!"

Mae sighed and shook her head.

"This isn't about what Sam will or won't do. It's about you.
Don't you see you can do whatever you want? You're a woman!
You hold all the cards here. Lying to a husband is a hundred
times easier than lying to a mother. And when you learn how to
be careful you can have Sam, Val, or just about any other man
you want. Cecily, what do you want?"

The girl looked out the window again. "I don't know . . ."

Mae felt a taste of contempt, metallic and cold, in her throat.
Maybe Cecily was even thinking about Sam, but Mae saw that
whatever she was turning over in her little mind, her girlish at-
tachment to Sam wasn't really love. She was telling on herself
by the way her gaze wandered onto Val on the ball field. She
was probably trying to figure out what she could hold on to
even as she took more—a child at a table of treats. Why, Mae
wondered, did people always equate ease with taking candy
from a baby? Really, the easiest thing to do would be to give the

baby more, not take anything away, because faced with such bounty the baby would inevitably drop the piece you wanted for yourself.

Mae moved away from the window and lit a cigarette, giving Cecily more space to ponder Val's physique. Mae had to release her of the suffocation she most likely felt from having the weight of a man on top of her. She had to feel the possibility of floating underneath him, traveling to the place Mae had no doubt Val had shown her that night.

She turned back to Cecily. "Then let me make it easy for you. Do you want to be a grown woman? Do you want to run your own life? Or do you want your mama telling you how it's going to be from here on out? Now is when it happens, Cecily. Now is when you decide."

The light from the window behind Cecily silhouetted her profile, accenting her long neck and high cheekbones. She rose from the window seat and walked over to Mae with new and confident steps. She seemed at least two inches taller. At the same time Mae heard the lumbering sounds of her cousin approaching the door. Mae rubbed Cecily's arm.

"I think your mother is coming. No more crying, all right?"

Cecily nodded. She clasped her hands in front of her and the muscles of her face relaxed. Mae was impressed. In the next moment Gladys entered the room without knocking.

"How are you now, Cecily, honey?" The effort of climbing the stairs had left a sheen of sweat on Gladys's upper lip. She dabbed at it with a blue polka-dot handkerchief.

"I'm feeling much better, Mama." Cecily even managed a faint smile. "Cousin Mae has put my mind at ease."

"Thank the Lord, I knew she would!" Gladys put a thick

arm around her daughter and drew her into her ample bosom. "But you should rest now, baby. You look so tired."

"No, I'm fine."

"I think you should listen to your mother." Mae reached out and touched one finger to the girl's shoulder. "For now."

Cecily responded to Mae with a slow, deep nod. "Thank you, I'll do that. I'll see you later, Mama." She walked over to her door and held it open for them to leave. The confused look on Gladys's face as she obeyed her daughter's dismissal delighted Mae, and her jubilance radiated in the smile she shone on Cecily when she left the room.

CHAPTER 32
Cecily

Mercylands, Mid-July 1947

After she closed the door Cecily returned to the open windows and gulped the fresh air with an eagerness that made her want to eat the sweet grass that scented it. The smell reminded her of Anselm, and the thought of Anselm prompted her to return to what she learned of her body there, that her body had rhythm and reason and was not as strange to her as it once was.

When she had left her aunt's house, Cecily felt she was beginning to understand, even trust, her body. The sensations blossoming within her could only be natural and good. But in Harlem Mama put high heels on Cecily's feet so she could no longer feel the ground beneath her; paraded her in front of Frank Washington who, along with Mama, seemed to tell Cecily that she had to think and be a certain way that had nothing to do with what she was learning about her body. Cecily took on what Mae had said because this thinking seemed to be her instructions, the words she had been waiting for to tell her how to be in the world. She loved Sam because he saw Cecily for herself, and she'd hoped all she had to do was find a way to replace Frank Washington with Sam in this picture of life Mama wanted her to create. That she could even still be acceptable and loved and learn to walk in those shoes.

But this thinking, of what was acceptable and what a proper girl should and shouldn't do, failed her on the night with Val Jackson. Her body hadn't reacted in the ways her mind told her it was supposed to, bewildering Cecily to the point of scaring her witless. The split shocked her because the one part of her had no hope of supporting the other. Her body wouldn't fight the way her mind insisted it should; her mind couldn't cope with the sensations her body was feeling. Where was her anger? Where was her indignation or fear? Only one thing stayed with her with frightening clarity, devastating her so much she barely admitted it to herself. It was what drove her from the dining room at breakfast when she had the faintest sense of it coming again—deep pleasure. She couldn't think about it because it made thinking about Sam torture.

She had paced her room for hours trying frantically to sort out what it all meant. Did she really love Sam in the way she thought? And if she didn't, what did that say about her? Did it make her a whore, a dirty, uncaring thing?

What terrified her more was that her body seemed to desire Val Jackson beyond reason. What if she couldn't stop herself from feeling this way? Would she be bound to this man forever?

But then Mae—and Cecily was grateful she was so wise— recognized the pleasure right away and pushed aside the veil of shame so Cecily could see the truth of it. It was such a comfort to her that her cousin understood everything. And to know what she had felt was desired by—and even withheld from—other women gave Cecily a kind of satisfaction. Mae seemed to be telling her she could be confident in this feeling, and this feeling allowed her to see there was only one place to be—in her body. She could trust her body more than she thought, could listen to it, and believe it ahead of anyone else, even ahead of Mama. If Cecily could figure out how to stand strong in her body she wouldn't have to worry about Mama taking her away and controlling what happened in her life. But in order for her to possess herself in this way, Cecily knew she had to allow herself to think about what had passed between her and Val Jackson.

She took in another breath of air, then closed the windows and the drapes. She got into bed, under the soft sheets, and lay on her back. The dark would help her concentrate. In the bed she felt safe, safe enough to listen.

In all the time she daydreamed about Sam, it never occurred to her what they might do together beyond kiss or hold hands. She knew there could be more, sensed it by the way Mama went out of her mind whenever Cecily seemed close to understanding the mystery. But why had she never gone far enough to even guess what they might do when they were alone and free to do whatever they wanted? She conjured his face above her in the dark, imagined him on top of her where Val Jackson had been. Her hand reached up to caress the empty space and she smiled. She felt the soft flesh between her legs awaken, and her fingers quickly found it. She used to lie like this in Anselm. She had touched herself down there and felt herself becoming another being, but she never thought of Sam doing the touching, that he might guide her on that journey wherever it might lead. Then the face above her changed and suddenly, once again, Val Jackson loomed over her.

Cecily gasped, turned onto her left side, and pressed her thighs together. Val Jackson had touched her down there—and with his mouth! Their soft spots of flesh, hers and his, seemed akin to one another, both moist and warm, both sensitive and strong. It was inevitable that one flesh should be upon the other with the same life-giving energy. And it made sense to Cecily when she thought of it at last that whatever touches you down there must be alive in the same way.

She remembered Mr. Travis and how he had pushed himself into the dirt. What could be more alive than the earth itself? Maybe that's why her struggle had been half of what it could have been. As her arms tried to push him away, they were weakened by what was going on below. The sensation grew stronger, overtook her, and when she couldn't breathe she gave in to it, the wonder of it, because she seemed to be growing, blossoming. When she reached the pinnacle of this exquisite ache she felt herself burst open like a bag of sugar and the sweetness flowing away from her as though blown by a soft wind. Her tears fell freely then because Cecily thought something had been broken and didn't see how the sweetness could ever be retrieved again.

She had grieved the loss of the sensation even as Val Jackson moved over her, kissing her tears, kissing her breasts. She lay in full surrender then because she didn't see the point of fighting anymore. There was nothing left of her, nothing but emptiness and ashes. Val Jackson may as well ride over the spoils of her landscape, laugh at her, proclaim his victory. Sometimes the word "no" had squeaked from her throat, but there had been nothing behind it. Her hands grasped the back of his neck, her nose filled with the smell of him—sweat and salt but something else she couldn't place. The scent was dark and deeply sweet—familiar like molasses or even some aspect of her own skin. Something about the smell comforted her even as she thought to herself, *This must be over soon. It will be over soon.*

Then he entered her.

It felt like a searing beam of light parting her, separating her from herself, seeking deeper as though insisting she give up something, only she didn't know what. Cecily instinctively spread her legs wider because if she didn't give it more space it would surely burn her up from within. But she couldn't do it, couldn't open up far enough, and yet it didn't matter because the light had already gone surging down into her, down so far that now it only wanted to come up and out of her, from the top of her, as a crystalline, soundless scream.

She was alive again and whole. Her body responded, partaking of him with unabashed, unmitigated greed. Cecily wrapped her legs around his back and held on. Only then did it seem she gained some sort of power over Val Jackson because she felt him change. The fluidity of him that made him melt into her thighs disappeared and his body tensed, like something about to set off. She held on tighter because she didn't want him to leave her in the strange new place. He chased the light, rode it down to its dimming, until everything went out and they were only themselves again.

Afterward he lay there on the bed smoking a cigarette as though waiting for her to say something. Cecily couldn't move but didn't know if her frozen state was out of fear or because she had forgotten how to move. He finally got up, put on a robe, and gently pulled Cecily's nightgown down over her. Then he lifted her up in his arms and, without a noise, carried her back to her room and placed her on the bed where she lay now.

He whispered to her before he left, "You can come back if you want."

She found herself nodding—nodding! What was she agreeing to do? What would he expect of her? Perhaps she felt disarmed by the way he had carried her, so friendly and gentle. She didn't know how to be unkind to him. That last self-betrayal and failure gnawed at her the rest of the night. If she tried to sleep both the burning between her legs and the unease of her mind would shake her awake again. By morning she was a ghost of herself, making her way through the house as though walking on ice.

Last night had felt like the end of the world, but after Mae's visit and now that she could think clearly, Cecily saw openings, a new world to explore. Nothing would be hidden from her anymore. As she thought about this Cecily's hand flew out in shock as she realized she didn't know what Val Jackson looked like down there. She wanted to know what had penetrated her, and she found herself grasping the air, reaching for him as though she could discover it now. This also made her fully aware of her ignorance, how silly she must have seemed to Mae. That was when she knew for certain she wanted Val Jackson again. Now she had questions. She wanted to know his body and how exactly it had fit into hers. Cecily figured the more she knew, the better chance she had of having a pleasurable experience with Sam when their chance to be together finally came. The fact that she could think of Sam once more without guilt made Cecily relax and soon she grew sleepy. She would give in to it. A nap now would be helpful because she knew that night she would return to Val Jackson.

CHAPTER 33
Mae

Mercylands, Mid-July 1947

Val's baseball game had already ended by the time Mae made her way down the stone steps of the terrace and onto the lawn. As much as she liked turning heads she enjoyed such moments when she could slip into a scene unnoticed. Any greeting or attention would go to Gladys, a few steps behind Mae, who would make her way to the table of icy pitchers containing sweet iced tea and gin and tonics. Gladys would accept the more potent concoction, deem it necessary for her worried nerves, and explain that Cecily, feeling much better, was now taking a nap. Rose Jarreau, sitting in her throne-like chair, would receive this news with pleasure.

Mae sauntered across the grass and folded herself into the gathering. She shielded her eyes with her hand, looked over the property, and pretended to enjoy the view. She didn't have to work too hard at the pretending—Val and his friends in tight T-shirts, their sweaty arms shining in the sun, made for a delicious spectacle as they jogged about retrieving equipment and joking with each other. At times they stopped and held still for a photographer Val had hired. Mae continued her slow walk knowing that Val would soon approach her. She wanted to make sure they were out of earshot when he did.

When Val saw Mae he tossed his glove to the ground and bounded toward her. He looked, she thought, like an actor leaving the stage, and this pleased her. He always removed the mask for her. It was her sign that they were on the same side, playing the same game. She adored his eagerness for it— relished his abandon and strength.

Mae clasped her hands behind her and smiled. She could tell Val appreciated the light blue cotton of her skirt and the way the warm breeze pulled it back around her thighs. "May I congratulate my star player on another fine victory?" she said. "How was your revenge?"

"Thank you, thank you." He gave her a small, playful bow. "I was at my finest if I do say so myself."

"Yes, well, I think you may find your pupil a little more willing next time."

"Oh, her fight was all for show."

Mae shrugged. "She was confused. The usual. But I've straightened her out for you."

They continued back toward the others as Mae scanned the lawn again. "So where is your latest project?"

Val scanned the grounds. "I don't know. She was just out here. But the game is on, don't worry about that. She's definitely in play."

"Yes, but it looks like we're heading into the ninth and you are not even on the field."

"For this part I almost don't need to be. She's the one call-ing the shots and she doesn't even know it." Val laughed and shook his head. "No, Mae, she's turned me into her god now. Everything she prays for—mercy, release, peace—she asks me for all that now. It's really a sight to see, watching her struggle like that, knowing it's all for my sake. She's trying to figure out how far she can go without a soul and whether it's a place where she can have me."

Mae smiled. "You spend so much time watching, Val, I wonder why you don't just go to the movies."

"And miss my role in the action? No way. Besides, our time will come soon enough, very soon. In the meantime I have our young friend to amuse me."

She crossed her arms and frowned. "Well, you better hurry. I'm bored and I'm not waiting around for extra innings."

He shrugged. "It's too bad our bet wasn't based on your as-signment."

"Oh, please, Val! You said yourself it was too easy! You don't score points just for stepping out of the dugout."

Val nodded. "I think even you will appreciate this victory when I have her. She doesn't see how silly it is, what she's do-ing. But this is the battle I told you about, her struggle between love and virtue. She's trying to hold on. She needs to believe in something and, hey, I'll give her that because I wouldn't give a flying shit about her if she didn't." He pulled a pack of Pall Malls from his pants pocket along with a lighter.

"But where is she?" Mae laughed. "Is she hiding?"

"She doesn't need to hide from me. She knows that." Val's face darkened, which delighted Mae. He so hated losing bets. He stared hard at the small knot of people gathered around the beverage table near his aunt. Mae looked that way too, making the same assumption: Elizabeth Townsend would be standing there drinking iced tea with Gladys and lending all her sympathy to Mae's chatty cousin. Neither Val nor Mae expected to hear Elizabeth's voice coming from behind them.

"Hey!" And then a laugh, light and crisp like a lettuce leaf.

Val turned first, and Mae followed his gaze and saw the woman who must be Elizabeth Townsend on the ball field approaching home plate. She wore blue dungarees, and a scarf printed with yellow roses held back her brown curls. She held a bat loosely at her side with one hand while she waved Val over to her.

"I've been practicing! You'll see!"

Val, without another glance at Mae, shoved the cigarettes and lighter back in his pocket and jogged over to the woman. He smiled at her and chucked her under the chin. This slight touch brought a flush of pink to her cheeks. She raised the bat and tried to stand taller. Mae stood frozen and dumbstruck. What had done it? But she saw it all too well. It was the ease of Elizabeth's movement, the flow of her arm floating out to Val to invite him to her, and then how readily Val went and fell into a synchronicity with her, like a river coming together at a confluence, leaving Mae bereft on its banks. Her insides felt pulled apart so what was left was all vitriol, scorching the center of her chest and pushing up bile into her throat.

She saw Val's mask, his true mask this time, fall away and suddenly he was no longer invincible. He could be moved, cajoled, touched, loved. The light he emitted was new. Before it had been like an electric bulb, one he switched off and on at will. But this light now was a natural one, the kind only seen in fire or the sun. Where had it come from? Had it always been there? Did Mae fail to see it before? No, she decided. He must have hidden it from her, made a choice not to share this wonder of himself with her who should have owned it by right, bound to him by prior claim for recognizing all he was—at least what she'd thought was all of him.

A sound rose in Mae's throat. It was the same sound sometimes pressed out of her by her masseuse who, as she rubbed Mae down, her hands sliding across Mae's well-oiled skin, would come to a spot between her shoulder blades, down about where her heart center would be, and when she kneaded the muscle there Mae would stifle a cry. That was the only time she allowed herself to think of Alice, her childhood friend. This touch, though manufactured and medicinal, made her feel half broken, as she had been when she lost Alice's love. But Mae always remade herself by the end of the session— remade herself again and again, gaining strength with each new rendering. Only now, because it was so unexpected, Mae didn't know what to do with the sound other than tamp it back down.

Val went to the pitcher's spot and picked up a ball and a glove. He walked toward the plate a few steps. "Are you ready?"

"I'm ready!"

Val tossed her a soft underhand pitch. Elizabeth Townsend swung the bat, twisting her tiny hips as she turned and made contact with the ball. It shot past Val into the infield and he could only watch it go. Then he looked back to the woman again. She was laughing.

"Well, all right!" he said. "All right! Wait right there. I wanna see that again!"

He started to go for the ball then stopped. "Hey, Marcus! Marcus, come take a picture for me! Over here!"

The photographer obliged and Val jogged over to Elizabeth. He threw an arm around her and pushed his glove into her hands. "Hold this for me," he told her. "We have to preserve the moment Mrs. Townsend learned to play ball!" The flashbulb made them blink and laugh. Val looked at her and from where Mae stood she saw time had stopped for him and Elizabeth Townsend. They would hold their breaths if they could, stay in that sunny moment until the day died and reminded them to go back inside. And then what would they do? It almost didn't matter because they owned everything in that moment; Mae felt it as her hand, balled into a fist, went to her stomach. The look wasn't long—that kind of thing always lasted just a second or so—but it was enough to turn Mae's face to stone.

Val took his glove back and ran out to retrieve the ball. Elizabeth, suddenly looking shy and embarrassed, turned toward Mae but Mae retreated, walking with a careful, regular pace back toward Gladys and Rose, and preparing a smile for her hosts. She had released her fist and her hands floated at her sides like open flowers. This way she could accept the glass of tea handed to her by Gladys. She maintained the cool look of holding ice just under her tongue. She could stand the wait, however long it would be, until she could be alone and plan.

* * *

HER PLANNING ALWAYS centered on anticipating what her adversary wanted, then making it seem they were on the verge of getting it. Of course that was the most delightful moment—savoring her opponent's premature satisfaction, then watching their joy wither and their heart shrink as they came to see how the situation really stood. But with Elizabeth Townsend, Mae saw a very different kind of rival. She was someone whose wants weren't exactly clear, even to herself, and it would be difficult, Mae decided, to strike such a person directly. It would have to be done obliquely, and this pleased Mae because she saw the opportunity to at last obtain the answer to a question she had long pondered. Val would be quite useful, of course. Mae needed him to prove the truth of the answer once she found it. In fact his actions would tell her everything she needed to know.

The situation between Val and Elizabeth Townsend, though, required she leave Rose Jarreau's estate. Mae doubted she could hide her disdain for long if she were further subjected to Val's activities. She also knew that for a puppet master's strings to work properly, they have to be far enough away from the puppet to create tension.

"Well, Val, I'm happy to see you have so much to keep you occupied up here in the country," Mae said the next morning as she finished tying a filmy red scarf around her hair and watched Lawrence put her bags in the Packard. "How will you keep up with your pupil while you pursue Mrs. Townsend?"

Val, dressed in his robe and pajamas because it was still early and he'd insisted on jumping up from the breakfast table to accompany Mae to her car, opened the door and reached out for her hand. "I'll manage. Don't you worry about me. I'll keep you posted."

"You better."

She slipped into the car and Val bent his head in close. She moved toward him and lifted her chin as though she meant to kiss him. But Mae only smiled and withdrew into the car.

"Goodbye, Val."

"Goodbye for now. I'll see you soon for that little visit of our own."

Mae nodded and settled back into her seat. She crossed her legs and put on a pair of sunglasses. "We'll see."

The car pulled away down the drive. As it accelerated Mae gripped the edge of the seat to keep herself from looking back at him.

CHAPTER 34
Val

Mercylands, Mid-July 1947

Val had known in the moment Marcus's flashbulb had turned the whole world blue that he would tell his friend to make two copies when he printed the photographs.

"My aunt will want one."

The lie had slipped from his lips so quickly he'd given no thought to why it was even necessary. His mind had been elsewhere. On the yellow of Elizabeth's headscarf and how the color made her skin glow. He also marveled over the tiny buzz of delight that had leapt into his stomach when he had seen Elizabeth holding the bat and waving for him to come over. The casual way she'd done it had proved his theory that she might feel more comfortable if there were more people around. He should have demanded Mae's compliments for a well-played move. Still, it had been a surprise—her beckoning like that and seeming so unafraid.

And when she got that hit? Oh Lord, he'd felt like he'd

been the ball and his seams would split with joy! Then to see her look so proud, like she wanted him to know she'd learned the language he spoke—the only language that truly mattered to him—and she would always understand. His first instinct had been to reach out with both hands and seize the moment so he could hold it like a shiny marble swirled in orange and red. He wanted to hold her to him and capture that smile— that smile—which left him awash in light, the same light he saw almost every morning in the rising sun. Could he really find every possibility he'd ever hoped for in that smile?

It was night, four days after they took the picture, and the feeling still drove about in circles in his mind. Val stood at the window, overlooking the lawn and sipping a glass of whiskey. He heard the tiny knock at the door and sighed. Cecily's timidity had melted like morning frost in the heat of the sun. This made his job easier, of course, and enjoying the girl was indeed pleasurable. But hearing her then made him feel as though he'd been rudely awakened. Crankiness prodded him as he watched how quickly her nightgown flew up over her head and he decided to take a more instructive tone for the evening. She wrinkled her nose at the sound of the word "lesson," and flipped her coltish legs up and under the covers.

"What else is there to learn?" she whined. "Why can't we just do it?"

"Because it's not just about 'doing it.'" Val removed his robe and slid between the sheets. His right hand found the soft flatness of her belly and traveled the length of her torso, up to her breasts. "That's childish and stupid."

Cecily's look darkened and Val realized he would embarrass her if he kept on like that. He moved up and over her until his mouth found hers and he kissed her until her arms encircled his neck and tightened him against her. "Besides," he whispered, "if you think like that you'll get bored pretty quickly and you're much too young for that. Cecily, it's all about what else you do, how you do it. It's about putting excitement into it and getting pleasure out of it."

"And Sam or Frank Washington? They would be able to tell? They'd like it?"

"Like it?" Val laughed and kissed her again. "Cecily, if I do my job well enough, a man would be willing to kill for you."

"What?"

"Sure, sure. Why do you think these guys run around Harlem pulling guns on each other like they're in the O.K. Corral?"

Cecily lay back against the pillows and shook her head in wide-eyed wonder. "I don't know."

"It's usually over some woman. A man can be willing to die for a woman because of what happens when they're in bed together. If it feels like he can't get that anywhere else in the world, he'll kill the man who might take it from him."

"That can't be true." Cecily rolled over onto her belly and hugged a pillow beneath her. "You're just making fun of me."

Val propped himself up on his left elbow and put his right hand over his heart. "Cecily, I swear, it happens. I remember this one time, and this would have been before you were born, it got ugly in one of the finest nightclubs in Harlem. It was all because of this woman who should've known better."

"Why was it her fault?"

Val counted on his fingers. "Because she had a boyfriend, she had herself a backdoor man on the side, and then on that night she had the nerve to get a third guy on the line.

"She's on the dance floor getting all hot and heavy with the third guy when he sees the other two men coming toward them from opposite sides of the room. Any fool could tell what was about to go down there."

"What happened?"

"Well, the guy did the only thing he could do. He grabbed her and hit the deck just as those Joes start blasting away at each other. One guy went down pretty bad. Turned out that was the boyfriend. Next thing you knew, she was crawling all over him wailing like it was the end of the world. That boy was laid up for months. Some say she married him because she had guilt eating away at her so bad."

"That can't be true! How awful!"

"I know it's awful, but it is true." Val lay back again into the pillows and pulled Cecily on top of him. "You can ask your mother."

"How would she know?"

"Because she was the woman."

"How do you know?" Cecily leaned over and took one of Val's earlobes between her lips.

"I was the guy she was dancing with!"

Cecily's face shot back in front of Val's and she gave him a look he had seen many times and cherished—a look that said someone had given you the keys to the world. Her laughter then was like bubbles spilling over from champagne.

"All right now?"

She nodded and nuzzled her nose into the side of his neck.

"Since you're already there, let's take it from the top."

* * *

THE NEXT DAY Val sat at his desk. He took out a pen and paper to anchor him there because he knew Elizabeth would be out on the grounds looking for him, and he wanted to make her wait. He felt her expectation growing, like a child waiting for Christmas, and this anticipation was the best gift he could give her right now. She would soon learn, he hoped, that this edge of suspense was where you drank the real juice of life. Mae knew this. Mae, whose name was coming to life in the loops underneath his hands on the paper. It would be Mae who would hold him in his seat and take her share of this moment.

Here we go, Mae.

> *It's time to play ball.*
> *The game unfolds just the way I planned it. She allows herself a little bit of time alone with me every day. We walk. We talk. We're cool. The relationship is what it is, but we both know the status quo can't hold up for long. It's like she keeps drawing circles around herself and telling me, "You stay out there." Then I step over the line.*
> *So she draws another one, this time farther in. I step over that one too. She keeps drawing, but the lines keep getting closer. Pretty soon there's going to be no place to go but in. Her defenses are gone, baby, gone.*
> *For now we haggle over words. What is "friendship," the word she likes to use when we talk about what we are to each other? I use the word "love" and she will start into a long speech about why I shouldn't. It's funny—I even laugh at her! She knows damn well*

she's stopped asking me to leave, and whenever there's a chance for us to be alone she never avoids it. But I let her go on because she can do all the struggling while I save my strength for the big moment. She won't have any strength or anything left to say when the time comes.

I think you left here too quickly. I thought you would have wanted a front-row seat to this game? But then it would have been too much—conquering my little player, instructing Cecily, and cashing in on our bet, all under the same roof! Aunt Rose would have me thrown out of here so fast my bare ass would be rolling down the highway and Sebastian would have to floor the Caddy to catch up and find me. But you would enjoy that, wouldn't you? So why leave?

I'll stop wondering. I know you have your reasons. I'll go back to my work and just hope you're not too lonely.

Soon, Mae. Very soon.
Val

Writing the letter gave him the resolve to wait a half hour longer before he went outside. And when he did he went in the opposite direction of where Elizabeth might be found. He was surprised to see a tinge of red on the tips of a few leaves. July was more than half gone. In six weeks his aunt would be closing the house and moving back to Harlem for the winter. Of course she did this every year, but for some reason Val now felt a sadness with the thought. He took the bat in his hands and put it up behind his neck, slinging his wrists over each end, and continued his walk down the lawn.

"Val?"

He waited a moment before he turned. "Yes, Mrs. Townsend?"

"I'm not disturbing you, am I? You seemed lost in thought."

"Well, I was thinking." He began to laugh. "Isn't that funny—me, thinking?! I'm not used to doing a lot of that!"

"Oh, I bet you're a guy who does a lot of thinking." She wore a blue cotton dress with tiny buttons that ran all the way down the front. Val couldn't help noticing how it hugged her hips as she fell into step with him.

"Well, maybe I did a lot of thinking, but I was still thoughtless." She laughed at that and he knew he could go a little further. "You know, I almost wish— Never mind, that's just dumb." He shook his head.

"What? Tell me."

He still held the bat behind his neck. It might make her feel safer, he thought, less vulnerable, if he remained semibound. He ventured a bashful sort of smile. "I almost wish you knew me before. You can't appreciate how much I've changed because you just don't know. My boys are all talking about it."

"Your friends—your boys—they're important to you, aren't they?"

"I hadn't thought about it, but yeah, we all answer to the crowd in one way or another. You care about the people you know at church, right? They're important to you too."

She grasped her hands in front of her and nodded.

"Yes, Val, I do. But at the end of the day I can't care about what they think to the point where it interferes with my life. I have to do what I feel is right, and that will always be between me and God."

Val looked at her with surprise and pressed his lips together as though considering her words. "That's pretty bold of you to say so for yourself. But what about me? You think I care too much about what a bunch of guys running around on a ball field think about me?"

Elizabeth smiled and clasped her hands behind her back. "I think your friends are important to you."

She didn't say anything else and Val didn't encourage her. The line of questioning confused him. What was she getting at? The puzzle annoyed and charmed him at the same time, but he didn't want to go carelessly skipping down a road that might have a dead end.

He released the bat from his shoulders and held the knob of it so it swung like a pendulum from his right hand. When he did this he noticed the path beneath their feet ended and the woods lay before them. He used the bat to point into the trees.

"There's a lake right through here. Gethsemane Lake. Have you seen it?"

Elizabeth tilted her torso to the right so she could peer into the underbrush. "Only from the house. Not up close. Rose doesn't like going off the paths when we walk together."

Val used the bat to push back a large bunch of Queen Anne's lace. "Yeah, it wouldn't be easy for her now, not at her age." He held out his other arm toward Elizabeth and smiled. "It's really pretty. You should see it."

He liked how she seemed to smile from only the corner of

her mouth, but still she moved toward the space he opened for her. "I'm sure it is," she said.

In the woods she stepped with care over the dead leaves, fallen branches, and stones. He offered his hand when a rock or a vine threatened her balance and she didn't hesitate to take it. This was a good sign.

"I loved being out here when I was a kid," he said. "Always seemed like I was the only person in the world."

When they reached the mossy ground Elizabeth took off her shoes and sank her toes into the soft greenery. She smiled at him and continued to the edge of the lake. She dropped her shoes and stood with her hands on her hips. She rose up on her toes and drew a deep breath. It was shady and cool under the trees. The water shimmered in the afternoon sun.

Val stood on her left side and let the bat rest between his feet. They were quiet for a few minutes. He liked the sound of the ripples gently kissing the shore. Elizabeth finally turned to him.

"Why is it called Gethsemane?"

"Oh, my aunt did that," he replied. "My uncle—I don't remember him well, he died when I was only three or four—she told me he would come down here to pray when he was troubled about something. He fished too." He pointed with the bat. "He used to have a boat launch down the way a little, but my aunt took it out after he died."

"Why did she do that?"

"I don't know. Maybe she didn't want anyone else out on the water. Might fool herself into thinking he was still around."

She nudged his arm with her left elbow. "And what about you? Did you pray out here?"

He shrugged. "When I was younger I didn't think to do it. When I was older—well, I wasn't always alone then."

"Oh?" She turned her head and raised an eyebrow.

He shrugged again and smiled. "Okay, yeah, I brought my female company down here. I used to pick a girl up, act like I was gonna toss her into the lake. Let her scream her head off."

Elizabeth, to his surprise, laughed. "You must have been some date."

"I was something else." He gauged a level of ease he hadn't seen in her before. She looked like a country girl with her bare feet on the ground and her hair tossed in the breeze. He decided he would take a chance and venture back to their previous conversation. "What did you mean back there when you said my friends are important to me?"

She shrugged and he wondered if she were mimicking his gesture.

"I just think you do care about what people think about you. You care a lot. I'm guessing more than most people."

He shook his head. "Not more than a woman."

"What are you talking about?"

He shifted his feet beneath him. "A woman is always fussing over what she looks like. Do you think that's because of what she thinks about herself? No. It's because she's worried about what others—men especially—are gonna think of her."

She tilted her chin up toward him and laughed. "That's ridiculous! One doesn't have to do with another. Yes, some women are vain but some men are too."

"I know for a fact looks come first for a woman." He pointed out at the lake again with his bat. "That's all those girls cared about when they thought I was gonna throw 'em out there."

"Well, not every woman would be so silly."

He looked at the ground and kicked at a stone with his shoe. "Yeah, well, I don't think you know what you're talking about."

She moved so fast he almost missed it—the way her left foot pushed down into the earth and her right one popped up and out of his view. In one second she was waist deep in the lake. In the next her arms shot forward and she dove all the way in.

Then a deep laughter welled up from inside of Val and burst forth hard enough to make him bend over and grasp his knees. He couldn't stop laughing or draw breath. This woman! Who was this woman? He'd never been so delighted, never in his life. It made him feel new to laugh like that. She swam two or three strokes before turning around and splashing her way back to the spot where she could stand. Water streamed down her head and torso, plastering her hair to her scalp and making her dress cling around her hips and thighs. She swiped her wet locks away from her drenched face.

"Are you gonna help me out or what?"

"Oh yeah. Yeah!" He straightened himself and reached out to grasp her hand. She used her other hand to pull her skirt above the knees so she could step onto the bank. Her face seemed to glow in triumph and she laughed with him. She put a fist on her right hip and stuck her hip out as though posing for a photograph.

"Well, Mr. Jackson? How do I look?"

"Beautiful. Just beautiful." He shook his head in wonder. Everything in his head and heart seemed to distill down to one single focused desire—he wanted to take the sun of her face in his hands and kiss her.

"Ha!" She picked up her shoes with a big flourish. "That's

nice but I don't give a damn!" She marched past him with her chin in the air.

He happily followed.

Just before the terrace came into view she turned and looked at him.

"I'm just wondering," she said. She walked backwards slowly, achingly slow for Val. "If you've really changed, as you say you have, when are you going to appreciate it for yourself?"

She raised an eyebrow just enough to make him want to grab her and tear at the little wet buttons on her dress. But he saw his aunt and her guests sitting down to tea on the terrace. Elizabeth turned around and skipped up the steps. He heard the exclamations before he could finish the climb himself.

"Elizabeth!"

"Good Lord, child, what happened?"

He leapt over the last couple of steps. "I didn't do it, Aunt Rose!" He raised his hands to proclaim his innocence but Gladys Vaughn stared daggers at him. She got up from her chair and put an arm around her friend to lead her into the house. Cecily frowned and looked confused. Aunt Rose's eyes shrunk into a narrow squint.

Elizabeth laughed and waved off Gladys's hulking figure. "It's true, Rose. I did it myself. I wanted to make a point." She looked at him and nodded. "And I think I was successful, right?"

He stuffed his hands in his pockets, lowered his head, and bowed. "Yes, ma'am." He sighed. "Point made."

"Good."

Annie stepped through the terrace doors with a stack of fresh towels in her arms. Elizabeth took one, thanked her, and buried her face in the cloth. Then she tossed it over her shoulder. "I'll see you all at dinner."

* * *

TWELVE DAYS LATER Val stood staring into the full-length mirror in his room. The white short-sleeved shirt stretched over the muscles of his chest and revealed through the unbuttoned collar the dark skin underneath. The creases of his navy blue pants were pressed hard and perfect. A flash of white from the lightning outside danced across the floor, but Val ignored it. On his desk lay the ivory sheet of paper decorated with the monogram "M.M." in bloodred ink.

The letter was brief but he had spent the afternoon reading and rereading it. He was certain Mae's laughter had been sewn into every word.

> *My dear Val,*
>
> *Oh, tell me you can't be serious. Walks in the garden? And do you drink afternoon tea? But then I've forgotten: you are visiting your aunt. I suppose this is how older people spend their days. Is that right?*
>
> *I'm thinking of traveling abroad in August. There's nothing interesting to hold me here unless circumstances change. Do you think they will? Of course I can't tell the future like Mother Jenkins does in her storefront on Lenox, but I see things staying just the way they are. Nothing stands out to make me think anything else.*

Of course I miss you, but neither of us has time for the obvious. Not when there's still so much to do . . .

Mae

Val walked toward the door.

* * *

ELIZABETH SAT AT the grand piano in the library where the sound of thunder rolled around the room. But she didn't seem concerned with it. Her left forearm lay draped atop the piano and she leaned against it, tapping out a few notes with one finger of her right hand. She wore a sleeveless white shirt decorated with a green paisley print and a dark blue skirt. White sandals showed her bare heels, her feet crossed at the ankles. Val stood patiently and waited for her to notice him. When she did, she sat up but kept her seat at the piano.

"Oh, hello."

"Good evening. Where is everyone?" As if he didn't already know. As if he hadn't already discerned this shining moment of opportunity. He looked around the room anyway for her sake.

"They called it an early night. You know, the weather and all. Good sleeping weather." She tapped on one of the piano keys.

"And what about you?"

"Just sitting here enjoying the quiet. I was wondering why Rose has this piano here. I haven't seen anyone touch it all summer."

Val moved toward her and ran his hands over the varnished red oak of the piano's curved side. "That's because it's mine.

My aunt bought it for me back when I was a kid. I used to play all the time."

"You don't anymore?"

He leaned his elbows on the instrument and clasped his hands in front of him. "Let's just say I got distracted by other things."

"Play something now! Please?" She got up to clear the bench for him and indicated she wanted him to sit, but he stayed put. He had to consider the move. It was unexpected and a little too easy. But then, he thought, maybe he could use that to an even better advantage.

"Oh, no." Val shook his head. "I'm not falling into that trap."

"What trap?" She positioned herself on the other side of the piano. "You're being silly."

"No, no." He shook his head. "I see what's coming. I start playing something nice and you'll start accusing me of making up a seduction scene or something. I'm no fool." He put his hands up in front of him and backed away.

"No, I wouldn't do that." The back of her right hand rested on top of the piano. Her fingers, relaxed and open, looked, he thought, like a water lily. She slid them toward him, a gentle offering. "I promise. Look, I'm the one doing the asking. I really would like to hear you play."

Val stared at her. He hadn't played in a while and wasn't sure if there was any music left in his tainted fingers. But then she might find it endearing if he let himself try, if he made a few mistakes in front of her.

"Okay, okay." He moved toward the bench but kept his eyes locked on her. "Let's see here."

He sat down, tapped at a key, and thought about what simple tune he could plausibly execute. Then he remembered the song Sam had sung at the Swan all those weeks ago. He heard the words in his mind as he found the notes beneath his fingers.

Val was hesitant at first, but the melody wasn't difficult. He found it easy to lay more notes on top of it until the music grew into full-bodied sound. He leaned into the piano and pressed harder with both hands. It was such a strange song, but there was something he liked about it, something that drew him in like he was being wrapped in a quilt. He allowed the song to build until his fingers, electrified, wanted to fly up from the keys. But he insisted his hands remained grounded and he pounded onto the keys, enjoying the opposing pulls of flight and gravity. Then, too suddenly, the lyrics came and pierced him:

> *The greatest thing you'll ever learn*
> *Is just to love and be loved in return.*

Val pulled up from the keys as though the ivory had burned his fingertips. He moved a hand across his face and was startled to find a thin film of sweat on the surface of his skin.

"I don't remember any more." He didn't want to look at her. He turned his head and closed the lid over the keys.

She laughed. "You're a liar!" She playfully hit him on the arm.

He couldn't see. Purple spots mottled his vision and he stood. "Yes," he said slowly. He rubbed his eyes and moved away from the piano bench. When he could see her face he saw it was streaked with confusion and her hand, the water lily hand, now reached out to him. "I am a liar."

He wheeled around and left the room. The gallery hallway felt like a tunnel sucking him forward as he walked away from her in long regretful strides. He reached the main stair and started to climb. "Wait!" he heard her call. Her voice echoed behind him and bounced from the high ceiling above their heads. He kept climbing but she was fast—so light and so fast. He reached the second floor and she jogged up the last few steps and kept going until she had gained a few steps on him on the landing. When he saw how she had put her body so boldly in front of him to interrupt his escape, he realized this was where and how it would all play out.

"What's wrong?" she asked, putting up a hand to make him stop. It landed on his chest and he allowed it to stay there.

He looked down into her face and almost believed himself when he said, "I can't do this anymore."

"Do what?"

He pushed his chest into her hand as though to move past her. "Just leave me alone."

"No!"

Elizabeth took him by the arm and pulled. Of course he knew her room was closest to the stairs, but he didn't know how small hands could wield such strength. They felt like bands of iron tugging on him.

She let go of him and closed the door.

"What's wrong, Val? What's wrong with this? I thought being friends was enough for you." She touched his arm, but then backed away from him.

Val kept his hand on the doorknob. He wanted her to see he could leave at any moment. "Yeah, and that was a big lie, a whopper. I'm sorry, but I can't go on pretending I just want your friendship when I want more. A lot more." He leaned his head back against the door. What he said was so full of truth and lies it seemed his head would roll off his neck with the heaviness of it.

She covered her face with her hands and shook her head. "This is my fault. I thought it would be okay, that we could be together and this wouldn't happen. God is punishing me."

"What's going on, Elizabeth?"

She turned her back on him and started to move away, but he grabbed her by the wrist.

"No!" He pulled her until her ear was just under his mouth and he half whispered, half hissed into it. "I want to hear you say it! I want to hear it from your own lips!" She tried to shake loose from him.

"No! I can't! I can't!" He had her then and he knew it. He had to concentrate hard and pull carefully. This is where he would take her out of herself and what he would see, he was certain, would be shimmering, elemental, and his.

He wrapped his other arm around her waist and held her to him. "You tell me, Elizabeth! What is it? What is it?"

She paused her struggle and gasped. She pointed her chin down and away from him. But the words came, hushed and trembling: "I love you."

Val's features remained rigid. He picked her up and could feel the sobs rolling like waves up and down her body. He placed her on the bed, and saw her face soften and the tears subside. He moved faster, pulling her top out from her skirt and undoing the small buttons with his thick fingers. She stopped crying altogether then and watched him. When he had the shirt free and pulled open he looked into her eyes, deep brown and large, and suddenly his fingers froze. He stared down into her irises and a sickly acidic taste rose into his mouth. What he saw in her eyes made him feel as though he had been caught doing an awful and pernicious thing. Then he heard the music again, clear and insistent, as though someone had continued the song as he'd left it on the piano downstairs.

He looked away from her. "I— Elizabeth, I'm sorry."

Val pushed himself up from the bed. His knees folded like cardboard beneath him and he stumbled away from her. He managed to right himself enough to get out of the room, leaving the door ajar.

CHAPTER 35
Elizabeth

Mercylands, Late July 1947

The lightning broke in shards of white across the floor of Elizabeth's room. Rain fell in sheets and made the dark night darker. Elizabeth gave way to her sobs again and melted into the depths of water upon water. She could only hope there would be cleansing in such water, so she let herself sink further in.

When Val had picked her up she'd surrendered to a wave of exhilaration that quickly joined one of guilt, and the combined force of the two had bored into her soul so deep it'd anchored her to the ground. On that ground began the battle where she ripped herself in two as she struggled to let go for him, to give in to him. But she also remembered all she had lost in that moment—her marriage, her place in the world, her peace of mind, her connection to the Divine. What struck Elizabeth though was how wildly she fought to move away from the grief and toward Val, even hoping he would know how to help her.

And he seemed to try. He was so close to her. His lips full and brown floated above and she, split between agony and ecstasy, waited for the kiss. But then he seemed to see something far away from them, and even in the low light she saw the shadow passing over his face.

He was toying with her.

Or was miserable, miserable as she was.

Which was it? The question tormented her not because of what one or the other meant, but because of the base fact she cared at all. She did care. More than that, she *loved* him. She loved Val Jackson and told him so. What she couldn't tell him was how much he filled her up every single day, how the world sparkled with hope whenever he smiled, and how much she consciously, diligently, had to cut herself off from that hope and feeling of wholeness because she knew to love him would be impossible.

She didn't hear Rose's footsteps as she entered Elizabeth's room. Elizabeth smelled her scent of rosewater first, then felt Rose's hand, cool and comforting on her shoulder. Her touch brought Elizabeth back to some semblance of a present mind and she tried to quiet her tears.

"Honey, are you all right? I was going downstairs because I thought I heard Val on the piano." Rose lowered herself onto the side of the bed and Elizabeth moved over to make room for her. She wore a blue satin robe and her hair was twisted into one long gray braid that hung down over her left shoulder. "I was so surprised. He hasn't played in years."

Elizabeth nodded as she sat up and wiped her eyes. "It was him. We got a little carried away."

"Elizabeth, what's the matter?"

She looked on Elizabeth so kindly that Elizabeth wanted to turn away and hide in shame but she forced herself to look into the eyes of her friend.

"Rose, I love him." She breathed the words carefully because she felt them heavy and full of fear and wonder within her.

The elderly woman rocked back on the bed and sighed.

"Yes, well, I expected as much."

"What should I do? I feel terrible, like the guilt will eat me alive! It's unbearable."

"What can I tell you?" Rose shook her head. "As old as I am, it just seems to me the story is the same and nothing helps."

"But why should that be?"

"Do you really think men ever meet us halfway when it comes to love?" Rose's wrinkled, blue-veined hand patted Elizabeth's hand as it lay prostrate on the bed's yellow quilt. "Oh, they make a good show of trying, but they can't do it. They just grab up all the love in their fists and take all the happiness they can." She balled up her hand and it looked like a little world covered with tiny blue rivers. "They leave the guilt and the fear and everything else up to us. And what do we do? We take it like the fools we are. When was the last time you saw a man cry for love? They only think of themselves." She released her fist and took Elizabeth's hand. "My nephew is an extraordinary man and I love him like he was my own child. But I have to say for your sake, honey, he's the worst of them all."

Elizabeth's chin sank down into her chest. "I know. I've been so foolish. I can't believe I let this happen."

"Now, wait a minute, don't you go doubting yourself." Rose wrapped her thin fingers around the curve of Elizabeth's chin and raised her face to meet her own lively brown eyes. "This hasn't worked out for Val either. You're not like all the other women he's gone stomping after. You gave him something he didn't expect to find. I do know him, and whether he knows it or not, he's been looking high and low all these years for something to prove to him that this life is worth living. He's looking for hope and joy, like he's looking for a kind of light. Ain't no different than the flowers in my garden, looking to turn their heads toward the thing that will make them grow. That's probably why he loves baseball so much, because it's a safe place where he can feel a little bit of joy. But when he's really in his joy, it's like it's so beautiful he can't stand it. That's why he doesn't play the piano anymore. It's like he thinks he doesn't deserve being able to make music that beautiful."

"Yes! I had to talk him into playing and when he did play he seemed to get upset. He stopped right away. And then we argued a little." Elizabeth pulled her legs up and hugged her knees to her chest. "We ended up in here."

"Elizabeth, he sees that light in you. He thinks I haven't been watching, but I see what he looks like after you two have been out walking together." She nodded toward the door as though Val were standing there listening to them. "He doesn't come in with that smug, cat-ate-the-canary look he usually has when he's been with a woman. You have him thinking. I'm not sure, but I'd guess you're making him feel there are light and good and beautiful things in the world, and it's all out there for him. That's hope in a nutshell. Now, does he think he deserves you? That's what I want to know."

Elizabeth's eyes widened. "Maybe that's what just happened. A few minutes ago—" She pointed at the door and for a moment felt she too could see Val. "He could have taken advantage of me and he didn't. He seemed sad. I think he even felt sorry for me." She lay back again on the pillows and turned away from Rose.

"I'm so ashamed. I can't even look at you."

Rose placed her hand on Elizabeth's shoulder. "Well, you're going to have to look at me, honey, because you need somebody to talk to about him."

"But he's your nephew . . ."

"And you're like a daughter to me. Seems to me I'm the best person to know."

"Oh, Rose." Elizabeth sat up again and hugged Rose to her. "Thank you. You would be the best mother I could ever hope for."

Rose pulled away from the embrace but held Elizabeth by the shoulders.

"Then listen to me when I tell you, you can't go beating yourself up like this. For all you know, child, you could be saving Val's soul."

"I don't understand. How?" Elizabeth was surprised because this was close to how her friendship with Val had begun. She really had wanted to save Val somehow and she still thought it was vain of her to have ever believed she could do it.

Rose pointed at Elizabeth's chest and Elizabeth's heart ached recalling Val doing the same thing weeks ago.

"They say when you see the face of God for the first time, you see Him in the face of someone you love. That's not been possible for Val because he never loved anyone before. Now he can put two and two together because I know he can't have sat up there in that church every week like I know he does and not scooped up anything."

"But that's like saying a wrong makes a right. I can't be with him, Rose. I'm married. How can I even set foot in church again?"

Rose leaned back and looked at Elizabeth. She seemed to be appraising her face. "You think God would condemn you for loving someone?"

Elizabeth laughed wryly and shook her head. "I know a number of people in our congregation who would say that's exactly where I'm headed."

Rose waved a hand as though she would swat such people away from her. "Then they don't know anything about love— God's love or any kind of love. Is love what other people say it is, or is it what you feel in your heart? I admire you, child, for being capable of it." Rose gently touched Elizabeth's face again. "I pity you too because I know how much it hurts and that you have a long road ahead of you."

A single tear spilled from Elizabeth's left eye and streamed down her cheek.

"Tell me what to do."

Rose sighed and shook her head. "Well, I know Val won't like it, but it seems to me you should get away while you can."

She tugged on Rose's hands. "Oh, can I do that? He would be so angry! He already thinks I treat him badly."

"We can't be concerned with him right now." She searched Elizabeth's face once more. "The question is, can you handle being gone?"

Elizabeth looked down and shrugged. "I don't know. It already hurts to think I might not see him tomorrow."

"But you won't always be here, will you?" Rose leaned in and cupped Elizabeth's cheek with her right hand. "I know it

won't be easy to be separated from him. All these days of seeing you two together put me in mind of my younger self. Lord
knows I didn't expect to be remembering something like love
at my age, but you got me thinking about it and I do know what
you're feeling, child. I know you'd rather jump out that window
right now than go more than a few hours without seeing him.
But you're going to go home one day, that's just the fact of the
matter. You have to find out what you're going to be, with or
without him. That may as well start now, don't you think?"

Elizabeth stared at her friend a moment longer. She took a
deep breath and nodded.

"Yes. Yes, you're right, Rose. I've got to go."

She moved as though she would get up and walk right out of
the house, but Rose pressed her forearm and said, "You rest a
bit. I'll send Annie to pack your things."

Rose got up and kissed Elizabeth's tearstained cheek. "God
bless you, child."

Elizabeth nodded and watched as Rose padded out of the
room on her small, quiet feet. She felt the exhaustion beginning
to settle over her, but she wouldn't give in to it, not yet.

"Yes. Thank you."

CHAPTER 36
Val

Mercylands, Late July 1947

Val stood on the terrace with his head back and his mouth open as the rain poured onto him and into him. He thought if he stood there the water would run deep enough to find what had failed him on the brink of victory. But when he swallowed he only tasted the bitterness of his own body and didn't know anything more than he had before.

He spit on the ground and sat down in one of Aunt Rose's wrought iron chairs.

Elizabeth loved him, and she was, as of a half hour ago, willing to go to bed with him. He saw her in the fray as a shining angel, sword in hand, fighting toward him with all her brave and beautiful might. Was that what had moved him? That didn't make sense. He'd seen women fight for him, one straining to grasp the other's perfectly straightened hair in her fists. They would tear at dresses, throw shots of Jack Daniels in faces, and grapple on the floor until their underwear showed white and voluminous above their thighs. Val would hoot, turn to the bartender, and order another gin and tonic.

He had laughed then, but he was far from mirth now. Still, he felt he was on the edge of something that hurt and tickled him at the same time. It seemed if he looked up he would see it coming, loping along the horizon like a new rising sun, a joyous thing coming to take hold of him. He had known that sensation before in the moment right after pushing a needle into his arm. It felt like a tiny wave of happiness and he rode it on a fire horse galloping madly through his veins, bucking and stomping when it arrived at his heart. How could he have that feeling while sitting there in a storm like a miserable fool?

As if in response, the rain lessened and stopped. The night air, thick with the smell of water, hung heavy over him. Val shifted his wet feet beneath him and sat back, closing his eyes. Elizabeth felt so light in his arms, so light. And he wanted her, without question—had defied the demands of his body when he walked away from her. That made him grateful for the rain on the terrace, grateful for the cool water helping him to settle.

He hoped Elizabeth would be grateful for his self-control, then he laughed at the thought. He had been anything but in control of himself. However, he had spared her, and he fully expected her to recognize the obligation she owed to him. He needed to make use of it.

"You shouldn't sit there like that in those wet clothes."

Aunt Rose carried two large, thick pink towels folded over her arm and held close to her side. She handed one to Val and slowly draped the other over a chair before lowering herself into it. Val put his towel over his head and leaned down over his knees. He couldn't look at her just then.

"Aunt Rose." He put his hands on his head.

"I know, honey." She patted him on the knee and smiled. "You don't have to say anything."

Val pushed the towel back and around his neck. "Something's different. It's different this time."

She reached out and touched him on the arm. "You're in love, Val. After all your years of playing around, you'd think you'd recognize it when you're in it."

"No, I'm not!" he said, the words too fast out of him, a shot.

Rose sat back in the chair and clasped her hands over her belly. "You say that like they are the only words you know how to say because you've been saying them your whole life. Don't sound a bit like something you meant to say."

"I'm sorry. I didn't mean to snap at you, Aunt Rose. But I know what I'm saying."

"And I know you. If you didn't care about Elizabeth you'd be in bed right now sleeping like a baby. Instead you're out here drowning yourself. And she's upstairs ready to jump out of her own skin."

Val leaned on his left elbow as his hand went to his mouth, his fingers folded just at his chin. "Is she? What else did she say?"

She reached out, lightning quick, and slapped the side of his knee. "I didn't come out here to go telling tales on that poor child."

Val, surprised, recoiled. "All right! I was just asking a question."

"Then let's all ask questions." Rose raised her arms to the sky then pointed at Val. "Here's one for you. What do you think you're doing then, if you're not in love?"

Val pulled the towel from his neck and sat back, but said nothing.

"I remember a time when you were about ten and you came running in here with a turtle you found under the bushes." She pointed as though a young Val would appear on the lawn in front of them. "Your mama said you could keep it so you put it in a box full of green leaves with a dish of water and you kept it under the lamp in your bedroom." Aunt Rose laughed and shook her head. "You were so proud of that turtle. Talked about it so much you almost busted my ears over it. Never saw you happier than when you were taking care of that little thing. What'd you call it?"

"Shell. I named it Shell," said Val, astonished by his ability to recall it.

"Shell, that's right. Then one week later—" Rose raised her arms again. "Poof! No more Shell. Gone. I asked you where that turtle went and you just shrugged and said you put it back under the bushes where you found it."

He shrugged. "Yeah, I did. Why you talking to me about some old pet?"

"Hush, I'm trying to tell you something." She pointed at him. "Like I said, I know you. When something makes you happy, you drop it like it's hotter than coal. I've seen it. There are times when you strut around like the world was made just for you. But when you take it in your hands you only want to hold on to the parts that don't mean a thing." She shook her head. "You don't keep anything good—anything hopeful."

Val shifted in his chair. He was beginning to feel chilled by his wet clothing.

"What if you were in love, Val? Would that really be so

bad? Love don't come knocking at your door every single day." She lowered her eyes at Val and peered at him over her glasses. "You *do* know that. Why can't you let yourself enjoy it a little bit, even if it can't last? In my book it's always a good day when you get to hear someone loves you."

"Aunt Rose," Val said slowly, "love isn't exactly convenient for a man with my reputation."

"It may not be." She shrugged and laughed. "Could be all the more reason to try. But Val, you deserve love, you do, whether you know it or not in that hard head of yours. You may not believe it right now, but that's God's honest truth."

Val looked down and stared at his hands.

"All right, Aunt Rose. I'll think about it." But how did anyone think about being in love? Val wondered. It seemed like a senseless vocation, like something you couldn't think about because it was more likely to sneak up and sink you before you knew you were in it. Then he thought of the feelings that swirled in him just before his aunt arrived. Was that what was coming to him?

Rose moved in her chair as though settling into a thought. "And what about the Malveaux woman? What would she have to say about it?" Her eyes laid into him, hard and stern, a look he hadn't seen since he was a teenager.

Val shook his head. "She doesn't have anything to do with this."

"Doesn't she?" She peered at him again over her glasses. "Oh, be careful, Val."

He waved her off like a pitch he didn't want to throw. "It's all right, Aunt Rose. She's . . . she's something else to me."

"You're on dangerous ground." She grasped the hand Val

floated through the air and made him look at her. "There are people in this world who can never get other people to love them the way they want to be loved. It's like they spend their whole lives on their knees in the dirt in the woods trying to light a wet match. Can't spark nothing. The more they can't, the more they want to burn the whole forest to the ground. I can tell she's one of them." Rose tapped her index finger on his knee as if to focus his attention. "They're dangerous. They know they'll always be second rate, and they'll try to make you and everyone else pay for it. Be careful of that woman, Val. Just be careful."

Val wasn't sure he understood what she was talking about, but he was also old enough to know better than to dismiss anything she had to tell him. "I will. I promise, I will."

"All right then." She looked at him a moment longer before she put her hands on the chair arms and began pushing herself up. Val jumped up to help. "Thank you, honey," she said, and kissed him on the cheek. "Good night. And don't stay out here in those wet clothes."

"I won't. Thank you, Aunt Rose."

Val didn't go inside.

He began to walk along the terrace. Happiness—what was Aunt Rose talking about? He liked his life just fine. Who cared if he didn't go around chasing some sunny-side up business? He enjoyed what he enjoyed at a level where he could be safe and still keep hold of his own mind. This way he didn't have to be a slave to worrying he was going to lose something important to him. If that's what Aunt Rose saw in him then she was right. Whether he did or didn't deserve it had nothing to do with it. It was about being a man in the real world where loss was on the menu every day.

He knew he used the word "love" a lot with Elizabeth, but only because it meant something singular and precious to her. He needed to hold it out to her as an innocent offering like a single-stem rose, knowing she would ignore the thorns and grasp it at her peril. He enjoyed how she weakened each time he uttered the word. The thorns had become his chisel and he'd chipped away at her bit by bit until tonight, when finally she took on the shape he had worked toward so diligently.

Val sat again, crossed his legs, and stuffed his hands in his pockets. If this were love then he had indeed worked for it. Didn't he achieve—no, *create*—something that wasn't there before? Who was he other than a bad piece of gossip to Elizabeth Townsend before they had met? He had been no different to her than the man who delivered her mail. And now she couldn't sleep because of Val Jackson. She struggled so hard to love him. His angel.

What if you were in love, Val? Would that really be so bad?

No, Val thought. He could linger here awhile and enjoy it like a pleasant walk in a garden. He had earned it. Then he could fully, truthfully embrace his angel. The thought of doing so released the feeling he had earlier and, as though he'd given it permission to bloom, it spread throughout his being and warmed him. It felt good, perhaps even necessary. He stretched his legs out in front of him and fell asleep.

In his dream he thought he was waking to the morning sun. The backs of his eyelids glowed orange-red and he felt a blowing hot wind on his face. He rubbed his eyes and opened them only to find a black night sky. Then he saw it—a dragon. It was covered in silver and green scales and when it reared backwards, revealing horrible blue claws, it opened its mouth and split the sky with an inferno. Val fell to the ground, too stunned to cry out. He only stared at the beast and shielded his face from the heat with his hand. The beast laughed then, and the sound boomed down onto the lawn and bounced over Val, filling his ears. He covered his ears with his hands and tried to push himself backwards into the house. He wanted to cry. The dragon laughed like a woman, and there was something in the laugh Val found achingly familiar. It reared up into the sky once more then dove, dove fast and hard toward him.

His whole body shook with terror. No—he realized only his shoulder was shaking, moving back and forth of its own volition. Val opened his eyes and saw Sebastian shaking him by the shoulder.

"Sir, sir, you gotta wake up."

"What? What's going on?" Val struggled back up through the clouds of sleep. It was no longer dark, but not yet daybreak. He began to focus on Sebastian's face. He looked calm, but urgent.

"Sir," Sebastian said crisply. "Mrs. Townsend is leaving."

"What? Where is she?" He pushed himself out of the chair.

"I think she's already gone down to the car, sir."

Val, his still-damp clothes clinging to him, ran across the terrace, down the steps, and across the lawn to the driveway. A car, its lights on, was already far down by the gates. Val sprinted hard toward it, but the car slipped through the entrance and was gone. He kicked at the grass and swung at the air, wanting so badly to throw or hit something that the emptiness of his hands burned. The sound of the dragon's laugh came to him then, loud and persistent. This time he placed the voice with precision. Mae's laughter filled his head.

When Sebastian joined him in the driveway he had regained his breath and was able to speak with the concrete-hard tones he knew to be his own.

"Follow her," he said. "I don't care how you do it, just follow her. Report back to me as soon as possible. I want to know everything—everything! You understand me? She stops for milk, you tell me how big the bottle was."

Sebastian quickly scanned the road in the direction Val was looking. "Yes, sir!" he said and ran off to the garage.

Val walked back toward the house, the sun now rising behind him.

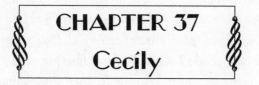

CHAPTER 37
Cecily

Mercylands, Mid-August 1947

Dear Sam,

One of Mr. Jackson's servants just knocked and told me he's getting ready to go back to Harlem. He's got some business he has to take care of at his club. The man said if I could write a letter real quick, Mr. Jackson would take it to you. So I'm sitting here writing as fast as I can.

I know you've asked about coming here, but it won't work out. If Mr. Jackson had stayed longer he could have helped us figure out a way. Frank Washington, Mama tells me, will be visiting us any day now. Besides, I will be back soon. I think it's better for us to wait—if you came here and we got caught Mama would send me away forever. Please don't ask for what I can't give you. It hurts to have to tell you no. And if you think I'm doing this because I'm starting to like Frank Washington, I'm not! I don't like him and never will.

But Mama may still make me marry him and when that happens, please don't worry. I love you—that won't change. As long as you still love me, and I hope and pray you do and you will, then everything will always be fine between us. We will be able to find a way to make it. And in a few weeks we will be together! I know Mr. Jackson will help us, and Cousin Mae might take our side too. So just be patient, Sam.

Mrs. Townsend left over a week ago now. Mrs. Jarreau told us she took sick in the night and went home. I'm sad about it and I miss her. With Mr. Jackson leaving too it will be just me and Mama here with Mrs. Jarreau. When Mr. Jackson came he brought lots of friends with him and we got to sit outside and watch them play baseball. Now I don't know what we'll do. When Frank Washington gets here it will be worse. But I'll be okay because I'll be thinking about you and singing our music in my head. Bye for now.

Love, Cecily

CHAPTER 38
Val

Harlem, Mid-August 1947

After Elizabeth fled Mercylands Val stayed on for ten more days, despite the steel cord in his being that pulled on him to dash after her back to Harlem. But he knew this would only result in useless scenes where she would doubt her own heart and his intentions. He admitted to one mistake early on: he'd written a couple of notes to her soon after she'd left. The correspondence went unanswered, but that was before he realized he had a more effective line of communication through Aunt Rose.

She coyly said nothing to him, but he was certain she was calling Elizabeth and checking on her. He believed Elizabeth would ask about him so he had been careful to craft his actions so Aunt Rose would deliver the image he wanted to paint. He stayed in his room as much as possible. The sacrifice wasn't hard—during the day he couldn't stand the thought of spending any time in the company of Gladys Vaughn and at night he had the young and eager Cecily to amuse him. In fact Cecily's visits—she often stayed until three or four a.m.—had the un-expected benefit of making him sluggish and his eyes heavy-lidded. One morning at breakfast Aunt Rose seemed taken aback by his transformation.

"Oh, Val, honey," she had said, her eyes dark with concern. "You've got to take better care of yourself."

He had patted her hand on the table, thanked her softly, and said he would go back to bed after he had eaten. And that's what he had done. He'd fallen asleep confident his aunt would soon relate the little scene to Elizabeth.

He had planned to leave Mercylands after two weeks, the appointed period his subtle calculations told him would be the time to return to Harlem. But if he were true and confident in his design he would have shared the date with Sebastian. Some part of him knew it might not be possible to wait.

He fell short by four. He realized even if he couldn't see her he wanted to be closer to where she was, to have the possibility of seeing her at church or the soup kitchen. They packed quickly, left quickly. But he applauded himself for having the presence of mind to send word to Cecily to write something for him to take back to Sam. He knew he couldn't return to Mae without a contribution to her game.

* * *

THE DAYS WERE growing shorter. Val looked out onto the street and noticed how the mere suggestion of cold weather—for it was only a chilly day in August—was enough to make the people down there quicken their steps. Men shoved their hands deeper into their pockets; women walked with one hand on their heads to keep their hats from being whisked away on the wind.

He had left his aunt's house a week ago. Once again he measured out time carefully, marking the days off on a calendar, following the passage of each hour on his watch. He felt the days shortening, not only because of the season but also because he knew he had to reach Elizabeth soon, and there would be fewer opportunities to do so. He had to be patient, though. As much as he would have loved to run up on her the moment he set foot in town, he knew that would ruin everything. He had to let her marinate in her escape, or what she thought was her escape. But he couldn't wait too long.

"Is her husband back yet?" he asked Sebastian, who reported on whatever details he could dig up. It wasn't easy. Besides a cleaning woman, there were few bribable people who had access to her. Still, Sebastian managed to find what Val needed.

"No, sir. And she doesn't see anyone. Hasn't been to church. The cleaning woman says it doesn't look like Mrs. Townsend has touched a thing in the kitchen. She believes she's not eating."

"Okay."

Val took a few bills from his wallet and gave them to Sebastian.

"Good job. I'll see her on Thursday. Make sure she's alone, though. I want to know first thing if she has any visitors."

"Very good, sir."

The phone rang and Val turned back to the window. Sebastian answered it. "Sir, it's the doorman," he said, his hand cupped over the receiver. "Miss Malveaux and Sam Delany are downstairs."

Val dropped his chin to his chest and sighed. "All right."

This would be the first time he'd seen Mae since returning to Harlem. He didn't often summon her—she didn't like it—but he thought the news he had for her would make up for it. He also didn't want to wait for an invitation from her to deliver it. But why was she bringing Sam with her? Val wanted to hate him and feel sorry for him all at once. He had read or overheard all his communications with Cecily and found that Sam truly seemed to be as guileless as the girl. Were love and life really so uncomplicated for him? If that were so, Val envied him for it. There must have been a time when it was the same for Val, when the world was open and simple and easy. But he couldn't remember it and he keenly felt the loss.

Sam bounded into the room. He shook Val's hand like he would bounce his arm off, like a child loving his favorite toy to pieces.

"Sam, my man!" He nodded at Mae. She was dressed immaculately in a Christian Dior outfit with a long black pleated skirt and a yellow jacket cut close to her slim waist. She pulled off her black gloves, touched a hand to the wide-brimmed black hat on her head, then sat down so gracefully in his armchair it seemed she was blessing it with her bottom.

"Hello, Val," she said, giving him a small smile.

"Mr. Jackson, I don't know what to say! How can I thank you for all you've done for me and Cecily?"

Val playfully punched him on the shoulder. "Oh, man, think nothing of it! Cecily just can't wait to see her Sam again. They'll be back from Aunt Rose's place soon."

"Yes, I know! It was in the letter you brought to me."

Mae tilted her head up at Sam.

"Two weeks! I think I might go out of my mind having to wait that long. I swear I've worn a path in my carpet, I've been pacing around my apartment so much."

Mae reached up and touched Sam's arm. Val couldn't help noticing it—Mae was stingy with physical contact, like she was some kind of Midas. Only she didn't turn people into gold. It was more like she was the gold and you could only hope she passed over some of herself with each touch of her fingertips. "Don't worry, my dear," she said to Sam. "I'm sure we can come up with something to distract you. Now, can you wait downstairs for me? I have to talk to Mr. Jackson in private for a few minutes."

"Oh yeah, sure. I am so grateful to you, sir. Cecily and I will always be grateful to you." He reached for Val's hand again and shook it.

Val smiled a real smile for him. He decided there was something refreshing about Sam's happiness and he would allow himself to take it in. "Well, your gratitude is enough for me. Don't think about it, man. I'll see you later."

Mae smiled at Sam, and the door closed behind him.

"Such a good boy."

"Yeah, he's all right." Val opened the humidor on the table and pulled out a cigar, but put it back when Mae frowned. "Hey, I've got some news for you. Thought you'd want to hear it firsthand."

"Oh?"

"I think Frank Washington's firstborn is gonna be a Jackson."

Mae lifted her chin and eyebrow at the same time. "Cecily is pregnant?"

"She's late and I don't think she knows it yet, but I'm pretty sure she is."

"How wonderful." Mae leaned back in the chair and clasped her hands out in front of her like a happy cat stretching in the sun. "Oh, people are going to laugh at Frank until his dying day and he won't even know why!"

Val rubbed his hands together. "Dumb jerk deserves it. But then again, does Cecily have to marry Frank? Like you said, Sam is a good guy."

"*No!*"

Mae's eyes flared hot and her cheeks hardened. It was all Val could do to stand his ground. He remembered the dragon and the fire in the sky. But then she smiled.

"You've had your revenge. Now I get mine and I want Frank's utter humiliation."

"Come on, Mae," Val said softly, surprising himself with his words. He spread out his hands like a peace offering. "Give the kids a break. You could find a hundred other ways to make Frank Washington miserable."

"Yes, but they would all lead back to me."

Val dropped himself onto the sofa and leaned toward her. "A woman scorned, Mae? I don't know—the part doesn't suit you. And the man's not worth it."

"That may be." She crossed her arms and Val knew what to expect next. "In any event I do have to thank you for doing your job so well. But I must say when you called me over here I thought you wanted to tell me something else."

Val retreated a little. He sat back and crossed his legs.

"I called time out on that one."

"Oh?"

"She was down and ready to give in and I saw something in her eyes."

"What?"

Val drew his hand over his face and sighed. "It was me—I saw a reflection of me in her eyes. It was like I could see what I was about to do and I couldn't stand it. I couldn't do it."

"How disappointing." Her hand floated to her mouth as though to suppress a laugh.

"She left my aunt's house." He nearly swallowed the mortifying words.

"I don't blame her!" Mae laughed and shook her index finger at him. "I would have done the same. She went through all that with you and finally surrendered and what did you do? Nothing! You walked out on her. I'd see that as an insult and I'd leave so you wouldn't have the chance to be so stupid with me again. You expect all women to respond the same way to all your old tricks. But every woman is different and you have to be prepared for anything. I'm surprised. And you a ball player! I would have thought you knew how to be quick on your feet, but that little prude got the best of you."

"Yeah, but not anymore." Val got up, went to the window, and stuffed his hands in his pockets. When he spoke again he couldn't tell if he was talking to Mae or to himself. "I'll go over there to her in the next few days and you'll see. No mercy."

Mae smiled but said nothing.

"And then it'll be over and I can—"

"What?" She raised her chin to him expectantly.

Val felt like he was looking for something out the window, like an answer would come sashaying down the street and shout up to him and tell him what was going to happen. He shook his head. "I'll be able to breathe again. She's in my head all the time. It's like a damn puzzle I can't put together. She's there in my sleep. She's there when I wake up. Why the hell is that? Why is it like that when she's—"

"Just a woman?"

Val turned back to Mae but couldn't say anything. He seemed to be looking past her, beyond her, still searching. Mae rose.

"I have to go," she said as she pulled on her gloves.

"Mae." He advanced on her a few steps until they stood directly in front of each other. "I'll finish it," he said, nodding. "And when I do I'll come see you after for another little visit."

"Make sure you do that, Val. Don't bother me otherwise. I don't want to hear another account of impotence."

He opened the door for her but she stopped just on the threshold and looked over her shoulder at him.

"Once upon a time you were a man." She smiled and walked away, her hips seeming to taunt him as they swayed pertly with her every step.

Val closed the door and found himself staring in the mirror on the wall next to him. His brow was furrowed and his eyes slightly bleary. He was disappointed he'd shown such a face to Mae.

CHAPTER 39
Elizabeth

Harlem, Mid-August 1947

Elizabeth couldn't pray, not even to say her mother's name. She knew praying was what she should be doing, using every sacred word as a tiny beacon to help see her way through the fog in which she persistently dwelled. She even knew which prayers would be best—she kept a small book of psalms on the table by her bedside—but she couldn't bring herself to open it. The New Testament was out of the question. The words "love," "compassion," and "peace" were too abundant there and since they were now blended in with her confusion— sometimes these words impelled her to run straight back to Val—she couldn't bear to read them. And she was absolutely certain Christ's words in the Book of Matthew, "Be ye therefore perfect, even as your Father which is in heaven is perfect," would break her in half.

But she thought often of the Book of Revelation, specifically the gift of the little book taken from the hand of an angel and how it tasted sweet as honey in the mouth, but turned bitter in John's belly. Because Elizabeth felt she was experiencing both the sweet and the bitter—she had tasted both constantly in the days since she left Rose's house. She thought so foolishly that she would come back home and move about her life just as it was when she left it. But the moment she stepped out of the car and into a world that so clearly did not contain Val, she'd stumbled and skinned her knee on the sidewalk. The doorman had come forward quickly to help her up, but she could tell she no longer knew how to put one foot in front of the other. She went upstairs and stayed upstairs and hoped from day to day that the feeling would pass.

Then, she surmised, if she stayed in long enough, she could go out and withstand the possibility of running into Val. She might even be able to endure looking at him and recognizing by the cast of his eyes how she was nothing to him anymore. The difficulty would be his recognition, because he would easily ascertain that she and her heart still stood exactly where he'd left them. Her humiliation would be complete.

But wasn't humiliation what she deserved? She had done all this to herself; that was the worst of it. Yes, Val was charming and magnetic, but she was the one who'd thought herself woman enough to redeem him. And, she must admit this to herself now, she *did* enjoy the fact he seemed so taken with her, even admired her. What she missed most was how, as she moved through the rooms at Rose's house and passed plates at meals and played cards with Gladys, he was always looking at her. She knew it despite not being able to meet his eyes herself.

She felt something comforting about his attentiveness; it was like having an earthbound deity watching over her, and she warmed in his sun constantly shining on her. Coming back to Harlem, she knew she would be giving this up, but she didn't expect to feel so devastated by the loss.

Kyle had called her on her first night back home. His calls to Rose's house had become irregular as the summer wore on. He said it was because he knew she wasn't alone and was in good hands. He seemed irritated that she was in Harlem again.

"What are you doing home, Elizabeth? I thought we agreed you would stay with Rose at least until I could come up for a break."

She gripped the black receiver in both hands as she sat down in his desk chair.

"I just wanted to go to church here. I was tired of driving all that way and back so early on Sundays." Her voice seemed small and high in her ears. *This is what a lie sounds like,* she thought.

"All right then. But I spoke to Rose and she'll take you back the minute you get tired of sitting there all by yourself. So you call her if you need to. You promise?"

"I will. I promise."

He continued speaking the way he usually did, in large swaths of monologue that required little response from her. This used to bother her, but now she was grateful for it. She didn't know what tone to use—what would conceal and what would give her away—so she thought it best to stay as silent as possible. Only after they hung up did she realize that not once did she say his name.

She knew then she could only love Val from afar. She just wanted his happiness. It didn't matter how despondent she was. But as long as Val's life was better, it comforted her knowing she'd played some role in making that happen.

And what of her own well-being? She had to make some effort. She saw by the way the cleaning woman looked at her cross-eyed she knew Elizabeth hadn't been cooking. Somehow she had to bring herself to eat again. She decided to take the approach of pretending she was a child again. She would eat simply, starting with plain things that would be warm and settling like grits with a little butter. Then she would learn to walk again. In the morning she would take a short trek, perhaps just around the block. She would have to go slowly and see what it felt like to have the presence of other people around her. She could acclimate herself to the sun again and accept its light as her guidance.

Next she would read once more, starting with the psalms by her bed. But what else would she read? Not poetry, not novels—both would only serve to keep her suspended in a dream world. She went over to the table by the front door and thumbed through the copies of the *New York Clarion* that had piled up while she was away. If she read the newspaper it would draw her out of herself and back into the world where people were working at jobs, passing laws, committing crimes, selling furniture, and renting apartments. She would be reminded of the problems of others and this might inspire her to go back to church and maybe even take on more volunteer work. She would be back in the mix of life then—active, functioning, and alive.

The beginning of this journey would start tomorrow, she

thought. She liked the plan for its simplicity and was proud of managing to think of it in the depths of her distress. It allowed her to go to bed on a hopeful note, and gratefully she crawled between the cool sheets and fell asleep.

* * *

BUT IN THE morning she found her grief refreshed, as was her desire to hold on to its exquisite pain. She liked how her world was pared down to this six-room apartment that held all of her needs and memories. If she wanted to dip a toe into the city all she had to do was look out the window and see all the people harmlessly walking back and forth. She could always start her journey back tomorrow. That thought became her litany and her journey was always slated for tomorrow, but she didn't take one step in that direction. She did read some psalms but after a few she always put the book down and sat on the couch staring at the pattern on the rug at her feet.

One day, just as she managed to finish some broth for lunch, she heard a knock at the door. The noise startled her and caused her to drop the bowl into the sink. It shattered. Would Val come to her? She hadn't considered the possibility and now that a meeting could be imminent she trembled. She moved toward the door slowly, leaning on a chair and then the couch as she went. Her heart pumped like a freight train engine.

"Mrs. Townsend? Are you all right in there?"

She stopped, and a tear fell down her cheek. The doorman. She shook her head at her silliness and opened up to greet him. Jack stood there looking smart in his green uniform with yellow braid. He tipped his hat.

"Good afternoon, ma'am. The mailman said your box was full so I thought I'd take the liberty of bringing your letters up to you."

"Oh, thank you, Jack!" She took the stack of letters and went to her pocketbook to get a dollar for him.

"Thank you! You let me know if you need anything else." Jack smiled, tipped his hat again, and left.

She began to flip through the letters but the thickness of one of the envelopes drew her attention. She recognized the shape immediately and when she saw the familiar handwriting she let the rest of the mail fall to the floor. It was a letter from Val. She smiled as another tear fell and she marveled over the handwriting and how the little packet of paper felt like the arrival of an old friend. She turned it over and over in her hands, her fingers rubbing the texture of the fancy envelope and the way its fibers absorbed the ink that displayed her name and address. Her heart seemed to be humming in a happy way and she knew it to be the anticipation of opening the envelope and hearing his voice again through his words. She held the letter to her nose but it carried no scent of him.

She put the envelope down on the table near her pocketbook and sighed. This tiny bit of joy made her realize she couldn't open it. As sad as she was, she knew it meant something that she was now a week old without Val. Each day she endured was precious. Though she still loved him, every day she didn't see him was a day in which she had learned something, even if it was just a minuscule thing, about living without him.

She thought again about the steps she could take to get her through the ensuing days: eating a simple breakfast, going for a walk, reading her father's newspaper. But despite the simplicity of the plan it suddenly seemed too much, too ambitious for her. And yet she could be feeling this way because she was tired. She decided to take a nap. As she settled herself on top of the bed coverings she thought about the next day.

Tomorrow—her journey back would begin tomorrow.

CHAPTER 40
Val

Harlem, Mid-August 1947

Two days later Val slid a fifty-dollar bill into the doorman's left hand just as he was about to lift the receiver with his right, and whispered, "Don't announce me."

The man immediately replaced the receiver and removed his green hat decorated with gold braiding and tucked the money into a seam inside the cap's lining.

In the elevator Val ran his fingers back and forth over the small folder he held in his hands but his eyes remained straight and steady. He stared hard at the door in front of him. The timing of this visit had to be right on target. Two days earlier would have been too soon. Two days later would have been too late. He figured right about now Elizabeth would be reaching the lowest depths. Now she would make the critical decision of whether or not she would ever see him again and he had to be there to push the point. It was all a cycle, just like anything in life. These past two weeks she'd been on the downturn, hiding out in her apartment, according to his information, and rarely eating.

He'd interrupted her process by sending the letters from Mercylands. He knew she wouldn't read them. In fact he was so sure of it he even copied one of the letters and resent it a few days after he'd sent it the first time. He enjoyed that joke for himself. But the letters would serve to nudge her, to remind her he was still seeking a response, an explanation for her sudden departure. He also liked the idea of his letters in her hands and how she probably worried over them every day because she didn't know what to do with them. Her slide would continue until she got to the bottom, at which point, Val was certain, she would have the strength to climb up again. Then she would realize how long she had already gone without seeing him and gain courage that she could continue to exist in his absence. He couldn't let that happen.

When Elizabeth opened the door, Val's heart felt like it wanted to leap right out of his chest and into her hands. He'd seen the dress before—the blue one printed with flowers—but it hung a little bit looser on her frame. Translucent shapes lay on the surface of her skin, traces of where her tears had been. He wanted to hold her and let her sleep because she looked like she hadn't done so in days. And yet these changes only made her seem more like an angel, more beautiful than he had ever remembered her.

"What are you doing here?" Her voice scrambled out like a handful of gravel, as though she had to recall how to speak. "Who let you come up?"

"Didn't have a choice." He walked past her quickly, finding his way down the short hall and into her living room, talking as he went. "You don't take my calls, you don't answer my letters."

She closed the door and stood with her forehead against it and her back to him. "How can I?"

"Well, that's why I wanted to see you." He spoke over his shoulder and faced into the room. This, he hoped, would draw her away from the entrance. "I realize I must have offended you real bad. Why else would you run away like that and not even say goodbye?"

She was silent a few moments. Then he heard her footsteps on the parquet wood floor. She walked all the way back into the room until she stood in front of him and raised her doleful brown eyes.

"I'm not sure 'offended' is the right word."

"No? Then what is?"

She lowered her gaze and said nothing. Val recognized the empty moment and quickly held out the object he'd brought specifically to fill it. He put the folder into her pale hands.

"Anyway, that's what I figured. So I wanted to tell you I'm sorry. And I wanted to give you that." When she touched the cardboard he held on to it for a moment longer so it connected them. "I'm sorry," he said again.

"What is it?" She turned the folder over. The words "Marcus Nelson Photography" were printed in gold script on the cover.

He shrugged. "Let's call it a memory of happier times." He looked around her living room. It was full of shadow because of the late afternoon light. Remnants of tissues were scattered on the floor.

She opened the folder and her right hand flew to her mouth. She moved over to a nearby table, turned on a lamp, and held the folder under it. Elizabeth examined the image closely. It was the photograph they had taken on the lawn at Aunt Rose's house. Val saw by the way Elizabeth's right index finger traced the border of the folder that he'd been right to bring it. The picture had turned out well. They both wore wide smiles, unaffected and innocent. Val thought anyone who didn't know them might look at it and think he must have kissed her right after the shot had been taken. There was nothing in this image of them that suggested anything else. And he loved it for that—how it held so much possibility of what he and Elizabeth could be and perhaps already were to each other. But he didn't let himself go too far down the road with those thoughts.

He gestured toward the picture with his finger. "I'm glad you like it. It's a goodbye present, really."

Elizabeth pulled her eyes away from the photograph and focused them back on him. "Where are you going?"

Val held his hands up as though the answer were obvious. "California. I could open up a club or two on the West Coast. I'll scout out some cities, live in Los Angeles for a while. Then maybe I'll move on to San Diego or San Francisco. It's a pretty big state." He moved toward her and shrugged his shoulders. "And it's far enough to run away from you. What do you think, Elizabeth? Would three thousand miles between us be enough?"

She dropped the photograph on the table. "You can't do that!"

"Why not? There's nothing left for me here." He shook his head and put his hands in his pockets. "If I stay in Harlem all I'll get is the misery of seeing you around all the time. I don't want that."

She took a step toward him and stopped. She wrung her hands in front of her stomach, her fingers twisting about each other like little lost vines. "But your life is here. Your friends are here."

"And what? Look, my friends, the people who really care, will be able to find me wherever I am. Why do you care unless—" Val suddenly gleaned a different tactic and smiled. Then he nodded. "Oh, I see. This is an ego thing for you."

"What?"

"I see it now. You like the idea of having some poor guy like me mooning over you and worshipping you like you're some high-and-mighty goddess."

"That's not true!"

Val saw the blood flush into her cheeks and knew he'd hit a rich vein. He was so close. "It's not? You said so yourself at my aunt's house. It's about God punishing you for being all vain and stuff."

"No, no! It's not like that at all!"

Val shrugged again. "Well, whatever. I don't have time for guessing games. I came to tell you I was sorry and I did. Everything I've done, I've done out of love, which is more than I can say for you. Getting out of here is the last thing I can do to prove it, short of killing myself."

Val turned toward the hallway but Elizabeth's hand, strangely strong and firm, grasped his arm.

"No! Don't go! You have to wait!" Fierce lines stamped

across her forehead and her eyes flashed. Val felt a rush of heat surge up from where her hand touched his skin.

"You just don't get it, do you?" The feel of her touch made him bolder. He drew the next words out so each one thumped with its own steady pulse. "I am sick of being in love with you." He knew then to pull hard away from her. He heard her nails scrape the cotton of his shirt as it came free of her hold.

"Val, stop it! Don't say that!" She threw her arms around his neck and her voice dropped into a whisper but the words were fast, urgent. "I do! I do care! Don't go, don't go, don't go."

She kept repeating the words but Val held himself rigid. He knew not to return her embrace. He had to listen right now. He had to listen—and wait.

He waited for a gesture, a look, a word, indicating permission. This permission would show she'd swept away all resistance, all barriers, and laid open the road to her conquered being. Then he could freely take possession of everything, as was his right as the victorious player. And he would set about proving why this was inevitable, how he had willed this moment into being. He saw himself as merciful, able to give her pleasure and at the same time release her from her struggles. He would reward her for giving in, and forgive her for holding him off so well for so long. He wanted to laugh at her desperate eyes, to tell her she could let go and she would soon feel better, all would be better, because he would make it that way. He wanted to lean his head back and preen in his confidence, to enjoy the sensation of being on the verge of fulfilling his brilliant plan. But he held himself still. He focused on her eager energy and waited for it to take its course.

Then Elizabeth put her hands on his face and in that moment he felt as though he were being pulled up out of himself, his essence stripped bare until he was nothing but raw shining light pulsing between her palms. Her fingers, strangely, were cool and firm—the touch of someone snatching a gift she knew rightly to be her own. He disintegrated in the grip of her confidence and thought he would collapse at her feet. This confidence, this knowing, was so shocking in its clarity. No woman had ever held him like this, face-to-face, eye-to-eye, as though every pretense had been wiped away and they saw clear down into each other's souls. He wondered how he had not seen it before: he was completely, utterly, hers. He'd been blind, stupidly blind. His whole life, which he finally saw with truth and transparency, had only been a long waiting—waiting for her to take possession of him. Tears welled up and stung his eyes. He forced himself to look down into her. He knew he had to go once more to the place that had unnerved him that night at Aunt Rose's. As much as he sensed truth he couldn't trust it until he saw the proof in the only place he knew to seek it. He dove into her brown eyes and this time, with relief, he saw himself mirrored there—and he saw love.

"You're the one who doesn't understand," she said. "Don't you know I can't live with you being miserable? The only way life makes sense to me is if I know you're happy."

Before, with other women, Val would reach the threshold of her surrender and hear a word toll in his mind like a perfect single chime: *now*. But this time he didn't need to hear the word and he didn't wait for it. His mouth was on hers and he wanted to consume her whole, to cool his parched insides that he realized had been dying. This was not some needy pawn throwing arms like steel bonds around his neck and choking the life out of him because she wanted so badly to be loved, to have his life within her. Was that why Elizabeth had always seemed so different than the others, because of what she didn't need? He had thought it was all about chipping away at her morality, her virtue, and demolishing the wall that made her inaccessible. But now he felt it. The thing that drew him to her took hold of him then and almost knocked him off his feet—*she was free*. And her freedom captured his spirit and showed him in one instant how he was the one enslaved to ego, flesh, society, and even his reputation. In her hands he wanted to renounce it all. Suddenly he was the one whispering fast, telling her as well as himself, "It's okay, it's okay. We'll be okay."

He wanted to begin his journey anew. It started first with the touch of her hands and then the next one—the touch of his lips to hers. The third—her hands again, light and beautiful butterfly wings, floating down to his hands. He quickly relinquished them to her. She looked up at him and nodded and smiled like the sun. She pulled him farther into the apartment and toward another room. When he realized where they were going he took her up in his arms and carried her in.

When he placed her gently on the bed she rose up on her knees. Again she put her hands on his face and her fingertips guided his lips up to hers. He undid the buttons of her dress and pulled it along with her beige silk slip down from her shoulders. Her hands remained where they were. He removed his own clothing. Then she leaned back on her knees and his face drifted down to explore the mysterious space below her breasts and above her belly. The softness of this one sweet spot bewitched him. It rose and fell with her every breath, and he felt safe. He pushed his face into this softness and thought if he could engulf himself there then nothing harsh in the world could ever break against him and Elizabeth.

Her left arm brushed his shoulder; her right hand rested against his head. She drifted backwards still, her thighs braced against his stomach. He could feel the strength of her muscles beneath him. He imagined she could lie all the way back, kick her legs out, and he could fly above her supported on those legs. But instead he wrapped his fingers around her torso and lifted her until she fully unfolded beneath him. He pushed her dress and undergarments all the way off.

Then he met her there, body-to-body, chest-to-chest, lying there as though on the first bed of his being. *Home*—the word not spoken but singing, singing throughout his skin. It was all there—sun and earth and the waters of Gethsemane; the salt and warmth of her rose from her skin as some healing balm blessing them both.

He was a navigator out of his element, beyond his carefully charted maps and courses. And yet he wasn't lost or fearful. The contours of her body were as familiar as his own, as though he had been dreaming her into form long before she filled the void of his ever-seeking hands. He wanted to enjoy this voyage so he took his time and allowed it to be a long while before he entered her. He wanted to wander over every area, every scent of her and to remember, remember, because it seemed he knew her before and had only forgotten her, had been out of his mind for centuries until this moment when he recalled where he should be.

How could this be? He thought he would've been comparing her to women of his past, eager to judge which motions of hers were too quick, too needy, or too awkward as he had witnessed in others before. But none of these thoughts existed. His mind was clear enough now to see how none of his life before Elizabeth mattered. Only this moment, here, with her in his arms was real.

At the same time shame—searing, heart-wrenching shame—poured through his veins. His vanity and pettiness attacked like rabid canines and their bite wouldn't let him forget how dishonestly Elizabeth came to be there. Could he ever deserve her? Could he walk through the world with his faults so fully exposed? But he stepped around these thoughts. He had to believe none of it mattered, that the shame was a last-ditch attempt by his former self to reclaim him. He stuffed it down and resisted. He was determined to live only in this new world and show her how much he belonged there.

Once he understood his surroundings he slid a hand down over her belly, between her legs and into her. He wanted to know where she lived and mark the place where he would stay. The lower part of him responded in envy and hardened. It coveted the place, silky and close. She lifted her arms above her and her hands perched like little brown birds on the bed's headboard. She pushed against it and her hips slid down allowing him to slide his hand deeper into her. She sighed.

He took this as an invitation to travel further. But he was careful to sense, to linger, to appreciate every measure he took of her being. He found the tiny starburst blot of scar tissue above her left knee, and the thin long one on the knob of her right elbow, and the rest of the cosmos of sights and smells that told him he would arrive and know what this place was and who he would be once more when he entered. *Home.*

A home that was her, but really him too, a part of him

returned he hadn't known was missing. The recognition of the unity was more than he could bear. His body burned with this wholeness. He knew such energy could not remain in him and the only place for it to go, the only place that made sense, was into her. When he released into her, it was in utter surrender. She drained him of essence, of ego and shame.

He wept. He held her tightly with his face buried in her hair so she wouldn't see, but he felt her chest billowing against his and realized she was crying too. He pulled away and saw her eyes shone bright in their own pools. She gulped and laughed. Her warm palm cupped over his cheek and brushed away his tears.

"Oh dearest," she said. "Please don't cry. I am here."

But her words only broke the dam and he cried harder. He didn't need another moment beyond this one. He could happily welcome the apocalypse, watch the world consumed in floods and fire. He didn't care. The disaster would only confirm the one certainty, the one thing in his whole life he now knew to be true: he would never leave her.

CHAPTER 41
Elizabeth

Harlem, Mid-August 1947

When Elizabeth awoke she found herself still burrowed against Val, his arm around her. Her head was half on the pillow beneath him and half lying against the dark and smooth skin of his chest. She didn't want to move and considered falling back asleep, but then she realized she wanted to just be there and turn this little bit of happiness over and over in her hands like a child with a snow globe. She had thought she would feel like another person, a stranger, when she saw herself making love to Val, reaching into him as if she could step inside his very skin. Isn't that how women usually saw themselves when they were consumed by fits of passion? They said things like, *I didn't know what I was doing; I was out of my mind; That wasn't me doing that.*

But Elizabeth felt down to the marrow of her bones that she was herself, truly, blessedly, boldly herself, perhaps for the first time in her whole life. She had reached for what *she* wanted and received it glowing and whole. And perhaps because of that sensation she feared neither pain nor punishment. She didn't know how to resolve that with her long-held beliefs about right and wrong. She knew only that she didn't see how anything bad could happen to her when she felt so strong in her body and so present in her mind. It was the Elizabeth who existed before this moment who seemed like a stranger. The new Elizabeth didn't want to confront or blame this relic—she only felt sorry for her, for how little she knew of herself. What was it she had been struggling against? What had she been trying to hold on to? It could only have been a wan sense of contentment that provided neither solace nor peace. In the drab landscape of "before," she'd considered herself happy because of her untroubled mind. Really it had been unstirred and flat. And she'd carried this lackluster way of being throughout her days with Kyle, thinking this had been good enough. That she hadn't had the right to ask for more.

But to her everlasting surprise she learned she didn't have to ask. It was there, presented to her with love and glory. It found her when she thought she was hidden. It humbled and softened her. It scolded this Elizabeth who'd seemed content with keeping her heart in one small box when all the time it had been whispering for more space—and she had refused to listen. Or she hadn't known how to respond. She was like a mother whose hungry child had asked for food, but she had none to give. She knew with all her heart she could never tell the child they had nothing to eat. She would dance over the words, toss up distractions, play games, anything to distract from the emptiness gnawing at both of them.

But her heart, refusing such controls, finally leapt out of its box. It made her reach out to Val the way she did. Yes, she ached at the thought of him going away and being sad and lonely because of it, but her heart acted jealously, desperately, because it knew how cold and constricted everything would be when he was gone.

She felt the wetness of him between her thighs and considered her body—she'd never known it was capable of such pleasure. And yet when she reached the moment of its peak, when her body felt so full of electricity she thought it would burst into tiny pieces of light to be absorbed into the earth, it seemed obvious the body, divinely designed as it was, would have such potential. This physical aspect of love made her feel human— she didn't know how she would have described herself before, but now she was freshly human, walking in Eden with her eyes open in awe and wonder of what she sensed of the world.

One day she would have to find words for this—words she would write down and send to him. She saw how ridiculous her earlier letters had been and she wanted him to have meaningful words from her, not lies and evasions. She decided to begin collecting the thoughts and tucking them away. When she had gathered enough she would take them out and write to him.

In small increments she lifted her chin so she could see his closed eyelids and feel his soft sleeping breath sweep across her forehead. He seemed peaceful, his body heavy in deep slumber. She wondered when was the last time, if ever, he slept so soundly? He was happy. *He was happy!* The thought gave her deep satisfaction, even more so than the physical epiphany she experienced earlier. She found what she'd sought for so long: purpose. Not a high purpose, such as feeding the hungry or guiding a lost spirit, but a purpose uniquely her own.

Only she could fulfill it. He was happy because of her, and her life, as such, carried a new preciousness to it. She would carefully preserve her life because it had this single, shining use: to love him.

He stirred. "Uh?"

She stroked his chest with her fingertips. "Shhh," she whispered.

The room darkened as the late summer sun waned. She knew she should sleep too, but the room still teemed with their energy. She thought she could see it, like shooting stars or a host of fireflies darting about before her eyes.

She draped her arm across Val's torso and pulled herself closer. He might tire of her someday. She wouldn't delude herself into thinking he was another kind of man. He could easily decide his happiness no longer depended on her, a decision he no doubt had made countless times before her. But she would deal with that decision and whatever it told her about her life when the road presented itself. She only knew she wouldn't be divided from him. She didn't know what that thought meant or what she might have to do to stay in his arms. But then she realized it didn't matter. His tears had been real. The way he'd held her had been real. She had touched him and seen the effects. He would never be able to deny this and make her believe it. Val could get up tonight and still go to California but he would never go alone, not really. Now she was within him, and he lived in her. Separation as she knew it no longer existed.

CHAPTER 42
Mae

Harlem, Mid-August 1947

Mae saw Val's arrival, of course. She'd been looking for him every day since she walked out of his apartment. She knew Valiant Jackson like she knew herself—they had roamed the inner rooms of each other's minds enough to know. Val's sense of shrinking time would push him to the point where he would come to her. But he didn't do so as quickly as she had expected, and she was surprised when she saw Val skipping— truly skipping!—up the steps to her front door. She stood at the window mulling over his energetic display when Justice showed him in.

"Well, my conquering hero!" She offered him a bright smile but he had already thrown himself onto the sofa with his feet up and his hands behind his head.

"Yes, ma'am, that's what I am!"

"How was it?"

"She was sublime."

"Is that so?" Mae slowly walked over to the table of cocktails and poured herself a half a glass of gin.

"Total release on both sides," Val said. He grinned like an idiot. "Joy! Just sheer joy! I swear I've never felt anything like it. It was the drink after the drought, the feast after the fast." Val paused and at first it seemed like he was searching for a word but then Mae realized he was going back into the memory. Finally he finished: "Just happiness."

She said nothing and sipped her drink.

"And don't you know I almost believed it all? Almost forgot it was a game." Val laughed and put up two fingers pinched together. "I came this close to proposing! Can you believe it? Me. But I got ahold of myself. Then it was over. And what was the first thing I did? Rush right over here to deliver the news."

"Oh, did you?" Mae looked at him hard. "You've got a funny way of rushing. I know for a fact you went to her on Thursday. It's Tuesday, Val, in case you've lost track."

She had thrown him. She saw the moment of hesitation right before he jumped up from the sofa. Val knew well not to get stuck in a vulnerable position like that. When in doubt, best to get up and move. That's what he did. He walked right up to her, took the glass of gin, and sipped from it before placing it down.

"Whatever. What matters most is I can now claim my reward."

He tilted his chin down and toward her face, but Mae turned away.

"Oh, so you brought your proof? May I see it?"

"Oh. That."

She poked him in the chest. "Yes. That. Remember our terms. Or are memories being worn short these days? You'll probably call me a stickler for details, but it's how I know I won't be taken for granted."

"Taken for granted?"

"Yes." She shrugged. "Otherwise I'll be just an easy conquest and you'll run right back to your 'sublime' other."

Val laughed. "What? You think I care a flying hoot about her?"

"Yes, I do. You're in love with her."

He touched the back of her neck. "You're crazy. And maybe a little jealous?"

"Do not toy with me, Val. And stop trying to hide it." Mae gently touched his face. "Remember, I know what you look like in love. I used to be the only woman who knew."

"You think I don't love you anymore?"

Mae felt a tiny twitch under her left eyelid and she lightly touched her middle finger to it.

"It doesn't matter. Besides, I have my own distraction at the moment."

"Yeah? Who?"

"Another time, Val. I'm in no mood to share secrets today."

"Well, I am in the mood for a lot of things." He kissed her on the forehead. She endured it. "I know what I want. And you could be right. But things being as they are—" Val threw up his hands, shrugged his shoulders, and grinned. "I just can't help myself."

Mae froze.

"What did you say?"

He shook his head and laughed. "I said I just can't help myself."

Mae nodded slowly. "All right." She smiled and crossed the

room to the door. She called for Justice to see him out because the last thing she needed was to see Val's back walking away from her after saying those stupid words. "Goodbye, Val," she said.

Before she turned she saw him open his mouth to say something but she was out before he had the chance to draw breath. She didn't want to hear it, not even his goodbye.

Mae climbed the stairs. When she reached her bedroom she stood for some minutes in the hall with her face in her hands. She needed to shift what she was feeling into other places where it wouldn't distract her. She took a deep breath and rubbed her temples between her fingers. When she lifted up her face she knew it showed the picture of calm punctuated with her trademark smile. Only then could she grasp the doorknob to her room and go in to where the eager young man awaited her.

"Mae!"

Sam lifted her up and whirled her into the room. She detested when he did this. Mae didn't like being off the ground and out of control. But Sam displayed such joy in picking her up, and he seemed to recognize the privilege of being so free with her that she allowed him the indulgence. This time she even went so far as to put her arms around his neck and kiss him while he still held her aloft.

"When do we leave?"

"Tonight." She kissed him again.

"And we're really going to Paris?"

"Yes." She nodded and he kissed her back.

"Yes!"

He twirled her around one more time before setting her down. She unbuttoned his shirt.

"What's it like, Mae?"

"Paris?" She glanced up at him.

He nodded.

"It's still August. Parisians enjoy the summer. We don't know how to do that here. There will be music and dancing everywhere. Paris is still waking up from the war, Sam, and you'll feel like it's waking up just for you." She ran a hand along his chest. "That's how I felt when I first went. It's not like here. Black, white, doesn't matter there. We can be who we are."

He picked her up again and placed her gently on the bed. "They say it's called the City of Lights." He kissed her between her breasts.

"Lights everywhere."

Mae smiled and relaxed beneath him. She noticed immediately how different making love with Sam was now compared to the first night when she met him. Back then they both acted out of lust and hunger. There was a naked aggressiveness to their desire—she didn't mind because she was in charge and he most likely followed her lead. Many of her assignations took on this quality. But making love with Sam now showed her the hollowness of that brand of tryst, and she would continue to fall through the emptiness again and again without ever reaching bottom. If she didn't steel her heart she would be sad at this realization. In Sam's arms she didn't fall. He caught her and wrapped her up in a cocoon so charming she felt like a girl again. Sam touched her reverently, and explored her with genuine curiosity.

If she could bring herself to be charitable, Mae might have felt some compassion for Val because she could only think he was having a similar experience with Elizabeth Townsend. He was smitten with the joy of a guileless lover, someone who saw him as being much, much better than he really was. Now Val was suffering from the delusion that he could be the person Elizabeth saw in him. In doing so he had betrayed Mae and, what's more, he didn't even know it. He could have easily followed her example. Sam was entirely devoted to her, but Mae still kept her wits and knew who she was and what she wanted. She would never neglect Val the way he'd neglected her. Trying to lie to her today had been the height of his disrespect.

Five days. Five days he'd spent with that woman and then had dared to play it off as an overnight victory he could hoot about. She would continue to make her moves.

* * *

IN THE MORNING, while Sam dressed and the servants took their bags downstairs, Mae wrote a quick note at her desk.

My dear Val,

> *I'm sorry we parted on such ambiguous terms. I'm leaving town for a few days, so let me be clear. When I return, provided that you've obtained the proof I require, we shall have that magical one night together. I can't promise anything beyond that, but we are the choices we make. I trust you will hold up your end of the bargain?*

M.

When they were ready, Mae and Sam got into the Packard, and Lawrence drove them to the airport. Once there, Lawrence helped her out of the car and as he did she slipped an envelope into his hand.

"Make sure Mr. Jackson gets this," she whispered.

Lawrence nodded.

Val's response found its way to her home quickly, but since Mae left no orders to forward her correspondence the note would remain stacked with other papers on Mae's desk to wait for her return.

> *As always, Mae, your wish is my command. But don't stay away long, okay, baby? New York ain't the same without you. And baseball season's almost over too. I guess I'll just have to be satisfied with getting your proof and finding other ways to have my fun.*

CHAPTER 43
Val

Harlem, Late August 1947

Val buttoned his shirt. Louise tugged up her stockings, pulled the skirt of her dress down over her thighs, and flopped herself back down on the sofa.

"I was so glad you called, Val. You know a girl like me needs her steady business."

"And you know a man like me gets very busy. But I always come around, don't I?"

He leaned down and kissed her. She took the chance to loop her arms around his neck and hang on.

"Mmm-hmm, yes you do."

To his relief, the intercom phone rang. The sound reverberated through the apartment. Val extracted himself and picked it up.

"Yes, Mr. Jackson, you have a visitor."

Suddenly the doorman's voice became distant.

"Miss! Excuse me, miss!"

When his voice returned the doorman sounded rushed and urgent.

"She's on her way up right now! I'm sorry, Mr. Jackson, she wouldn't wait."

Val nodded. "Don't worry about it, George. Thanks."

He hung up the phone, turned to Louise, and motioned for her to get up.

"You gotta go now, baby. Someone's coming up."

"Another woman?"

Val grabbed their glasses and the half-empty bottle of vodka and hid them in the liquor cabinet.

"Yeah. One who wouldn't exactly appreciate you being here."

He was about to grab Louise's pocketbook when Val caught himself and paused. What was he doing? He was Val Jackson, not some henpecked fool whose wife came home early. He couldn't believe Elizabeth was making him forget himself. If he wasn't careful she would have him on a leash parading him down Lenox Avenue. He stole a quick glance at Louise. She probably couldn't wait to tell her friends what she saw. Val Jackson tamed—how would that look? No, Val decided. He had to maintain appearances, and make Elizabeth pay for her insistence.

"On second thought, I really don't know how far her appreciation goes. Let's find out. You wanna play?"

Louise nodded and rose from her seat, and Val's doorbell rang. He put his fingers to his lips, positioned Louise where he wanted her to stand near his desk across the room, then went to open the door.

"Elizabeth!" He grabbed her arm quickly before she

tried to embrace him and led her into the room. "I'll be just a minute."

The entrance hallway in Val's apartment was long and the living room large. When Elizabeth finally reached the vast expanse full of light it took her a moment, Val thought, to notice the woman standing on the far side of the room.

Val continued to watch her out of the corner of his eye as he went over to the desk where he'd left Louise. He took out his wallet, put some money into an envelope, and handed it to Louise. A cloud descended quickly over Elizabeth's face.

"There you are, Miss Louise. Thank you so much for coming by. I hope I'll see you again soon."

"No, thank *you*, Mr. Jackson!" Louise tossed her shoulders, perhaps a little too sassy for Val's taste, but she was trying. He couldn't expect bronze to turn gold at the snap of his fingers. "You are so generous, as always! I'll catch you later."

Louise, taking her time to sashay slowly past Elizabeth, walked out, but all too clearly Val heard her laughing as she closed the door behind her. When he finally embraced Elizabeth it tickled him to feel her stiffness. She drew back fast and hit him on the arm.

"Don't touch me! How dare you!"

"Elizabeth!" He smiled and gamely deflected her half-hearted blows. "What's wrong?"

"I know who that woman is! She's a prostitute!"

"She is?"

"Liar! Liar! Don't ever come near me again!" She managed to land a blow to his shoulder.

"Ow! Okay, okay, you're right, she's a prostitute but it's not what you think."

"I know exactly what to think!"

He loved the way her eyes flashed, indignant and resolute. She had the dark brown eyes of a fine Arabian thoroughbred. The transformation captivated him.

"Yes, and that's what I was afraid of! How could I trust you would believe the truth?"

He moved away from her and, as casually as he could, went over to the liquor cabinet to pour himself a whiskey. He tossed ice into the glass.

"Truth?" She looked confused. He was delighted.

"Yes, the truth," he said as he poured the liquor. "Do you think women like Louise sell themselves because they want to? Louise, it just so happens, is trying to support a sick mother and go to secretarial school. I respect that kind of diligence. Some of our friends told me about her and, naturally, as a result of your good influence on me, I offered to help her out *without* her having to supply any favors in return."

Val took a sip of his drink and shrugged as he sauntered back to her. "Sure, I give her a few bucks from time to time. If it keeps her off the street a few nights a week, she'll be that much further along to going legit full time."

"This is true?"

Val saw the struggle in her face. He knew she was working hard to justify him and watching her do so made him love her even more than he thought possible.

"You're not paying for a child?" she finally asked.

Val put his chin down and spoke slowly because this was the point where most guys would get caught. Only liars spoke fast.

"Louise doesn't have any children. Elizabeth! I knew you were coming up. The doorman said you were on your way.

Wouldn't I have gotten her the hell out of here if we were doing anything wrong?"

Of course this fact was his ace in the hole. A little bit of truth always made a lie palatable.

Elizabeth absorbed his words. She nodded and seemed embarrassed. Val found this even more endearing as her face softened.

"I'm so sorry, Val. I just didn't know what to think."

He put his drink down and embraced her. Elizabeth's heart thumped hard in her chest as though it would leap out and join his own. The sensation weakened him and he realized how much he had risked and how stupid he'd been. She really was of his flesh, his other self. Why else would he treat her so callously? What had it gotten him? He had tried to hurt her and he was the one who had ended up feeling lousy. Because she was now grateful and loving, happy to be in his arms again. He couldn't deny her. This little slip of a woman managed to be so much bigger than he was and deigned, with so much sacrifice, to show him what he had resisted for so long—that he was loved. He promised himself that her sacrifice would never be for nothing.

"No, it's my fault." He buried his face in her hair, wanting to hide himself. "I'm sorry. I should have told you about Louise a long time ago. I'm just a dumb ass."

* * *

THE NEXT MORNING the sun wakened him, as it always did, when it reached that certain sweet spot right outside his bedroom window. He rose from the bed and stepped into the golden light. The heat felt cleansing, satisfying. He heard Elizabeth turn over in the bed and knew she was watching him.

"What do you see out there?" Her voice sounded soft and sleepy.

"Possibility." He turned around and looked at her. "I love this time of day. I love the way the light looks, how it makes everything look fresh and perfect and new. It seems like anything is possible. Maybe it makes me see the way I want the world to be. It's a way I never thought the world could be, but you made me believe in it. You make me see it."

"You look beautiful in the light," she said. She smiled and leaned back into the pillows. "I love you so much."

He sighed. He wanted to crystallize the moment—the light, how she looked, her words—and set it like a diamond in a ring to wear for the rest of his life. "That's what makes anything possible, isn't it?"

She nodded and held out her arms.

"Yes."

CHAPTER 44
Mae

Paris, France, Late August 1947

Mae had no illusions she and Sam would walk moon-eyed, hand in hand along the Seine or sigh at each other over cups of coffee at a tiny table on a wrought iron balcony overlooking the Eiffel Tower. Such images were for fools who believed in romantic fairy tales. They invested so much in the belief that when life finally proved it a lie you could see the graying veil of disappointment fall over their faces. Mae also knew, because she had seen it, people like that could leave Paris and return with the belief once again intact. She supposed it had something to do with the white gravel walkways or the carefully tended greenery or the city's clean lines that made them feel Paris opened its arms to them each time and made them new. Whatever it was, she knew the city had an energy she respected. She would use it to bind Sam to her, and she had to do it before Cecily returned to Harlem.

Mae was certain this was the right strategy because she

recognized Sam to be a sensualist—he was moved, deeply so, by riots of color, assaults of mind-bending scents, or simple, knee-weakening beauty. It was what made him sing the way he did, what made him bowl through the world gathering up life's wondrous experiences. He reminded her of Alice in the way he saw the world as so completely his own. She and Alice had wanted to go to Paris together, to take hold of it as a confirmation of their beauty, youth, and power. She could never give that to Alice. Perhaps she could give it to Sam. And he would love her for it.

They bounced around on the clouds on a late-night Air France flight. The turbulence fascinated Sam, and Mae was impressed that though it was his first airplane ride, he wasn't afraid. He didn't seem to have time to be afraid. He was determined, she thought, to feel the magic of the city. When they arrived she was certain he'd be disappointed. She saw right away Paris was still struggling to right itself after slouching through years of war. Women wore shabby summer dresses and careless thin sandals and walked barelegged down the Rue de Montaigne because stockings were hard to come by. Many of the buildings, dirty and hulking over their heads, were in need of repair and painting. Grass grew between the cobblestones of Le Marais. Something in Mae wanted to mourn the drab state but she didn't, perhaps because it all still looked like a storybook to Sam. He craned his neck out the car window to breathe the morning air. He stared at the people, the heavy arms around waists, the public displays of kissing. When he saw the Eiffel Tower, Mae thought he would cry out. But instead he sat back and just nodded. He reached for her hand and squeezed it.

Rationing was still in effect so she was glad she had the foresight to book them in a hotel, the Gerard, whose managers had the right connections in the black market so their guests would have coffee, milk, eggs, bread, butter, and cheese. Once in their room, Mae and Sam undressed and submerged themselves in the soft white sheets of an enormous bed. They made love and slept all day, an electric fan blowing a cool breeze over their naked skin. Then they ordered supper, roasted chicken and green beans, and ate it atop the bed.

"I know we're not going to leave here without hearing some music," she said.

"Mmm," he replied. He licked his fingers and wiped them on one of the linen napkins. "Let me find the place, Mae! I'll find us the hottest jazz in the whole damn town."

"All right." She leaned back into the pillows and smiled. "You go ahead and do that."

He took his time. In the meanwhile she indulged him with the tourist haunts. They rode to the top of the Eiffel Tower, and watched the barges slowly float down the Seine. When they listened to the bells of Notre Dame, Mae glanced at Sam and saw him wipe away a tear. They steered clear of the Folies Bergère and all of the 9th arrondissement. She didn't want to compete with the spectacle of nudity.

Over the next few days Sam managed, in both English and broken French, to communicate with bellhops, food cart vendors, strangers sitting in plazas, and elevator operators. He was able to glean that Montparnasse, once the heart of the city's music scene, was considered passé. All the hot spots held court in the Saint Germain area and Tabou, on the Rue Dauphine, reigned supreme. Of course Mae could have learned this with one telephone call to the concierge, but she allowed Sam the joy of his hunt. It would make Paris feel more like his own.

* * *

TWO SETS OF letters marked the name of the club. The first towered over the top of the door, the word "TABOU," garishly lit by lights shining underneath it. The second, a vertical column of singing yellow neon, glowed bright enough so one could locate Tabou the moment he turned onto the Rue Dauphine. The façade was dark and windowless. Tall men in loose-fitting jackets, their hair cut short at the sides but left longer on top, leaned against the walls and smoked. One of them stood up and held the door open when Mae and Sam approached.

"Thanks, man," Sam said. He slipped an arm around Mae's slim waist and guided her in.

Once inside, Mae paused. The place looked like a tomb. The stone walls rose from the floor and arched all the way across the ceiling to form a chilly dark cavern. Round tables hugged the sides of the tunnel and couples dancing filled in the floor space at the center. Mae peered through the smoky haze. She saw gray-faced men who looked like they were far along the road to being drunk, and women with stick-straight hair that they pushed behind their ears when men lit their cigarettes. How did people breathe in this hole? She turned to Sam to suggest they try another club, but he was already snapping his fingers to the groove pulsing from the other end of the room. He grabbed her hand and pulled her toward the sound. She felt the buzz beneath her feet and thought the music scuttled across the floor like beasts crawling on their bellies.

They sidestepped a couple spinning in tight circles and made their way to a table near the front, within shouting distance of the band. Mae figured the table was ignored or abandoned because the pool of light from the small stage spilled onto it. The people in Tabou tucked themselves into the dark corners like bats. Sam didn't seem to care. He sat in the light, ordered drinks, and pulled out cigarettes. He handed one to her and lit them both. He blew out a stream of smoke and began rapping on the table as though it were a set of drums. He was happy so Mae decided to be satisfied. She sipped her gin and tonic and listened to the saxophone player, a dark-skinned musician with a pencil-thin mustache, slide artfully through an improvisation as easily as a snake shedding its skin.

A jazz band in this setting was so different from the Swan. The musicians could have been in their own living room— that's how relaxed they looked, with glasses of whiskey within reach and burning cigarettes set carefully on ashtrays on the piano or on the floor. The drummer took off his jacket and rolled up his sleeves. The trumpeter, who wore his hair in a stiff black crew cut, had large ovals of sweat blossoming under his arms. The bassist, tall and thin like a straw, rocked back and forth with his instrument, plucking the thick strings with skinny fingers. Sam cheered them on and provided a running commentary: "All right now! Don't get too hot! You'll burn this place down." They laughed with him and tossed back his teasing. "Aw, man, you didn't come all this way to be cool!"

By one a.m. the band grew playful, improvising along the lines of Cab Calloway's "Boo-Wah Boo-Wah." The trumpets wailed bright like the noonday sun. Sam howled.

"That's old jive!"

The bassist stretched his giraffe neck down toward Sam. "Yeah, but it's still nice and hot!"

Now the saxophone perched on the edge of the stage and crooned at them like a great gold bird. To Mae's surprise, Sam jumped up and answered it. He didn't use words, just the notes, the music. He scatted out a long line of nonsense and it sounded gorgeous. His honey-toned voice rippled through the room like a fast bubbling river. The saxophone player smiled so wide Mae thought he would break his mouth. Then he put his mouth back to the instrument and blew a syncopated rhythm that delighted Sam. Soon a call-and-response flourished between them. The pianist waved Sam up to the stage and he gladly made the small leap onto the platform. He continued scatting to the frenetic rhythm and the saxophone responded. The audience ate it up.

The music took hold of Mae too. The liquor must have made it easier, made her stickier so this could happen. She didn't realize her shoulders popped up and down like pistons and her feet tapped underneath the table. But someone noticed. She didn't know where the voice came from, whether the stage or the audience. She only knew the command was meant for her.

"Danse! Allez! Vas-y! Danse!"

Mae stood and pulled the navy blue skirt higher on her legs. She kicked off her shoes and gyrated her hips. The sensation of the movement felt so good that she put her foot on the chair and stepped onto the table. When she knew it would hold her weight securely, she wrapped her arms around herself in a delicious embrace and tossed her head back in defiance. Then she danced. The drums rose thickly in her ears and the rhythm spoke to her and told her what to do. A wave of cheering washed over her but she didn't hear it. Only the drums got

through, only the drums played for her. Her motions felt familiar and she realized she was doing an imitation of a Josephine
Baker dance, from the jungle scene in *En Super Folies*.

Whistling rang in her ears. "Bravo! *Bravo!*"

She was shocked by how well she remembered the moves.
She danced for the memory of Alice. She danced for the triumph of being once more in Paris, only this time with a man
who could love and would love her if he didn't already. She
danced because she was free. Mae threw her arms open and
thrust her chest forward. She lifted her skirt and kicked out her
bare thighs in mad ecstasy.

The strange hand crept up her inner thigh. She felt it clutch
her skin and it dragged her back to herself. Her instinct was to
turn and kick—kick the face of the offender until it was soft
mush like grapes beneath her bare feet. She was about to do it.
Then a flash of light—shining brass—swept through the air
in a golden arc and found the man's face in its path. His cheek
exploded. Blood spurted from his mouth and stained Mae's
dress. She whirled and there was Sam, the trumpet held fast
in his hands. He breathed hard like a bull and stood over his
victim and poured epithets upon him.

"Mutha fucker, you're gonna keep your damn hands to
yourself now, aren't you? *Aren't you?*"

The man groaned, covered his bloodied head with his arms
and balled himself up on the floor. He was white with a shock
of blond hair and a light gray suit now soaking up his blood.
Mae jumped off the table and found her shoes. She pried the
trumpet from Sam's fingers and threw it down.

"Sam!" she said and tried to take hold of his arm.

The rage reddened his face like a ripening bruise. The

words, all nonsense now, still spilled from his mouth. The crowd pressed in on them.

"Il est mort?" she heard. *"Il est mort? Quelqu'un appelle la police!"*

Mae tugged harder until Sam's feet started moving. Then they moved fast, as though he wanted to catch up to the language he spewed throughout the cave. Mae pushed through the people coming forward to gawk at the man on the ground. Soon they were on the street. The night air hit Sam and silenced him. They moved away from the glowing neon letters and Mae looked up and down the street for a taxi.

* * *

HE REMAINED QUIET all the way back to the Hotel Gerard. Inside their room, he stripped the bloody dress off her and kissed her hard. His teeth nipped at her lower lip as though he would devour her. He pushed her onto the bed. She allowed it. He didn't hurt her and she knew he needed to do this—mark her, reclaim her. And wasn't this what she wanted? He was attached to her—she could feel that, deeply so. He'd gone mad for her, had shed blood for her.

Afterward she poured soap into the tub and ran a hot bath for herself. He put on one of the fluffy white hotel robes and sat on a chair near her while she soaked in the water. She leaned back, being careful not to wet her hair, and put her feet up on the side of the tub. The suds, looking like strands of clear pearls, draped around and slid down the skin of her legs. Finally she looked at him. He sat with his head bowed down, his chin to his chest—a chastened figure.

"This isn't the first time you've done this."

He slumped forward. "No."

Mae's eyes drifted up to the ceiling. She let her legs slide back down into the water and she waited for him to speak again. When he didn't she prompted him.

"Who was she?"

He sat up and shook his hands out in front of him. "I didn't know her! That's the damn thing about it, Mae. She wasn't even my girl."

She nodded and closed her eyes.

"It was in St. Louis. I grew up near there, in Jefferson. I was with some friends in a bar. They were sitting in a booth across the room, but you could hear them arguing down the street they was yelling so bad. I turned around and looked at them because I didn't know why somebody wasn't throwing them out. They were spoiling the nice night for the rest of us. I remember she had this big red flower in her hair, kind of tucked in behind her left ear. And I got caught up in staring at the flower. It was real pretty, with these long petals with yellow streaks. Must have been some kind of lily, like something my mama had in her garden. So I was thinking about that, my mama and her garden and how she loved her flowers and that's when he just reached out and wham! He hit her. That flower got knocked off her head and it went spinning on the floor. She fell over in that booth like a rag doll."

Sam sat up again and shook his head. "And the thing that got me was the way people just glanced at them and turned away like nothing was going on. Like none of them ever had a mother or a sister or an aunt. Maybe they didn't. I don't know. I just know I dragged him out of that booth and I hurt him bad. I didn't kill him, just hurt him real bad. Wanted him to see what it felt like to have somebody bigger whaling on him."

Mae opened her eyes to see Sam twisting his fingers together then pulling them apart like he wanted to find the man and pummel him again. He stood up and paced the short length of the bathroom.

"The police came and grabbed me, but no one mentioned how that woman had a shiner big as the sun on her face," he said. "We have laws where they'll pick you up for crossing the street wrong, but no one cares if you lay hands on a woman. Guys like that dumb-ass fool aren't punished and yet they can do more damage and get away with so much shit. Well, not in front of me they don't. Makes me so mad I can't see straight."

"How do you know?"

"Know what?" Sam stopped pacing and looked at her.

"About the damage."

"I got a mama, don't I?" He started pacing again. "But don't ask me about my daddy."

"Sam."

"What?"

"Please sit down."

Sam looked down at himself like he didn't know he'd gotten up in the first place. He dropped into the chair and crossed his arms. Mae closed her eyes again and made her calculations. She filed away the information about Sam for future reference. His strength and energy, not to mention his tendency to wield it with such force, could be useful. But his explosiveness had to be managed and she had to learn how to ignite it when necessary. She made plans to send money to Tabou to pay for the trumpeter's horn. She thought about what they should do the next day. When she came to her decision she asked Sam for a towel and she climbed out of the tepid water.

* * *

THE NEXT MORNING they slept late. When they awoke Mae saw from the way the sun slipped through the blinds and drew stripes on the floor it was already high in the sky. They ordered a late breakfast from room service. When they had dressed and eaten, Mae called for a car.

"Where are we going?" Sam asked. He wore khaki pants and a short-sleeved white shirt pulled over his broad chest.

"My choice today," she answered. She looked into the hall mirror and positioned a light blue hat on her head. She smoothed the skirt of her Dior dress and straightened the light blue belt at her waist.

The drive was a short one. Mae knew they didn't have to leave the city limits. The walls of the Musée Rodin encircled a haven of quiet and beauty within Paris. She would dip Sam into this place as if it were a hot bath and it would help bring him back to himself. When they got out of the car and he removed his hat and looked out at the gardens as though he were about to enter a church, she knew she'd done the right thing.

She took his arm and led him down the walk. "Do you know anything about art, Sam?" she asked.

"No, not really." He craned his neck to look back at *The Thinker* and Mae stopped so he could examine it better. "Damn," he whispered. "He looks so real."

"This is the Musée Rodin," Mae explained. "These grounds and the mansion behind these walls used to belong to a great artist, Auguste Rodin. I thought you might enjoy being here for a while."

She took his arm again and continued. The path opened up into a circle with a pond and a statue in the middle. When Sam saw the mansion before them with its broad façade and towered points on both ends, he sighed a breath of awe. Mae smiled but said nothing. She listened to the gravel crunch beneath their feet. They came upon a series of four statues of men, each on their own short pedestals. Three were nude but the fourth was draped in a fabric that seemed to be falling off him. The limbs of the statues floated in graceful gestures as though Rodin had captured them in mid-dance. Their dark color glistened in the sun.

Sam stood before them and stared. "Mae, they look like black people," he said.

She thought the angular noses and deflated asses on the men made them unmistakably white, but for a novice like Sam she understood the impression. "Yes," she responded. "I can see that."

The trees were still trimmed into the perfect conical shapes she remembered. She and Sam passed archways festooned in leaves. "It's like we're in a room." He whistled softly. "We're outside, but we're in a place. It's like the Garden of Eden."

"Yes." She remembered when she'd first visited the mansion years ago and how it had seemed the statues challenged anyone who viewed them. She'd seen people turn their heads because they couldn't endure the intimacy of *The Kiss* or the weight of a woman holding her head in grief. Or they would stand by the fountain and couldn't stop looking at the horrifying sight of a man about to devour his children. And yet she had cherished the experience because it was like Rodin had put these terrors and delights before them so they could master them. They taught her what was possible so she could react coolly when she came upon the terrors and delights of real life. But no one else had seemed to take away the same lessons. They couldn't get beyond their staring and their shock. She smiled and shook her head. She could tell from Sam's bowled-over expression when he gaped at the grotesque and melded heads of *The Three Shades,* he would be no different. But that was fine. She didn't want him any other way.

In the rose garden he stopped in front of the massive bronze doors depicting *The Gates of Hell.* Mae drifted to a bench and sat down. She knew the door well and knew Sam could stand there studying it for a long time. Of course the piece was fascinating. The figures teeming all over the doors belied the heaviness of the bronze. They floated, flew, loved, and writhed. Rodin had crafted a miracle. She wondered if Sam would notice *The Three Shades* were here too looking down at him from the top of the door. What was their message? *Abandon hope.* That was it. *Abandon hope, all ye who enter here.* She smiled. If she had been able to stomach the strange torque of the bodies she would have bought a copy of the statue and mounted it above her bedroom door.

"Look at this, Mae!" Sam waved his arm, beckoning her back to his side. He pointed to the figures he'd been studying. The man cradled the woman's head in his hand; she tilted her face up to receive his tender kiss. The fingers of his other hand sought to grasp hers. It was passion and terror entwined. "That's what it looks like to love," Sam whispered. He looked up at the suffering figures above him. "Does this mean the people who love will all burn in hell?"

Mae didn't point out to him the related figures on another part of the door that would seem to answer his question. The woman was swept away from the man into a swirl of despair. Instead she said, "I don't believe in hell." She strolled over to a bush and plucked a velvety red petal from a rose. She held it to her nose and enjoyed its perfume. Then she looked at Sam and smiled. "At least not in the way you think. I think it's all right here, right now—heaven, hell. The world is whatever you decide to make it. As far as I'm concerned I get up every morning and make my own heaven. Where are we right now? You said it yourself—Eden. I'm here; you're here. This is heaven. Why should I be worrying about hell?"

She strolled away from him and expected him to follow. But Sam remained. The bronze door, it seemed, had enchanted him. She heard him humming "Nature Boy" under his breath.

CHAPTER 45
Cecily

Harlem, September 1947

Cecily pulled the hood of the voluminous brown raincoat over her head and walked as fast as she could. She'd seen her chance the moment Mama, who'd stood in the hallway tying a pretty red-and-white scarf over her freshly pressed curls, said she would be back at two o'clock from her lunch with the ladies of the church. Cecily knew she had to leave right then and use the precious empty time to make it to Val Jackson's apartment and get back before Mama returned. When she reached 7th Avenue a blast of warm wind swept up from the south. It pushed her dress and coat around her ankles and made her suck in her breath. She turned the corner and joined the press of bodies hurrying down the busy street. She kept her eyes low so she saw only a bustle of soaked pant legs and dress hems and below them galoshes and stained shoes rushing past her on the wet pavement. The rain fell harder, in gray sheets, and she whimpered in dismay. If she ruined her hair, which had been straightened only the day before, Mama would know she'd gone out. But Cecily hadn't thought to bring an umbrella.

Nothing was the way she thought it would be when she got home from Mrs. Jarreau's house. It wasn't that she expected to see Sam grinning like a birthday boy and waiting for her on the stoop with a bouquet of pink roses or anything of the sort. But she wanted something to seem different. Maybe she wanted moss to spring up under her feet when she climbed the front steps, or to find Mama's houseplants had grown wild in their absence, the snake plant standing in the parlor, its spikes like giant green sentinels, as tall as Cecily, and the devil's ivy spilling over its pots and reaching out to trip them the moment they stepped over the threshold. But there was nothing so outlandish, nothing to hint there was any extra life in their home. Instead Mama closed the front door and followed Gideon, who took their bags upstairs. Cecily stood at the parlor window and listened as the house settled into silence again. She didn't know what to do with herself. She held the white kid gloves she'd worn in the car, and chewed on her lower lip. When Mama came back downstairs and scolded her, telling her to change her clothes, Cecily sadly realized she'd only been waiting for someone to tell her what to do. She felt a shrinking inside her, like everything about her that had stretched and grown over the past few weeks was being balled up like a piece of paper full of mistakes. Would she have to throw herself away and start again?

But Cecily had done everything Mae said to do, right down to making Mama believe she'd be willing to give herself to Frank Washington. She endured his visit to Mercylands and managed to conjure a look of friendliness for him. She smiled at him the way she figured she might do for Sam, and did not pull away when he wrapped a heavy arm around her shoulders as they walked across the lawn. He smelled syrupy sweet like fake mint and she tried not to think about what it would be like to have that scent in her nose night and day, for the rest of her life. She had seen Mama watching them from the terrace and Cecily waved at her in a way she hoped would seem contented and cheerful. But Mama's face, instead of being pleased, had looked pinched and broken. Later she said they would go home in the next day or so. Cecily felt so grown-up then, and so smart. She started packing before she went to bed that night and wondered how she would get word to Sam she was coming home.

She had drifted through three aimless days in Harlem. On the third night she was slouching up to her room, consigned to another lonely, childlike sleep, when she opened the door and found Val Jackson standing there. She nearly screamed. He held his long dark fingers up to his lips to shush her. He pulled her into the room, took a quick glance out into the hallway, and closed the door.

They sat atop the thin patchwork quilt on her iron-framed bed and spoke in whispers. Cecily shifted uncomfortably. He smelled warm like chocolate and his skin shone smooth and bright like a new penny. His presence seemed too large for her girlish room with its flowered wallpaper. And her dolls lined up on the shelf above the white vanity table suddenly seemed out of place. She hoped he wouldn't notice them.

"Are—are you staying?" she stammered. Two horses reared up in her heart, each one kicking its hooves in an effort to overcome the other. The one was glad to see Val, and only needed him to give her the smile that seemed to light up the world to make her spread herself out on the bed for him. It would ensure that the new and very physical part of her she'd discovered at Mercylands was not a dream or a mistake. He would smooth out what had been shrunken since she returned and be her reward for fooling Mama and Frank Washington into satisfaction.

But the other horse wanted all her thoughts and all her desire to be focused on Sam. It wanted her bed to be their own; where she imagined she would share her new womanhood with Sam in hushed whispers. And Harlem would be the place where she was his and his alone, Frank Washington notwithstanding.

Val smiled as though he knew what she was thinking. Her fingers grasped at a piece of the quilt near her knees. "No, I can't stay long. This is just a reconnaissance mission."

Her hand relaxed and the rest of her body followed suit. "A what?"

He pointed to her windows and doors. "I'm checking out the house—had to find out how to get in, and where your room is. Now that I know I'll pass it on to Sam."

Her face brightened. "Sam! Have you told him I'm home?"

"No, I can't find him." Val shook his head. "He hasn't sung at the Swan in nearly two weeks. No one's seen him. But don't worry; he just doesn't know you're back. He's probably off moping somewhere. When I find him I'll get word to you."

She bunched up a piece of the quilt again in her fingers and sighed. "You will?"

"Oh yeah. He'll be here before you know it."

He kissed her and smiled. Then he went back to the door and put his ear against it. She tiptoed over to him and listened too. When he opened it she watched him slink quietly along the hallway and then down the back stairs.

But another week had slipped away. September arrived and Cecily was still alone. It bothered her that Mae hadn't been in touch, not even to visit or offer a few words of encouragement. She hadn't been to church, either. Cecily did manage to sneak a call to her one day when Mama was taking a bath, but the maid who answered the phone only said Mae wasn't available. Cecily didn't know what that meant. Was her cousin at home? Could Mae call her back? The maid wasn't much help and Cecily didn't want to get Mae mad at her so she didn't try again.

Then came the awful realization, after carefully marking a tiny pocket calendar day by day, she'd missed her period. She sat on the toilet and wiped at herself again and again, looking for the faintest sign of pink, some sign that she was wrong and her flow was about to begin. But there was nothing and Cecily felt sad and alone. For days afterward she dreaded Mama's eyes and her touch, as though she could divine her daughter's condition long before the baby grew enough to show. The word "trouble" took up residence in Cecily's mind and crowded out any sense of womanhood she'd once had. She was a girl again, a girl "in trouble," which was the phrase she used to hear whispered among Mama's friends when they gossiped over cards and thought she was out of earshot. At night she lay in bed and tried to imagine the size of Mama's wrath, and thought how it could only be immense, and deeper than anything Cecily had witnessed before. Most likely it would sweep her away like Noah's flood. When she slept she dreamed the bed moved, heaving and shifting because the waters were already rising beneath her.

One night the dream changed and Val stood on a rock looking down at the water swirling around him. Cecily struggled to hold on in her rickety boat, but then she saw Val and he smiled at her like the brightest beacon. The light shone in her face and she woke up blinking, her eyes stinging. She knew she had to get to Val and tell him. Since she didn't know if or when he could return, she had to risk meeting him during the day. She praised herself for that bit of clear thinking and for recognizing her chance when it came.

On the last block she started running until she reached the shelter of the foyer of Val's building. As she stepped in, she caught her reflection in the glass of the door. Her eyes looked wild and frightened. She frowned and leaned her back against the stone wall. She waited to catch her breath. There was something lopsided and wrong about the way she looked. How could she be running scared from her mama and about to be a mama herself? It made no sense. She made no sense. What kind of mama would that make her? Would her child be as scared as she was? The thought squeezed a knot in her stomach and she wanted to cry. Instead she rubbed her tired eyes and stood up straight.

Inside the doorman raised an eyebrow when she asked for Val Jackson. He seemed to hesitate, and his sharp eyes cut up and down her figure before he finally picked up the phone. She couldn't hear what he said because he turned his back to her and hunched over the receiver. Then he motioned toward the hallway in the back to his right and told her to go up. He spoke the apartment number in a dark, low tone. Cecily pushed the hood off her head and tried to walk to the elevator looking as dignified as possible. She sighed with relief when she made it to his floor and Val opened the door.

"Cecily, what are you doing? How did you get here?" He stuck his head out into the hallway and surveyed the corridor. "Did anyone see you?"

"I ran, I think, most of the way. Mama went to a lunch with some friends, but I have to get back soon." She peeled off the dripping raincoat.

"What's wrong?"

She took a deep breath and let the words pour out in an overflowing stream. "I'm pregnant! I've been checking and waiting for my period but it's not there. It's just not there! I don't know what I'm gonna do. Mama's gonna kill me!"

"Stop it! She's not going to kill you." He turned his head and called into the apartment. "Sebastian!"

He appeared so quickly and quietly it made Cecily jump. Val handed him Cecily's raincoat. "And bring a towel," he said.

Cecily put her hands up to her hair. She hadn't given any thought to what she must look like. She tried to think about what a mature woman would do. She pulled her shoulders back and took a deep breath as she followed Val into his living room. It helped that there was something soothing about the smell of his apartment. She couldn't tell if it was cologne or aftershave but it smelled warm and earthy and spicy all at the same time and it made her feel a little better. Val looked distracted and she wondered if she had interrupted him. What did Val do all day? It never occurred to her he might not be there. She could have risked the trip for nothing. She could have called.

So stupid of her. She saw papers on his desk—taking care of business? Is this what men did? Write orders? Send money?

He led her to a large blue sofa with black and white cushions. "Now sit down," he said. "And calm down. Stop going on like that."

She lowered herself onto the couch and nodded. "Have you found Sam yet?"

Val shook his head and sat next to her. "Sebastian is still asking around, but right now it looks like he skipped town."

She covered her eyes and began to think. She ran over every word Sam ever said to her. He'd given her no indication of being unhappy with her, of wanting to go away. If he had a club date with a band, people would know. Sebastian could find that out. Of course she and Sam hadn't seen each other in weeks, but would he really abandon her? He wouldn't unless he . . .

She looked at Val, her eyes wide.

"Do you think he already knows?"

He paused as though he were considering the possibility. Cecily felt her stomach go sour. Finally he said, "Don't be silly, how could he? You haven't told anyone, have you?"

"No, no one!"

Sebastian returned and presented Val with a thick white towel. Val handed it to Cecily and dismissed Sebastian. She mopped at her damp cheeks and pressed both palms into the towel to absorb the sweat on them.

"All right, now, Cecily." Val put a firm hand on her shoulder and the pressure of his touch helped her to focus. "I want you to listen to me. We'll find Sam, all right? He's bound to turn up somewhere. Then I'll set it up so you two can spend the night together."

"How?" Her hand flew to her mouth. The moment she said it Cecily knew it was a silly question. Val had been able to find his way into her house and into her bedroom without Mama knowing about it. Why couldn't Sam?

"You let me worry about that. Once we square that away, all you have to do is wait a few weeks. Then you tell him you're pregnant with his child."

She wrung the towel in her hands. "But that's not true!" It was bad enough she was lying to Sam about being true to him. She had been able to make herself feel better about it by thinking what happened with Val was a temporary and necessary situation. But could she lie about a child? For a whole lifetime? She could barely think about being a mother—how could she look Sam in the face and tell him a lie like that? It felt sinful, sinful in a way she couldn't fit around lying about sleeping with Val. That was different. But why? Maybe because this kind of lie would hurt people. It would hurt Sam and it would hurt a little baby who hadn't hurt anyone. The burden seemed too big, bigger than the Empire State Building.

Val pulled the towel away and took hold of her hands so she had to look at him directly. "Cecily, I need you to grow up here. Your mama is making plans for you to marry somebody within the next six months. Who would you rather marry, Sam or Frank Washington?"

She shook her head as though he should know the answer was obvious. "Well, Sam of course! I love Sam."

Val touched her face with his warm fingertips. "All right then. This is the only way you're gonna make that happen. And to fix it so that your mama doesn't kill you. You got it?"

Cecily stared back into Val's dark brown eyes and realized Sam wasn't the only answer to her problems. She thought about the dream that inspired her to seek out Val. She had to be truthful to herself—what did she expect in coming here? Did she want Val to help her get rid of the baby? Lord no! And she wouldn't have told him about being pregnant if she thought he would want that. Val Jackson was her baby's daddy, and she must have known in the bottom of her soul if she still wanted a life with Sam, she needed Val's help—and his willingness to let his child be raised by someone else. Now here he was being that beacon of light and giving her the words, the permission, for what she'd really wanted all along. Suddenly she felt the weight of what he was doing. She felt selfish and ashamed because she would be the one to get what she wanted. She bowed her head and nodded. "Okay."

"Great." He lifted her chin with his fingers and smiled. "Cecily, it will be all right, I promise. We just have to find Sam."

Warmth flowed into her face and she believed him. "Yes."

CHAPTER 46
Val

Harlem, September 1947

September 3, 1947

Dear Val,

 You may be surprised to receive this. Why should I write when I have the complete joy of seeing you every day? But I do believe a letter is necessary. I can't stop thinking about the way I behaved that day when Louise was there. You must have been so disappointed in me. I know I showed every sign of having no faith in you. I'm sorry. Love can't exist where there's no trust so I must mend this breach. The best way I know how to do that is to put down on paper the depth of my love for you.

Val, I've searched my whole life for something to do that matters. No one has ever let me even try to do meaningful work. Not my father, not my husband. But you have seen meaning in me, enough to inspire you to change your life. It made me happy because you shone a light on me and showed me that I exist and I'm important—me, Elizabeth. You seemed to be able to take something good from every little thing you've seen me do, from praying and serving in the soup kitchen to cutting flowers and hitting a ball. You act like all the things I do hold up the universe for you.

And why shouldn't I do this for you, my dear other self—yes, I even give those words back to you!— because I realize what I do benefits you and what you become enlivens me. Can there ever be a more perfect match? When we make love I feel I am home. Your skin has the scent of warmth and inevitability, as though I've always known you and have only been marking time waiting for you to arrive, waiting for my life to begin. Now here you are. Here we are.

My excuse for that terrible day can only be jealousy—stupid, naked jealousy. You have to know it's my own insecurity, my own doubts about measuring up to such a striking woman. Please don't think for a moment I ever stopped loving you.

I'll close here because I expect you at any moment and I want to put this in the mail. I'm too embarrassed to hand it to you myself. See how silly and timid I still

*am? But be patient with me, Val, please be patient. I
promise I will atone.*

> *All my love,*
> *Elizabeth*

Val sat alone, his feet propped up on the desk, reading
the letter over and over. He had it at last, the proof Mae demanded. The feeling of victory pumped through his veins and
he wanted badly for it to be enough. Because if it were enough,
if he could just be satisfied in knowing that he had won, then
there would be no reason for him to betray Elizabeth.

He could keep the letter, and cherish it, and feel blessed. But
what did it say about him that he was still thinking about giving the letter to Mae? If he were truly a better man, wouldn't he
dismiss the thought outright? If he weren't a better man, then
the letter only proved Elizabeth a fool for believing in him. It
pierced his soul to think this of her. Once again she proved to
be so much bigger than he was. How was it she fought so well
for him and he couldn't lift a finger to protect her? Scum, that's
what he was.

It was getting late. The shadows were growing long over the
buildings outside his window. He had to make a decision soon.
He didn't know how, but it might be possible Mae already
knew of the letter. She would gain the upper hand if he withheld it from her. Maybe it was better this way, that he finished
things with Mae, closed out accounts. He might be in a better
position to protect Elizabeth if he played the game to its natural
finish. If he did that, he saw no reason why he shouldn't end up
with his love.

Val stood up and called for Sebastian. He would need to know the latest information on Mae's whereabouts.

* * *

THAT NIGHT THE rain fell steadily but Val stood beneath the stairs at the brownstone's ground floor, and was grateful for the cover. He knew it wouldn't be possible to get a key, even though Sebastian had wanted to try, but Val knew the trouble that would run through the house like a tornado if its owner discovered disloyalty. Besides, he had the smarts to work a lock himself. After a few minutes he gained entry.

The house was as it had appeared from the outside, shut up and dark. Using a flashlight he found the back stairs and made his way up and along the corridor until he reached a certain door he once knew well.

He opened it quietly. They were there, the two forms on the bed, just as he'd thought they would be, but they weren't asleep. He waved the flashlight over them and Mae, quick as ever, turned on a lamp. She wore a long ivory-colored negligee and a matching robe over it. Sam was shirtless but, Val was relieved to see, wearing pants. He thought about what Aunt Rose had said and wondered if Mae really wanted the same thing he had with Elizabeth—a pure, joyful experience of love. If that were the case, and they were fighting essentially for the same thing, then this might turn out to be a battle royal.

"Oh, here you are!" Val feigned cheerfulness. "Don't you know how worried I've been? The house all shut up, no word for weeks."

Mae stared calmly and, Val noticed, didn't move the arm

she held possessively over Sam's chest. "I told you I was out of town."

"Oh, that's right! Well, maybe I forgot. I'm getting on, you know. My mind isn't what it used to be. But really I was looking for this guy." He nodded at Sam. "My talented friend here, Mr. Delany."

Sam got up like he'd been shot out of a gun and began putting on his shirt. Val enjoyed the stunned look on Mae's face.

"Uh, me, Mr. Jackson?"

"Val, it's late." Her note of warning was unmistakable but Val ignored it.

"I know, I know. And I wouldn't have come if it wasn't so important. Sam here would want to know about Cecily."

Sam fumbled with the buttons of his shirt.

"Cecily? Is there something wrong with Cecily?"

"Aw, come on, man, what do you think? She finally gets back after being gone all summer and you know the first thing on her mind is 'Where is my man?'" He pointed at Sam.

Sam put a hand to his chest as though he had to remind himself of something. "That's me."

"Of course, you dummy. You'd think the world was gonna end, the girl's been crying so hard. Almost made herself sick."

Sam's eyes widened into saucers. "Cecily is sick?"

Val wanted badly to laugh but that could wait. Instead he shrugged. "Naw, she's fine now. She'll be even better when she hears from you."

"Man, thank you, Mr. Jackson! You're right, I was so stupid to go away like that."

Mae sat up then and Val moved over to Sam and grabbed

his hand before he could detect her wrath. Sam shook it vigorously.

"I better get going. I can't thank you enough, Mr. Jackson."

"It's all right, man." Val chucked him on the shoulder. "Come see me tomorrow."

Sam started to leave the room, hesitated, and turned. "Uh, Mae, I mean Miss Malveaux—"

"Oh, don't worry, Sam." Val clapped him on the back and guided him to the door. "I'll look after Miss Malveaux. She and I have a lot to talk about."

Val closed the door behind him.

Mae lowered her chin and frowned. "Just what do you think you're doing?"

He recognized the look, her bullish one. But he had already decided: there would be no destruction tonight. He waved the letter in front of her face. It was his ticket, his protection—proof of his obedience. He dropped it into her lap. A twinge of doubt, hot and sharp, pierced his stomach. He ignored it.

"You told me not to waste your time." He sat on the bed, watched her face as she read, and wondered what would come next. Mae was right about him. He didn't deal well with curveballs. She was a master of the unexpected. It would be a matter of staying focused and trying to catch what she threw at him. But giving up the letter freed him. It meant he'd held on to nothing. His hands were empty and waiting for Mae.

"How very basic," Mae said at last, folding the letter and handing it back to Val. "She's not one for creative phrasing, is she?"

Val smiled. This was a cheap shot at Elizabeth, but one

easily fielded. He took the letter and tucked it back into the pocket of his jacket.

"Oh, I'm willing to bet your piano playboy hasn't gone beyond the 'wham, bam, thank you, ma'am' stage yet."

Her chin rose up, full of defiance.

"Sam is devoted to me! And he's much more interesting than you are."

Val laughed and shook his head. "Oh, Mae. Are you trying to back out of our deal?" He touched her leg under the sheets. "And here I thought you loved me."

Her face softened. Her mouth opened slightly and her fingers gripped the sheet next to her. He thought she looked brittle, even vulnerable.

"I do love you," she said.

His smile faded. Blood rushed to his groin. He held his breath. He didn't dare move. She seemed to sense this because she rose and positioned herself behind him. She whispered words he hadn't heard in years.

"Don't *ever* think I don't want you."

He leaned back into her and exhaled.

"But do you want me?" she asked. "Do you want me in the way we've always wanted each other? If I could believe you did, it would be so easy for me to honor our agreement. So easy."

She ran her hands over his shoulders and down his chest. She kissed the top of his right ear. He forced himself to keep his eyes open. He stared up at the white plaster of the ceiling.

"You know I do. I always have."

Her arms tightened around him.

"I don't know. That woman—she's changed you."

"She doesn't matter. You mean more to me than she does."

"Then why are you still with her?"

"Hey, it's not like I haven't tried to dump her. She's even caught me red-handed with another woman."

Mae's lips touched the curve of his ear. She whispered, "And what happened?"

"She forgave me. She's like that—that's how she loves me. I can do no wrong."

Mae pulled herself around to glide to the front of his torso until she sat on his lap and he held her.

"You should have expected her to be sticky like that. But I can help you."

"How?"

"You'll have to follow my directions exactly or it won't work. Promise?"

He nodded. He didn't use words because he didn't want to hear himself agreeing to whatever came next.

"This is what you do."

She kissed him lightly on the brow just above the top of his nose. He closed his eyes.

"You tell her you're bored. It's time to move on. She will be shocked. She'll want to know why. You will say, 'I just can't help myself.'"

He opened his eyes. Her hands cupped his face but she gazed away from him at a spot in the air just to his left as though she were looking to pull her words out of the void.

"She will cry. She will ask what she's done wrong. They always ask that. You will say this is how you are. 'I just can't help myself.' And that would be true, wouldn't it, Val?" She ran the soft pad of her thumb over his lips. He nodded slowly.

"Yeah."

"That's what will make it easy. A truth well told is much more effective than a lie."

He tucked his head and nuzzled his face into the warm skin of her chest.

"But why do I have to do all that? Why can't I just drop her, stop seeing her? It's not like I haven't done that before."

She reached down and smoothed a hand over his forehead. When she got to his hairline her fingers pinched a piece of his hair and pulled so he had to look up at her. He winced. She ran her long slim finger down the center of his nose. Her eyes bored into him with a hard, shining brightness.

"Because it won't be finished. She'll come after you. Drag it out. She'll want to understand. You'll have to play it all out sooner or later."

She slid off him and back onto the bed.

"You may as well do it now. Be in control. Keep your reputation intact. Otherwise—" She began to laugh.

A coal in the pit of his stomach began to burn.

"Can you imagine what your friends would say if you started going around Harlem with Elizabeth Townsend? Would she even set foot in your club?"

He chose to ignore these words. "She'll be crushed."

"Yes, well, at least she has a husband to take care of her. Besides, what do you care? You don't love her." She shrugged and sighed. "Goodness, Val, I'm tired. Since you let yourself in I'm sure you can let yourself out."

She climbed back under the sheets and arranged the pillows beneath her. "Good night."

In the dark corridor, leaning against the wall, Val sank down to the floor and covered his face with his hands.

* * *

HE HADN'T BEEN to his club in weeks. But after leaving Mae's, Val decided he needed to be there. After walking all the way in the rain, he felt wet and heavy when he arrived. He shook the water from his coat and handed it to the girl, who would know to dry it off further and have it sent up to be hung in his office. His stride felt short and hesitant when he first entered the main room. But his step soon took on the bounce of the Louis Jordan song playing, and his feet accepted the more confident rhythm as he made his way across the crowded dance floor.

> *I don't care if you're young or old,*
> *Let the good times roll!*

One hand touched his shoulder. Another reached out to shake his. The greeters had to shout to be heard over the raucous footfalls of the dancers.

"Hey, Val! How's it goin'?"

"Jackson! How 'bout them Dodgers? They got that pennant in the pocket."

"Man, where you been?"

A big-bottomed girl with sleepy eyes and a toothy smile shimmied into his path and tried to engage him in the dance. He obliged her for a few steps, but then went on his way. As he crossed the room he saw friends, dancers, and patrons, continuing to hail him as they always had before, smiling and waving. A few times, though, he found he had to shake his head and look again because the faces seemed contorted and grotesque, with their mouths gaping. He thought the waving hands closed into fists or pointed fingers and he heard in the music an under-current of laughter—of people laughing at him.

But he knew this couldn't be true and he managed to shake off the feeling. Once he did, he felt better by the minute. Eventually the club, the dancers, and the atmosphere did what he needed them to do: pump him full of bravado and remind him of his name—Val Jackson. Because as Val Jackson he saw no reason why he couldn't field the play Mae had put in motion in such a way that would allow him to best her and still have Elizabeth in the end. He could cut Elizabeth loose now, but it would only be temporary. He had no doubt he could win her again. It wasn't just because of his abilities that he knew this. He was simply that certain of her love. Forgiveness and mercy charged through her blood. She had forgiven him several times and, he was willing to bet, had done so countless times more for infractions she'd kept to herself.

But what about Mae's assessment of his reputation? He eyed the people juking around him as he cut through the dance floor. Would they really dare laugh at him? Again, his ego came to his rescue—even if they did, he was fully capable of shutting them up. They would all bow down to him when the details of his machinations became public. For him to juggle so many women, and of such varying ages and sensibilities—well, the whole affair would make him legendary. He laughed to himself because the word felt good: "legendary." And in this final assessment the hurt he would inflict on Elizabeth would feel like a mere pinprick. The pain would be momentary, his fame everlasting. He knew, though, this would be the last time he'd ask such a sacrifice of her. He knew grace, at least for him, extended only so far. He would gladly acknowledge he'd put her through purgatory and then hell and she had survived it like no woman—ha, like no person!—he'd ever known. She would have earned his undying devotion then. He would happily give it.

He made his way through the crowd and up the stairs to his office, where he slammed the door closed behind him. He sat in his chair, lit up a Montecristo, and put his feet up on the desk. He rocked a bit and thought about what he had to do. What would be the best way to do it? Mae had given him the script. He saw no reason not to use it. Such a detail would play in his favor—it would be easier to disown the words when the time came. And Mae would like knowing she had a significant role in the scene. It would further ingratiate him to her.

He turned the words over in his mind, particularly the curious phrase, "I just can't help myself." He didn't like it. It made it sound like he couldn't control himself when he had been nothing but controlled all summer. His choices had all been good—gaining Elizabeth had proved that. But the very thought of his gain, and the memory of its consummation, caused him to suck in the cigar smoke too quickly. It stung his throat and he sat up coughing. He recalled his tears and her own and her words: "I am here."

He could write a letter. The benefit would be the advantage of being able to turn over a copy of the missive to Mae, another token of his sincerity. But then he would have no way of knowing how Elizabeth had handled the news. Could he stand that? If he couldn't he might be driven to see her somehow, and foreseeing the result would be tricky. He might feel moved to placate her, to begin too soon the work of luring her to forgive him. She had her own way of working, and he respected her enough to know he wasn't totally immune to her ability to seduce him. If he gave in that would anger Mae— she would certainly find out about such a betrayal, however minor, and that would destroy everything.

No, he had to see Elizabeth and see her just once. He had to rip off the bandage fast and clean. He could make his little farewells that would allow him to step away from her. He would observe her carefully and take mental note of what he might perceive as bread crumbs he could leave on the path that would eventually lead him back to her. This bit of hope would help him withstand her inevitable tears and, for the moment, view her as just another of the women he'd known who had wailed over the loss of his company. He would make himself see Elizabeth as the ordinary woman Mae insisted she was. Of course he knew better, but this tiny delusion was necessary for his performance. With this thought he grew more confident in his ability to pull it off. As long as he prepared himself well, he saw no reason he couldn't come out of the event shining.

* * *

THE NEXT DAY Val waited for Elizabeth to go out before he bribed the doorman to let him into the apartment. He planted himself on the sofa and stayed there, leaning back and staring at the ceiling. He needed to be alone, in her rooms, to empty himself of her as much as he could and prepare for what he needed to do. He unraveled himself through one hour and then the next. He could have used a third hour but then he heard Elizabeth's key in the lock and in another moment she rushed, breathless, into the room.

"What a surprise! I didn't expect you. When the doorman

said you were here I was so excited, the elevator couldn't go fast enough!" She threw herself onto him, her arms around his neck. "It was like time stood still. Do you ever feel like that?"

"I feel like that right now."

She didn't notice he hadn't touched her, and he knew he had to keep talking because if he didn't he would touch her. If he touched her he wouldn't be able to do what he came to do.

"I've been feeling it the whole time I've been sitting here. Like I'm stuck. I've been a fool to think I could ever change. I just can't help myself."

Elizabeth hopped off him and flopped down on the sofa next to him. She laid her head against his shoulder and smiled. "What are you talking about?"

"Me. I'm talking about me. I just can't help myself. I've realized I'm done with you."

"What?" She raised her head.

He homed in on the piece of sky, calm blue, he saw through the window.

"It's time. The only change I can ever make is to move on to the next woman. It's time. I just can't help myself." Having the phrase helped him stay focused. When he didn't know what to say, he would say it and it kept him moving where he needed to go.

She was staring at him, waiting for the joke that would surely follow. But when he didn't laugh, she seemed to choke on what she said next.

"What are you saying? You don't love me anymore?"

He shook his head slightly. "I don't know, Elizabeth. Was it love? Because if it was, it had a hard time outlasting the win once I had you."

He stole a quick glance at her—bad move. He saw the tears already present in her eyes. But they had yet to run down her cheeks. He turned his attention back to the ceiling and delivered another line.

"I just can't help myself," he said. Then he shrugged. "You can't seriously believe you're the only woman I've been seeing?"

"The prostitute?" Her left hand pressed on his chest. He was going to have to move and do it soon.

"Right, but she doesn't matter. There's another and she *is* all that matters." He pushed her hand away and got up from the couch. He felt a reluctance in his leg muscles and thought he would fall back toward her. He managed to make it to the brown wingback chair near the hallway and he put his hands on its back to steady himself. He would need to be able to go quickly so he was glad to be closer to the door.

"Look, she's a jealous woman," he said. He surprised himself by laughing a little. "Even more so than you! She won't share me so I have to give you up. That's all I can say. I just can't help myself."

"Liar!" She shot up from her seat, the words hot from her lips. "I can't believe you. This isn't you talking! Why are you doing this?"

"Me?" He laughed fully then and shook his head. "I don't think so. You need to look in the mirror. I . . . am . . . a . . . snake." He said the words slowly, deliberately, as though he had to remind himself as well as her of the truth of them. *A truth well told is much more effective than a lie.* "You knew that! When you get close to a snake and the snake bites, whose fault is it? You knew I was a snake. And I'm still a snake."

He shrugged and shifted his feet. He repeated Mae's phrase again, but he felt the words, dull and flat in his mouth. "I just can't help myself."

"It's not true." She pulled at her hair and bit her lip. "And even if it is— Val, I know I'm not like the women you're used to. I'm not as pretty or as interesting, but I can change!"

He put his forehead down on the back of the chair and wanted to scream so he wouldn't hear her words. There was a kind of blasphemy to them and he couldn't bear to hear it, not from her.

"You changed! You know you did! You're no more a snake than I am. Val, please—"

He straightened himself and was horrified to see her coming toward him. That silly, adorable curl hung over her eye as she looked down to unbutton her shirt.

She said, "If you can change, so can I."

He wanted to grab her right then and there and make her stop. He wanted to whisper, as though Mae might overhear, that the hurt wouldn't last for long. He wanted to plead with her not to make this so hard for him. But he knew her so well—so very, very well. It wasn't her nature to stop, because she loved him, and she would be determined to make things right for him because that was what she wanted for him. If her love had been a selfish one she would do what he had experienced before— she would be throwing lamps at him, and trying to punch him or claw at his eyes. That's what the ordinary women did.

"Look, your husband will probably be back soon," he said. He shuffled his feet backwards so he could maintain the space between them. "Or you can find yourself another man. It's your choice, but from now on I can't care about what you do. I've never regretted anything, not a day in my life, and I'm not about to start now."

She reached for him, but Val ran. He shut the door before she got there and in another moment he was around the corner and flying down the building's steps. His heart banged in his chest and he knew how close he'd come to failing. If he had looked at her, if he had touched her, he would have taken it all back within a moment. He felt like a thief running from the scene of a crime. He had to put as much distance between them as possible but he knew as he rushed down the street with tears stinging his eyes that however far he ran, it would never be enough.

CHAPTER 47
Mae

Harlem, September 1947

Mae sat writing letters at her desk and waiting. It was a Friday night, almost mid-September. She thought for certain Val would be at her door sooner. Her handwriting floated onto the paper but she couldn't focus on it. He had paid what she assumed to be the fateful visit on Monday. She didn't expect to see him that night or on Tuesday. He had to have his show of being in control and she could allow for that. But Wednesday slipped by and then Thursday. She thought about the possible reasons he hadn't come. Each one annoyed her and made her fidget in her chair. Was he checking on the woman? Or had he been truly moved by her? Maybe he didn't dare show his face because he didn't know how to hide it. But this thought made Mae smile. She pushed on the tip of her pen and punctured the sheet of paper.

No. She was certain he would have the nerve to stand in front of her, to celebrate his actions, and to try to deny Elizabeth Townsend ever meant anything to him. She marveled at how he could sustain himself with the delusion but then, of course, he was a man. It seemed to be their natural way. They liked to believe they were in charge and entitled to all they beheld. Wasn't that what had made the creep in Tabou touch her? And likewise, wasn't it Sam's reason for doing what he claimed was defending her? When all was said and done, the fight, as noble as Sam may have been, was really about each man claiming ownership of Mae. As if there was ever a chance in hell of that happening! She laughed out loud and kept writing.

She didn't look up when the parlor door burst open and smacked against the wall. Instead she carefully shaped her face to seem calm and bored. She took a deep breath and laid down her pen. When she felt she had affected the right look she raised her eyes and leaned forward on her elbows. She hoped he would make it interesting.

"Really, Val, all this breaking and entering isn't becoming to you."

He threw off his coat and unbuttoned his shirt. Mae felt a twitch between her legs and pressed her thighs together.

"It's done," he said. His voice sounded gravelly.

Mae smiled and got up from the desk. He'd barged in as though he'd come straight from Elizabeth Townsend. *Why would he do that?* she wondered. He obviously had to pump himself up to burst in the way he did. She guessed he'd received some news about the woman—news he didn't like. Now they would begin.

"I'm sorry," she said. "What's done?"

"I dropped her—with your words, your script. Exactly."

She laughed and put a hand to her mouth. "Oh my."

"I said I just couldn't help myself. It's over. Are you happy now?"

She crossed her arms. It always had to come back to someone else. Like he had nothing to do with any of it.

"Why would I be happy?"

"Because that's what women are about. Win the man, be happy."

He took off his shirt and at first Mae wanted to hold her breath. But she let the air move through her lungs, slow and controlled.

"Well, there is some truth to that. When one woman strikes at the heart of another? That's power." Her hand rose to his chest, a dangerous move, but she couldn't resist. "The loser almost never recovers. And as you know, I never lose." She leaned in just close enough to blow gently on his left nipple. "But what if the man wasn't the prize? What if the man were merely the object?"

He glanced down at her. "The object? What are you talking about?"

"Yes, Val." She looked up in his eyes and smiled the way she knew he loved her to smile. Here was all of it—every perfect aspect of what she and Val were, distilled down to its cool and bittersweet essence. She would taste it now. She would savor it. And so would he. "It was all about you. How about that?" She poked a finger into his chest to stress her every word. He would have to enjoy it eventually—to know that even as he lied to her, betrayed her, tried to outthink her, he had been the target of her singular enduring focus. One day he would understand. This was what he wanted all along. "You—and me making you give up the first true love you've ever felt in your sorry, little, life."

His arms hung loosely at his sides and she was disappointed. He looked too defeated too soon. Maybe she'd made a mistake in using the words "true love" but she wouldn't believe they would totally deflate him. Finally he pushed her away. The force of his hands made her suck in her breath. She managed to force the air out of her throat again with her laughter.

"What the hell do you think you're doing?" His voice rose.

"Why do you have to ask? What have *we* been doing? What have we always done?"

"She's messed up now! Messed up, you—"

Mae raised a hand to silence him. She couldn't let him go further. She would not shoulder his blame. "Now, Val, I didn't do that. *You* did that. Go ask yourself why you did it. What did you want? Do you have it now?"

He grabbed her by the neck and pushed her back against the wall. She stared hard into his eyes. She knew she could not look away. She could not show fear.

"I'm not going to be the one to point fingers," he said. His other hand moved down and he tried to pull up her dress and grab between her legs at the same time. "But yeah, I wanted something. I'm gonna get it now."

She held herself perfectly still. She didn't want to struggle. She allowed his fingers to fumble as he tried to strip her and maintain control of her at the same time. "Do you like hurting women, Val?" She squeezed the words out through thin lips. "Trying to go two for two?" He tried to kiss her but she turned her head away.

"I don't have time for this," she said. "I'm expecting a better man tonight."

She tried to push him away but he tightened his hold.

"Oh," he whispered into her face. His breath stank of whiskey and sweat. "I don't think so."

"What do you mean?"

He kissed her hard on the neck. His mouth felt hot on her skin.

"I mean baby boy Sam is not coming. He's busy."

"What?" The statement threw her off. A flash of frustration overtook her and she tried to slap at his hands. She needed him to stop moving, to stop talking.

"Yeah. He came to see me and he asked me for help with Cecily." He kept kissing her as he spoke. "I set it up for him to be with his *true* love tonight."

He laughed. *Laughed!*

"Yeah, he's so devoted to you."

"Stop it."

She felt her jaw clench and the muscles of her neck tighten. Her left eyelid fluttered.

He loosened his grip on her and smiled. Mae steadied herself against the wall. She had not seen his smile this close for so long.

"Yeah, let's stop it," he said. "Come on, let's get nicer."

She shook her head. "Oh, I don't think so."

He moved closer to her again. His groin pressed against her. "We had a deal. You're gonna pay up, Mae. Or—"

"Or what?" Mae laughed and felt the charge rushing through her body. The thrill of wanting him and not wanting him burned through her. She held on to the feeling. It felt like life. "Do you want to be my enemy, Val?"

He raised an eyebrow. His fingers rubbed the skin at the nape of her neck. "Mae, I don't think you want to be *my* enemy."

She sighed. "It could be a lot of fun."

He tugged at a piece of her hair near the back of her neck. Her eyes widened with the bright sharpness of the pain. "I can think of better ways to have fun. What's it gonna be?"

She smiled. "Oh, Val."

She raised her knee fast and hard and connected squarely with the soft flesh of his groin. The impact reverberated up her thigh and the sensation of it released an "Ah!" deep and satisfying from her throat. He crumpled like a rag doll. He managed to stay on his feet, but he was bent over, coughing and sputtering.

Yes, she thought.

Yes.

She put her hands against his back and pushed. The door, which he'd left ajar, swung open and he fell out. She quickly gathered his coat and shirt and threw them out into the hall. When she did she was disappointed to see he had caught himself, grasping the rail with his fingers, before he rolled down the steps. She slammed the door closed and locked it behind her. She leaned against it and laughed. Her face glowed.

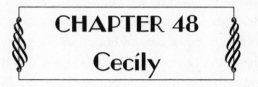

CHAPTER 48
Cecíly

Harlem, Mid-September 1947

The night Cecily waited for Sam her nerves were so bad, she couldn't hold a glass. It didn't help that the mid-September evenings now held a chill that sank right into her bones once the sun went down. She thought about starting a fire in her fireplace, but it was too early in the season. She shut her windows and stood rubbing her arms and wondering what else she might do. She had already removed the shiny-haired dolls from the shelf above her vanity and wrapped them lovingly in tissue paper. They now resided in a box on the floor of her closet. A simple blue bedspread replaced Aunt Pearl's quilt and she had laid a large square of rose organza over her lamp to soften the light in the room. When she finished these preparations she had nothing to do but stare at her bed. Val's note, which she found under her door the day before, had said Sam would arrive around nine p.m. Her clock on the night-stand said it was not quite eight. She didn't even have to worry about Mama coming in and finding them. She was with Mrs. Townsend, who wasn't feeling well.

She paced the length of the room twice. When she started the third time she caught a glimpse of herself in the vanity mirror. Her eyes were pushed wide open as though she were startled to find her own face and body walking around in real life. Her brown dress with the pink and white flowers looked stiff and formal. She thought about changing for bed and this brought her to a better thought—a bath might help.

The water ran into the tub and sounded like a chorus of murmuring voices. She listened to the shimmering flow and how it seemed like the bathroom was full of people whispering, passing judgment on her nakedness as she sat there. She thought about Mama, a hovering dark cloud; Val, a sharp blade of clarity; Sam, her blanket of comfort; Frank Washington, an old entitled toad; and her unborn child, voiceless yet expectant. They closed around her with steady, fervent gazes and crowded in on her so much it seemed they all sat right there on the rim of the tub, the baby too, with their feet soaking in her bathwater. She hugged her knees to her chest and shut her eyes as the tub filled. She tried to transform the voices back into water, the sound of running water, water rushing over stones like the river in Anselm.

Then she remembered the sound of splashing, of Mr. Travis thrashing about in the river. And with a movement that was almost unconscious she reached out a hand and slapped at the water. The splash was like a tiny explosion that stung her ear and died too soon. So she did it again with her other hand and again achieved the satisfying whoosh that broke through the accusing whispers. Then both hands attacked the water in unison. She kicked too. Her long legs fluttered in front of her and soon she was ensconced in her own maelstrom. Invigorated by the noise, she kept going, pushing her arms up and down and kicking her legs until the water sloshed up to her chest and spilled over the sides. She enjoyed the oblivion and wished she were submerged in more water, living water, like the currents running through Anselm, the same ones that enlivened Mr. Travis. She thrashed like a spiteful child and didn't care about the pools forming on the floor or the streams running down the walls. She shut her eyes tight and pressed on.

When her arms grew tired and heavy she let them drop into her lap with a final slosh. Then she turned off the faucet and listened. The waves settled; the final drops plinked to the surface; then silence. Cecily took a washcloth, wet it, wrung it out, and held it over her face. She breathed deeply. The quiet settled around her, as did the warm water. She sighed and opened her eyes. She took in the empty room—she saw the smoothness of the rectangular spring-green tiles on the walls, savored the coolness of the porcelain against her back, and noted the black pane of window reflecting the falling night. All of these pieces and sensations were hers. They were hers because no one else was there—not Mama or Frank Washington. Even the baby, nestled somewhere deep inside her, wasn't really there yet. If she could somehow remember that and stay in a place of knowing she was all by herself and safe, maybe she could pretend everything was as it was before Mama found out about her and Sam—that she remained untouched and wasn't pregnant, and everything about Sam held the excitement of possibility. That she didn't have to be afraid of anything. She wasn't sure if she could deceive herself so well, but it would only be for a little bit, a couple of hours at most. Certainly she could have this clutch of time so she could enjoy herself with Sam. She leaned against the side of the tub and rested her cheek on her hands.

After sitting in silence a few minutes longer she got out, dried herself, and mopped up the water on the floor with her towel. She went back to her room and pulled on her yellow nightgown, the sleeveless one, which she could now wear because she was no longer cold. She sat on the edge of the bed and listened and waited. Before long she heard slow and careful footfalls stepping along the hall and coming closer to her. The doorknob clicked quietly and turned. Then there was Sam.

He walked through the door like he was coming home. He tossed his hat on the vanity, which was just to his left, and removed his jacket of brown tweed and laid it there as well. Cecily couldn't move. She stood there drinking him in with long, slow sips as if he were a soothing hot tea. They had never been alone before, not truly alone, and she realized her earlier views of him had been so chopped up—no more than a series of glances and stolen glimpses—never a simple, uninterrupted time of just looking at Sam. His skin was tawny like caramel and the soft reddish curls of his hair, slightly crushed from his hat, lay flat against his temples. When she met his eyes, straight on, for the first time, she suddenly felt whole, like her mind was no longer split between what had happened and what would be. This one moment, so similar to what she perceived in the bath, was the only moment and she was so alive and so awake that she could dwell in it forever.

He raised his arm, perfect and muscular under the vivid white sleeve of his freshly pressed shirt, and she saw it as pure invitation. She knew immediately she belonged in that warm

place, snuggled right underneath his arm and her face caress-
ing the skin of his neck. She went to him to claim it. He folded
her in his embrace and she marveled at how he was so much
taller and heavier than she was and yet he felt light, so light. His
touch didn't press on her, didn't consume her or smother her.
Instead she seemed to rise in his arms and they floated together
in the lamp's pinkish haze.

His kiss, summery and ardent, tasted like coffee but in a
way that seemed new, like she had never relished a man's lips
before. But as she fell against the pillows she realized neither
she nor Sam existed before this moment, not as the people they
were now. They were creating each other anew with every de-
gree of heat generated from skin against skin, and they did this
together as equals. She was no longer the student being cajoled
and led by Val—her hips pushed here, her head and arms adjusted there. She loved this freedom, like flying, this newness.
Sam smelled of fresh earth, and she imagined walking barefoot
in the woods of Anselm and with that thought in mind she gave
herself to Sam, as she would submit to the sun under the sky in
a field of fresh-cut grass. She thought they could be doing this
outdoors, in Central Park, and it wouldn't have mattered to her.
That's how right it felt—not shameful, not something needing
to be hidden. She wanted people to see, to show them, *This is
what love looks like*. But she knew no one would be able to see
beyond the raw nakedness of their bodies. They would only see
what scared them, what they didn't understand. She could only
take what would be left after they were done—the glow she already felt rising to her face—and wear the light wherever she
went. She didn't care if Mama saw it and knew what she had
been doing. She didn't care how most people wouldn't under-

stand what they were seeing. But she refused to believe this fire
she and Sam ignited would be without purpose. Somebody
or something would be changed by it. She would carry it forth,
a flaming torch, and see what burned in her wake.

When they were done she lay on her belly, her hand beneath
her cheek, and watched his chest bellow up and down with each
breath.

"Sam?"

"Uh-huh?" The fingers of his right hand reached over and
smoothed the hair on the back of her head.

"Where have you been?"

He rolled toward her and propped himself up on his elbow.
"Paris, France! How about that? I never thought I'd ever get to
say something like that, but it's true! I was in Paris."

Cecily raised her head from the pillow. "What were you
doing all the way over there?"

Sam laughed and rolled his eyes to the ceiling. "What
didn't I do? I saw the Eiffel Tower and heard jazz like they
don't dare play it here. Damn, there's so much music in Paris
it runs through the streets like a river." He talked about nightclubs made out of caves and houses turned into museums and
statues that looked so alive he thought they would follow him
around the grounds. His dark eyes shone and Cecily absorbed
the light and the flood of words. But for all his talking there was
something she still didn't understand.

"Were you there with a band? To sing?"

Sam ran his fingers down the skin of her back and no longer looked at her face. "No," he said. He swallowed. "Miss
Malveaux took me."

Cecily frowned and he spoke faster. "We went because of you, Cecily. She knew—she knew I was so broke up over you and I was doing nothing but waiting and waiting for days and days. She was the only one I could talk to about you. She's been a good friend."

Her chin, full of doubt and inquiry, dipped. "She has?" The sting to her heart surprised her. She supposed it was jealousy—what else could be so sharp? And why else would Mae Malveaux's face, serene and confident, suddenly amble through her mind?

Sam's hand settled on her shoulder. "She was, Cecily. She *was*."

Cecily closed her eyes and settled her head on the pillow again. Her mouth felt dry and a metallic taste settled under her tongue. She wanted to cry out and complain but she knew the protest, if she made one, wouldn't live long. She'd spent their weeks apart in another man's bed, with enduring results Sam knew nothing about. But Mae knew the truth and, Cecily suspected, had taken advantage of her infidelity. Now Cecily understood her silence and thought it echoed around them in the room.

"Cecily."

She opened her eyes. Sam stroked the side of her face. "I'm here now. I love you. I'm not going anywhere. We'll figure out how to stay together. We have to—I know that now. We're supposed to be together."

Cecily nodded and said nothing.

"Where do we go from here?" Sam asked. "What do you think?"

She sighed and turned over. She draped an arm over his torso and pulled herself against him. "I don't want to talk about it tonight," she said.

"Yeah, but we should. It feels like everything is about to change. It's like . . ." He looked around as though searching for the words. "It's like summer and us being separated was a dream, a strange dream. Now it's over and we have to get ready for winter."

Maybe so, Cecily thought to herself, but she had a tiny spark growing within her.

CHAPTER 49
Elizabeth

Harlem, Late September 1947

Elizabeth lay in bed listening to a key being worked into the lock of the outside door. But she didn't move. Instead she listened to Gladys repeating the words "Oh my Lord." She must have seen the darkness of the apartment and found the broken dishes in the kitchen.

"Elizabeth? Are you here?"

Still Elizabeth didn't respond because she wasn't there, not really. And she didn't know how to explain such a truth so she stayed lying on her stomach watching the door and waiting for her friend to come find her.

"Elizabeth! Why didn't you answer me, honey? Kyle is worried sick about you. He says you haven't been answering the phone. And now I see it's off the hook. Why is it so dark in here?"

She moved to open the curtains but Elizabeth couldn't allow her to do that. Gladys could do anything else she wanted, but the curtains would stay closed.

"No!" she shrieked. "I don't want the light." The tears began again and Elizabeth sank back into the bed.

"Elizabeth, honey, what's wrong?" Gladys asked. She ran her cool hands over Elizabeth's face.

"I should've listened to you . . ."

"Honey, you're burning up. I'm calling a doctor."

She picked up the telephone and started dialing while Elizabeth buried her face back into the sheets.

Elizabeth heard the voices, male and female, through a fuzziness in her brain, but then she slept again. Next she heard Gladys telling Cecily she would be staying the night.

"Are you awake, honey? How are you feeling?"

Elizabeth reached out her hand and Gladys took it.

"I know what will make you feel better," Gladys said. She held on to Elizabeth's hand and used her other hand to reach for the telephone. She dialed. "You can talk to Kyle."

Elizabeth suppressed a whimper. She wanted to stop Gladys but she heard the ringing on the line and the drone of Kyle's deep voice. Gladys turned away from her and spoke quietly into the receiver. Then she turned back to her and pressed the receiver into Elizabeth's hands. She managed one word.

"Yes?"

"Elizabeth? What's going on? Gladys says you're not taking care of yourself. What's the matter? Why didn't you go back to Rose's house?"

"I'm sorry." She closed her eyes and pinched the top of her nose between her fingers.

"I'm not mad. I just need to know you're all right."

"Well, then why can't you just come home? Come home for a little while."

He was silent. She heard what sounded like papers being shuffled around. "Look, Elizabeth, you have to pull yourself together. The case is at a critical point; I can't leave now. Maybe when you feel better you can come down here. But you won't know anyone."

He went quiet again. Then he said, "And I can't rightly say it would be safe for you."

Elizabeth shook her head. *Safe!* What did that word mean anymore?

"You just need something to do," he said. "I've asked Gladys to stay with you a couple of days. Maybe she can help you find some work to keep you busy. You could volunteer on another committee at church since you seem to be hell bent on staying in the city."

Work. He had no idea how hollow the word sounded. The word "work"—and the word "love" for that matter—had taken on new meaning because of Val Jackson. Work wasn't work and love entwined with purpose. She had lived a brief, light-drenched moment when her work had been to love, and she had performed it so well it had absorbed her being.

Kyle seemed to be waiting for an answer.

"What am I supposed to do?" Every muscle in her body felt thick and heavy. She wanted to sink into bed and stay there, unseen.

"Woman, I don't know! What did you do all summer? Go back to doing that."

"I can't."

She heard the telephone shift in his hands. His voice sounded clipped, impatient.

"Why?"

"Because it's finished."

"Well, it's done. Good. You're done. Elizabeth, you gotta move on to something else. Figure out what makes sense to you. I know you can do that."

She pushed her forehead into the pillow so Gladys couldn't see her face.

"All right." She handed the receiver back to Gladys. Her friend turned around and murmured a few more words into it before hanging up. Elizabeth reached for her hand again.

"Gladys, I can't see. It's like I've been in the light too long and now there are spots and shadows in front of my eyes. I tell you, he's here. He walks through my mind like you just walked across this room."

"Who, Kyle?" Gladys looked around and patted her hand. "There's no one here but us. The doctor was here, but he left a little while ago. He's said you're going to be just fine. You do need to eat something, he said that too. Let me go in here and find something to cook for you."

Elizabeth watched her friend step quietly out of the room. She wanted to call her back, but Elizabeth saw Gladys would never have a clue in God's heaven what she was talking about. Elizabeth would never be able to make her understand—she had lost the beauty of language and began to see how she was now exiled and living on foreign soil, separated forever from her family and friends because she could never relate the deep-down hurt now woven so tightly throughout her being.

Had he known it would be this way? Did he intend her to suffer so?

For days when these questions came she would go back again to his letters, his precious letters, and read them in search of the words that showed his cruelty lying dormant. But she figured he must control the words as he controlled the lie because she could find nothing that would have warned her. She went over each word that had the possibility of indicating endearment—"dearest," "cherish," "thank you," "love"—and the phrase that always sent her to the floor on her knees when she read it, "other self," because that had been the most right, the most true. It explained how she suffered, torn in two, never to be whole because a full side of her had been ripped away.

Strangely enough, this was also her slight comfort—they were indeed exactly the same, two parts of a whole, and she held to the belief that some aspect of him grieved as she did. She thought this most in times when it seemed she felt better, but then a heaviness would come over her, silent and dark. For such a feeling to come unbidden she could only think this: *He is hurting right now too.* He must be thinking of her and she, his other self, picked up on his pain as clearly as any radio signal. She would go to bed then, even if it was broad daylight. She would curl her body into herself like a conch shell and huddle there under stacks of blankets, cradling the hurt like a living product of their failed love.

Then she would get up and rummage madly through the clothing on the floor to find where she had last thrown down her pocketbook. She would pull from it the picture he'd given her and study it again under lamplight. In the photograph Val had thrown his arm around her, but looking at it now she was surprised to see how close they were. She fit perfectly under his arm and could have laid her head on his shoulder or buried her face right into his neck. The framing of the picture made it feel like the borders had conspired to push them even closer together, hunched into this small space of intimacy that was theirs alone.

Elizabeth had thought to burn the picture but couldn't manage to hold it near the stove. There was something about Val's eyes that made her stare at it for hours. The Val in the picture didn't echo false bravado or a pained effort to be cheerful—she had seen such pictures in Rose's library and in the newspapers. There was something about this Val that was like looking at a Christmas tree—something shining, no, *glowing* with hope and possibility. She felt his life popping out of the picture so much that Val Jackson became more alive than anyone else she knew. Everything and everyone else felt dead by comparison.

And what about herself in the photograph? She held something in her hands and Elizabeth remembered it was a glove— Val's baseball glove. He had shoved it into her hands when he called the photographer over and she had held it against her stomach like a small bundle. She peered at her face—did she always smile like that? Her past pictures—even her wedding photograph—sat grounded in a formality that seemed to preclude smiling. But the smile wasn't the only thing. She too looked full of light and lightness, like she could float off at any moment and Val held her so she wouldn't fly away.

When she came to that thought, delight filled her heart and she smiled again much as she smiled in that photo. She would place it carefully back into its thick envelope and put it in her purse. She didn't know if this was the right thing to do, but she liked having the picture on her person.

In the worst moments she abused herself for her stupidity. She would remember her life before him—even just the day before she first saw him—and stare longingly into that memory to see herself with a peaceful, untroubled mind. She smacked herself on the side of the face, thinking how horrible she had been to let herself lose her calm soul.

But almost in the same moment disgust flooded her being, because the woman she was seemed like such a simpleton. Then Elizabeth hit herself for being that person in the first place.

This was terrible because her former self should have been a key. There was a way of living before Val. Why couldn't she find her way back to it again? Perhaps she didn't want to. Perhaps this ruinous ache was the child she couldn't starve because it told her in sad and haunting whispers: *You have loved—you have lived.* This thought held tiny pieces of light but she feared it as though the lights were really warning flares.

She thought about her mother then. How did she know when she had done what she was meant on this earth to do? A warmth flooded Elizabeth's body. She relaxed and remembered her mother's face, so placid and clear. She had been fearless, Elizabeth realized, because she had loved. She had felt complete. She could release her life fearlessly, like a feather on the wind. Elizabeth felt as though she herself had been walking a very long road, one that was meant to arrive at this one sweet point—she had loved. She had lived. And if she had lived this meant she was done. If she was done, all that was left was darkness.

* * *

When Elizabeth awoke the next morning she realized she had done so because of the light—a gorgeous bright sun shone through the window. Though she had shunned it for days, the sun seemed willing to forgive her, and it reached out with arms of blazing gentle warmth. She had been so cold and so empty for so long that she couldn't help but respond, rising from the bed and going to the light-filled window. Now she saw it, the possibility, the hope Val had always talked about, surrounding her in glorious rays and making her feel the misery of the past weeks would be burned off and she reborn.

She would not ignore this invitation; she knew that immediately as she threw open the window. In doing so it seemed the sun smiled and she knew with perfect, utter clarity it was ready to receive her. She presented herself on the windowsill and smiled back, raising her arms like a child expecting to be hugged, and leapt out into the light's comforting, infinite embrace.

CHAPTER 50
Mae

Harlem, October 1947

When the huge gold box of yellow roses arrived, Mae instructed Justice to take it into the dining room. She followed Justice in and watched her place the box on the table.

"Bring me a vase with water and a pair of scissors."

"Yes, ma'am."

Mae pulled the box over to the other side of the table so she could face the doorway. She opened the box, removed the two dozen stems, and laid them out. She had ordered the flowers for herself because she had an important scene to play with Sam, and she needed to prevent him from impulsively lifting her again. If her hands were occupied, and she kept the table between them, she could execute more effectively.

She turned around and peered into the gold-framed mirror that stretched the length of the table. She adjusted the neckline of her white collared shirt and unbuttoned another button. Then she untied and retied the large bow on the left hip of her straight navy skirt. She didn't want to entice Sam, but she did want to look fresh and untroubled. She was done with seducing him. The possibility of his love that had seemed to exist for a few shining days in Paris was now smashed, and she had Val to thank for it. But Sam had betrayed her too. He'd tricked her into thinking he had gone past the point of seeing her only as his consoling friend. Perhaps she mistook his constant flattery and expressions of gratitude, but that was unlikely. Whatever the case, Sam was in the unfortunate position of being able to deliver her revenge on Val. She'd long ago accepted that when she played at lining up dominoes, all would have to fall eventually.

The doorbell rang. Justice brought in a vase of fine blue-and-white porcelain and placed it in front of Mae, then handed her the scissors.

"Mr. Delany is here, ma'am."

"Thank you, Justice. You can send him in."

Mae picked up a rose, cut the stem an inch from the bottom, and put it in the vase. She picked up another, held it aloft as though about to cut it, and waited for Sam to enter.

"Hello, Mae!"

He wore the new dark brown suit she'd bought for him in Paris and held the matching hat in his hands. He put it on the table, and started to come to her, but stopped when he saw what she was doing. She smiled and continued to cut the roses.

"Good morning, Sam. I trust you had an enjoyable evening?"

"Yes, I did! And I owe it all to you."

She looked up, held a rose to her cheek, then to her nose.

"Really? How so?"

"Because you helped keep me and Cecily together. If I didn't have someone to talk to about her, I probably would have tried to move on and forget her. But getting to talk about her with you and hear about her from Mr. Jackson gave me hope."

"Interesting."

Sam touched the hat on the table, running his fingers along the brim. He shifted on his feet. "I want to thank you, Mae, for taking me to Paris. You don't know how much it meant for me as a musician to be there. And to see it so soon after the war!"

"I'm glad you appreciated it."

She slowed down. She wanted to make sure the flowers lasted their entire conversation. She chose another rose and used it to point at Sam.

"But Sam, I was disappointed in how fast you ran out of here the other night. I know Cecily is important to you." She shrugged. "I just thought I was becoming more important."

"You are important to me." Sam put his hands on the table as though he wanted to vault over it and come to her. "You are! But you introduced me to Cecily so I just thought you were okay with it, that you thought it would be good for me to be with her."

She nodded. The man was insipid. She couldn't believe she'd gone to so much trouble for him. It would make the rest of her plan easier to accomplish, but she couldn't help but feel a deep disappointment. She would emerge from the fray with neither Sam nor Val. Sam could be replaced easily enough, but Val was another matter. She already accepted he would no longer be there as her comfort and safety in later years. At the present moment, in his upset state, he was a danger to her. He knew too much about her and had correspondence to back up any accusations he might make if he decided to destroy her in public.

She smiled at Sam. "Tell me, how did Cecily seem when she was with you? Was it awkward? It can be that way sometimes for the very young."

"No, not at all. She was relaxed. It was quite wonderful actually." Sam picked up his hat and turned it over and over in his hands. He looked around the room.

"Ah, so she was experienced?" She cut another rose and put it in the vase.

Sam cocked his head to one side as though he were trying to remember something.

"Cecily . . . " he started.

"Seemed to know quite a lot for a virgin, didn't she?" She laughed.

Sam's hands were now crushing the hat's brim. She kept a firm grip on her scissors.

"What do you know, Mae?" He stood up straighter, bracing himself.

She kept cutting the roses. "Where was Cecily for so long?"

"At Mrs. Jarreau's in Westchester."

"And where was Val Jackson?"

"You already know—he was at Mrs. Jarreau's too."

"Both of them at Mrs. Jarreau's and then they come back and are so eager to find you. Why do you think that was?"

"Because Cecily missed me. She wanted to see me."

Mae pointed the scissors at him.

"She wanted to bed you. And fast."

Sam put his hands on his hips and stared at the floor, thinking. She could see the breath begin to move faster and higher in his chest.

"Do you know what yellow roses represent, Sam? Friendship. I have always been your friend. And as your friend I simply can't stand by and watch them make a fool of you."

Sam put the hat over his face and bent over as though he'd been hit in the stomach.

"Cecily's pregnant?" he asked. He dropped his hat and steadied himself with his hands on his knees.

"Yes," she said quietly. She cut another rose.

"And Jackson did it?"

She nodded. "Do you see how easy it would have been? All they had to do was arrange for you to sleep with Cecily. Then in a couple of weeks you'd get the news you were going to be a new daddy. Simple, right? How would you have felt about that, Sam?"

Sam straightened up and made a sound that seemed to be a cross between a roar and the howl of a wounded animal. He kicked over one of the chairs at the table and sent it smashing to the floor. He glared at her and stalked out.

A moment later, Justice rushed in. Mae put up a hand.

"It's all right, Justice. Mr. Delany just left. Pick up that chair and put these flowers on the table in the hall. Then you can clean up."

"Yes, ma'am."

Mae wiped her hands, went into the parlor, and pulled back one of the curtains. She didn't see Sam on the street and surmised that he must have run away from the house. *Why did men always want to run somewhere?* she wondered. They'd get there soon enough. When you ran, you didn't have the strength to do what you needed to do when you got there. She dropped the curtain and went upstairs. But perhaps Sam would have more than enough energy. He was young.

CHAPTER 51
Val

Harlem, October 1947

Val sat at the bar in the club drinking through his fill of bourbon. It had become his habit of the last several nights to exist unfed, unshaven, and unwell until the bar closed. Then he would go to Elizabeth's apartment building and stand across the street, staring up at her windows until well past noon, when his legs threatened to unravel with exhaustion and Sebastian arrived to drive him home for a few hours of miserable sleep.

He was stunned by how quickly his certainty of winning her back had turned to dust. She withdrew from the world so completely, even more than before, and he of course had assumed he could find some way of putting himself in front of her, of showing how wrecked he was in body and soul, and begging her for mercy. But he'd stopped trying to call when she took the phone off the hook. He could only hope to see her, to speak to her in person, but her doorman, who must know the state she was in, had become resolute and wouldn't let Val past the threshold. He had to wait for her to come out and so far she had not.

Instead she taught him a new lesson—this was what a broken heart felt like. This was what happened when love and faith took a backseat to vanity and foolishness. He couldn't believe how well Mae had played him but his reaction to this thought frustrated him because it so clearly delineated who he was before and after Elizabeth's influence. Before he would have been hell bent on revenge, and looking for ways to burn that superior mask on Mae's face. Mae didn't matter, though. He saw that now. She had struck him like a tornado, but her storm would move on. His job was to repair what he could, salvage what he couldn't, and find a way to rebuild from the pieces.

When Gladys Vaughn showed up at Elizabeth's building in all her lumpy-bodied glory, she went in and stayed and for once Val was actually grateful for her. He knew Gladys would care for Elizabeth, make her eat and bring her out into the world again.

He missed Elizabeth like he would miss the sun. He'd wandered in darkness ever since he left her, but for the most part he found the darkness comforting because it hid from him the wretched state of his soul. He used to think he didn't have a soul because of the way he went through the world, unable to feel anything or anyone really mattered to him. Always, though, there had been the glimmer of hope he glimpsed in the early morning sun. Elizabeth had fulfilled the promise of that hope. He couldn't bear knowing how he'd waited for this precious hope for so long only to throw it away when she finally arrived.

While he sat on the barstool or stood on the street, he played back in his mind each and every time he had made love to Elizabeth, cataloging the different smells of her skin and the delightful discovery of freckles or moles that looked like random chocolate dots on her body. In the summer, at Aunt Rose's, Elizabeth had smelled like the sun, warm and familiar, when her skin seemed most like his own. Then, as autumn came on, she smelled of cinnamon and cocoa butter—the scents she smoothed over her skin to keep it soft and supple as the air grew dry.

But it was only when he was back in bed, exhausted and on the verge of passing out, that Val allowed himself to remember exactly what it was like to be inside her. She was wet and blossoming, folding and unfolding as he pushed into her deeper, but there was always a point where he couldn't tell if he had stopped because she seemed to be pulling him in more and he couldn't resist. Val would fall asleep with these memories and in the morning, in the dredges of half sleep, he would grow hard and rub himself into the sheets trying to make the last notes of his dreaming as real as possible before he fully woke up to nothingness.

* * *

WHEN ELIZABETH HAD come to the window that late September morning, Val thought he could be, at that moment, the happiest man on earth. It was the first time he had seen her in so long. He wanted to call out to her but he only stared. Her hair hung down around her shoulders and the long white nightgown she wore made her look perfectly ethereal: an angel, a fairy. She was so beautiful.

Then he realized his lips were moving and he was talking to

her and to himself. "Elizabeth, Elizabeth, Elizabeth," he whispered over and over.

He savored the sound of her name. By seeing Elizabeth and saying "Elizabeth," he tasted her again and remembered her laughter, light and airy. He smiled for the first time in days and raised his arms up toward the window.

He added to his litany: "I am Elizabeth. Elizabeth is me. I am Elizabeth. Elizabeth is me." Though his arms ached to hold her again, all Val really wanted was to tell her of all the terrible things he'd done, of all the lies he'd told her. Calling her his other self had been the one true thing. How else could he have treated her the way he did? He knew so well how to attack her because he knew so keenly how to hurt himself. And he'd discarded her heartlessly because that's what he thought of himself. If only he could have fully believed in how she saw him. But then, just in that moment, Val saw his error.

Elizabeth was part of him.

All he really ever had to do was have faith in the part of himself that was her. That part would know how to fight as she did. That part would know how to see as she saw the world. And that part of him would certainly know how to love. Now he burned to tell her this discovery. He thought if he could just tell her that, and not even *I love you*, she would understand everything.

As she opened the window, Val thought he would have his chance. He stepped forward and was about to call up to her when Elizabeth climbed onto the windowsill. Her toes seemed to grasp for the ledge like a baby standing for the first time and trying to understand the strangeness beneath its feet. Her arms flew up just as they had done whenever she wanted to embrace him.

"Good God, no."

She did it easily, bravely. He found himself marveling once more over her glorious strength. She did it like she knew for certain she could fly. And because she was certain, he was certain too. He fully expected her to catch a current of the morning air in the folds of her nightgown and come floating down to him like she would in his dreams. She would look at him with pity and forgiveness and love. He would weep at her feet.

He moved toward her so she wouldn't have to fly so far. A truck hauling fruits and vegetables stopped to let Val cross the street. But the truck wasn't the only thing that stopped. Now everyone saw his angel, and they swirled in an ocean of color beneath her. Some, like the uniformed sanitation worker with beefy arms and a face enshrouded in hair who jumped from his truck, looked up. Others, like the woman wearing the black trench coat and pumps and clutching the hand of a small boy, ran away.

Someone shouted and Elizabeth took flight. The hollow croak resonated in his chest and Val realized the cry was his own.

"No, Elizabeth! No!"

She seemed to slow on her descent, and he remembered the lightness of her body, how small and dear she felt next to him. Now she was again walking on the lawn with him in Westchester, and he remembered how she had warned him about caring too much about what others think. He would tell her she was right and not because it was something he thought she wanted to hear. He would say it because it was true. But he hadn't listened to her and now because of his pride, caprice, and arrogance, Elizabeth, his angel, fell to earth.

Val didn't hear the screams around him. He didn't hear the car horns or, when they eventually came, the sirens. None of it mattered because soon they would move on without him and Elizabeth. He dropped to his knees and lifted her to him. Her head lolled to the right and fell against his chest. He held it there with his chin. He kissed her head, rocked her, and kissed her again. His arms ached with the pain of finally, finally, being able to hold her.

* * *

VAL STAYED IN bed and didn't leave the apartment. He stared for hours at his blood-stained shirt and pants still hanging on the valet where he insisted Sebastian leave them. On his bed-side table in a silver frame sat the photograph he'd taken with Elizabeth on Aunt Rose's lawn. These things and her lovely letter were all that Val had left of her. Going to her funeral was out of the question. As much as he longed to see her pretty face again he stayed away from the open casket visitation. Her family and friends, including Kyle Townsend, newly returned, would point and accuse him. If they didn't, Val would have asked them why they weren't doing so. Kyle Townsend should have tried to have him arrested by now, but he hadn't. But then Val realized these thoughts were just the vestiges of his ego kicking, making him think these people had him topmost in their minds.

One week later Sebastian brought the wood-encased Philco radio into Val's room and turned it on.

"What are you doing?" Val lifted his unshaven face from the pillow.

Sebastian leaned over and adjusted the tuning with his slim careful fingers.

"Sir, the World Series is on. Game four. They're at Ebbets Field."

The voice of Red Barber, the Dodgers' radio announcer, filled the space with his barking cadence. In the bottom of the ninth inning, when the Dodgers threatened to pull ahead, he seemed to be attacking the microphone.

"Wait a minute . . . Stanky is being called back from the plate and Lavagetto goes up to hit . . . Gionfriddo walks off second . . . Miksis off first . . . They're both ready to go on anything . . . Two men out, last of the ninth . . . the pitch . . . swung on, there's a drive hit out toward the right field corner. Henrich is going back. He can't get it! It's off the wall for a base hit! Here comes the tying run, and here comes the winning run! Friends, they're killin' Lavagetto . . . his own teammates . . . they're beatin' him to pieces and it's taking a police escort to get Lavagetto away from the Dodgers! Well, I'll be a suck-egg mule!"

The Dodgers won, 3–2. Val glanced over at his dresser and remembered the set of tickets sitting there waiting for him. He didn't understand how they could still be there, or why baseball games still were being played. Why did the world go on, relentlessly it seemed, when Elizabeth was no longer in it?

But the fact of the World Series roused him in an unexpected way. He recalled the day in April—Jackie Robinson's tipping of his cap, his stand-up attitude despite the epithets raining down around him. The man had seen and experienced worse as the season progressed, but he remained resolute, going about his business month after month until he had arrived at the pinnacle of his profession. When had Val ever done such a thing? But he was awake enough to recognize his chance might be there now. And if he did what needed to be done, the results would be important for others and not himself—just as Robinson's actions meant more for so many others. It seemed right that the man who showed him what a life could mean would remind Val how his own life, even in its current state, could have meaning as well.

Because he knew a sacrifice had to be made, but was it really a sacrifice if what he would give up had no value to him? He had a hard time believing his life was worth living. Not when he awoke daily hoping to see once more the light of possibility, to find his soul unstained, to know that miraculously Elizabeth was alive, her heart unbroken, and he could go to the soup kitchen and see her tie on a yellow apron, push back her wayward curls, and smile, radiating her divine light. But the memory of her smile convinced him he would craft some sort of value for his life—he would mend what was worn and prop himself up. It would be fine enough for the moment he foresaw coming. It had to be.

Because the only light possible now would be emitted from the ones he saved with his last move, his greatest play. It would require he ditch everything he knew because the only way to help Cecily and Sam and Cecily's baby would be to throw Mae a curve she'd never expect. She wouldn't anticipate it because though she knew Val's vanity so well, she could never understand love. Aunt Rose had been right about that. He had a lot to do, though, to prepare this move. He had to be about his business.

He pushed back the sheets and reached for the phone beside his bed.

* * *

THE OFFICE OF Lenny Potts, Val's lawyer, looked out onto 7th Avenue. Val walked there with Sebastian and thought about how different the street looked and smelled in broad daylight. No one lingered. Everyone shuffled or strode at various speeds. The blare of car horns precluded any friendly shouts. The smell of oil and car exhaust snuffed out the scent of cooking from the restaurants.

Then he saw the tiny whirl of a girl toddling toward him. She sped along not looking where she was going because she was too small to know any better. She would have collided with Val but he bent down in time, as though fielding a bunt, and swept her up in his arms. One of her thick black braids flopped over her eyes and she moved it aside with her little fat fist. She appraised him quickly—her shiny brown eyes darted over his face. She seemed to like what she saw because before he could say a word, her warm and chubby cheek pressed against his and she kissed him, leaving a sloppy spot of spit and joy on his skin. The gift of her, so perfectly exquisite, pinched his heart and made him grieve afresh. Tears began to clog his throat.

"I'm sorry, sir." The father pushed his hat back on his head and showed Val brown eyes identical to hers. He reached for the girl. "Come here, Breena!"

She happily shifted over to his arms and she waved at Val when she completed the transfer.

"She likes to run," the father said. He shrugged and adjusted her higher in his arms.

Val coughed before he could speak. "Oh, that's all right, man! She made my day."

When they walked away Val thought he heard a whisper within him: *Life.* Then a memory took shape in his mind—a sunny day in the Bronx, rolling knolls of grass—

"Are you all right, sir?" Sebastian's arm on his shoulder scattered the thought. But Val knew it was important. He would find his way back to it again. There was work to do first.

"Yeah," he said. He tilted his head in the direction of the building's door. "Come on."

Lenny Potts, the jacket of his brown pin-striped suit unbuttoned, opened the door himself, and led the men into a large conference room where a long polished wood table held several neat sets of papers. Val scanned the whole room and nodded his approval. He shook Mr. Potts's hand.

"Thanks for coming in on a Saturday, Mr. Potts."

"No, this is good." He scratched his thick gray beard and waved his hand over the papers. "It's good to have a day open. We can focus, get it all done fast, just like you want it. Have a seat. Let me get my secretary so she can take notes and type up any changes."

Three hours later when they were done, Val told Sebastian he would make his way home alone. He walked west until he found the edge of the Hudson River. The sun on its autumn trajectory dipped steeply in the sky and bathed the bankside in a liquid golden light. A man with a wool felt cap pulled low over his eyes packed up his tackle box, nodded to Val, and waddled away with his fishing pole.

The memory returned then, just as Val stuffed his hands into his pockets and gazed into the muddy brown waters. He had been in the Bronx, and the grassy knolls were the grounds of Woodlawn Cemetery and he had stood on them before his parents' flower-strewn caskets and heard the words that came back to him now.

"I am the resurrection, and the life: he that believeth in me, though he were dead, yet shall he live: And whosoever liveth and believeth in me shall never die."

He remembered when he first heard them he had thought, *How? How?* And it surprised him now to think it never occurred to him to not believe the words. He'd just wanted to know what he needed to do to make them work, to make them ease the grief sitting heavy in his heart and help him walk away from the graves of his mother and father knowing he had not committed them to an everlasting darkness.

Now the words were with him again and he whispered them to himself, laying them out like a kind of bridge to uphold him over a deep cavern.

"'I am the resurrection, and the life: he that believeth in me, though he were dead, yet shall he live: And whosoever liveth and believeth in me shall never die.'"

He didn't doubt Elizabeth had known these words too. How else could she have been so bold going through the world radiating love the way she had? Most people would just as soon spit on each other as show the kind of love she'd held out for common strangers every single day. He had taken advantage of that. And the only thing he could do now to make it right called for him to crack himself open and prove the truth of the words he had written so shamefully in one of his letters—love mends. He would do it because her spirit called upon him to be better than himself. He would do it because she had shown him what was possible when one truly loved. Now he just needed a touch of her courage.

He watched the water's strong current running busily, as though it had somewhere to be. A tiny brown tugboat, a red stripe painted on its side, floated past and pulled a great flat barge loaded with a backhoe and a crane. The sun on the river broke up in the ripples of its wake, and the pieces of light danced on the surface and disappeared.

He wouldn't sleep that night or the next. Instead he sat on the roof of his apartment building. He pushed his overcoat collar up around his ears and waited for the midnight blue sky to fade into a flat gray coin and then for the sun to stain it blood pink as it crept over the eastern horizon. He stayed until it was high enough to warm him, to make him feel certain it would come again the next day, and then he would utter his prayer: "'I am the resurrection, and the life: he that believeth in me, though he were dead, yet shall he live: And whosoever liveth and believeth in me shall never die.'"

He remembered what Reverend Stiles had said about listening for God's voice. He was supposed to listen so he would know what to do. It was too late for that. There was no chance for him to hear, not now. And he wasn't sure he would believe anything good there was to hear. But the words he prayed did comfort him. He had the sense he was running hard in preparation for a leap, like an athlete performing the long jump. Only he couldn't see where he would land. The prayer helped him to know he wouldn't leap into a void.

* * *

IN THE BOTTOM of the seventh inning in the seventh game of the 1947 World Series, a man named Robinson knocked a fly ball into left field allowing Billy Johnson to come in from third base and score, giving their team a 5–2 lead. But even Val in his fog knew it wasn't Jackie Robinson. It was Yankees catcher Aaron Robinson. The crowd in the second tier of Yankee Stadium where Val sat with Sebastian near left field engulfed them. The deafening roar testified to the over seventy thousand spectators packed in for the event that afternoon.

But Val and Sebastian kept to their seats.

He'd chosen to attend the game because anyone who knew him knew he wouldn't miss it. And he wanted for once to make himself easy to find. He sat hunched over, his hat low over his eyes, his hands in his coat pockets. The noise reminded him of how much smaller Ebbets Field was—just half the size of Yankee Stadium. It was also farther away, in Brooklyn, but Val had appreciated it more. The approach to Yankee Stadium wasn't as inviting as the one at Ebbets Field. Instead of soft, welcoming curves, a great stone wall loomed large as the front of Yankee Stadium. Straight walls stunted all the other curves in the ballpark as well.

The mass of overcoats and hats made him feel invisible, and he wanted the kind of oblivion it offered. He felt Sebastian fidgeting and knew he was worried. Sebastian was a good man—Val didn't expect him to be any other way. The directions he had given Sebastian earlier in the day would have made any caring person worry. Val had shown him all the drawers, locks, and inner workings of his desk.

"You know I haven't been well lately, Sebastian. Mr. Potts will know what to do, but you may need to access this information. Here, this is a spare key for you, just in case."

Val had tried to hand it to Sebastian, but he'd kept his hands clasped behind his back.

"Sir, I don't think it's necessary."

"And I say it is. Please take this key, Sebastian. That's an order."

"Very well, sir."

Sebastian had put the key in the pocket of his vest.

He'd been so unhappy about receiving the key Val wasn't surprised when Sebastian insisted on accompanying him to the game. But then, sharp as Sebastian was, Val knew he hadn't failed to see the .22 Val had taken from the shelf of his closet and put in the pocket of his coat.

At the top of the eighth inning, after two quick outs by Eddie Stanky and Pee Wee Reese, Jackie Robinson came to the plate. Val watched him stand strong in the batter's box and get ready to swing. He had remained hitless in the game so far. Val didn't see why it should be any different and he was right. Eventually Robinson hit a fly ball out to center field and Joe DiMaggio caught it to put the Dodgers away for the eighth. Yankees fans were on their feet all over the stadium. Val's seat rumbled beneath him.

"Dodgers are gonna lose this series," he shouted in Sebastian's ear. "Yankees pitchers are too good."

Then Val realized—he should have known a lot sooner he would lose to Mae. She was too fast, too clever. That's why he was waiting for Sam Delany to come after him. He wondered what was taking him so long. Or, more accurately, what was taking Mae so long to throw her switch. He figured once she knew she had lost Sam, Mae would tell him about Val and Cecily. He only saw the potential for the play when he found

Sam and Mae together that night and it made him remember what Aunt Rose had said. But there was one more move Val could make, and he would do it for Sam's benefit, and Cecily's. The waiting, though, bothered him because he felt he was being cowardly. He was used to being a man of action, of taking charge of the field. But Elizabeth had shown him taking charge had nothing to do with fighting battles. He didn't understand how to go to combat with both his heart and his head working together in full force. Mae had taken him down to prove it. But maybe he'd finally learned something.

Val stood up and pulled his coat closer around him.

"Come on, Sebastian, this game is over. I don't want to stay for the celebration."

"Yes, sir."

Sebastian pushed his hat onto his head and followed Val down the stadium steps.

They folded in with like-minded Dodgers fans who were all leaving the stadium. People shrugged on coats and shuffled toward cars and subway trains. Their relatively slow movement made it easy for Val to spot fifty yards away what he had been waiting for.

Sam Delany crossed East 157th Street and charged hard toward him like a mad bull. Val sighed with relief to see him coming at last.

"Sir." Sebastian stepped forward and Val saw he was about to move between him and Sam, but Val put an arm in front of him and pushed him aside.

"Don't worry, it's all right," he said to Sebastian. "I'll take care of this."

The .22 he'd loaded that morning weighed down his pocket

and had seemed to pull on him the whole afternoon. But when Val drew the gun it slipped out easily and felt light as a dream when he held it up high and straight in front of him. He heard gasps and screams and the charging bull froze a few feet from Val.

This gave Val the moment he needed—it was a flickering of an instant just when everyone had moved safely away and just before Sebastian, who was two steps too far, could reach his arm. In that moment Val turned the gun into his own chest and fired.

The sky rushed up and made everything blue—blue like the world was when Marcus's flashbulb had lit it; blue like the dress Elizabeth once wore.

He didn't hit the ground. Someone's arms held him aloft and he suspected they were Sebastian's. Then a face, Sam's face, filled the sky. Val grabbed him by the arm.

"Don't think you know everything, man." He choked out the words and tasted metal on his lips. "Don't think you know everything. Don't make the mistake I made."

"What . . . what . . . what do you mean?"

Sebastian was yelling for someone to call an ambulance, but Val held Sam fast as more people came running and he felt the moment slipping through him.

"Mae Malveaux. She played us all for fools. The devil couldn't do a better job." He felt himself draw in a breath, but felt it go nowhere, a welling in him, the breath only a grab at a straw, one last thought. "You gotta love Cecily. Love that baby she's gonna have. Sebastian will help you. Don't make the mistake I did. Don't let your pride keep you from love."

Val sighed. His eyes lifted up into the blue, and didn't come down again.

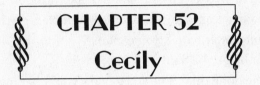

CHAPTER 52
Cecíly

Harlem, October 1947

Cecily heard the sound of shattering glass and went downstairs to see about Mama. Ever since Mrs. Townsend had leapt from her window it was as though her mama's fingers no longer knew how to grasp the hard surfaces. In public she cried, yes, but still she had ordered the women of Mount Nebo around as she organized Mrs. Townsend's wake and the gathering after the funeral. But in private Cecily noticed how when they arrived home Mama moved slowly and in increments. She prodded Mama to eat, reminded her to go to bed.

Cecily found her in the parlor. She was sunk down in her chair like every muscle in her body had failed her. She looked gray and defeated and if it hadn't been for Mama's constant murmuring of "Lord, have mercy," Cecily would have thought she'd suffered a stroke.

"Mama, what's wrong?"

Then she heard the name "Valiant Jackson" and Cecily

turned to face the tall walnut cabinet of the radio that stood across the room from where Mama sat. More words pushed through the static and they included "shooting" and "dead" and they grasped Cecily's heart like a childhood nightmare. She fell to her knees and heard *"self-inflicted gunshot wound after an encounter with a young man."*

Sam. It had to be Sam.

Had she done this? The story, Val's voice, her own laughter rolled back to her. *What are men willing to die for?* What had she done? She saw herself pushing over a domino like a child at play, only she'd been unaware of the falling. Now it was coming toward her, she could feel it, as though the force of the coming wave would knock over the radio on top of her.

Dead? Could he really be dead? Her hand flew to her mouth. She felt a bitter taste rising in her throat. Only a month ago death had been nothing but a word, not even a shadow to her, and she had no way to begin to think of it because life pulsed so hard around her and within her, including the child growing in her womb.

She pressed her ear to the speaker. She wanted to hear Val's name spoken again, as though somehow a final spark of him were inside it and could be released by the sounding of his name.

"Cecily, I don't know what this world is coming to." Mama pushed herself out of her chair and Cecily stood and took her arm to steady her.

"Yes, Mama."

She stared at Cecily and Cecily thought for a moment her eyes drifted down to her midsection. But Mama said nothing. Instead she climbed the steps as though they were an afterthought, her mind far away. Cecily followed her.

Cecily couldn't remember the last time she'd been in Mama's bedroom, or rather the last time she'd really looked at things in there. Now she noticed, pulling back the covers, how the mattress was worn down on only one side. She could only assume the other was where her daddy once slept.

Mama sat down on the bed and Cecily kneeled to pull off the pumps misshapen around Mama's swollen feet. She peeled the stockings down over her thick thighs and calves and rolled them into a black cloud-like ball before putting them in the dresser drawer. She climbed onto the bed and unbuttoned Mama's dress at the back, and it fell down around her waist. Cecily undid the clasp of the brassiere and she realized she had not seen her mother's naked body since Cecily herself was a child. As Mama's breasts dropped free from their restraints she felt a new tenderness for her mama drawn forth by the soft mound of flesh that looked like it might melt from the grief heaped upon it. Cecily knew Mama once had her own affection for Val Jackson and she wondered if she were recalling it now, how they danced on the night Cecily's daddy was shot.

She put her arms around Mama from behind and she cried then, her tears wetting the skin on the back of Mama's neck. Mama patted Cecily's forearms and the dampness of her fingers said she was weeping too.

"It'll be all right, baby. Lord willing, it will be all right." She turned so her lips could graze the top of Cecily's head.

Cecily squeezed her tighter then pulled aside the sheets so Mama could raise her legs up onto the bed and settle underneath them. She kissed Mama's cheek and was about to turn out the light.

"Cecily, honey," Mama said. She lay back against the pillows, her arm covering her small and tired eyes. "Read me Psalm 23 before you go."

"Yes, Mama." She nodded and picked up the Bible from the night table and sat down on the side of the bed.

The Bible, covered in worn red leather with Mama's name embossed in gold capital letters in the lower right-hand corner, was another artifact she had not touched since childhood. When Cecily opened it an antique small rose from the pages and made her feel small and childlike again, marveling at the red and black type on the pages as thin as butterfly wings.

"'The Lord is my shepherd; I shall not want. He maketh me to lie down in green pastures: he leadeth me beside the still waters.'"

Here she thought of Anselm and her feet tingled to feel the soft grass beneath them. She wanted to leap into the river and thrash madly because she wanted to feel clean and she saw that's what it would take—a full immersion, a new baptism, where she had to throw herself headlong into a point of reconnection to wake her up and help her live despite all the dying.

It wasn't that she felt dirty—no—it was more the need to shed old layers of herself, like skin that she needed to beat and scrape away—the parts of her that had been needy and fearful and ignorant of herself. Those parts had to go so she wouldn't feel shame or regret over what she once was. She had no time for it—and it didn't matter anymore. With the old gone she could think clearly and perhaps hear what the new part of her wanted to do and where she would go.

"'He restoreth my soul: he leadeth me in the paths of righteousness for his name's sake.'"

"'Yea, though I walk through the valley of the shadow of

death, I will fear no evil: for thou art with me: thy rod and thy staff they comfort me.'"

Mama whimpered quietly at these words and Cecily held the Bible on her lap with one hand and she rubbed Mama's shoulder and arm with the other. Her voice remained calm and clear, and she wondered if the words explained why she herself wasn't falling apart, why she wasn't rolled up in a ball of grief in her bed. She felt the ache of it, the desire to give in to the sorrow hanging dark and heavy on her like a shroud. But Mama was already doing it and there was no room for her to do the same, even with Mama sleeping on only half the bed. Something sustained her, though, made her feel capable.

"'Thou preparest a table before me in the presence of mine enemies: thou anointest my head with oil; my cup runneth over.'"

What did she have? A baby on the way, its father dead. But still love and hope in her heart and nothing about any of this felt catastrophic, although it should. She had to hold on to this feeling, stand up for it however she could.

"'Surely goodness and mercy shall follow me all the days of my life: and I will dwell in the house of the Lord for ever.'"

"Amen," Mama said. The word flowed out on a breath that sounded like a sigh of relief. Her arm moved away from her eyes and she turned onto her side, her back to Cecily.

"Yes," Cecily said quietly. "Amen, Mama." She put the Bible back on the table and stood. She kissed Mama on the cheek and pulled the blankets up over her soft rounded shoulder.

After Cecily closed the door she stood in the dark hallway and listened.

Surely goodness and mercy will follow me.

Yes, follow her wherever she went. She had to believe that. Cecily went to her room and pulled the quilt from her bed. She climbed another flight of stairs and then the metal ladder. At the top she unlatched and lifted the door and opened it. She pulled herself out onto the roof. She wrapped the quilt around her. The cold air rushed over her in soothing waves. To the south she could see the treetops of Central Park, their leaves silhouetted against the light of the city buildings. The streets seemed to buzz beneath her feet and she wondered if the sound came from people celebrating the end of the World Series or people gossiping about Val's death. Most likely they talked about both because of the close proximity of the two events.

She sighed. Mrs. Townsend had kissed the sky and now Val Jackson was following her. Cecily sensed the empty spaces where these two people once stood and wondered if they, now released from their physical beings, could be anywhere or everywhere. Could they see her? Could they know what she thought? Were they judging her?

Then she remembered the photograph. Mama had sent her into Mrs. Townsend's room to straighten it up and retrieve the clothing Mr. Townsend had requested for the burial. Neither of them could bring themselves to set foot in the place where Mrs. Townsend last stood.

The sheets on the bed were still shaped in the twisted curves in which Mrs. Townsend had left them. When Cecily pulled at them to strip the bed she saw the corner of what looked like a thick envelope just under the bed and partially hidden by the sheets. She picked it up.

She was shocked by how familiar it was. She recognized the day—she had been there, at Mercylands, when the picture was taken. She half expected to see herself walk through in the background. But she hadn't seen the photograph being taken. She couldn't stop looking at it. She knew and didn't know them at once. Mrs. Townsend didn't look serious in the way Cecily had seen her. Val didn't look cool and collected. It was like some surface of both had been cracked and their smiles, their joy, could then flow freely through. Were they in love?

She felt no jealousy over this and she had meant to ask Val about the picture. At first she did wonder how he could feel such emotion for Mrs. Townsend and still be in bed with her, under the same roof. But hadn't she done the same, enjoying herself physically while still holding her love for Sam? Who was she to judge, especially when the woman who would have been her rival was gone? And there was something hopeful about the way they looked, bright and happy like children. She had wanted to protect them, to not have unkind fingers touching the picture or the owners of those fingers saying disapproving words. So she'd hidden the picture in her coat and had intended to give it to Val when she had the chance.

Now that would never happen. She would keep it hidden. She would keep it safe if only to show her child someday what her real daddy looked like. What did it mean to her that Val Jackson was dead? She could only guess that for her he could never be fully, truly gone. His last spark was ignited within her. In fact she was certain she could feel, day by day, the heat of this new sun burning within her. A piece of him lived.

If dominoes were really falling toward her, as she had felt when she heard of Val's death on the radio, then the one coming for her would be Sam. He must have found out about the baby. Until he appeared, every moment would be about waiting for him, looking for him. She wasn't afraid or worried. It seemed inevitable. She didn't believe he would hurt her—she was well aware she herself had done the hurting. She had to stand up for that and to do so seemed as obvious and inevitable as taking and hiding the photograph of Val and Mrs. Townsend. This was more out of necessity than anything else. She had no one to turn to but she was also well aware that she had moved herself, all alone, into this swirl of events. Though the thought made her sad and ill, it was also helpful. Because little by little, she began to understand that she also had the power to walk out of this, with her child, and go where she chose and not where Mama chose to move her.

That's when the thought came to her, and it seemed whispered from the stars above her head and not from the hum of the streets below—she would be in Anselm come spring. Her child would be born there. Something in these deaths released her, pulled from her a rising that seemed to take her out of herself, stretching her even taller than she was before if that was possible. She felt stronger with the thought because she knew she would go no matter what happened next, no matter what Sam did or said when he arrived.

* * *

THE NEXT MORNING Cecily stood at the parlor window and rubbed her belly with her right hand. She wasn't really showing yet, but she saw her stomach was beginning to thicken and her hand seemed drawn to the area now. The gesture calmed her and helped her to concentrate. She looked down the street again. Sebastian's message said Sam would come to the house this morning. She moved aside one of the window's wooden shutters and saw Sam coming down the street. He carried a large box in his arms in front of him. Just a few months ago she would have rushed to the door to open it before Sam could even ring the doorbell. Today this Cecily, who was tired of running and tired of being fearful, did not do it. So she let Sam ring, and even allowed him to wait for Mama to open the door when she came downstairs from her room where she'd just finished dressing.

"What are you doing here?" She sounded more confused than angry. It seemed to Cecily that Mama didn't have the strength to be mad at anyone anymore.

"Good morning, Mrs. Vaughn," Cecily heard him say from the hall. "I'm sorry to disturb you. You probably know Mr. Jackson died yesterday."

"Yes, I know that, God rest his soul," her mother said, and Cecily thought she could hear in her voice that this was the truth: she wished him peace.

"Mrs. Vaughn, I have in this box some of his personal papers. I brought them to you because some of it concerns Cecily and myself."

"What are you talking about, Sam? What concerns Cecily?"

"If I could just come in I think we can answer those questions together."

Cecily got to the door in time to see Mama step back and open it wider for Sam. When he walked in Cecily realized she hadn't seen him in the house in broad daylight since the last time he taught her a lesson. It seemed so long ago and now they both seemed older, so much older. Sam's eyes looked heavy, as though he had been crying. His shoulders, stooped and sad, made her yearn for the lightness of the music they once played.

"Hey, Sam." She held her hands clasped in front of her to stop her fingers from lifting over imaginary piano keys.

"Hey, Cecily. Come on. Follow me."

He walked through into the dining room, where he put the box down on the white lace tablecloth. He turned to Mama.

"Mrs. Vaughn, I want you to know my intentions toward Cecily have always been honorable. We only wanted to be together."

Cecily stood next to Sam and put her palms flat on the table and waited. Mama crossed her thick arms and nodded. "Go on."

He pulled open the cardboard flaps of the box. "I've got here some letters that belonged to Mr. Jackson. If you read them you'll see someone used our situation to take revenge on other people. One of those people is you."

"What? Who are you talking about?" She tilted her head toward Sam as though that would help her understand him better.

Sam swallowed and his chin dropped down to his chest.

"Mae Malveaux."

Cecily looked at Mama, whose arms fell to her sides. Then she gripped the back of one of the dining room chairs.

"You're talking nonsense now," Mama said. She shook her head. "Mae don't have any reason to want revenge on me."

"Are you sure, Sam?" Cecily asked quietly. But she already knew the answer. It must be why her cousin never responded to her messages.

"Yes. But that's why I brought the letters, so you can both read them all yourselves." Sam dipped his hand into the box.

"They're her letters, in her handwriting. I also have some bank statements here. She's been letting everyone believe she's been giving all this money to the church anonymously, but it wasn't her at all. That money came from Mr. Jackson."

Mama's hand flew to her mouth. "Lord have mercy."

Cecily pulled a chair out for her and, with gentle pressure on her shoulder, guided her to sit. Then Cecily sat down next to her.

Sam laid the letters and documents out on the table. They read and sorted through the papers for two hours. Cecily tried to read in what she thought was a calm, grown-up way, but her face burned when she saw how Mae had scoffed at her, had acted like her innocence was nothing but a pawn to be knocked off a chessboard. And she could barely hold her seat next to Mama when she read of how easily she had been taken, and the description of how Mae had pacified her at Mercylands. Her heart thumped in a way that sickened her and she tasted bile in her mouth. Worst of all, Mama didn't seem surprised when they got to the information about her pregnancy.

"Cecily, you should try to eat something," Mama said when Gideon brought them a platter of sandwiches and set it in the middle of the table. "You'll regret it later today if you don't. I still remember what it's like to be with child."

Cecily stared at the table. She wasn't ready to look her in the eye. "Mama, did you already know I was pregnant?"

Mama spread a large napkin onto her lap. "I suspected," she said. She reached over and grasped Cecily's hand and squeezed it. "You're not showing much yet, but a body still changes. Like I said, I remember."

Cecily finally lifted her eyes and saw Mama's face wasn't

twisted or blowing with anger. She looked placid and tired. "I didn't say anything because I was waiting for the two of you to say something first." She paused and sighed. "But now we know your baby's daddy is dead."

Cecily nodded sadly. "Yes, ma'am."

Mama turned to Sam. His plate still sat empty.

"Actually, Mrs. Vaughn, Mr. Jackson's last words were about Cecily and the baby."

Cecily looked up and leaned closer to Sam across the table. "What did he say?"

"First he warned me about Miss Malveaux. Then he said I shouldn't be too proud to love you and your baby."

Suddenly he pushed back his chair, scraping it noisily over the floor. He rushed around the table to Cecily and dropped onto his knees next to her chair. He took her hands so she had to look at him and see the sad sincerity draped over his eyes.

"I aim to take his advice and do that. I already love you, you know that. I can't hold no grudge against a baby who knows nothing about all this. Is that all right, Cecily? Will you still have me?"

She ran a hand over his head, and sighed. "Isn't it strange how we've been through all this and now it all comes down to me answering a question I could have answered months ago? Here I've been depending on older people to tell me what to do," she said. "And all the time they're running around acting like children themselves."

She turned to Mama without letting go of Sam's hand.

"With all respect to you, Mama, I should have trusted what I knew would be best for me."

Tears welled up in Mama's eyes and Cecily thought about

how she and her mother both must look like chastened children. "I understand, honey. But you're just a girl. You did what you could do."

Cecily shook her head. "No, Mama. I did what I could do here, up north, in Harlem and Westchester. This wouldn't have happened if I had stayed in Anselm. This place makes no sense. It's like a viper pit of people lying, people pretending, people just being out for all they can get. I know Westchester is fine, but here nothing grows and the streets are dirty."

She looked at the piles of paper on the table.

"Everything is dirty."

Sam rubbed her arm. "What are you saying, Cecily?"

She sat up straight and let go of his hands, then set hers on the table.

"I'm saying I won't raise my baby up here. I want to go back to Anselm."

Sam frowned and looked at Mama. But Cecily held up a hand to stop him—she didn't want to hear any argument. "We can have a good life in Anselm."

She rubbed her belly again. "Mama, I'm going to call Mrs. Jarreau and talk to her. Val was her heir. I'm sure she will be willing to make some arrangements for the baby since it will be her relation too."

Mama crossed her arms and looked at her intently.

"You're right, Cecily. But we should all just get in the car and go see that poor woman. She's going to be heartbroken. And she needs to know about all of this." Mama shook her head. "It's not going to make her feel any better, though."

Sam sat back on his heels then stood up. He looked uncertain. "We have to talk to Reverend Stiles too," he said quietly.

"Yes," Cecily said. She got up and pulled Sam to her. She put her hands on his face and kissed him. "Sam, I love you. But this baby and I are going to Anselm. You can come with us or not. But if you come with us we'll be all right, Sam. We'll figure it out."

* * *

THAT AFTERNOON SAM held Cecily's hand while they sat with Mama in Reverend Stiles's office at the church. The preacher, his round wire-rimmed glasses perched on his nose, carefully read through sheet after sheet of the selection of papers they had brought to him. Then he picked up the small leather bankbook Sam had placed on his desk.

"How did you get these, son?"

"His butler, Sebastian, gave them to me." Sam coughed and looked at the floor. Cecily reached to his back and rubbed it gently, encouraging him to go on. "He said Mr. Jackson wanted me to have them. I showed everything to Mrs. Vaughn first."

"That's right, Reverend," Mama said and dabbed at her eyes with a handkerchief. "Because of Cecily and all."

Cecily felt the minister's eyes on her and she met them.

"Why tell me at all? I would have thought you'd keep all this quiet because of your daughter."

Cecily sat straight and tall, her feet crossed beneath her. "Reverend Stiles," she said. "I'm not proud of what's in these papers. But I'm grown enough to know more people could get hurt if we don't say anything. And you should know where the church's money is really coming from."

He nodded at her. "Well, all right then. You're a mighty brave young woman."

"Thank you," she said, but Cecily didn't feel brave. Her insides quivered and she took Sam's hand so Reverend Stiles wouldn't see how much her own hand was shaking.

He turned back to the bankbook. "And you say this account is in the church's name?"

"Yes," said Sam. "The way Sebastian explained it, Mr. Jackson always maintained this separate account and all the funds he donated anonymously came from that. He paid for the addition with it and everything."

"He even made it a joint account with his name and the church's. Imagine that." Mama shook her head. "Now that he's gone it all belongs to the church free and clear."

Cecily watched the reverend to see what he would say, what he would do. Carefully he removed his glasses and looked at the three of them. She could feel the sweat in Sam's palm and was grateful she wasn't the only one feeling nervous and scared.

"Why do you think Sebastian gave you all of these things together?" Reverend Stiles asked. "There's more here that concerns you all directly; it's not just about church money."

"I think the bankbook was supposed to help support the truth of who Mr. Jackson really was, so we would believe him when it came to Miss Malveaux." Sam shifted in his chair and dropped Cecily's hand. He crossed his arms. "I know I didn't want to believe him at first."

Reverend Stiles nodded. "If I'm to understand what the truth is here, then you all—and Cecily here—have some troubles of your own."

"Yes, sir." Sam looked at Mama, then at Cecily. He leaned toward Reverend Stiles. "But it's nothing we can't handle ourselves, with a little help from you."

He smiled and stood up from his chair. "Then let me go find my wife and we'll have ourselves a wedding," he said. "Is that all right with you, Cecily?"

She looked at Sam. For the first time that day she saw some light in his face. He kissed her on the forehead and she felt hopeful. "Yes," she told Reverend Stiles. "That would be just fine with me."

He moved toward the door, but then he paused as though something had occurred to him. He turned back and put a hand on Mama's shoulder. "Gladys?"

"Yes, Reverend?"

"I know this is so quick on the heels of Mrs. Townsend's homegoing, but after we get Sam and Cecily set to rights here, could you see your way clear to helping us organize a proper goodbye for Mr. Jackson?"

Cecily was pleased to see how Mama lit up at the request. "I sure will," she said. She lifted herself from her chair as easily as if she were a girl again. "I'd be happy to." The change in her made Cecily want to remember—there would always be some small saving grace in having a job to do.

CHAPTER 53
Mae

Harlem, Mid-October 1947

Mae chose to wear to Val's funeral a chocolate brown suit with a flared skirt and a fitted jacket. She put the lace veil of her matching hat tucked up and away from her face. She didn't want to show signs of particular mourning—she and Val, to the rest of the world, were only acquaintances—but she knew to look respectful. She sat at her vanity mirror and waited for Lawrence to bring the Packard around. After staring at her reflection for several minutes, she clenched her hands into fists on the table in front of her. She took a deep breath and pushed away the tears threatening to well up in the back of her throat. She refused to grieve for Val Jackson. She'd intended to dispose of him and it was done. She grieved instead for what he'd been to her. She doubted she could find his equal—*her* equal.

What perturbed her more was that the dominoes had fallen messily in ways she hadn't expected. Sam should have killed Val. He was supposed to be sitting in jail at this very moment, according to her plan. But how could she have fore-seen Elizabeth Townsend would take her own life and inspire Val to dispose of his own?

Was this what love really did to people?

Mae chuckled under her breath. If so then it was ridiculous and inconvenient. She was glad her affair with Sam hadn't worked out. But where was he now?

She heard a quiet knock on her door. Justice's muffled voice found its way through to her.

"Ma'am, Mr. Lawrence is downstairs with the car."

Mae stood, checked herself one last time in the full-length mirror by her bedroom door, and descended the stairs.

* * *

THEY ARRIVED LATE. The service seemed to be much better attended than Mae had expected, and Lawrence had a hard time getting the car to the front of the church door. By the time she entered a sea of faces packed the sanctuary and the organist pumped out "Amazing Grace." Six of Val's friends, including Sebastian, bore his casket of polished mahogany down the aisle. This left her in the awkward position of walk-ing behind the pallbearers. She sensed the glances made in her direction and, determined to ignore them, she faced strictly forward. When she made it to the front she tried to claim her usual seat.

Gladys and Cecily were already seated there—and so was Sam Delany. Mae's lower eyelid twitched to see them all to-gether, but just as she decided to smile and greet them warmly, an usher grasped her elbow.

"I'm sorry, Miss Malveaux," he said. "This section is reserved for family."

"Oh."

She looked sharply at the trio in the front pew, all of them staring straight ahead without acknowledging her. That's when Mae noticed Sam and Cecily holding hands, and the wide gold band encircling the third finger of Cecily's left hand. She opened her mouth to say something, but the usher was already leading her away. Four rows back, he deposited her in a seat near the aisle.

People were still filling the back pews and soon the doors stayed open so the ones who couldn't find seats could spill into the street. The wait gave Mae time to think as she glared at the heads of Sam, Cecily, and Gladys. When did Sam and Cecily marry? And why didn't Gladys tell her? Her anger paired with her disappointment. This would have been when she would have appreciated Val's presence. Once upon a time, he would have shared her frustrations, and maybe even found a way for them to laugh at Sam and Cecily. He would have helped her topple them once again into the game she played so well. She tugged at her black gloves, and reminded herself she let go of Val long ago.

Reverend Stiles stepped into the pulpit and the music and the murmuring died down. "We're here to celebrate the home-going of our own Valiant Jackson," he said, "a young man of our faith gone too soon. He led a complicated life, I'll tell you that right now."

Several people around her nodded and Mae wanted to scoff at them. No one knew Val like she did.

"But I'm going to tell you a little story, a little story from the

New Testament. I think it will help us understand what Val Jackson, and maybe some other persons, were about."

He took a breath, closed his eyes, and sighed, looking like he was offering a silent prayer of his own before he began.

"There once was a man with two sons. He said to his first son, 'Please go work in the vineyard.' The son shook his head and said, 'No.' But the young man later thought better of it and he went to the vineyard to work."

People nodded again and many said, "Uh-huh. He sure did."

"The man then said to his second son, 'Please go work in the vineyard.' The son said, 'Yes, of course.' But he did not go. Which one did his father's bidding?"

A murmuring rose from the pews.

"The first."

"The first, Lord Jesus."

"The first one!"

"Yes, the first. And what does this story mean?"

Reverend Stiles came out from behind the pulpit so he could put a hand on his hip and roll himself forward to point and to testify. He pointed the index finger of his other hand into the air.

"That there are *some* who pretend to do God's bidding, but *don't*."

He bounced both of his hands to his hips, leaned forward, and looked straight at Mae. His sharp brown eyes seemed to pierce through his glasses and stab Mae in the face. She felt the hairs rise on her forearms. He kept going.

"And there are others who, if we just look at them on the

surface, look like they aren't doing God's work. But all along they are."

The reverend moved down the steps from the altar and placed a hand on Val's casket.

"I'm here to tell you today, that our brother Valiant Jackson was such a son. He was all the while, toiling for God, giving this church the money it needed, while disguising himself under a cloak of vanity and disinterest. But God always knew the difference, and we're here to acknowledge that our eyes are now open and we see. We will make amends for seeing our poor brother too late. Can I have an amen?"

"Amen!"

"Hallelujah!"

"Amen, Lord!"

"And I thank the Good Lord that our eyes are now open. Because we can see!"

Another cry from the crowd: "Yes! Thank you, Jesus!"

"We can see so clearly," said the reverend, bending backwards and raising his voice to the rafters above. "We can *see*!"

"Yes, we can!"

"You're right!"

"And what are we seeing, my brothers and sisters? What has God given our eyes to see here, right here, in the seat of our church, *Jesus's house*?"

"Tell us!" The congregation now buzzed. "You tell us, Reverend!"

He stood up straight and shook his head.

"We can now see, my brothers and sisters, that we have a viper among us!"

His gaze swung sharply back to Mae again. She jumped back in her seat and turned away from him. But, to her horror, every eye in the sanctuary was trained hotly on her.

"A viper that has sown poison in our midst!"

"Lord have mercy!" Mae heard some say, and heard too others cluck their tongues. Out of the corner of her eye she saw some shake their heads.

"Who has sought to *rend* the sacred bonds of love between a husband and wife, between a mother and child. A viper of *discord!*"

"Christ protect us!" people murmured in the crowd.

"One who wore the face of virtue, while all the time flourishing in a hellhole of sin! Who did not *hesitate* to further that sin among us."

At this some women put their hands to their chests. "Oh my Lord!"

"Have mercy!"

"So I tell you again, brothers and sisters, there is poison running fast through the veins of this congregation. We must stop it before it makes it to the *heart!*"

He raised his arm again.

"Can I get an amen?"

"Amen!" the congregation cried. "Preach, Reverend! Go on and preach!"

Reverend Stiles stomped his foot in rhythm.

"When there is poison in a body, *what must we do?*"

He stomped a beat to each of his last four words.

"Cut it out! Cut it out! Cut it out! Cut it out!"

A woman behind Mae said the words so sharply Mae felt

her spittle on the back of her neck. Mae cringed into the pew, singed by the heated anger focused on her.

"Cut it out! Cut it out! Cut it out! Cut it out!"

Now the congregants batted their paper fans and hands on the tops of the pews. Ugly, contorted mouths threw words into her face.

"Jezebel!"

"Sinner!"

"Temptress! That's what you are! A temptress!"

"She's a Judas! A woman Judas!"

When she tried to face forward again, Mae saw Cecily. She was looking back at Mae, her hand on the pew, her chin on her hand. She didn't smile or frown and she didn't call out like everyone else was doing. Her expression was serene, almost expectant. She tilted her head as though waiting for Mae to do something.

"Pfftsst!"

The warm wet spittle sprayed Mae's face. She looked down and her veil dropped over her eyes.

"Stop it!" she finally cried out. "Stop it! You're all crazy! Crazy!"

She got up and brushed past Reverend Stiles in the aisle as she rushed out of the sanctuary. The fans and hands continued to bang on the pews to accompany her exit.

The moment she reached the pavement a stiff wind blew and knocked her hat off. Her once carefully coiffed hair loosened and blew about her face. No one from the overflow crowd ran after the hat for her. A little boy laughed.

Mae looked around. Her car was nowhere on the crowded

block. All she saw were faces staring blankly at her. She moved to get out of sight and stumbled in her high heels. She regained her footing and tried to walk straight and tall. But Mae felt shrunken and vulnerable, even older. A single tear ran down her cheek.

She wrapped her arms around herself and walked away down the street and around the corner.

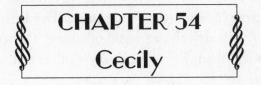

CHAPTER 54
Cecily

Anselm, 1948

Aunt Pearl's voice slipped through Cecily's postlabor drowsiness with the clarity of a small beacon. "Let her sleep," she said. But then Cecily supposed the light piercing through her eyelids could just have easily been the full moon shining through her window that Friday night when she gave birth, April 23. The only other pieces she remembered were the baby's crisp and lusty cry, and its thick tuft of black hair that felt slick beneath her chin when Aunt Pearl tucked the tiny girl into Cecily's arms. Her aunt repeated those three words of grace many times in the ensuing days. With those words she midwifed Cecily into motherhood much the same as she'd helped her bring the baby into the world. Because of this tender attention Cecily never sank to the too-tired depths where she would have felt blue about nursing throughout the night. She could surrender to the cycle so necessary to them both: feed the baby. Sleep. Feed the baby. Sleep.

One morning Cecily awoke to the scent of crabapple blossoms wafting through the bedroom's open window. And because she didn't want to miss the rest of the spring she rose carefully so as not to disturb Sam, padded downstairs, and, for the first time in ten days, went outside. Her belly felt large and heavy as though she were still pregnant. The soreness between her legs made her move slowly. But the wet fragrant air revived her and the dew on the grass soothed and cooled her bare feet. She walked along the clothesline in the backyard. Her fingers reached up and slid along the white cord and she watched the sky blushing pink with the impending sunrise. Then she turned and made her way back to the house where she settled herself on the steps. She didn't notice the light on in the kitchen, but she wasn't surprised when Aunt Pearl opened the door and handed Cecily a glass of water with a lemon slice floating to the bottom. She lowered herself onto the step next to her.

"I like being outside," Cecily said. She sipped from the glass.

"Hmm. It's good for you too." Aunt Pearl rubbed her hands together. "Well, I should get some breakfast started."

"Aunt Pearl." Cecily's left hand grasped a piece of the woman's red flowered housecoat between her fingers. "Am I ever gonna want to be with Sam again? In bed?" She shifted uncomfortably on the step. Aunt Pearl leaned toward Cecily and kissed her on the forehead. Her thick lips felt pillow soft on Cecily's skin. "Oh, honey, you're gonna heal up just fine," she said. "Give it time."

The time did pass and the time did arrive when she could be with Sam and have it be pleasurable. Still, Cecily worried about him. She could see he loved the baby. He even surprised Aunt

Pearl with his willingness to change a diaper or walk the floor rocking the child when she was fussy. And he didn't give Cecily a moment's trouble about naming her Valerie Rose when he could have demanded she be Samantha or Samuelle. Then there was the matter of where they lived. When she and Sam moved to Anselm they didn't buy their own house, though they very easily could have. Val Jackson, as it turned out, had left a will bequeathing his wealth to his child and Cecily. But when she made it clear she wanted nothing to do with Val's clubs or businesses, Aunt Rose took on the task of having her lawyers dismantle the estate and transferring the funds as they came in to Cecily in Anselm. So they could easily afford not only a house, but land of their own. Aunt Pearl offered them a lot to build a house on just down the road so they would be "in spitting distance," she said.

But Cecily liked being with Aunt Pearl and Uncle Menard again. Their house was big enough, warm enough, and she was certain her child would better thrive in this fertile ground with plenty of loving family around her. Cecily knew herself well enough to know she couldn't make a home. Yes, she remembered or relearned everything Aunt Pearl taught her about ironing, baking, and growing snap peas, collard greens, and tomatoes. But Cecily sensed it took more than housework to make a home feel safe and full of love. It wasn't something she could learn like the number of eggs you used to make corn bread. She had to grow into it—grow into it until it was just who she was automatically. Aunt Pearl was like that, and Cecily was willing to stay under her roof until she had acquired this grace herself.

She could tell Uncle Menard enjoyed Sam's company. Ever since they arrived in Anselm that January he would drive Sam around the countryside, acquainting him with the property, the farm animals, the town. And when the spring work began Sam accompanied him still. But Cecily didn't know how long he would last. Sam was no farmer. She didn't want to see him dissolve into uselessness. This would be the burden, she thought, that would prove too much for him.

Then one day, like an answer to her prayers, a dirty panel truck with markings that read "Gianelli Brothers Moving" rolled to a stop in front of the house. Sam and Uncle Menard went out to see what the driver wanted and Sam returned with a small blue envelope he handed to Cecily.

"It's a piano!" he said before running out again. He jumped off the porch steps and yelled to her. "Your mama sent us her piano!"

Cecily saw the men opening the back of the truck. She pulled open the envelope and drew out the sheet of paper.

> *I thought you might want this. It was only sitting up here gathering dust. I know you and Sam will get some enjoyment out of it like you did before.*
>
> *Love, Mama*

She was pleased to let Sam take charge of the process of assembling and placing the piano in Aunt Pearl's living room. Then he drove into town to buy the tools to tune it. He spent the rest of the afternoon on the task and was ready to play it for them after supper that evening. He played and sang for them every evening and there was no end to Uncle Menard's pleasure in hearing him. "You know," he said one night after Sam finished singing "Nature Boy," "there's not a lot of places where our people can go and hear music like that."

"I know." Sam sighed. He pressed a key with his index finger. "But they're here. Louis Armstrong plays in North Carolina. Ella Fitzgerald too. Places like Asheville."

Uncle Menard sat up and waved a hand through the air. "But not in places we can go. As a matter of fact, Ella Fitzgerald performs in those places, but they won't even let her walk through the front door."

Cecily sat on the couch with Aunt Pearl, stitching a small quilt for Valerie. She stopped and looked at Sam. His fingers had grown still over the keys and his forehead was creased deep in thought. "Sam—" she began.

"It won't be like one of Val Jackson's clubs," he said quickly. He spun around on the bench to face her. "I can make a nice joint, like the Swan, a classy place where people know they have to behave themselves, where musicians like Lena Horne or Louis Armstrong would thank the Lord they can have a nice place to perform, and even stay—we could have rooms for them."

She thought about Sam's hands. They weren't meant to be blistered and calloused like the mottled landscape of Uncle Menard's palms. And here she had taken him from what he knew, given him a child not his own, and asked him to love her and the baby just the same. It wasn't fair. He deserved his bit of sunshine and if this club was going to be it, she couldn't deny it to him.

Cecily smiled. Aunt Pearl said, "As long as you don't sell moonshine, I gather it would be all right."

Cecily laughed and went to Sam and put her arms around him. "Yes. I think it would be all right too."

Uncle Menard leaned back in his chair and grinned. "Then I guess Sam and I need to take a drive into town and see about where you might want to make this club!"

"Yes, sir!" Sam turned and ran his fingers along the keys in a rising riff. "I know just how I want it. It'll be really pretty and simple, like the places I saw in Paris. Something fitting for a new decade."

Cecily blinked. Her sense of time had dulled in Anselm. She hadn't given a thought to the decade soon coming to a close. She only paid attention to the seasons—when to plant what and whether the baby would be warm or cold, when they could next walk down to the river with Rex ambling along with them.

Cecily felt most herself, the most content, when she had Valerie wrapped close to her in a sling Aunt Pearl had fashioned out of a swath of soft yellow cotton. When she helped Cecily put the sling on for the first time she rubbed her niece's back, shook a nimble finger at her, and said, "Now, some of those prissy women at church might go running their mouths and say you're gonna spoil that baby by carrying her so much. Don't you listen to them. I carried my babies like this." She stood back and examined the sling's placement just below Cecily's breasts. Then she picked up Valerie from the little bassinet by the bed and gently placed her into it. She adjusted the sling's tightness and suddenly the baby pressed close to Cecily, snug and secure. Cecily walked around the room and was surprised by how much it felt like when she was pregnant. She could carry Valerie with her arms free, but even better, she could hug her or pull her close at any time.

Aunt Pearl laughed. "Humph, women been carrying their babies in the fields for years because there was no one else to hold them. Now they sit up there with their noses in the air and act like they know what it is to spoil a child. They too cold and stingy to have to worry about spoiling anybody! You carry her as much as you want. Right now you can—she'll get too big for it soon enough. But she'll remember that you did it. It's good for her. It's good for you. Blood on blood is the best medicine in the world."

Cecily knew Aunt Pearl was right. She had felt something of this contentment before Valerie was born, when her belly had grown so the baby was unmistakably present and, with her frequent sharp kicks, eager to make her presence felt. When Cecily was still in Mama's house she had hummed and walked around with one hand rubbing her belly while she prepared for her and Sam's journey to Anselm. Cecily enjoyed the feeling of wholeness that came with having her baby, her flesh and blood, so near. She loved the complete security of knowing exactly where her child was. In sensing this Cecily grew a fresh compassion for her mother. She couldn't imagine what wrenching of the heart had to be done, what wounds acquiesced to, in order to let a child go away. And here her poor Mama had to do it twice in as many years. Cecily showed her every kindness, writing to her often and reminding her of how much she would be expected and welcomed in Anselm for Christmas and any other time she could make the trip down.

Mama filled her letters with news and replies. She said she would come in the winter to escape the cold. Another time she said Mae had shut up her Harlem home. There were rumors she had moved to Paris for good, although, Mama wrote,

"I don't know what good can come of anything that woman does."

"Still," the letter went on, "she is family and so I pray for her."

Cecily wanted to do the same for the sake of her own Christian spirit and, truth be told, her cousin's machinations had brought Cecily back to Anselm, the place she loved most, with the man she adored. And having a baby had made Cecily able to look at grown-up faces and see the helpless innocents they once were. They were all somebody's baby once, Mae too. But then Cecily thought about how beautiful Mrs. Townsend once looked in her blue dress and swinging a bat on the lawn at Mercylands. And she remembered Val's smile and dark eyes and how her daughter would never see how his had originated her own, and her heart felt encrusted in stone. Its heaviness made her feel sad in a way she just couldn't shake. Until she did she wouldn't be able to forgive Mae Malveaux—or herself for that matter—for all that had happened.

She thought about it on her walks in the woods with Valerie. Once the weather got warm she went out every day just as she used to. Sometimes she went in the morning; sometimes she walked in the sleepy afternoon. The trees still enclosed her in a sky-filled room. The leaves still yielded with a satisfying crunch beneath her feet. Valerie's cooing sounded just as soothing as the river flowing past them. But Cecily was aware enough now to know none of it was really the same. She could tell she was different, but not different in a way she'd expected, like being older or wiser. It wasn't like that at all. Something inside her hurt from the hard edges of resentment she felt because of Mae. Something wanted to resist the hurt but didn't know how.

Being back in Anselm, Cecily wanted to lay herself open to the world, to believe again as she once did in the kindness of people. The urge to leave Harlem had bothered her in the sense that she knew it wasn't an evil place just because of the people in it. If that were true then Mae might doom Paris with her very presence. And Sam's new nightclub might reveal the meanness of some of the people in Anselm. If moving from one place to the next were the answer, then the better life would always be somewhere else because she'd always be seeking nicer people somewhere else. People were who they were. Wouldn't Aunt Pearl say that?

Cecily had to figure out how to make that better life within her. She didn't know how she knew that or how to do it, but she did and would. Then she could take it wherever she went, the same as carrying Valerie with her now. If she could do that, she could teach her daughter how to do the same. Rich or poor, this was the best gift she could give her. She tried not to worry about it too much. She thought the person who might be able to help her learn what she needed to know might be nearby. Whenever she sat by the river she listened carefully for a frantic rustling of leaves, or for the explosion of a mighty splash in the water. But there was none. The closest sounds to her were the quiet sucking ones Valerie made while Cecily sat in the thick grass and breastfed her.

Then finally one day, the last day of June, when she went to sit by the water, Cecily saw the shoes, her long-abandoned shoes, placed at the base of a tree like they'd been waiting for her return all this time. She was almost afraid to touch them. The mud had been wiped from the heels and the tops were polished to a fantastic shine.

"They might be a little tight right now."

The voice, still airy like a sigh, startled her. She turned. Mr. Travis was sitting on the riverbank with his legs crossed beneath him. He wore jeans and a short-sleeved shirt, perfectly pressed, with a light blue-and-white plain print. He shifted his seat to face her.

"I've seen that—women's feet go up a size or two when they have a baby. But they'll go back down in a year or so."

Cecily stepped over to where he was and lowered herself to sit next to him on the grass. She settled Valerie in her lap. "I've been waiting for you," she said. "Ever since I got back I've been hoping to see you."

His lips pressed into a kind of shy smile and he plucked at a blade of grass near his ankle. He looked younger than she remembered. But up close she saw now how his thinning hair and broad forehead had fooled her. He was older, but not as old as she had thought. Not much older than Val Jackson was.

"Why?"

She shrugged and rubbed Valerie's back. The baby slept in her arms. "It seemed to me you needed a friend."

He tilted his head back and seemed to contemplate the tops of the trees. "I thought the same thing about you."

They sat a little longer in silence.

"I'm Cecily," she said finally. She touched his knee. It seemed right—right in a way that shaking his hand would not. It would have been too formal. "Maybe you don't remember, but that's my name."

He nodded and looked at her with a straightforward, earnest gaze like, she thought, he wanted to get this right too.

"Cecily," he said. She liked the way the soft Cs of her name slid off his tongue. "I'm Isaiah. You can call me Ike. And who is this?"

"Oh!" She pulled back the cloth of the sling a little. "This is Valerie."

He reached into the sling and laid a hand on the baby's head and looked like he would bless her. "Hello, Valerie." He smiled and they were quiet again. They watched the water flowing calmly on the windless day.

"Ike," she said after a while. Tears, a small and unexpected stream, stopped up her throat. She put her hand on his knee again. She shook her head and wiped her eyes. "Ike, I've got some sadness in me. It's wrapped up tight, I think, but it's in there."

He tugged at his right ear in the thoughtful way she had seen when Aunt Pearl asked him for a pair of boots. Something about the motion made her feel a tiny crack had wedged open in her heart and she knew they were beginning.

"Well, Cecily, you just have to wait for it to come out. I'll be happy to sit with you until it does." He took her hand and squeezed it.

"Thank you," she said through her tears. "I would like that. I'd like it a lot."

* * *

THEIR MEETINGS CHANGED little from that first one. They talked in what Cecily thought seemed like a long, ongoing conversation. Each time, even if it was days later, they picked up where they left off as though they'd spoken only an hour before. The words didn't pour out between them as they often did for her and Aunt Pearl. Sometimes they didn't say anything at all. She never again discovered him thrashing about in the water or touching himself the way he did before. She didn't know if he just stopped doing it or if he was careful to do it where she wouldn't find him. Either way, she liked that he seemed to be considerate of her in this. She never asked him about it. Instead she focused on how she and Ike seemed like children playing with blocks, putting one on top of the other and then spending days considering the move before they added another. She liked it. She liked how the knot inside her untangled a little more each time they met.

One morning she noticed the calm river's shimmering surface disturbed intermittently by a dot or two of bubbles.

"What is that?" she asked.

"The fish," he replied. "They're rising."

She nodded and hugged Valerie to her. "Me too," she said. "Me too."

ACKNOWLEDGMENTS

Several years ago my friend, the screenwriter Jenny Lumet, during a conversation about my obsession with *Les Liaisons Dangereuses* and its various incarnations, said there needed to be a version of the story with an African American cast. I knew I could do it and I knew it had to be set in Harlem in the 1940s. She doesn't remember the suggestion but I never forgot it. The story finally blossomed for me when I met Leslie Lewis, who became my muse. Her fierce and gorgeous energy fed the streams of my imagination from which Mae and Elizabeth emerged. I would not have embarked on this journey if not for Jenny and Leslie.

I'm grateful for my family, Darryl and Tain, who have allowed me to shape a world where, when I'm not with them, they know Mama is either writing, reading, sleeping, or exercising. And doing some teaching as well.

Thanks to my wise and stalwart literary agent, Brettne Bloom, and to my excellent editor, Lucia Macro, who loved this novel from the first. I have endless appreciation for everyone at William Morrow who worked on the book and helped bring it into the world.

I wrote this book while an MFA student at the Vermont College of Fine Arts (VCFA) in Montpelier. I'm grateful to Ellen Lesser, the advisor who worked with me when I generated the first draft, and Bret Lott, who oversaw/edited the revisions leading to the manuscript I eventually submitted to Brettne. Mary Ruefle, Clint McCown, and Martha Southgate read excerpts in workshop and provided insightful feedback.

David Hicks, Raphael Matto, Janet Simmonds, and William R. Smith were my trusted readers who dove into the manuscript and came up with the fresh perspective I needed. I will always appreciate the time they lovingly provided.

David is also my writing partner, and since 2013 he has sat with me through most days of my writing life. He knows nearly every high and low I experienced in the creation of this book. I am lucky to have him.

I thank Peyton and David Cooper for sending me postcards from Paris—that's how I first learned of the Rodin Museum. And I'm grateful to dear Maria and Thea Trotta, whose visit there and gift of a framed image of Rodin's *The Eternal Idol* inspired me to put the museum in the book.

I thank these friends for their ongoing love and support: Katy Kjellgren, Kathi Brown Wright, Vaughn and Gail Buffalo, Anupama Amaran, Yana Syrkin, Heather Jackson, Rob Berkley, Debbie Phillips, and all my Women on Fire sisters. The same goes for my writing allies: Peter Wright, Donald Quist, Michelle Webster-Hein, and Mathieu Cailler. Special thanks to Mathieu for providing the French translations I used in the text.

Thanks to Pastor Kathie Adams-Shepherd and my faith

community at Trinity Episcopal Church in Newtown, Connecticut.

I thank Vinny, Julie, and Paige Caggianiello for looking after Tain when I needed a few extra hours to write.

Thanks to the libraries that provided both books and space to write: the Gary Library at VCFA, C. H. Booth Library in Newtown, and Southbury Public Library.

The following books were particularly helpful: *The Art of Seduction* by Robert Greene (Mr. Greene's analysis of the methods used by the original Valmont character informed the strategy I created for my Val), *This Was Harlem: A Cultural Portrait, 1900–1950* by Jervis Anderson, and *On Her Own Ground: The Life and Times of Madam C. J. Walker* by A'Lelia Bundles.

Last but not least I'm forever grateful to my dear friend Jane Brady, who helped me see I'm all about redemption, an observation that led me to understand the heart of the book I wanted to write.

About the author

About the book

Insights,
Interviews
& More . . .

Meet Sophfronia Scott

About the author

Rob Berkley

SOPHFRONIA SCOTT hails from Lorain, Ohio—a hometown she shares with the author Toni Morrison. She was a writer and editor at *Time* and *People* magazines before publishing her first novel, *All I Need to Get By* (Griffin), in 2004. Her short stories and essays have appeared in *Hotel Amerika*, *The Timberline Review*, *Killens Review of Arts & Letters*, *Ruminate Magazine*, *Saranac Review*, *Numéro Cinq*, *Barnstorm*, *Sleet Magazine*, NewYorkTimes.com, and *O, the Oprah Magazine*. She has an essay collection forthcoming from Ohio State University Press/Mad River Books, and a spiritual memoir, *This Child of Faith: Raising a Spiritual Being in a Secular World*, cowritten with her son, being published by Paraclete Press.

Sophfronia teaches creative writing at Regis University's Mile-High MFA and the Fairfield County Writers' Studio. She speaks and teaches at literary events such as the Hobart Festival of Women Writers in upstate New York, the Frederick Buechner Writer's Workshop at the Princeton Theological Seminary in Princeton, New Jersey, and the Fuller Seminary in Pasadena, California. She blogs at www.Sophfronia.com, and is a guest blogger at RuminateMagazine.com.

Sophfronia holds a BA in English from Harvard and an MFA in writing, fiction, and creative nonfiction from Vermont College of Fine Arts. She lives in Sandy Hook, Connecticut, where she continues to fight a losing battle against the weeds in her flower beds. ∽

Story Behind the Book

Against the glamorous backdrop of 1940s Harlem,
two wealthy people—Mae Malveaux, whose mother
built the family fortune through a hair care product
business, and Valiant Jackson, whose money comes
from sketchier means—play games of sexual intrigue to
feed their sense of ego and power. But their amusement
takes a poisonous turn when Mae is slighted by a former
lover.

This lover, Frank Washington, is engaged to marry
Mae's young cousin Cecily, recently returned to Harlem
after spending time with relatives in North Carolina.
Understanding that the girl's virginity is what Frank
values most, Mae orders Val to seduce her.

The world-weary Val, feeling restless and dissatisfied
after witnessing Jackie Robinson cross baseball's
color line, hopes to inject new life into his pursuits by
seducing Elizabeth Townsend, the virtuous wife of a
civil rights attorney. He lies to Mae about his true focus,
and when she discovers his dishonesty, the game crosses
the line into war.

Love, faith, lost innocence, and the nature of each
character's sexual being all drive the narrative as they
learn what is most important just when they have to
risk it all.

BACKSTORY

I can't do this for most films, but for some reason I can
remember the first time I saw *Dangerous Liaisons,*
starring Glenn Close and John Malkovich. I remember
the theater on the Upper West Side of Manhattan
and I remember the people who were with me, and
I remember the film wasn't my choice and I knew
nothing about it. But the story and its characters
burned such an impression into my brain that I felt
impelled to read the original novel by Pierre Choderlos
de Laclos, *Les Liaisons Dangereuses,* published in 1782,
and in the years to come consumed nearly every version
of the story that came down the pike.

I keep a television in my office and there came this
time that the film *Cruel Intentions* was in rotation on

cable, and I found I was watching it over and over again. One day my husband came in and asked, "Why are you watching this again?" I said, "I don't know. I think I'm going to write something." When I mentioned this to my friend, the screenwriter Jenny Lumet, she said there needed to be a version of the story with an African American cast. I knew I could do it and I knew it had to be set in Harlem in the 1940s. The idea sparked a flame in me because I recognized it as the perfect vessel to contain the vision of how I see this centuries-old narrative.

Dangerous Liaisons has always been considered a cautionary tale, but I see it as a love story. As a writer I am obsessed with love—how we want it, fear it, are paralyzed by it, will go to amazing lengths for it. The Valmont/Val Jackson character fascinates me because at the start of the story, the measure of the man appears to be the measure of his deeds. By the end of the story the measure of the man turns out to be the measure of his love. But why does he fall in love? Elizabeth brings about this change in him. He already has an inkling that there might be good in the world, a good that has nothing to do with money.

She shocks him by confirming that not only is there good in the world, there is good *for him*. The woman not only captures his heart— she captures his spirit and he is a stronger, better person for it.

This is also a story about sexuality and how the way we wield it can be the deepest expression of our human nature. In writing the book I realized I also had an opportunity to articulate some challenging thoughts about sex. I feel as a society we are too disconnected from this important aspect of our humanity and because of that, the potential for trouble is huge. Mae and Val understand this weakness and a lot of what they do is simply a manipulation of people by taking advantage of it. In North Carolina, Cecily is just beginning to learn about and feel more connected to her physical self when she is suddenly whisked back home by her mother. The confusion and sudden disconnect she feels makes her susceptible to Mae's machinations because no one has been honest with Cecily about her body or helped her learn about it.

But what happens when we take ownership of our sexuality? Elizabeth is changed when she finally does. And Cecily eventually learns to be awake and aware in her physical being, and it causes her to act accordingly. I found it thrilling to watch Elizabeth and Cecily emerge as actualized women, assertive in both love and sexuality. Cecily especially becomes her own hero in a way I didn't expect. She became this great representation of the power of sexuality. What does your sexuality reveal about you, and where can your sexuality take you when you claim (or reclaim) it? These questions are why the story of *Dangerous Liaisons* is still so relevant and captivating today. We are still on this quest when it comes to exploring sexuality. ▶

I originally wrote the story as a screenplay because my first experience of it had been a film. I had this shimmering image in my head of Val revealing the beautiful baseball field he's created on the vast lawns of Mercylands. But by structure a screenplay is sparse—you have to leave room for the director and the actors to fill in the spaces. Only about a quarter of my vision made its way to the page. When my agent suggested I write the story as a novel, I was more than happy to do so because I could finally make that journey of discovery that is part of the novel-writing process. *Unforgivable Love* fulfills my original vision in both scope and story.

ON THE SETTING

I wanted to write a story where money obviously wasn't an issue, and to create settings I wanted to spend time in: lush gardens, large gorgeous rooms filled with sumptuous jazz music. I like having the sounds of Duke Ellington, Louis Jordan, and Ella Fitzgerald flowing through the book's pages. I wanted to relate a vision of elegance, of well-dressed people strolling down the street or through a park. I love such images. So I chose a place—Harlem—where such beauty and art would have existed during a time—the late 1940s—filled with its own inherent glamour. This moment in history was so full of potential. World War II had ended and all of society was still adjusting. People were figuring out who and what they would be in this time of change.

I also knew Jackie Robinson would be a pivotal figure for Val Jackson, so the date of the novel's main action had to be 1947—right when Robinson crossed baseball's color line. I saw Val being present for the event, and having it change him in ways that plant the seeds for what happens to him with Elizabeth.

An architectural note: I modeled Aunt Rose's house after The Mount—Edith Wharton's house in Lenox, Massachusetts. I know I could have used Villa Lewaro, a palatial estate in New York's Westchester County that really was the home of America's first black female millionaire, Madame C. J. Walker. In fact Walker's wealth and hair product business served as inspiration for the character of Mae's mother. But the Mount has a modesty I felt was more appropriate for Aunt Rose. And I found it easier to imagine my characters moving about through the rooms and on the grounds of Wharton's beautiful property.

The author Bret Lott was my advisor during my last semester of graduate school, and I did a lot of writing and revising of the novel with him. He turned out to be the perfect person to work with because he loves baseball and jazz music, and has an encyclopedic knowledge of both. Actually, it was a blessing and a curse: a blessing when he helped me avoid what could have been embarrassing mistakes in my references to baseball history, and a curse when I wanted to reference a song in a scene—it was hard to find music that both fit the scene and existed at the time of the novel—and he would vexingly be able to say, "Well, yes, that song did come out that year, but it didn't make it to the nightclub circuit until late the following year." ARRGGGHH!! Can you hear the sound of me banging my head on my desk?

Ann Petry's novel *The Street* plays a role in my book, and I didn't expect that to happen. I initially read it for research purposes because it was published during the timeframe of my novel, but when I realized how much the dark and sad nature of *The Street* affected me I knew I should put it in my novel and use the emotions I felt for one of my characters and see where it might take my story.

I feel there's a richness to *Unforgivable Love* in that it can be enjoyed on more than one level. It can be read as a straight story of love and romance. It can also be read on the literary level, as historical fiction, and as social commentary. But at the end of the day I will admit it: this story is for me. I wanted to tell myself a story I could tell myself again and again with the same sort of passion Zora Neale Hurston poured out when she wrote *Their Eyes Were Watching God*. Her passion overflowed and the ensuing waves flooded the world, leaving us forever steeped in that story. I can only hope readers will likewise feel my love and passion for this novel in equal abundance. ❧